Christ in Khaki

Christ in Khaki

Theresa Murphy

ROBERT HALE · LONDON

© Theresa Murphy 1999
First published in Great Britain 1999

ISBN 0 7090 6432 2

Robert Hale Limited
Clerkenwell House
Clerkenwell Green
London EC1R 0HT

2 4 6 8 10 9 7 5 3 1

Typeset in North Wales by
Derek Doyle & Associates, Mold, Flintshire.
Printed in Great Britain by
St Edmundsbury Press, Bury St Edmunds, Suffolk.
Bound by WBC Book Manufacturers Limited, Bridgend.

'Look! Christ in khaki, out in France, thrusting his bayonet into the body of a German workman. See! The Son of God with a machine-gun, ambushing a column of German infantry, catching them unaware in a Lane and mowing them down in their helplessness.'

Dr Alfred Salter, Labour Leader, 24 September 1914

Author's Note

Making the usual claim that the characters in this story are fictitious, and the situations they are involved in are imaginary, requires qualification. The historical figures of World War One who are included in these pages were, of course, real. In some instances meetings and locations have been invented for these figures so as to facilitate the flow of the story. For the same reason, a minimal number of the speeches made by them have been slightly altered, although care has been taken to ensure that the content, meaning and the opinions held by the orator remain intact.

It must be emphasized that descriptions of the inhumane treatment of conscientious objectors in that era have not been sensationalized for effect, but deliberately underplayed. The full truth might well offend, and would certainly be distressing for the majority of the readers.

My major source of authenticity came from remembered conversations with a relative, a Roman Catholic who suffered terribly for refusing to submit to military discipline in the Great War. In acknowledging his, sadly posthumous, help, I must also express gratitude to those who sharpened my memory, including the friendly staff at the Colindale Newspaper Library who made contemporaneous magazines and newspapers available.

One

Leon ceased his hammering at the anvil to listen. The metallic clanging echoed in his ears as glowing red sparks dropped like falling stars around him. From outside came the bawdy sound of accordion music, the scuffling of booted feet, and the laughter of a crowd. Curiosity took him to the door of the forge. Tiny meandering snowflakes fell slowly and the December air chilled the sweat on his brow as he blinked in disbelief at a scene that held all the absurdity of a dream.

Normally drab in winter, the street had taken on the gaiety of a funfair. The musician was an elderly man whose neglected appearance of a tramp was belied by an aristocratic bearing. With long white hair flying behind him wildly as that of a circus clown, he led a single-file procession of three soldiers. As if fleeing an overrun Flanders' trench, they were dressed in torn, muddied and bloodied uniforms. Immediately behind the leader, was a one-legged soldier on crutches. Second in line, clinging to the shoulders of the one-legged man with both hands, was a soldier whose head was wrapped in soiled bandages from the nostrils upward. Bringing up the rear was a soldier who, though apparently physically uninjured, had the vacuous expression of an idiot on his face.

Up and down they went in front of a growing crowd. As he did a high-kneed prancing, the animated leader swung his upper body from side to side puppet-like to the beat of his own lively music. With his entourage he had turned a terrible war into a travesty. Although the crowd laughed and occasionally applauded, there was an eeriness to the strange parade that made Leon's scalp prickle icily.

'What's going on?' Bruce Seldon arrived at Leon's side to ask in his quiet way. With him, anxiety etched deeply into her pretty face, was Judith, his wife.

Greeting Judith with a smile, but having no answer for his schoolteacher friend, Leon shrugged. The three of them stood together, not so much isolated from the townsfolk by distance as by Leon and Bruce being of military age while remaining as civilians. Heavily muscled arms folded across his chest, Leon gave an involuntary gasp as a mishap changed the unintentional comedy into an unplanned tragedy.

Carried away by enthusiasm, the white-haired man made a sharp turn that took his three trailing disciples by surprise. The gruesome carnival went swiftly from bad to worse. Worn rubber shoe of a secondhand crutch catching in the rough road, the one-legged soldier tilted at an alarming angle. At first it seemed he would recover, but when he looked down with an expression of horror, as if realizing for the first time that he had lost a leg, he crashed face first to the ground. Deprived of his guide, the sightless soldier staggered about with hands outstretched in front of him in the way of a blindfolded child playing a party game. A few young people in the crowd chuckled cruelly as he collided with a lamppost, his head hitting the metal with a meaty smack.

'Bastard! Bastard!' the blind man complained loudly, holding his hurting face with both hands. Mothers all around hurriedly placed their hands over the ears of children.

Stopping his playing, the white-haired man reached for the blind soldier. But it was too late. Tripping over the prone body of his comrade, he fell heavily on top of him. Bending over to tug frantically at the two fallen men, the third soldier yelled excitedly at the white-haired man, 'Boche machine-gun. We're all that's left of C Company, sir!'

Both Leon and Bruce came forward with the intention of assisting the helpless, crippled soldiers. An angry shout from the white-haired man stopped them.

'Stay right where you are, young gentlemen!' His fingers

gripped the accordion so tightly that the knuckles whitened and his hands began to swell. 'I will not dishonour two heroes by permitting cowards to lay a hand upon them.'

Stung by the outburst, Leon glanced to where Anne-Marie Penny stood watching with her parents. They were in the company of the ancient, wizened and acerbic Brigadier Horace Lytton and his wife, Claudia. Anne-Marie's lovely face was expressionless, while her mother seemed to be both confused and embarrassed. But the Reverend Paulton Penny and the Lyttons openly supported those who were showing their appreciation of the man's condemnation of Leon Marriott and Bruce Seldon. Leaning against a low wall not far from them was Hubert Lytton, the brigadier's son, and Alexander Plummer. Both were smartly turned out in the uniforms of army officers.

Leon regretted the position in which his stand against the war had put Anne-Marie. It had earned him the contempt of her father, which made their relationship one of snatched, clandestine meetings that left each unsure of the other. Saddened by the rebuke from the accordion player, he reminded himself that only his convictions were important. It mattered not what anyone thought of him. Anyway, the pompous, war-mongering Rev Penny compared badly to Leon's father, who had died with the word 'peace' on his lips after a long agonizing illness. So brave a man must never be betrayed.

A fourth soldier suddenly appeared. He came down the road stooped over, rolling a beer barrel with his left hand, the right sleeve of his ragged uniform flapping emptily. In a deft one-armed movement, he flipped the barrel up on end. Awkwardly, the accordion strapped to his front like a grotesque pregnancy, the old man climbed up on the makeshift rostrum, his outstretched arms acting as wings until he found his balance.

Walter Hann came from his baker's shop preceded by a belly so huge that it was a separate entity, waddling on his short, crooked legs. His son, James, joined him. The two of them stood side by side, set apart from all others by the long white aprons of their trade. James said something to his father before leaving him to join Leon, Bruce and Judith.

'What's this, more government propaganda?' the young baker asked.

Though of sturdy build, James Hann looked frail by the power-fully built Leon, and intellectually inferior by the fine, academic features of Bruce and Judith. He was the odd one out, but the others were aware that the young baker possessed admirable qual-ities, and the four of them were staunch friends.

With a negative shake of his narrow head, Bruce replied, 'The way I see it this old fellow is going to cause us more trouble than Lloyd George ever could.'

'Things are bound to get tougher, so let him do his worst,' Leon offered a half-hearted philosophy.

The two soldiers who had lain on the ground were back on their feet. Uniforms dampened by the snow they had rolled in, they stood behind the old man. The blind man had his back to the crowd. Hands clasped behind him, he stood like a dunce in a schoolroom, his nose touching the HAPPY CHRISTMAS 1915 banner the Hanns had draped across the front of their premises.

Leaning down, the old man said something to the one-legged soldier, who balanced precariously on one crutch as he stretched a hand to turn his blind comrade so that he faced the townsfolk. Satisfied, he threw back his head and was about to speak when he was stopped by a wag in the crowd.

'Get your hair cut!' a young man shouted, causing laughter.

'Very funny,' the white-haired man sneered, sarcastically adding, 'I wonder if the boys crouching in the trenches would find you so amusing.'

'Perhaps. I'll ask them tomorrow when I go back to Passchendaele.' The heckler, wearing the uniform of a Cold-stream Guard, stepped from the crowd.

'My sincere apologies, young sir,' the old man mumbled in discomfort as the crowd readily applauded the KRR. man. Humbly saluting the soldier, he hesitated for a moment before beginning an oration in the booming voice of a preacher: 'My very dear friends! Never in its history has our country been in such deadly peril. At this very moment German ships could be heading for our shores . . .'

'If they are,' Bruce Seldon called, 'they will be steaming on coal supplied to the German Navy by South Wales mine owners.'

Peering down at him, the man observed, 'You are obviously a fit young man, but not wearing a uniform. Having already insulted one brave man in this town, I hesitate to offend another. Are you a serving soldier, young sir?'

'No. I am Bruce Seldon, a member of the No-Conscription Fellowship and the Independent Labour Party.'

There was booing and cries of 'shame' from the crowd. Seizing on this, the old man glared at Bruce. 'Your neighbours have passed judgement on you, young fellow, so nothing further is required of me. What of your two companions, are they also khaki-dodgers?' He pointed a finger at Leon. 'You, young sir, have the body of a Samson. You could slay a thousand Hun Philistines with the jaw-bone of an ass! Have you the liver of a chicken in that powerful physique of yours? Is that what makes you stay at home with the women?'

'I do not have to answer to the likes of you.' Leon glared at the accordionist.

'Indeed not, young sir. You speak nothing but the truth. But one day, you mark my words, cowards like you will be forced to answer to their sisters and mothers who have been ravished by the Hun,' the white-haired man shouted, his face reddened by anger. Then he moved his accusing finger to James Hann. 'And you, young sir, is life as a gentleman baker so comfortably rewarding that you are prepared to leave the defence of the country, the elemental duty of every capable citizen, to your peers?'

'I have my reasons for not enlisting.'

'No doubt, and we don't have to enquire as to those reasons. The colour yellow springs to mind,' the man smiled derisively, bowing to the crowd as they roared agreement and applauded his remark. He went on, 'Is there not one iota of patriotism in any of the three of you?'

'This is a capitalist war, mister. Germany is selling guns to France so that the French can kill Germans. I want no part of such lunacy,' Bruce said. 'Capitalism knows no country, has no patriotism.'

13

'I have not come to argue with Marxists, but to appeal to right-minded folk.' The old man, sensing that Bruce would easily defeat him in a battle of words, turned away from the schoolteacher and his friends to look out over the by now larger crowd. 'My very dear friends! Let me tell you something. Many say that war is murder. I tell you this is not so. War is not murder, but sacrifice; which is the very soul of Christianity.'

'Hear! hear!' Rev Paulton Penny called with evangelical fervour.

Acknowledging the clergyman's support with a respectful lowering of his head, the orator continued, 'I have brought with me today four soldiers who represent the courageous men of the British Army to whom we owe our lives, the honour of our women, and the sanctity and safety of our homes. But our military might undergoes a constant diminution, and unless reinforcements flow steadily and increasingly we shall have an army of so low a number in the field that it will be unworthy of the power and responsibilities of the British Empire. My dear friends, I bring you a message. . . .'

He stopped speaking as somewhere in the near distance an unseen person blew a sharp note on a whistle.

Leaping about excitedly, the mentally affected soldier cried out urgently and anxiously, 'Stretcher-bearer! Stretcher-bearer!'

The whistle blew once more. Swinging on his crutches, the one-legged man moved a little way out into the street to look in the direction from which the sound had come. Jerking to life in sudden panic, the strangely behaving soldier leapt at him.

'Get down, you bloody fool!' he shouted, as he landed on the one-legged man's back, sending him crashing down to the ground again.

The young guardsman and Rev Penny came forward to help both soldiers to their feet. The one-legged man's nose streamed blood, and the mentally disturbed soldier was nursing a painfully twisted arm while crying like a baby.

Following up on the whistle was a crunching of marching boots accompanied by a chorus of deep male voices singing 'Goodbye Dolly Gray'. A column of soldiers right-wheeled into sight round a corner and came marching down the street. Every so often they paused in their singing to roar out a mighty cheer. Pacing beside them, a deep-chested sergeant with a rigid backbone and the battered face of a pugilist, removed the whistle held between his teeth to yell the question 'Are we downhearted?' and the soldiers shouted a reply in unison, 'No!'

When the singing started up again, the people clapped their hands. The next time the sergeant shouted 'Are we downhearted?' the answering 'No!' was swelled by the voices of the townsfolk.

Breaking away from the crowd, four young women approached Leon, Bruce and James. Their walk was a dance to the beat of the soldiers' song, their faces were smiling, but the appearance of forward girls flirting with three handsome boys was deceptive: there was a maliciousness in the encounter. White teeth clenched in bogus smiles, the young women made a big show of passing the three men white feathers. They walked away, smiling genuinely now as those in the crowd who had witnessed the incident shouted approval.

Without looking at each other or anyone else, the trio of young men let the feathers flutter earthwards with the falling snow. Judith Seldon struggled to keep her feelings concealed, but she was betrayed by tear-filled eyes.

The whistle blew yet again, and then the marching soldiers were lost to the people of Marshlee as they turned left at the bottom of town. Disembodied, their song came floating hauntingly back on the soft air of twilight, a forlorn anthem for battlefield ghosts. Then all that remained was a distressing silence. A strange hush had settled over a crowd that seemed to be expectantly waiting for a non-existent bugler to sound The Last Post.

The white-haired man needed to rattlingly clear his throat several times before resuming his speech. Meditative eyes fixed on the place where the marching soldiers were last seen, he said, 'That group of brave men came in timely support for the message I bring to the young ladies of this fair town of Marshlee. You know how to deal with cowards – shun the blighters. No self-respecting girl should these days be seen in the company of a man not wearing a uniform. To you young men, and yes, I see you skulking there in the crowd, afraid to show your faces, my advice is enlist now before you get fetched. It is not too late to regain your pride, Hesitate any longer and you will be forever shamed. The day will surely come when your children demand to know what you did in the war. What will you tell them, eh? No man who has never served with the colours, never drilled with a regiment, never marched with a column, can come close to imagining the spirit of comradeship that exists among soldiers.' He gestured at the disabled men behind him. 'Lance/Corporal Brown lost a leg, Private Kelshaw an arm, Private Williams his sight, and Private Pearce his mind. Yet, given the chance, they would return to the front line tomorrow. You can ask them, although perhaps not Private Pearce. . . .'

This had the crowd laughing, and Pearce knuckled away earlier tears to laugh with them before snapping to attention and bellowing an order: 'Form up in column of fours!'

This caused further amusement, and the man shouted over it, 'It's up to you ladies! Force the cowards to replace the heroes that England has already lost. I will give you statistics that will shock, my dear friends. British casualties now total over half a million. There are nearly two million men available to serve who have not volunteered. There cannot be rights without duties. Freedom cannot exist where men are not prepared to defend it.'

Fingers busy at the accordion again, he started to play a song currently popular in the music halls and, as some in the crowd, mainly the women, began to sing he conducted the community singing by swinging and nodding his head. ' "We don't want to lose you – but we think you ought to go. . . ." '

When the song came to a close amid scathing laughter, the man bowed his head over the accordion to squeeze out the last note. Then he stared into the crowd for a long while before shouting, 'You have listened to me, and I beg you from now on to listen to Lord Kitchener.'

Softly playing the hymn 'Abide with Me', he let the music swell as the crowd once again gave voice. Stepping away from them, the

Rev Penny turned to face the people. Grey head tilted to one side, he waved his hands as if holding a baton, guiding their voices as he would those of a choir in his church.

As they joined in the hymn-singing, Leon, James, Bruce and Judith got enraged stares from the crowd. James Hann's voice faltered under the communal glare of condemnation. Nudging him in the ribs, Leon increased the volume of his fine baritone voice, and Bruce Seldon also sang more loudly. Gaining confidence from each other, the three men and one woman exchanged smiles and defiantly continued to sing.

As the last of the music faded and the voices fell away to silence, the crowd seemed oddly perturbed. In the grip of a disquiet that bewildered them, they showed signs of wanting to disband, to hurry away. Their emotions had been subjected to too many twists and turns.

Aware that he was about to lose his audience, the old man struck up the first few bars of the *National Anthem* to renew his grip on the people before addressing them with, 'Now I give every young man here today the opportunity to become a warrior; to be trained to arms, to serve his King and Country. Follow me, boys!'

Helped down from the barrel by the shell-shocked soldier and the one-armed man, he played 'Johnny Get Your Gun' and shouted, 'You young single men of Marshlee! When Britain calls all must respond. You are living in the great darkness of Egypt, but I, the new Moses, have come to lead you to the promised land where you will be ready at all times and in all places to guard and defend the national flag. Me and the boys are marching now. Fall in behind us and become heroes this very day.'

As the white-haired man and the trio of crippled soldiers stepped out to the martial tune, no one at first followed. Then a young boy, dulled into stupidity by generations of inbreeding, walked out, grinning foolishly, to join the parade behind the one-armed soldier. The lad's mother, her toothless face as broken as her dilapidated shoes, ran sobbing to clutch at his arm.

'Billy, you can't go, you mustn't go,' she howled her distress.

But the boy shook her off him roughly. She dropped to the

ground on her knees, weeping and wailing. Bruce Seldon stepped forward to halt the lad by placing his hand on his chest.

'Burden,' the schoolteacher said, 'you are neither old enough to be, nor capable of being, a soldier. Now stop this nonsense at once, go back to your mother and take care of her. I expect to see you in class tomorrow morning.'

Side-stepping the restraining hand, Burden started to hurry after the procession that was now gaining men fast. It was an ambling parody of soldiers marching off to war behind a military band. Seldon was making another grab for the boy when Rev Paulton Penny stopped him.

'You should be setting an example, Schoolteacher,' the clergyman said loudly enough for all around to hear, 'not spreading the contagious disease of cowardice. That boy will benefit greatly, physically, morally, intellectually and educationally from military training. You are a disgrace to your profession.'

'No, Mr Penny, no. It is you who has lost the message of your calling,' Bruce protested. 'The workers of England and Germany have no reason to fight each other. Next week, maybe the week after, that poor, backward boy will die with a bayonet thrust into his belly. Go back to your Bible, sir, to where it says "Thou shalt not kill", for it means what it says.'

'I beseech you to understand that he and the others will lie on the battle sward not to inflict death but to endure it,' Penny ranted before, with a glazed look in his eyes, shouting as if from the pulpit, 'They will be purged of savagery and transfigured into devotion.'

Breaking free of the clergyman's grasp, Bruce saw that it was too late to save Billy Burden. The boy was far along the line behind the accordionist, which had become a long, twisting crocodile of shambling local men. All around him women were clinging to each other, weeping. Several people were trying to lift the hysterically shrieking, prostrate mother of Billy Burden from the snow-covered ground.

A man was striding past Bruce, intent on joining the extended line of volunteers. Recognizing Ronald Fletcher, the clerk at the Marshlee railway station, Bruce blocked his path.

'Ronald, what are you doing?' he asked pleadingly. 'You are with us. You solemnly and sincerely affirmed your intention to resist military service, whatever the penalties may be.'

Unable to meet Bruce's eyes, Fletcher mumbled, 'I know all that, Bruce. But, like that chap said, one day my children will ask me about this war.'

'Dead men can't have children,' Bruce tried to tell him, but Fletcher had run off to get on the end of a line that had increased by three men in the short time that he had been delayed.

'The Pied Piper,' Leon came up beside his friend to comment grimly on the accordionist.

'Parade of the innocents! If only they were rats and not people he was leading away from the town,' Bruce Seldon said sorrowfully, taking his wife's hand as she came to him. Together they glumly watched the volunteers swallowed up by a new night that was as black as death.

Beth Marriott sat on the thick ledge inside of the window of the cramped bedroom that she shared with her mother. Disappointed that the fun was over, she clutched her doll to her and rocked back and forth. Cuddling Kipsy was made difficult of late by a swelling bosom that Beth hadn't welcomed, didn't like, and couldn't adjust to. Other things had been happening to her body, too. Alarming, upsetting things, and her mother become evasive when Beth tried to question her.

She had laughed with all the blissful ignorance of a 14 year old when the soldiers had fallen over. She had jumped up and down with excitement on seeing Leon and his friends, and had beaten time with her feet to the music. Beth's only upset had occurred when the squat, podgy figure of Mr Hann had come trundling from his shop. Cowering at the sight of him, she had given an involuntary breathless squawk of fear. Beth was terrified of the baker. Whenever she went shopping with her mother he would twist his bulging lips into a smile and reach across the counter to stroke her cheek with a finger as fat as a sausage. Her mother said that Mr Hann did these things because he was a kind man who was fond of children. Although incapable of forming a theory of her own, a pubescent intuition told Beth that her mother was wrong.

With a squeaking and a thud that shook the tiny house, the front door down below opened and closed. They had a visitor. Clambering off the window-ledge, Beth tiptoed to sit on the top stair. This was her favourite place in the house. From here she could hear everything that was said downstairs. Beth liked to live her life remotely, looking in on the world and its people rather than being a part of it.

'A lot going on out there today,' she heard her mother remark.

'It's awful, Mrs Marriott. That man has taken lots of boys off with him to join the militia. My Clarence says this sort of thing shouldn't happen, but he reckons it don't make a lot of difference as those boys would be going soon anyway.'

Beth recognized the voice of the visitor; it was her mother's friend, Mrs Crandal. She was a stout woman who smelled of onions and whose hair was rarely out of curlers. Her husband, a bumptious little man, was a clerk at the Marshlee Council Offices. Regarding himself as much more than a lowly pen-pusher, he gave the impression of running the Marshlee Urban District Council. Beth often heard her mother say derisively that 'Clarence Crandal thinks he knows more about the war than the Kaiser does.'

'Did you see anything of my Leon, Mrs Crandal?' Beth's mother asked anxiously.

'Oh yes, Leon and that schoolteacher chap, Bruce whatshisname, really gave that man what for,' Mrs Crandal replied. 'They had the good sense not to go like the others did, but, like the man said, they will be fetched afore long.'

A shiver so massive that it rattled her teeth, shook Beth at the thought of somebody taking her brother away. Leon was both a big brother and a replacement father. He was always there for her, ready to hold her in his strong arms. A cuddle from Leon comforted and reassured her. He was her security. She couldn't bear to lose him. Leaning forward so as to hear better, she listened.

'Not Leon,' her mother stated in a firm, denying tone. 'My boy is a Quaker, as was his father before him, and his father's father before that. Leon would no more take up arms than he would issue a single swear word, Mrs Crandal. And if they do start conscription, then it won't include married men, so Bruce Seldon won't have to go.'

'I'm sorry, Mrs Marriott,' Mrs Crandal said sympathetically, 'but from what my Clarence tells me neither of those two things you've said are correct. If Leon refuses to fight and they accept that, although I don't say they will, then they are going to get the likes of him to do work that will help the war effort but don't involve no killing. As for the schoolteacher, well, he didn't get wed until after the war started, and that don't count.'

There was the clinking of crockery and accompanying sounds that told Beth that the two women downstairs were sitting at the table. Her mother would be pouring tea. It was getting dark in the bedroom, making her nervous. She was worried that Leon might be taken away that very night.

'How on earth will you manage, Mrs Marriott,' Mrs Crandal said solicitously, 'if your Leon has to go?'

'Heaven forbid! We would get by. My Beth will be fourteen in two days time. She'll be able to go into service for someone.'

'I don't know.' Doubt drew out Mrs Crandal's words. 'No disrespect, Mrs Marriott, but your Beth is what we always used to call a *natural*. You must take great care with her, the utmost care, I say. Breasts the size of a nursing mother and a feeble mind make a dangerous combination in this immoral world. There'll be plenty of men ready to take advantage of that child, Mrs Marriott. Look at Hilary Beckett down at the corner shop, she expects another baby every time a commercial traveller calls.'

'I'll have you know that my Beth knows right from wrong,' Elsie Marriott said huffily.

'She's a sweet little girl, I'll grant you that, but the way she carries that doll around, Kipsy she calls it, don't she? is better suited to a child half her age. I think you'd have some difficulty placing her in employment.'

'There is nothing backward about my girl, Mrs Crandal.' Elsie

Marriott sounded angry like she did the times when Beth defied her. 'Beth may not be as quick as some, and she's a mite shy, but she's strong and healthy, and a good worker. I've already been approached by a tradesman interested in employing her.'

'Oh?' The disbelief in Mrs Crandal's voice came close to imputing that Beth's mother was lying.

Hearing this pleased Beth. As an eavesdropper she rarely heard anything good said about herself. Her pleasure was short-lived, lasting only until her mother next spoke.

'Yes, Walter Hann said that he would welcome a nice, quiet girl like my Beth to take care of Lou, his bedridden wife, and be a companion for her.'

'You mean she'll be living in?'

'Oh yes, but it's just across the street,' Elsie Marriott replied, 'and she'll have every Sunday afternoon off.'

Although having been frightened of just about everything all her life, Beth had never felt the kind of terror she was experiencing at that moment. Shaking from head to toe, she began to cry. A strident scream was building in her and she clapped both hands over her mouth to stifle it. Night was creeping into the bedroom, filling the shadowy corners with unspeakable horrors as its darkness crept into her mind. Only Leon could save her from Mr Hann, but from what Mrs Crandal had said he wouldn't be here to do so.

'Father tells me that the same little gang of conscientious objectors shamed the town and disgraced themselves this afternoon.'

Although an excellent dancer, Anne-Marie faltered on a step as her partner said this. A slow waltz made conversation possible, even desirable, and Hubert Lytton was smiling down at her in anticipation of her response to his words. In his smart uniform he was the epitome of military perfection. It was strongly rumoured that the lieutenant's insignia on his epaulettes was soon to change to the three pips of a captain. The bitter and the envious said the son owed his army prestige and promotion to the father's position of influence. The less unkind were satisfied that Hubert's ability as an officer meant that he required no assistance in forwarding his career. His was far from being the only uniform at Brigadier Lytton's pre-Christmas ball. Held at Farley Grange, the family home three miles out of town, the event had always been a much-loved highlight of Anne-Marie's year. This Christmas the war had ruined it for her.

The militarism that began with the brigadier host and spread like a plague through the younger officer guests of lesser rank, created an atmosphere of suppressed violence that unnerved her.

Some weeks previously, it had been rumoured that Lord Kitchener was to be the evening's special guest. That uncon-firmed whisper had proved false, and now it was known that the distinguished visitor was to be Andrew Bonar Law MP, Leader of the Opposition. It was anticipated that he would make a rousing speech in favour of a more vigorous prosecution of the war. This produced an excited expectancy from which Anne-Marie found herself separate.

The elegant surroundings and splendid orchestra was in total contrast to the corrosive street scene and somehow decadent accordion music of earlier that day. The degrading image of seriously wounded men being mercilessly used was still vivid in Anne-Marie's mind. In particular, the memory of the mentally wrecked soldier lingered. He was old enough to be the husband of someone, the father of children, but neither his family nor the world would ever see him as the hero he was. War had sentenced him to life as a buffoon, being laughed at by ignorant people.

She had hated everything about that afternoon – the marching, singing and cheering, and above all the vile abuse spat at Leon and his friends. It was ironic that those who professed to detest the German and all his doings held more hatred for their own people.

'I understand that Marriott chappy was there, flexing his muscles while displaying his yellow streak,' Lt Lytton went on, when Anne-Marie hadn't spoken.

She released an inward sigh. Hubert was about to become tedious yet again. His otherwise wittily charming personality was

23

marred by his obsessional dislike of Leon Marriott. In a way it was understandable, as from their schooldays it had been assumed that she and Hubert would one day marry. Both families were certain that it would be so, and Hubert's attitude evinced that he saw it as a foregone conclusion. Yet she had done nothing to encourage these assumptions. Hubert resented her friendship, if that was the word, with Leon Marriott, yet she was free to see whom she pleased when it pleased her.

Much of the misunderstanding stemmed from the few days she had spent on holiday with Hubert in London. It had been as a friend, and she was accompanied by her mother acting as a discreet chaperon. That was in August the previous year, a wonderful time lent a terrible magic by danger. The capital's streets had been packed with Americans fleeing from Germany. Soldiers were marching, singing and cheering on a much larger scale than in Marshlee that afternoon. Cars and taxis had been flying British and French colours.

That period, already an important date in history, had brought Hubert and herself closer than they had ever been. But soon afterwards, at the wedding of schoolteacher Bruce Seldon and Judith Petters, headmistress at the Marshlee infant school, she had come to know Leon Marriott. Previously, she had been only vaguely aware of Leon as the town's blacksmith. There had been an instant rapport between them. Despite finding the superbly built Leon to be gentle, Anne-Marie found that she was a little frightened of his raw masculinity.

Though her fondness for Hubert was no more than a hair's breadth from loving him, Leon had turned that fragile division into a barrier. As well as being uncertain of her own feelings, Anne-Marie was unsure of both her suitors'. Leon's faith made him a rebel who was at all times at the centre of some bitter controversy; in contrast, the Lyttons were highly regarded, although Leon had explained to her, as a fact and not a criticism, that the family had since the year 1066 callously traded their sons to the military in exchange for privilege and affluence. A pacifist at heart, Anne-Marie regretted that she lacked the courage to be a non-conformist like Leon, especially now that the war made it so emotive an issue. He refused to recognize the authority of either Church or State.

'I didn't really see or hear much of what was going on,' Anne-Marie said neutrally. Because she respected and admired the beliefs of Leon and others like him, she would never criticize them.

'Of course. Why should you concern yourself with such nonsense,' Hubert said, as the dance ended and he escorted her from the floor. He nodded to where Brigadier Lytton and Rev Penny were deeply engaged in conversation as they eagerly awaited the arrival of Andrew Bonar Law. 'Let's leave all that sort of thing to our fathers. I know mine is eager to deal with the likes of Marriott, Seldon, and Hann, and the Reverend Penny feels just as strongly, what?'

'Probably more so,' Anne-Marie said, with a bogus flippancy.

This wasn't a subject on which she wanted to dwell. Though an excellent, if strict, father in most ways, the Reverend Penny was positioned in the shadowy area between zealotry and insanity in some matters – his church in particular. Though they had not spoken of it to each other, Anne-Marie sensed that her mother shared her fear that he was suffering from incipient religious mania. With a weak mother, it was a heavy cross for an only child to shoulder.

At the punch bowl, Hubert was filling her glass when his mother joined them. Warmly greeting Anne-Marie, Claudia Lytton made small talk while using her eyes to tacitly convey some kind of message to her son. She wore her hair piled high and though the passage of years had aged her, an underlying beauty and elegance survived to make her special.

In demand and needing to circulate, she laid a gloved hand on Anne-Marie's forearm to say confidentially, 'You look absolutely stunning in that dress, Anne-Marie. Blue is your colour. I hear everyone here speak of you as belle of the ball. It makes me so proud.'

The old lady moved away, leaving Anne-Marie perplexed by what she had said. What reason would Claudia Lytton have to be proud of her? She was just another guest. Then she became really concerned as she recalled the silent signals the mother was sending to her son; signals that had made Hubert uncomfortable. The Lyttons knew something of which Anne-Marie was ignorant, but she had an awful feeling that she was soon to find out.

Holding her elbow lightly, Hubert guided her to a quiet space beside a wall turned into a massive Union Flag by an artist engaged by Brigadier Lytton. Those who knew Hubert as well as Anne-Marie, could easily tell when he had something on his mind. Even in the artificial lighting of the ballroom she noticed how tense and pale his face had become, a whiteness accentuated by his black moustache. She assumed that, though undoubtedly a courageous man, he was affected by the knowledge that he would some time soon be sent across to France. But Anne-Marie was mistaken.

'This is difficult for me,' he began, with a hesitation surprising in so self-assured a young man. 'It's obvious to all but the foolishly optimistic, Anne-Marie, that this war isn't going to be short, sharp and over by Christmas. There is no telling how long it may drag on. That is not of great concern in itself. However, with my being destined for France, what does worry me is where we might be when it eventually comes to an end.'

'We?' a curious Anne-Marie enquired.

'You and me,' Hubert, more confident now, replied. 'Maybe the poet can believe that absence makes the heart grow fonder, but a soldier can't. Separation, Anne-Marie, especially if prolonged, can create a gap between two people so wide that both find it impossible to get back across it. I don't want that to happen to us. I couldn't bear to lose you, Anne-Marie.'

Lose her! This was serious stuff that knocked Anne-Marie off balance. It explained the mysterious exchange between Claudia Lytton and Hubert. Having envisaged that one day, after the war had been won, Hubert and his parents might ask her to join the family as his wife, she guessed that was what Hubert was leading up to now. It was premature, and she didn't know how best to deal with it.

'You've confused me, Hubert,' she said to gain time, eyes darting to limited horizons in the hope of seeing someone to rescue her. 'What are you trying to tell me?'

'I can't get down on bended knee in front of this mob, but in my stupid, bumbling way I'm asking you to marry me, Anne-Marie.'

Anne-Marie was too taken aback to say anything. The band had begun playing a foxtrot. Couples were moving to the floor. She envied them their restricted thinking that went no further than the next dance. Hubert's shock proposal had presented her with a dilemma of immense proportion.

'When?' she asked hurriedly and foolishly, as if a date was her only consideration.

'As soon as possible,' he answered, delighted by what he took to be her acceptance. 'Certainly before I'm sent to France. There will be time to prepare a proper wedding, Anne-Marie.'

'But . . .' Anne-Marie stammered, coming close to saying yes. But that was a mere surface reaction; deep down inside of herself, where things really mattered, she knew that she had to handle this with caution. Not doubting that Hubert loved her, she was also aware that in a country fast losing its sons, his parents had accepted bereavement in advance and were planning the next generation to continue the family line. It was both very sad and extremely ugly. Anne-Marie had the dank smell of the grave in her nostrils.

Head swimming, the music and hubbub of the crowd fading in and out, Anne-Marie just didn't know what to say. A noisy interruption saved her from pleading for time to give an answer.

'Lytton, old chap,' a young. sweaty-faced man in the uniform of a second lieutenant put crooked teeth on show in a half-drunken grin as he clapped Hubert on the shoulder. 'Come along, bring the delectable Anne-Marie with you. Gladys and I are going slumming. The last chance to have some fun before a German bullet ends it all for us, what?'

The unexpected marriage proposal and the arrival of 2nd Lt Alexander Plummer and his wife was almost too much for Anne-Marie. Regarding the couple as obnoxious, she found their interruption to be as traumatic as what they had interrupted. Fighting the urge to flee, she heard Hubert rebuke Plummer, who was the spoilt-brat son of Marshlee's current mayor,

27

Raymond Plummer. Plummer senior was the wealthy owner of a flour mill.

'We don't want that sort of talk in front of the ladies, Plummy.'

'Quite right, old bean, quite right,' Plummer agreed with the exaggerated solemnity of a drunk.

'Yes, please don't say those terrible things, darling,' Gladys Plummer, fair-headed and insipid, hugged one of her husband's arms tightly, as if she was making love to it. 'I never want to lose you.'

'Tonight we'll lose ourselves. It's our anniversary, Lytton.' Plummer swayed, went to punch Hubert's shoulder but missed. 'One year the delicious Gladys and I have been wed. You should try it, Lytton old chap,' – he opened bloodshot eyes wide to ogle Anne-Marie – 'and make an honest woman of this dear girl. Good old Pater bought us a new car to mark the occasion. I've got it outside; a really spiffing Alvis, the latest model. Come on, you two, we're driving into town. We're going to liven up Marshlee.'

Hubert looked at Anne-Marie, wanting her to make the decision. Unable to bear the company of Alexander and Gladys Plummer, her initial reaction was to turn the offer down, but to stay would mean giving Hubert an answer that she as yet didn't have herself.

She said, 'I don't mind going into town, Hubert. It's up to you.'

'Father wouldn't be best pleased.' Hubert looked worriedly over to where the brigadier was jabbing a finger in the narrow chest of Reverend Penny to ram home a point. A bored-looking Andrew Bonar Law looked on.

'He won't even know that you've gone,' Lt Plummer giggled, swaying drunkenly. 'Him and Bible-puncher-Penny – sorry, Anne-Marie, old thing – will have finished fighting the bloody war for us by the time we return.'

'We should stay for the speech,' a doubtful Hubert said.

'What? Listen to political clap-trap?' Plummer was dismissive of Bonar Law. 'If Lord Kitchener had made it here then you wouldn't be able to drag me away, I'd be standing at attention, most probably saluting, throughout. This chappy won't say anything to interest us, Lytton, old bean, so let's make tracks.'

There was applause as Hubert's father introduced Andrew Bonar Law, and then Anne-Marie heard the Member of Parliament begin his speech.

'Before leaving the House to take up the kind invitation of my friends Brigadier and Claudia Lytton, I was able on behalf of the Conservatives to promise that the Government can depend on the unhesitating support of His Majesty's Loyal Opposition for whatever steps they think it necessary to take for the honour and security of the country.'

'Like I said, clap-trap,' a hiccuping Plummer said, too loudly.

Heads were turning their way. An embarrassed Hubert steered the staggering second lieutenant to the door. Hubert and Anne-Marie's decision whether to stay or go had been made for them.

They went out into a bright moonlit night that was so cold that Anne-Marie immediately huddled close to Hubert for comfort. As they neared a gleaming, brand-new car, he questioned Alex Plummer. 'Are you in a fit state to drive, Plummy?'

With the front passenger door open, Plummer clung to it as he indignantly turned to face Hubert. 'I'll have you know, old boy, that I'm likely to he seconded from the King's Royal Rifles Corps to the Royal Flying Corps. I'll be trusted to fly a Henri Farman biplane, Lytton, so you can rely on me to drive a motor car into Marshlee.'

Anne-Marie was apprehensive as Plummer ushered his wife into the front passenger seat and Hubert and herself got into the back of the Alvis. Settling down beside her, Hubert bent his head close to whisper in her ear, 'I expect your answer before this evening is over.'

Disorientated by their sudden exit from the house into the night, and worried about the drunken Alexander Plummer's fitness to drive, Anne-Marie heard her own voice speaking without her willing it to do so. She cringed as she heard the rash promise it made.

'You will have my answer, Hubert.'

Edward Lee's small motor coach was open-style. He was protected by a windshield as he headed back to Marshlee through the night, but his four passengers had no protection from the chilling 30 m.p.h. wind generated by his vehicle. They were returning from an Independent Labour Party 'Stop Conscription' meeting at Salisbury. All four of them had found speeches made there by Sylvia Pankhurst and George Lansbury to be inspiring. On the way out of Salisbury the four of them had continued singing 'The Red Flag'.

But the frost-laden wind made it too uncomfortable to sing. Soon it became too cold for conversation, and they huddled down inside their coats, collars turned up high, silent with their thoughts.

Leon's mind was troubled. Opposition to the war was growing. Those who had rushed to volunteer had learned a harsh lesson. People who had encouraged them to enlist were now tortured by guilt as the list of dead, dying and injured grew at a depressing rate. The tide was turning away from patriotism and mindless sacrifices in the trenches, but he knew that compulsory service would be introduced sooner rather than later. Kitchener had declared that he must have seventy full-strength divisions in the field, and it was obvious this could only be achieved through conscription.

Leon had a premonition of trying times ahead. He didn't fear for himself; whatever they attempted to do to him he would stand firm in his beliefs: his concern was for his mother and sister. Since taking over the forge when Bill Swinton, the man he'd been apprenticed to, had suffered a short, terminal illness, Leon had provided for his family reasonably well. Without him they would swiftly slide into poverty. Though willing and wanting to help, without him Beth would be a liability rather than an asset to their mother.

'Hullo, what's this?'

Lee's startled shout brought Leon swiftly out of his reverie. He sat upright with the others as the motor coach slowed. Up ahead a car had gone nose first into a ditch. It was at such an angle that the offside rear wheel was several feet up off the ground. The nearside front corner of the vehicle had crunched against a stone wall deep in the ditch. Two men in army officer uniforms were still waving their arms at Edward Lee, even though he had brought his coach to a halt.

'Lucky you happened along,' one of the officers called as Leon and his friends alighted from the coach.

'We were doing no more than ten miles an hour when for some reason the damned thing went straight off the road,' the other officer said as they approached.

Leon took that to be a lie, as the car had to have been travelling at considerable speed for the front to embed itself in the wall the way it had. He noticed that the officer's speech was affected by alcohol, and each time the soldier took a step he had a problem with his balance. Up close, Leon recognized Hubert Lytton and Alex Plummer. Bolstered by the wealth of their fathers, both were habitually arrogant and rude. Normally they would not have afforded Leon and his friends the time of day, but now they were seeking help. Leon was about to walk back to the motor coach. having no inclination to assist such a pair, when he realized there were two women standing further back, half hidden by the night. With a shock, he saw that one of them was Anne-Marie Penny.

It hurt him that she was with Hubert Lytton, but he told himself that he had no hold on her. Had it not been for the war it would doubtless have been different. As a serving soldier he would have hesitated to ask her for a commitment to him; as a conscientious objector it was totally out of the question. As his girlfriend, fiancée, or wife, Anne-Marie would be subjected to the same vile treatment as he endured.

'Do we help them?' Bruce asked Leon.

'That's Anne-Marie over there,' Judith exclaimed.

'Then I guess we help them,' her husband said with a rueful grin, and Leon gave a nod to say that they would.

Together, straining and struggling, with Plummer falling flat on his face several times, the six men got the car out of the ditch and back up on to the road. It couldn't be moved from there because the buckled nearside front mudguard was jammed tight against the wheel.

'Good old Pater will be terribly cross,' a staggering Plummer declared mournfully as he studied the damage. 'First time out, and the damned car's a wreck.'

Taking a wallet from the breast pocket of his tunic, Hubert Lytton said to Edward Lee, 'I'll pay you to drive us to Farley Grange.'

'I can't leave the car here, Lytton,' an anxious Plummer objected. 'Pater's at your place, and he'll throw a fit if I turn up without the jalopy.'

'He won't be too pleased,' Lytton remarked as he ran a hand over the crumpled mudguard, 'if you take it back in this state.'

A huddled-up Gladys Plummer muttered through chattering teeth, 'You'll have to do something, darling. I'm absolutely frozen stiff.'

'Sorry, darling,' Plummer said contritely, taking a step forward to peer into Leon's face. 'I say, what a stroke of damned luck! Aren't you the blacksmith chappy?'

Leon nodded.

'Oh, jolly good. You can do something with the damage, can't you, there's a good chappy.' Plummer rubbed his hands in pleasure at having found a solution.

'I can't help you,' Leon said flatly.

'I say, that's ridiculous! We'll pay anything . . .'

Leon interrupted Plummer, 'Your father, and yours' – he pointed at Lytton – 'now take all their work to the smith in Dennington. They say that they refuse to put money into the pocket of a coward like me.'

'I say, old chap,' Plummer began with an awkward little laugh, indicating his damaged car with a sweep of his hand, 'we can put all that nonsense behind us, what! You see the situation we're in: what would you have me do?'

'Go to Arthur Prince, the blacksmith in Dennington, the same as your father and the brigadier,' Leon suggested.

'Apparently you haven't taken the ladies into consideration.' Lytton nodded toward Gladys Plummer and Anne-Marie Penny as he spoke to Leon.

Taking time to think, Leon then gave a half-shrug as if in reply to a question he had asked himself, Then he walked slowly to the front of the Alvis. Getting a grip under the buckled mudguard with both hands, he braced himself. As Leon pulled upwards with all of his considerable strength there was a grinding creak of metal stretching. Bending to check, he was satisfied that the mudguard was clear. Then he sat on his heels to hold the wheel each side and wriggle it.

'It will drive now,' he said.

Chortling happily and drunkenly, Plummer got into his car, started the engine, and with a roar sent the vehicle spinning round in the road. It was only luck that prevented it from going into the ditch on the opposite side.

'He can't drive in that state,' Edward Lee said urgently. 'Stop him, Leon, he'll kill himself.'

'That wouldn't be much of a loss,' Bruce Seldon muttered.

'Here, this should more than compensate you,' Hubert Lytton told Leon, passing him a five-pound note and then walking over to where Gladys Plummer was getting into the Alvis.

Joining his friends, who were getting aboard the motor coach, Leon paused as he saw an undecided Anne-Marie standing in the centre of the road.

'We're ready for the off,' Lytton called to her, as Plummer revved the engine.

Leon's hurt and anger at finding her with Lytton subsided. Unable to let her leave in a car driven by a drunken driver, he called her name.

'Anne-Marie?'

Body still, she turned her head to look at him, then toward Lytton, who stood waiting with the back door of the Alvis held open. She didn't move, and Leon had turned his back on her to climb up into the motor coach when he heard her footsteps hurrying in his direction.

Going to meet her, he helped her into Edward Lee's vehicle. When he turned, Lytton was standing there in the night. Going over slowly to the lieutenant, Leon held out the large white banknote he had been given. He let it fall to the ground at Lytton's feet.

Staring at Leon for a long time, naked hatred in his eyes,

Hubert Lytton turned on his heel. Leaving the five-pound note on the frosty ground, he strode back to the Alvis, opened the back door and got in.

Two

Leon rowed the boat effortlessly. Sitting on the seat in the stern beside Judith, Anne-Marie watched him extend the power of his physique in long, slow strokes. The small craft eased gracefully along the river with a low, musical rippling of the water. Bruce sat at the bow, his poet's features set thoughtfully as he puffed steadily on his beloved pipe. The background of faint splish-splashing made by the dipping of the oars projected the serenity of the afternoon to a degree that almost fooled Anne-Marie. The peaceful scene was an out of time phenomena, a mirror image of a past for ever lost. If she could turn that image round and suspend it in space before her it would surely reflect the horrors of the world today.

Returning Leon's smile, she retrieved the hand she had been trailing in the river, needing to massage the pain from her fingers. The water was bitterly cold, belying the springtime appearance of a clear blue sky. Yet another illusion shattered. All life was in a state of flux. Of late, Anne-Marie had experienced trouble in separating the true from the false. Old values had either disappeared or were rapidly changing. It had become increasingly difficult to find a normality to measure the real against.

Since the night of Alex Plummer's car accident, she had spent much of her time with Leon. Regularly visiting his home, she had in several ways become closer to his mother than she ever had her own. The Marriott terraced cottage possessed none of the opulence of the vicarage, but had all of the warmth that was lacking in her parents' home. Most rewarding of all for Anne-

Marie was the friendship she had formed with Beth Marriott. Though painfully shy and difficult to reach, Beth had a depth to her that could never be found in those who dismissed her as a moron.

'I don't remember a time when I haven't felt like screaming, but I have never screamed,' Beth had once confided to Anne-Marie, and those were the most poignant words she had ever heard.

Leon and his mother had no option but to let Beth go into service, Though she believed that leaving home, admittedly only crossing the street, would take the girl out of herself, be the making of her, Anne-Marie was sure that Beth was in some way troubled about going to work for the Hanns. Despite many attempts, she had failed to get the diffident girl to reveal her worry.

Anne-Marie had also grown close to Leon's friends, and had more and more come to respect, even share, their pacifist views. Fascinated by Quakerism, Anne-Marie subtly questioned Leon on his faith at every opportunity. The emphasis on human goodness and the levelling of social classes appealed to her. Impressed by the Quaker love of truth, she found the absence of sermon, liturgy, and outward rites refreshing in comparison to the dogmatic, almost violent, Christianity that formed her father's credo. There had been guilt, too, over these past months. Not having seen Hubert since that time before Christmas, Anne-Marie's conscience was disturbed by the thought of him having returned to the army to fight in an increasingly ghastly war. She was also bothered, as a dutiful daughter, by her parents' recent and unexpected passive opposition to her going out with Leon. If anything, their new attitude was more troubling than the vehement verbal objection it had replaced.

Outside of her family there had been a price to pay for her friendship with Leon. Claudia Lytton had made several attempts to coax Anne-Marie back into the fold of the local gentry. These attempts were in the form of invitations to take tea at Farley Grange. Anne-Marie had made so many excuses that the last few had been palpably and embarrassingly false. In addition, she had been publicly snubbed by Gladys Plummer. Her husband having returned to his military unit, the officer's wife resented Anne-Marie's dalliance, so to speak, with a conscientious objector.

'Why does time have to pass?' Judith asked wistfully, her voice echoing as it ended a lengthy period of silence. 'I'd like this after-noon to go on and on forever.'

Removing the pipe from his mouth, tapping the bowl against the side of the boat, Bruce smiled lovingly at her. 'You would soon become bored, Judith. Just imagine, no work, no children to educate and shape for the future, no challenges.'

'All of the challenges today are the wrong ones,' Judith said sadly.

Agreeing with her, but saying nothing, Anne-Marie was unsure whether it helped her to discern that her friends were as . melancholic as she was. It seemed fitting that they were suddenly shrouded in shadow as the boat slipped under a bridge. Re-emerging from a temporary half dark into sunlight lifted her spirits. She tried to see Bruce and Judith not as they were at that moment but when totally absorbed in their work as dedicated educators. It helped to remember Leon in the forge, his mighty body and clever mind united in shaping red-hot iron. A purpose in life was essential. Leisure robbed people of some-thing vital.

Up ahead, James Hann was waiting on the tiny wooden jetty where they would disembark. Clad in a heavy white apron, the young baker paced restlessly up and down.

'The ferryman waiting to be paid,' Bruce said, intending it to be a joke. But even he didn't find his words funny once they had been spoken. In these times no one welcomed a reminder of death, even when spoken in jest.

The young baker wore a frown on his flour-powdered face as he came to the edge of the landing.

Leon's expression betrayed his worry as he said, 'There must be something wrong.'

In her present mood it was easy for Anne-Marie to share Leon's misgivings. She waited anxiously as James reached for the mooring rope. At this time of day he should have been at the

bakery preparing tomorrow's dough. Only a matter of importance would have brought him here to meet them.

After securing the boat, James took an envelope from his
pocket and waved it as a semaphored warning. This came for me
today. Leon and Bruce will have one waiting for them when they
get home.'

'From the War Office,' a grim-faced Leon suggested.

'Form W3236,' guessed Bruce, who had a head for figures.

'Yes.' James gave a nod of confirmation. 'It says I have to join
the colours forthwith. Anyone who fails to comply will be treated
as a wartime deserter.'

'And shot.'

Bruce said those two words so seriously that Anne-Marie
couldn't tell if he was joking; she had a terribly cold feeling that
he wasn't.

Mrs Lou Hann was so fat that it was difficult to tell where she
began and ended among the hills and valleys of crumpled bed
linen. She made Beth think of a gigantic candle that had melted
so that it drooped in huge uneven rolls of wax. The bed-ridden
woman smiled a lot, but a complete absence of teeth distorted the
expression so that it took a frightened Beth some time to convert
the grimaces into friendly expressions. Riding on the homely,
cosy aroma of a burning oil lamp was an overwhelming stench
that filled the bedroom. At first it made Beth feel so sick that she
had begun to retch, but, incredibly, after a few minutes in the
room she ceased to notice the smell.

The Hann home, of which the shop and bakery were an integral part, was generally much larger than the Marriott cottage. Yet
narrow passageways, small rooms, and low ceilings closed in on
Beth so that she felt in danger of suffocation. Despite having been
there for two days, Beth found the house to be a bewildering
labyrinth. Often she would find herself on the wrong floor,
entering the wrong room. Already claustrophobic, she discovered
that encountering Walter Hann anywhere in the building diminished her space so rapidly and effectively that she felt trapped.

Only when the fat baker had gone by, after stroking her cheek, did Beth realize she had stopped breathing in his presence. The shuddering intake of air that followed made her so giddy that she was in danger of collapsing.

'You'll start at six in the morning by lighting the stove,' Mrs Hann told Beth, sounding as if she was describing an adventure rather than giving an order. 'Mr Hann and Master James come through from the bakehouse for their breakfasts at seven o'clock, and I have my breakfast at half past seven.'

'Yes, madam,' Beth acknowledged, in the way she had rehearsed with her mother. The two of them had discussed at length what Beth should expect, her mother drawing on her own experience in service for a doctor many years ago.

'You'd best fetch the wood and coal in from the yard in the evenings,' Mrs Hann was continuing. 'That's the only heavy work you'll have to do, child.'

'Yes, madam.'

For all her physical grossness, Lou Hann was a kindly person. She beckoned for Beth to come closer to the bed. 'Your mother told Mr Hann that you have a favourite doll.'

Feeling her face burning hot, Beth expected her new employer to either mock or lecture her on the foolishness of a girl old enough to go into service but still playing with dolls.

'What's her name?' Mrs Hann asked encouragingly when the girl couldn't manage an answer.

'Kipsy,' Beth at last replied.

'Well, Beth, when you go to see your mother on Sunday, be sure to bring Kipsy back with you. I want you to be happy here, child. This is your home now.'

Hearing the woman put into words what she had forced down in her mind brought Beth close to tears. Maybe she was just yards from the house she had been born and raised in, but she was distressingly homesick. Having Kipsy with her would be no compensation for not having her mother to cuddle and Leon to rely on. Beth fought her tears and won.

'Thank you, madam.'

Wondering if she should now leave the room, Beth took a few

tentative steps toward the bedroom door. Lou Hann's voice stopped her.

'Just one more thing, child.'

'Yes, madam?'

Beth stood waiting, looking at the invalid woman through the upright rails of a brass bedstead. Linking the bars were scrolls resembling the ornamental ironwork she had often watched Leon create at his forge.

'Mr Hann works very hard. That dear man keeps the business going and takes good care of me. I've been a burden to him, child, but not one word of complaint ever passes his lips. He is a saint. There is no other way to describe Mr Hann.'

'No, madam; yes, madam.' A confused Beth didn't know what sort of answer was expected of her.

'Because of this war, Master James will have to leave here soon to become a soldier,' Mrs Hann was going on, the reminder that she was to lose her brother bringing Beth close to tears once more. 'That will put all the work of the bakery on to Mr Hann. It is too much for any one man, Beth, but he'll get on and do it. Mr Hann has always been ready to sacrifice himself for me or James. Crippled as I am, I can't do anything to help him. That is why I ask a promise of you, child. Are you prepared to make me a promise, Beth?'

'Yes, madam.'

'Good child. Now, listen to me, Beth. I shall rest easier here in my bed if I know that you are prepared to help Mr Hann. He is so kind, child, too kind for his own good, so he will not put too much work on you. What I do want you to promise, Beth, is that you'll do everything Mr Hann asks of you. This means a lot to me, child. Do you promise?'

'I promise, madam.'

'Good child, good child,' Lou Hann gave Beth one of her gummy smiles. 'Now, Beth, run along and get on with your work.'

Thinking sad thoughts of her home and the loved brother who would shortly leave, Beth, still disorientated in the strange house, needed to rub the back of a hand over her snuffling nose as she dusted ornaments and polished brasswork in the sitting-room. Watching her dourly, from a framed portrait on the wall, was a man in old-fashioned clothes who resembled James more than Walter Hann. Perhaps the man in the painting was James's grandfather, or even his great-great-great grandfather. Beth had heard Bruce Seldon tell her mother that Hanns had baked bread in Marshlee for Oliver Cromwell's men during the Civil War.

She hadn't finished her polishing when Walter Hann's working day came to an end. Shivering involuntarily when the baker entered the room, Beth turned her back on him to continue her work. With a mighty sigh that vibrated his thick lips, he closed his bulging eyes as he sat heavily in a worn armchair. Unable to leave until her task had been completed, Beth wished that James Hann would come into the room. As Leon's friend, James had always treated her well, teasing and joking with her whenever he came to the house. Now that she was a servant for his family he had to remain aloof. Nevertheless, he would flash her a friendly, encouraging smile in passing, and even had a pleasant word or two to say if his father was out of earshot.

Needing to use both hands and all of her strength to lift a large flower-girl ornament back up on to the mantelpiece, Beth had a creepy feeling of being watched. Turning quickly, she was certain she saw one of the supposedly sleeping Walter Hann's heavy eyelids slyly close.

Relieved to finish her work in the room, having been aware of her employer covertly observing her at all times, Beth took the empty coal scuttle out into the yard.

It was raining heavily, but she was too afraid of Walter Hann to go back inside for a coat. Shovelling the glistening wet coal into the bucket, she heard a cough from Mrs Hann come from a room on high. The sound signalled to Beth that she wasn't alone. It was momentarily reassuring, lasting only until she realized that a woman confined to her bed could not help her.

With the full scuttle in both hands, she struggled toward the scullery door. Shins bumping painfully against the bucket, she made it across the yard, only to freeze in horror, the weight of the scuttle forgotten as she saw Walter Hann standing in the doorway.

'I didn't know it was raining, girl,' he said, making no attempt to move so that she could enter the scullery.

Standing with the rain beating down upon her, Beth became suddenly and agonizingly conscious of the weight of the full coal scuttle. Letting it thud to the ground, she straightened up, hoping that Walter Hann would carry the scuttle into the house. Employed in that way he would be of no threat to her.

But he just stood there, looking at her, shaking his head as he took in how her rain-soaked dress was clinging to her. He gruffly told her, 'You should put on a cloak before going out in the rain, girl. Mrs Hann needs you to care for her, so we can't afford to have you fall sick, can we?'

'No, sir, I'm right sorry, sir,' Beth murmured contritely, making her longest speech since coming to the house, head drooping under a torrent of rain.

'No, we don't want you falling sick, girl,' he repeated, as he reached out to her with both hands, cupping a breast in each, his voice hoarse and shaking as he added, 'Can't have you catching a cold in these, can we?'

At his touch, Beth wanted to run, to escape to anywhere, to hide from this monster. Then he was squeezing and hurting her and she started to shed the tears that had been building up all afternoon. As his fingers manipulated her flesh, Beth went deep inside herself to find the resolve to flee from this painful indignity.

Walter Hann was breathing deeply and harshly as she stiffened her body and mustered the strength to escape. Then she heard the voice of Mrs Hann inside her head: '*I want you to promise to do everything that Mr Hann asks of you.*' She had given her promise. Hating every second of it, Beth stood meekly and let the man feel her with his fat fingers.

Then there was a surge of joy in her as she heard footsteps inside the house and James's voice called, 'Are you there, Father?'

Releasing Beth's breasts, Walter Hann bent to lift the coal scuttle as his son appeared in the doorway behind him.

'I came out to help this silly girl, James. Look at her, soaked to the skin.'

'You should have put on a coat, Beth,' James quietly advised, immense sympathy in his brown eyes.

'She'll catch her death,' Walter Hann grunted as he placed the heavy scuttle on the flagstone scullery floor. 'Go to your room, girl, and I'll bring you a towel.'

Wanting to protest that she was all right, that her dress would soon dry, Beth was too shy and unsure of herself to speak up. Moving like a zombie, dreading what was to come, she had reached the scullery door when her fear was eased by James coming to her rescue.

'Just a moment, Beth,' the young baker called, 'I'll get you a towel from the airer.'

Turning to wait, Beth's hopes were dashed when Walter Hann said, 'You go back to the bakehouse and grease those last few tins, son. Leave this to me.'

On leaden feet, Beth went to what was little more than a cupboard under stairs that shaped it strangely. When entering the tiny room, she had to incline her head to the left to avoid bumping it on the sloping ceiling. But then there was height enough to stand up straight, and space for the hard bed on which she slumped down miserably.

Holding her head in her hands, she sat sobbing quietly. Then she stopped crying and dragged in a squawking breath as she jumped to her feet. The sound of the heavy footfalls of Walter Hann came to her, and she closed her eyes and willed them to go on past her door.

They didn't. First she heard the footsteps falter, then fall quiet. Clapping her hands over a mouth that stretched jaw-achingly open, she shook from head to toe as the latch was lifted and the door slowly moved inwards.

It was a bad, sad morning all round. In a damp, grey, swirling mist, Marshlee mourned. Few people were on the street as folk sat sorrowfully at home and dwelt on what had ended in tragedy that day, but had begun with Union Flags flying on a hope-filled afternoon in January of the previous year. That was when Brigadier Lytton had offered the workers on his estate the bonus of a week's extra wages if they would enlist in the army. He drove all fourteen men into town that Saturday afternoon. With the townsfolk praising the brigadier's patriotism and generosity, and the bravery of the workers, thirteen had that afternoon joined the Montgomery Yeomanry. Rejected because of his club foot, only Jack Harlow remained behind.

This morning only Jack Harlow remained alive. News had come through early that all thirteen local men had been killed in the front line close to Bethune. Closed doors and windows could not mute the sounds of grief. The wet, heavy air that enveloped the town was rent by the keening and wailing of widows, and the mournful howling of orphans. The war had come of age in Marshlee. Celebration had conceded to desolation.

It was not the ideal day for the first sitting of the local tribunal set up to consider the applications of men determined not to fight. The tribunal itself was a shambles, as Leon, James and Bruce learned as they walked together toward the church hall. Bruce didn't intend to recognize the authority of the tribunal, while Leon and James expected to make up a total of ten conscientious objectors at the most.

They trudged along a street that the rain had turned into a morass of mud and horse-droppings, which hoofs and wheels had churned and spattered all over the pavements and buildings. The empty shop that had become a recruiting office and had known scenes of patriotic fervour, stood forlorn now when men were dying and bands had ceased to play.

Outside the hall, there was a queue formed by more than eighty men. They joined the lame, the halt, the sick, and the angry. The Secretary of War had sent out call-up notices indiscriminately to all young men of service age. Now the already exempt, the unfit, and those who had previously tried to enlist and had been rejected, were here to voice noisy protestations.

By the time it came to Leon's and James's turn, the tribunal had been turned into an abysmal slanging match. James was called first by the officious Clarence Crandal, who had been appointed, or had possibly appointed himself, clerk to the tribunal. Within minutes, the young baker came back out, his grim expression indicating that he had failed. There was no time to speak to or question him. The proceedings were rushed, which added to the disorganization.

The hall had become overheated and airless when Leon went in, with Bruce entering unobtrusively behind him. A tortoise stove glowed hotly and the burning coke could be tasted as well as smelled. The discarded trappings of a Christmas concert were heaped untidily to one side, their message starkly out of keeping with the tribunal. The board was made up of elderly worthies who sat behind a trestle that was more familiar with the sale of home-made cakes than the pursuit of war. The only young person among them, also the only female, was a sour-faced Gladys Plummer, whose Member of Parliament father was a devout advo-cate of conscription. As Hon. Secretary of the Marshlee War Relief Fund, the enthusiastic Gladys had so far raised £550.

All of them sat with expressionless faces as Leon made a slow approach. It was a peculiar half world that was ludicrous but at the same time perilous. Leon came to a stop in front of the trestle under the hostile glare of the Reverend Paulton Penny. Brigadier Lytton was at the clergyman's side.

'Name?' asked Clarence Crandal, a big open book supported by his left arm, pen poised in his right hand.

'Leon . . .' Leon began, able only to state his first name before the brigadier fiercely interrupted.

'Marriott!' the old soldier spat out the name. 'Today of all days you disgust me. I mourn thirteen men who were loyal employees, then brave soldiers, and now they are dead heroes, and you have the gall to stand before me cringing, afraid of donning the King's uniform.'

'It is not fear but principles that bring me here,' Leon said.

'Principles?' Gladys Plummer scoffed. 'As a member of the No-Conscription Fellowship you belong to one of the most pernicious bodies this country has ever known. You do Britain more harm than the Germans ever will. My word, I would readily embrace the Hun rather than shake the hand of scum like your-self.'

Leon Marriott stood firm under this tirade. As had been

predicted in respect of all tribunals, this one was biased and intolerant, prepared from the start to inflict flagrant injustices: the tribunal members were now also influenced by frustration and anger. Gladys Plummer glowered at Leon, who answered in a steady voice. With James Hann's application apparently dismissed out of hand, Leon knew that he stood no chance of gaining exemption. Nevertheless, he was determined to give these self-opinionated snobs a tussle.

'I am not a member of the fellowship to which you refer,' Leon replied. 'My application is made on religious grounds.'

'Religious grounds!' Reverend Penny snorted contemptuously. 'You blaspheme, sir. You exploit God to save your own skin, to keep you from having to defend your country and womankind. You ask the Almighty to stand by you as a coward and a cad.'

'I follow Jesus Christ. "Love your enemies", He said in the Sermon on the Mount.'

'You dare to argue with me, a man of the cloth?' Penny snarled, then raised both his head and his voice to cry, 'Our Lord declared "I came not to bring peace but a sword".'

Tiring of this theological exchange, the brigadier asked Leon, 'There is a new army order establishing a Non-Combatant Corps for conscientious objectors; would you be content with an exemption from combatant service only?'

'No, sir,' Leon replied.

'Don't be too hasty,' the brigadier advised. 'You could redeem yourself, at least partially, by working in munitions.'

'Whiteheads sold the Austrian Navy the torpedoes that are now sinking British ships,' Leon argued. 'Under no circumstances will I accept service in this corps, which will be under control of the War Office and in every sense part of the military machine.'

'You might well stand a better chance of exemption were you to have the humility to offer to accept work of national importance,' Lytton commented gruffly.

'The Secretary of War said in the House of Commons that the Non-Combatant Corps will be organized to relieve combatant soldiers for the front,' Leon pointed out. 'I will neither pull the trigger or have someone pull it for me.'

'By adopting this attitude, Marriott, you leave the tribunal little alternative,' Reverend Penny warned.

Bruce Seldon, who had been standing just inside of the door, stepped forward to address the tribunal. 'I believe this is a case where absolute exemption should be granted. To quote the first Military Service Act, Section 2, Sub-section 3, in part . . . there may be exceptional cases in which the genuine convictions and circumstances of the man are such that neither exemption from combatant nor conditional exemption will adequately meet the case. Absolute exemption can be granted in these cases if the tribunals are fully satisfied of the facts. . . . It is my contention, gentlemen, that this covers the case of Leon Marriott.'

'I recognize you as a schoolmaster, not a solicitor, which gives you no right to represent anyone here,' Reverend Penny said angrily.

'I recognize you as yet another coward,' Brigadier Lytton put in, adding sarcastically, 'so no doubt your turn will come to represent yourself before this tribunal.'

'My turn will not come before you or any other tribunal,' Bruce stated, 'for to do so would be to admit the jurisdiction of tribunals in an issue where the sole valid judge is the individual conscience.'

Jumping to his feet, an irate Reverend Penny pointed at Bruce and yelled, 'Then get out, get out, before you stretch my patience beyond the limit.' He swung his arm toward Leon and thundered, 'Application denied.'

'Compulsory military service is despotism, not democracy,' said Bruce as a parting shot.

'Get out!' Reverend Penny yelled, as the two friends headed for the door.

James Hann was waiting for them outside. He gave Leon a rueful grin as he enquired, 'A waste of time?'

'Beyond doubt,' Leon reported.

The mist was clearing and an ambitious sun was turning the cloudy sky yellow. There were a few more people on the street now. The elderly Mrs Sophie Bremmer, who had taken over from

Ronald Fletcher as the railway station porter, made a point of not looking their way as she passed by.

'What are we going to do now?' James asked, leaving his question open for either Leon or Bruce to answer.

'The next move,' Leon replied, 'is to go to the appeal tribunal.'

'That will only delay the inevitable,' Bruce remarked glumly.

'What are your plans, Bruce?' James enquired anxiously.

'Me?' Bruce shrugged. 'I will carry on teaching as usual. One day they will come for me, but until then. . . .'

'That's it,' Leon agreed. 'All three of us can only live by the day now.'

'By the hour,' Bruce Seldon corrected his friend.

'Can you manage?'

Balancing the tray of cups precariously, Anne-Marie replied with a half-confident smile and hurried off down the station platform. She had never seen her mother so absorbed in anything, so positive in her movements. The old lady was already filling a giant, two-handed teapot from an urn as Lottie Wainwright came back with a tray of empty cups.

The railway engine, a huge metal, hot-oil-smelling beast, hissed in frustration, keen to move off and regain the steady click-clacking rhythm it had enjoyed coming up from the South Coast. It would remain at Marshlee for just ten minutes, which meant that Anne-Marie, her mother, and the other women needed to move fast. Subdued by tiredness and wearied by battle, the troops crowded to the carriage windows to lean out and wait patiently.

At the leading carriage, Anne-Marie lifted the tray above her head with both hands. Aware that some of the steaming tea must have spilled, she knew that it mattered not. Soldiers reached out eagerly for the cups, smiles lightening their strained, dirt-streaked faces. She smiled back.

As she waited for the cups to be emptied and returned to her, Anne-Marie could see some of the soldiers taking tea into the carriage where bandaged comrades sat and lay. She could see two nurses moving about inside, turned into supernatural creatures by their unusual headgear. The ghosts of angels.

'Thanks a lot, miss.' A soldier, whose smile lost nothing because two front teeth were missing, put the last of the emptied cups on her tray.

'God bless you,' Anne-Marie said as she turned to hurry away.

On the way back to the table where her mother stood, she realized that she had come close to saying God bless 'thee' to the soldier in old Quaker style. Leon had explained that, though rarely used now, 'thee' was once opposed to 'you' to indicate the spirit of fellowship integral to Quaker teaching. It struck her as incomprehensible that she was thinking in a Quaker way while ministering to the victims of a war Leon's faith kept him from. For a moment she was between two worlds in danger of shattering each other.

'Lottie's done the second carriage, and Beryl the third,' her mother reported, deftly wielding the pot to refill the cups on Anne-Marie's tray. She gestured with her grey head toward the next carriage. 'You take these to the fourth, Anne-Marie. Look at those poor chaps, they certainly need some tea.'

'You, Mother, are a wonder!' Anne-Marie said in praise.

'I'm really enjoying myself,' Rachel Penny admitted with a happy smile.

'I can see that,' Anne-Marie chuckled, as she went off with a loaded tray.

It suddenly hit her that this was the first time for as long as she could remember that she had seen her mother apart from her father. That was why the old lady was so different. When the fire and brimstone Paulton Penny was around, his wife was both oppressed and depressed. Away from him, she came into her own. She was a different woman, and Anne-Marie liked her, no, loved her, that way.

'You must have come straight from Heaven, love,' a grateful soldier said, as he leaned out to take a cup.

'Sorry to disappoint you,' Anne-Marie laughed, still feeling really good about her mother. 'In fact, I come from the vicarage over by the church you can just see through those trees.'

'There, I was close,' the soldier grinned. 'Now, let me guess your name. I'm pretty good at this. I've got it – Mary.'

'Nearly. I'm Anne-Marie.'

'Ralph, Ralph Meadows,' the smiling soldier introduced himself, about to shake her hand, until an older man knocked his arm aside while reaching for a cup.

'A vicar's wife?' the older soldier asked, as he helped himself from the tray.

'A vicar's daughter.' Anne-Marie good-naturedly put him right.

'Ah, I know a joke about a vicar's daughter,' the old soldier said.

'Which we don't want to hear, thank you, Tommy,' the soldier named Ralph cautioned.

'Suit yourself.' Tommy shrugged narrow shoulders. 'Anyway, I think it was a farmer's daughter, nothing to do with a vicar. Yeah, that's it, a farmer's daughter and a commercial traveller . . .'

'And we still don't want to hear it,' Ralph warned, and Anne-Marie joined in the laughter.

She found it incredible that these men from the war-torn trenches of Europe had retained so much humour. Enjoying their company and being a part of the good clean fun that was devoid of any innuendo, she feared that her loyalties, though perhaps not divided, were confused. This was a war that encouraged sitting on the Home Front fence between two extreme factions.

Ralph paid her a compliment. 'I think it's really great of you and your friends to put yourself out for us like this.'

'It's the least we can do, after what you chaps have probably been through.' Anne-Marie was a little flustered by his praise.

'We didn't have a choice, you do this voluntarily,' the soldier answered, just as Gladys Plummer walked up.

'Another helper,' Ralph greeted the newcomer in his friendly manner.

'I'm afraid not.' Gladys Plummer gave him a scathing look. 'My husband is an army officer, and I feel that the onus is on me to warn you not to be so free with your flattery. This young lady consorts with men too cowardly to take part in the war. I doubt that she'll admit it, but her man friend is a conscientious objector.'

Totally humiliated, Anne-Marie lowered the tray just as a

soldier was returning the first empty cup. It fell on to the platform, shattering instantly. The smashing crockery was an explosion that made her cringe.

'Is that right, miss?' Ralph asked Anne-Marie.

Giving a curt nod of affirmation, Anne-Marie then lifted her head, tilting it so that her chin was held high. Leon had done nothing to be ashamed of and she would proudly stand by him. She was trying to think of something telling to say, when the soldier spoke again, astonishing her.

'Then I say good on him. I wish I had his courage.'

'And me!'

'Me too!'

Other soldiers were shouting. Anne-Marie couldn't believe what they were saying. She saw first shock, then rage on Gladys Plummer's narrow face.

'We have great respect for conscientious objectors, miss,' the first soldier told Anne-Marie. 'We admire the stand they are making against the authorities. We are the weak ones. We let ourselves be ordered into the trenches. All we'll do is prolong this war. It is those like your friend who will hurry peace along. Tell him from us to keep up the good work.'

This was supported by a mighty cheer from the soldiers who had been able to overhear. As if in agreement, the engine let out a roaring burst of steam, a whistle was blown and iron wheels spun on iron tracks as the train began to move off. Anne-Marie reached out her hand, fingers brushing those of Ralph. There was nothing sexual, not even flirtatious in the brief contact. Yet it meant much to them both. Then he was gone.

Anne-Marie felt no guilt over the exchange with the soldier. It was something that she would openly relate to Leon. It was something that the gentle Quaker would understand.

Taking a deep breath, expecting Gladys Plummer to be standing there aggressively, eager for further confrontation, she was surprised to see the other woman walking away. Anger showed in Gladys's stiff-legged gait, but Anne-Marie felt no animosity. The war affected people drastically and differently. She didn't envy Gladys her worry over a loved husband serving with the colours.

What Gladys and she had in common was fathers with extreme opinions. They differed in that Anne-Marie distanced herself from what the Reverend Paulton Penny preached, whereas Gladys perpetuated the rantings of Stanley Whitton, MP.

Dusk was settling when Anne-Marie got back to where her mother was wiping down her table while chatting to the uniformed Sophie Bremmer. A few yards away, a smartly dressed woman stood in the sparse light from a lamp painted blue under wartime regulations. Anne-Marie didn't recognize the woman, who appeared to be watching her.

With an uncertain little smile on her face, the stranger approached to ask, 'Might I have a word?'

'What can I do for you?' a mystified Anne-Marie replied with a question of her own, impressed by the business-like appearance of the woman. Possibly a few years Anne-Marie's senior, she was not pretty, but had an attractive face with strength that was close to masculine.

'I couldn't help overhearing that unfortunate incident at the train,' she said in a pleasantly husky voice, her manner completely feminine.

'It was nothing really,' Anne-Marie said, with an apologetic shrug, bracing herself for yet another virulent attack on pacifism. 'Feelings are running high, understandably.'

Anne-Marie's mother had been helped in packing the tea-brewing equipment away. Ready to leave, she was looking inquisitively in Anne-Marie's direction.

Noticing this, the woman said, 'I'm sorry, I won't detain you. Please don't think that I have any sympathy with what that woman said to you. Far from it.'

'She was once a friend of sorts,' a rueful Anne-Marie explained.

'A need to take sides severs all kinds of relationships,' the woman remarked, 'but I don't think that excuses your former friend. We are all ignorant, but some are more ignorant than others. They are the ones ignorant of their ignorance, thereby fooling themselves that they know.'

That was very profound; the kind of thing that Bruce Seldon came out with. Anne-Marie wondered if this woman was a schoolteacher. Glancing at her mother, who was ready to leave, she took a middle course by commenting, 'As they say, it takes all sorts.'

'Unfortunately,' the woman said wryly. 'Forgive me, I neglected to introduce myself. I am Vera Scanlon, maybe you've heard of me?'

'Yes.' Anne-Marie was staggered to be in such famous company. 'The Women's International League, and the su—'

Anne-Marie's hesitation caused Vera Scanlon to chuckle. 'You're right, and the suffragettes. Don't worry, I promise not to padlock myself to your garden gate.'

'That didn't occur to me,' a blushing Anne-Marie stammered. 'But I am wondering what someone like yourself would want with me?'

'Don't sell yourself short. You are. . . ?'

'Anne-Marie Penny. My father's the local vicar,' Anne-Marie answered and, proud of her mother for the first time she could ever remember, then added, 'That's my mother over there.'

Vera Scanlon looked in Rachel Penny's direction saying, 'A very distinguished lady. I can see the resemblance, Anne-Marie. Now, I came down from London to visit an aunt here in Marshlee. I shall be here for two days, and I wonder if we might meet for a chat at some time?'

'I'd love to,' Anne-Marie replied, 'but why?'

'I watched you with the soldiers at the train. You have both intelligence and compassion, Anne-Marie, and, if I can persuade you, I'm confident that you have much to offer our cause.'

'I'm not sure. I've never been involved in anything of the sort.'

'Then give me the chance to outline what we do,' Vera Scanlon said eagerly. 'Perhaps we could meet somewhere, a restaurant or whatever. It is difficult at my aunt's house. I'm something of a fraud, Anne-Marie, in that I preach patience and tolerance yet can't bear to spend too long with an inquisitive old lady who uses an ear trumpet.'

This made Anne-Marie smile as she offered, 'You could come to the vicarage this evening.'

'Are you sure that your parents won't mind?'

'Not a bit, but I must warn you that my father is likely to be totally opposed to all you believe in, everything you stand for.'

'Don't worry on my account.' Vera Scanlon rested a hand lightly on Anne-Marie's arm. 'In my time I've crossed swords on more than one occasion with David Lloyd George and Lord Kitchener.'

'I'm not sure even that will have prepared you to meet my father,' Anne-Marie warned her with a laugh.

Three

The two days since James and he had been arrested by the police at their homes had gone by surprisingly swiftly for Leon. Anticipating animosity at best, brutality at worst, the two of them had been treated civilly by the police. After leaving Marshlee, the arresting officers, a police sergeant and two constables, stopped at a café and ordered egg and chips for themselves and their prisoners. The sergeant paid, and the five of them chatted over a second mug of tea like old friends.

Imprisoned in cells overnight, the following morning they had been brought before the court together with five other conscientious objectors. One was a Quaker like himself, the other four were members of the No-Conscription Fellowship, including a young solicitor's clerk named Paul Rynedale. Although highly intelligent and articulate, the frail-bodied Rynedale preferred to remain in the background. It was his poor health that prompted the capable Rynedale to vote with the others to elect Leon as spokesman for the group. Leon, a man of action rather than words, would have preferred the more knowledgeable Rynedale to be leading them.

In court, the friendly relationship they had with the police was extended to the magistrates. Regarding them neither as cowards nor criminals, the bench afforded all of them respect. Two white-haired women sat on each side of the chairman. He too was elderly, and infirm, with the appearance of a man who had perhaps once been a colonel in days too far back for him to recall.

'As a man,' the chairman said sadly, looking weary of judging people and equally as tired of life, 'I am bound to say that I am not without admiration for individuals such as yourselves who have the courage of your convictions, be they religious or political. As a magistrate, however, I have to uphold the law, and the charge sheets before me state that you have failed to report under the Military Service Act.'

'Yes, sir,' Leon spoke for the others as the magistrate forlornly studied the large, yellow sheets of paper.

'And you have all chosen to plead guilty.'

'Yes, sir.'

The magistrate peered over the tiny lens of his spectacles at Leon. 'I would like to tender the opportunity of changing that plea. You do understand that if you are handed over to the military authorities, then the army will use force if you persist in refusing to obey orders.'

'We fully understand that, sir,' Leon assured him.

'Possibly you are unaware of just how drastic the measures taken will be.'

'We are prepared to stand by our principles, sir.'

Leon was disturbed by the magistrate's eyes. It was as if the old man saw him as a favourite son to whom he was reluctant to say farewell. The old amateur judge started to fumble with his hands, with his words, as he gazed beseechingly into Leon's eyes. Leon had the impression that something mystical was passing between them. Unable to tell what it was right then, he had a feeling that he would understand later.

Breaking the silent exchange, the magistrate said in a shaky voice, 'Each of you will be fined the amount of two pounds, and be held in police custody to await a military escort.'

As they were about to leave the dock, the chairman added seven words that though mild caused Leon's spine to run cold.

'You are now deemed to be soldiers.'

That statement became a reality the following afternoon. After a long and uncomfortable journey by motor lorry they arrived at an army camp in Cardiff. Under escort, they were marched along narrow roads flanked by green grass and rows of brilliantly white-painted stones. The place was like some mongrel offspring of a prison and a public park. But they were in no doubt about it being a barracks when they were lined up outside a guardroom that was a large red-brick, single-storey building annexed to a tall barrack block of grey stone.

On the far side of a low hedge facing them, was a main road that had traffic and pedestrians, all the trappings of normal life. It was no more than yards away, yet for them, deprived of their freedom, it was a parallel but unreachable universe.

The door was opened and they were marched in and left waiting in a dark, narrow corridor that was a dead end. They stood facing a blank wall, with a row of cell doors at their backs. A guard of just one corporal stood by the single door that led back out to the main room. All of them accepted that they must remain silent. Each of them was lost in his own thoughts, his expectations and his fears of what would soon happen to him.

'Pst!'

The attention seeking hiss came from behind Leon's head. Turning, he could see nothing but a Judas-hole in a cell door. Blaming the rogue noise on his imagination, he was about to face the front when the sibilant signal sounded again. Aware that the hiss had issued from the small hole, Leon first checked that the corporal wasn't watching, then moved closer to the door. Squinting into the hole, he found himself looking at a single eye.

'Got any snout, mate?' the eye whispered.

'I don't smoke,' Leon whispered in reply, feeling an absurd guilt at not being able to help the poor wretch in the cell.

'A match then?'

Leon whispered a request for a match to James at his side. The plea was relayed down the line, and a match was passed back. A cautious Leon fed the match through the hole in the door. Fingers as cold as those of a corpse brushed against his to take the sliver of wood.

'Ta, mate. They turns you over regular-like, but I managed to hide the makings for one fag, but I didn't 'ave puffin' to light it with.' The prisoner's voice was that of a man in pain.

'Are you all right?'

Leon's whispered question was pointless. He could offer no

assistance, whatever the condition or circumstances of the man in the cell.

'They've broke all me bleedin' ribs,' the prisoner gasped for breath as he answered. 'I'll give you a tip, mate. They beats you about the body so it don't show. Struggle as much as you can so they 'its you on the 'ead by mistake. That way they'll leave you alone and keep you out the way until your face 'eals up.'

As the door at the end of the passageway opened with a crash, Leon whispered into the hole. 'God bless you.'

'I don't reckon 'e will,' was the prisoner's despondent response as Leon was ordered out with the others.

The main room was large, with a desk, a stove, and an indefinable but sickening odour. On the wall above the desk hung a picture of the king, while a long, yellowing photograph propped on a shelf depicted three tiers of soldiers in the uniforms of a distant yesteryear. A burly sergeant was dipping a tin mug into a bucket of tea. Completely ignoring them, he sipped from the mug with a grateful sigh, belched, then lifted a leg like a urinating dog to rattlingly break wind. Drinking from the mug once more, deeper this time, he then placed it on the table and walked swaggeringly over to Leon and the others.

With a wide stretch of ribbons across his broad chest, the sergeant was every inch a military man. His stiff-necked stance and high collar gave him the snooty appearance of a country squire, but this hint of breeding was betrayed by a coarse London accent. When he spoke it was in an oddly detached way. With his bloodshot eyes fixed on a point above their heads, the sergeant seemed to Leon to be rehearsing his speech and not actually addressing them.

'Well, lads,' he said loudly, 'you've 'ad your fun and bin through the police courts; now it's time to stop all that ruddy nonsense, and it's my duty to make you into soldiers. First, let me advise you to ignore what you 'ear from the men in this 'ere camp. My name is Sergeant Wellstead, and they'll tell you I'm a bastard. That hain't true. Every week I sends money 'ome to me poor old mum. I'd send some to me dad, too, but I never learnt who 'e was. . . .'

Pausing for the laughter that Leon and his comrades denied him, the sergeant showed a touch of anger before he went on.

'I'm a reasonable man, and I leaves the choice up to you. You can have it real easy, or you can 'ave it ruddy 'ard. Like I just said, you do the choosing. Treat me right and I could be a father to you, the father none of you whore's gits never 'ad. You play ball with me, and I'll play ball with you.'

'The men have chosen me as spokesman, Sergeant,' Leon said in a conversational tone, 'and . . .'

'Who gave you permission to speak, laddie?' Wellstead roared in anger, his fat face colouring red and then purple.

'And I have to inform you that we now refuse, and will continue to refuse, to obey all military orders,' an undaunted Leon announced quietly.

Taking a step forwards, Wellstead brought his face so close to Leon that the tips of their noses made contact. There was a rage bordering on madness in the sergeant's small, red eyes. Issuing from a gap between his front teeth was a stench of half-digested food. Holding his breath in an attempt to avoid the noxious smell, Leon failed and resigned himself to the ordeal.

'Listen to me, laddie,' Wellstead said, in a grating half-whisper, 'what you sees before you is an old soldier who's seen it all and done it all. I was at the side of Lieutenant-General French when Kimberley was relieved. I soldiered with men who died bravely beside me, and shot Boers who breathed their last without a whimper, like real soldiers, laddie, like real soldiers. I've 'ad all types serve under me in a long career of which I am most proud. But today I am ashamed. Today is a new and 'orrible first for me 'cos I've been detailed to 'andle you yellow-bellies. Now, don't get me wrong; I'm a soldier through and through, and will do my duty without question for king and country. Even so, deep down where it counts' – he jabbed a finger into his own ample stomach – 'I take it as a personal insult that I 'ave to breave the same air as wot you lot breaves.'

'We refuse to obey all military orders,' Leon repeated.

'You do, do you?' Wellstead said, taking a step backwards. 'We'll see 'ow you feel about that once the medical officer's 'ad a look up your arse to see if your ruddy 'at's on straight.'

'We refuse to be medically examined,' Leon said.

'Right. I see, I see,' Wellstead said, pacing to left and right. 'You really are asking to 'ave it the 'ard way, is that right? Well now, I hain't going to push you.' Picking up a swagger cane from a table, he used it in a mighty swipe at the empty tin mug. Flying through the air, the cup hit the floor with a clatter that caused Leon and the others to give a small, involuntary jump. Wellstead pointed the cane at some papers on the table. 'This 'ere hain't asking much. All I wants is for each one of you to sign a ration form. It's in your own best interest, as you'll want to be fed. Come up to the table one at a time and put your name at the bottom of a paper.'

None of the seven moved. Outside there was a scrunching of boots as a squad of soldiers marched by. Orders were being shouted, close by and at a distance. 'Left-right-left-right . . . left-left-left-right-left. . . .' A freak breeze carried the faint playing of a military band, then snatched it away. Then there was absolute silence in the guardroom as Wellstead waited.

Losing patience, he screamed a one-word order at them.

'*Move!*'

'We refuse to sign anything,' Leon said, as the tail end of Wellstead's shout died away.

Not replying, the sergeant paced back and forth, then he walked up to face Leon once more. For a very long time he stared into Leon's eyes. Desperate to break the gaze, Leon recognized that to do so would give the army its first victory over him. A trivial triumph it might be, but it would still represent a defeat for the conscientious objectors. Leon was determined, as he knew that his fellows were, not to concede as much as half an inch.

At last Wellstead spoke, in the same rasping low tones as before. 'You don't know what you are doing, laddie. You don't 'ave any idea what's in store for you. Like I said, the men reckon I'm a bastard, but I can't be. If I was, then I wouldn't find it in my 'eart to feel sorry for you, like I does right now.'

For the first time since being arrested at his home, Leon was apprehensive. It wasn't fear: it was a numbing disquietude that brought him out in a cold sweat all over.

'Are you sure about this, Anne-Marie?' Judith Seldon frowned. 'I just can't imagine Marshlee without you.'

'I won't be leaving for good, Just for the duration.'

They were standing together in the bay window of the school-house, looking out to where the start of spring was rewarding Judith and Bruce for the long hours spent tending the garden that was part of the school grounds. Beyond and below the asphalt playground, a double-deck, open-top bus filled with soldiers rumbled along the road, a reminder for Anne-Marie of Leon and how much she missed him. The vehicle was one of the *Old Bill* type requisitioned from London Transport. As a parody of a peacetime excursion it was a depressing sight, and both women were glad to turn from the window as they heard Bruce enter the room behind them.

Since moving in after their marriage, the Seldons had turned the place, left vacant since the death of headmaster Stephen Henricks in 1910, into a warm, cosy home. Everywhere Anne-Marie looked in this tidy, inexpensively furnished room, she could detect the stamp of either Judith or Bruce. Anne-Marie liked visiting them. She enjoyed the hospitality, the warmth and the deep, meaningful debates. In the way of all things, the distinct prospect of losing this made it all the more precious.

Bruce placed a tray on the table and left it for Judith to pour three cups of tea from the pot. As a realist, Anne-Marie had always been sceptical of St Paul's philosophy that a man and a woman could be as one, but the Seldons came close. Now, as Bruce took a seat and Judith passed the cups around, it was a matter of unspoken co-ordination, an unconscious display of total har-mony.

Bruce looked questioningly at Anne-Marie. 'I didn't catch all of what you and Judith were discussing, Anne-Marie, but am I given to understand that you have been recruited to women's suffrage?'

'You know very well that's not true,' a laughing Anne-Marie pretended to punch him. Bruce loved to gently rib people, even his wife. Where he was concerned it was impossible to take offence. 'What I am intending is to do something useful for the first time ever.'

'I won't have that,' Judith protested as she offered a plate of biscuits. 'You are always busily engaged in something or other, Anne-Marie.'

'I haven't been in any kind of employment since leaving school, Judith.'

Dismissing this with a shake of her head, Judith said, 'You would have been wasted as a teacher, a secretary, or anything else, Anne-Marie. You have toiled harder than most, and there would be a lot of people around here who would have suffered were it not for your charitable work.'

Though modest to a fault, Anne-Marie had to accept the truth of this. She had put tremendous energy into the fringe activities of the church, initially as an aid to her father, and then on her own volition. Once she had been satisfied with what she had achieved, but in recent times her interest had palled. Never had her faith in God weakened, but she couldn't accept the prevailing remarkable Christian defence of war and military training. As a vicar's daughter she had been placed in an invidious situation by circumstances. In rejecting the Church of England she was denying her father. But that troubled her little, for Paulton Penny, who boasted that he was a 'liberal imperialist', had invented a God who favoured the British in all things, even the slaughtering of people of other races.

Anne-Marie much preferred the quiet, balanced-thinking company of her friends. She was certain that she would be blessed with a similar rapport with the new people she would be mixing with in London. However, what had to take priority over all else was her mother, who had been very ill in hospital for the past four days. Anne-Marie felt sure that the elderly woman had caught a chill when they were providing refreshments for the troops at the railway station. Dr Arthur at the hospital had advised Anne-Marie that her mother's heavy cold could develop into pneumonia. If this did happen, then the worst had to be prepared for. The doctor hadn't mentioned this worrying possibility to her father, and neither did Anne-Marie. Paulton Penny was a difficult man to speak to, and though she felt she should tell him how serious her mother's condition was, she couldn't bring herself to broach the subject.

'Vera Scanlon must have worked her magic on you,' Bruce remarked. 'You are a level-headed woman, Anne-Marie, but please don't rush into anything. She plays pretty rough, and those around her are likely to get hurt. These days it pays to be suspicious of everyone. Remember how the Kaiser invited King George to Berlin to see the German Army at manoeuvres in 1913? Look what happened a year later.'

Able to understand how people who had never met Vera saw her this way, Anne-Marie had formed a very different opinion while with the woman activist. The abrasiveness so essential in order to fight the battles she had been engaged in, was assumed and not even skin deep. The real Vera Scanlon was a sensitive, fundamentally shy, very sweet creature.

'I don't think we could class Vera and the Kaiser together,' Anne-Marie smiled, appreciating Bruce's concern for her.

'Of course not,' he agreed. 'But she lives dangerously with her defiance of authority.'

'She lived dangerously when she came to the vicarage,' an amused Anne-Marie said, 'and proved tough enough to face up to my father at his worst.'

Judith gave a tinkling little laugh. 'Do you know, I can't for the life of me picture Vera Scanlon and the Reverend Penny in the same room together.'

'I try not to think about it.' Anne-Marie managed a painful smile. 'His face was a picture when she told of how she had learned ju-jitsu, and had put it to good use by overthrowing a policeman. He was even more irate when she said this had cost her a night in the cells at Vine Street Police Station.'

'I'd love to have been there,' Bruce confessed. Then his face grew serious as he studied Anne-Marie intently. 'Even so, I can't see you as a revolutionary, Anne-Marie.'

'I won't be; I'll leave that kind of action to those better suited. I've always had a yen for newspaper work, and Vera believes she can find a place for me on *The Tribunal*.'

'The No-Conscription Fellowship's weekly.' Bruce gave his

head a shake of doubt, a perplexed expression on his face. 'That paper's not very popular with the government and military authorities, Anne-Marie. You might well be setting yourself up for attack. The powers that be get really vicious with anyone they see as a threat to the *status quo*.'

She shrugged. 'That doesn't worry me. Anyway, I might not even go to London yet. It depends.'

'On what?' Judith enquired.

On many things,' Anne-Marie replied pensively. 'I won't leave until my mother is well again, and then there's you two. You're my friends and I'd feel that I was abandoning you.'

'Nonsense, we've got each other,' Bruce scoffed. slipping an arm around his wife's waist, and she smiled up at him.

A lump in her throat and a stinging of incipient tears prevented Anne-Marie from saying anything for a moment. Bruce had done his best to appear nonchalant, but all three of them were starkly aware that he and Judith would not be allowed to stay together for much longer. She knew that the pair of them had been living on their nerves ever since Leon and James had been taken by the police. When she did manage to speak, she excused the trickle of teardrops down her cheeks by mentioning Leon.

'So much has happened, there is so much turmoil,' she said. 'I'm frantically worried about Leon.'

'We think of him constantly, of course, Anne-Marie. But he's a strong man. I wouldn't care to take him on, and I'm sure no soldiers would like to try,' Bruce said to reassure her.

'But he won't fight back in case he hurts someone,' Anne-Marie pointed out.

'Leon's Jerusalem is crumbling as he wanders through it, Anne-Marie. All is in ruins around him, but he will find something to grip, and he has the strength to rebuild everything he believes in,' Bruce insisted.

'I hope so,' Anne-Marie said fervently. Then she added, 'What about poor James? He hasn't got anything like Leon's power.'

Mentioning the name of James Hann brought Beth to her mind. The shy girl was another reason to deter her from leaving for London. Though missing her daughter, Elsie Narriott was both relieved and delighted by the way Beth had settled in at her job. Walter Hann praised her work and willingness, and had assured Elsie that her daughter's company had been the best tonic Lou Hann could wish for. Yet when she'd had tea with Beth and her mother the previous Sunday, Anne-Marie could sense that there was something terribly wrong with Beth. The girl hadn't complained, but there was an air of desperation about her. Most likely Walter Hann was working her too hard. Mindful of how much her mother needed money, Beth would not complain. It would be wrong for Anne-Marie to interfere, but she promised herself that she would if it continued.

'Leon will take care of James, Anne-Marie,' Bruce said, breaking in on her thoughts.

'If they are still together,' she grudgingly agreed. 'Do you think the army will have separated them, Bruce?'

'I wouldn't like to say. I confess to being ignorant of all things military, Anne-Marie.'

Placing her empty cup and its saucer on the table, Anne-Marie studied Bruce from under her eyelids. With his high forehead and sensitive face he looked exactly what he was, a caring man with a brilliant brain and a saint-like gift for lifting people to a higher plane. All life was precious, and Anne-Marie's heart bled for those who suffered and died in the front line, but it would be such a tragedy, so unforgivably wasteful, to consign Bruce Seldon, a man capable of benefiting humankind immeasurably, to the trenches.

At the outbreak of war, anxious about the future, she had asked Bruce his opinion on how he thought it would end, and what would it do to the people, to the world, before it was over. He had answered her by using the words of Francis Thompson:

> All things by immortal power,
> Near or far,
> Hiddenly,
> To each other linked are,
> That thou canst not stir a flower
> Without troubling a star.

'The flowers are being plucked, Anne-Marie, and man is greatly troubling the stars,' he had said then, and when she'd looked into his eyes she saw he was every bit as anguished as she.

That anguish was with him this evening. Though not noticeable in Bruce's face, mood or manner, Anne-Marie had grown close enough to him to detect it in his aura.

They talked for an hour or more, Bruce and Judith speaking of their plans for the school, for the pupils, and for themselves as if there was not even a minuscule blurring of the near horizon of their lives. They spoke so positively that Anne-Marie's concern for the immediate future slipped away. It threatened a return when the evening had grown long and a heavy darkness had settled outside.

Bringing a bottle of White Horse brandy from a cupboard, Bruce poured a drink for each of them but didn't lift his glass until asking, 'Can we trust our emotions sufficiently to toast absent friends?'

Moved by the consideration he was showing her, Anne-Marie's mind turned to Leon, where he was, how he was being treated. There was nothing to be gained by being tearful, and it seemed that her thoughts reached him and he sent her strength. She thought, too, though not with the same intensity, of Hubert Lytton, who was possibly suffering less than Leon but was in much greater danger.

'I'll drink to that,' she said positively, reaching for her glass.

'To absent friends.' Bruce held his drink aloft and she and Judith joined him in the toast.

At the door ready to leave, Anne-Marie was pleased by how the evening spent with friends had relaxed her. She was able to put parting with them if and when she went to London from her mind, but discovered that she couldn't walk away without whatever assurance Bruce was able to give about how he could deal with the army and the courts. Some time ago he had hinted that he possessed knowledge with which he could avoid conscription.

Desperate for something to cling to, Anne-Marie had to ask, 'What of you, Bruce? Do you know the way to beat the bullies you'll be facing?'

Bruce suddenly looked very old. Though he tightened the arm

he had around Judith, his customary bouyancy abandoned him. Anne-Marie was traumatized by the resignation in his tone as he replied softly, 'I know all the roads, Anne-Marie, but I don't think I'll ever arrive at the destination.'

After two days of starvation in solitary confinement, Leon and his six fellow conscientious objectors were lined up outside of the guardroom. All of them were totally naked and squirming with embarrassment because they could be seen from the road. Weak from hunger and bodily sore from sleeping on the floor of a cell that had no bed, Leon conditioned his mind to withstand this latest indignity and whatever else he was sure would shortly follow. His greatest worry was Rynedale. With no reserve of physical strength to sustain him, the solicitor's clerk had displayed magnificent courage. When they had temporarily been held with others in a detention area, Rynedale had taught the words and tune of the 'Red Flag' to more than twenty men, and then induced them to sing it with him. The stirring song had continued until four guards, soldiers no older than Rynedale himself, had knocked him to the ground and administered a kicking.

Since then Rynedale had deteriorated. This morning, when they had been brought from separate cells, he'd asked Leon to write a letter for him, as he was too weak to hold a pencil. The short letter was to Rynedale's parents, and every word of it was imprinted on Leon's mind:

My dear ones
A friend is writing this letter for me. We have been treated terribly and I lack the strength to write to you myself. Illegal and brutal acts have been perpetrated upon us, but I am pleased to be able to assure you that I have remained true to my principles of International Socialism. Do not waste your time in trying to write to me. What is hardest for me is leaving you, my dearest ones behind.
Goodbye.
Paul

Leon had suggested deleting the last two sentences and substituting a less final word for *Goodbye*, stressing, 'This letter will upset your mother and father unnecessarily, Paul.'

'You are right about it upsetting them, Leon, but not unnecessarily,' was Rynedale's feeble-voiced reply. From that moment on he wouldn't discuss his letter further.

All seven of them had refused to undergo a medical, resulting in them being stripped by soldiers and held down while the doctor examined them. Afterwards, a major, tall, pale-faced, and as cold as a dead fish, had come to lecture them.

'I am Major Chalmers, and I strongly advise you men to listen carefully to every word I say,' the officer told them. 'I am your last hope. You may believe that you are over the worst, that we have done all we can to you. You delude yourselves. The army can tame wild animals. When the country handed you over to the army it was on the understanding that we could do as we wish with you. Take my word for it, you men: carry on in this manner and you will all be facing a court martial and most likely the death penalty.

'I know that you all belong to some petty little organization – stop the war, no conscription, International Socialism, or whatever. These ridiculous societies are tiny minorities with no power whatsoever. With our heroes dying at the front in hordes, the majority of the British people wouldn't care a damn if we shot you the first time you refused to wear the king's uniform.

'The end is inevitable, so I am asking you now to give up acting the goat. I promise you that all your past offences, all the trouble you have caused the military authorities, will be forgiven and forgotten if you start to be soldiers from this moment on.'

Not one of the seven responded, apart from Rynedale who began to softly hum the 'Red Flag'. Giving them a contemptuous glare, the major had turned on his heel and left without another word.

What came next was a degrading mêlée, an unequal battle in which Leon and his comrades all received bloody noses as they were forcibly put into army uniform. Thrown back into solitary confinement, they had stripped off the detested khaki clothing at once. All seven had been left naked ever since.

'Wot a sorry sight!' Sergeant Wellstead said as he paced up and down in front of them. ' 'Ere am I, a soldier wot's stood four-square on the battlefield with men of the Coldstreams, Irish Guards, Lifeguards, and the Grena-ruddy-diers, stuck with you lot. Well, it won't do.' He raised his voice to a shout. '*Stand at attention!*'

When none of them reacted, Wellstead strode to Leon and kicked his ankles. Agonized by the sergeant's heavy boots, Leon pulled his feet together. Smiling at his victory, Wellstead shouted an order at the soldiers who were standing around him. They moved in to kick the ankles of James Hann and the others. Soon all seven men were standing with their feet together.

But once the kicking stopped they all followed Leon's example when he moved his feet apart again. This sent Wellstead into a rage that had him frothing at the mouth. He screamed out another order. '*Mark time!*'

None of them made any move, and Wellstead moved to begin kicking Leon's ankles again. This time he did it harder so that Leon involuntarily lifted each foot alternately as a boot cracked against his ankle. Soon, with Wellstead having found a rhythm with his kicking, Leon was marking time.

It wasn't long before James and the others were doing the same enforced raising of their knees as the soldiers kicked them. This was a tiring drill for healthy soldiers. For maltreated men who had eaten no food for days it drained energy fast.

'Hup, two, three, four – hup, two, three, four – one, two, three, four – hup, two . . .' the sergeant puffed and panted as he shouted the time while keeping the kicking going.

With the bones damaged, each time a boot collided with his ankles, Leon felt agony knife through his whole body. Aware that the skin of his legs had broken, he assumed that he was bleeding just as badly as his comrades. He could see them stepping in sticky pools of blood as their legs were forced up and down.

At last, because Wellstead and the soldiers were exhausted by their efforts, the marking time stopped. Drawing in deep breaths, the sergeant spoke, his voice still uneven from panting.

'I'll make ruddy soldiers of you lot yet. Stand up straight, Rynedale!'

Having been resting his skinny back against the wall of the

guardroom, the solicitor's clerk weakly pushed himself upright. But the upper half of his body dropped forward so that he was bent almost double. This enraged Wellstead more, and he was advancing on Rynedale when an explosive belching sound which seemed far too loud for his skinny body, burst out of the conscientious objector. Then Rynedale vomited. It was an eruption that splattered noisily on to the ground around him.

'You foul bastard,' Wellstead shouted, smashing Rynedale's mouth with a backhanded blow that knocked the sick man's head back against the wall.

Barely conscious, bleeding from lips that had been mashed against his teeth, Rynedale slid into a sitting position. But two soldiers yanked him to his feet, propping him against the wall, staying with him until satisfied that he could remain upright unaided.

'A fighting soldier is a fit soldier, and none of you lot are fit,' Wellstead said. 'Fetch them a blanket each, Corporal Smythe.'

Minutes later, Leon and the others, each with a blanket wrapped around them, all weak from hunger, with Rynedale staggering like a drunken man, were being taken at the double toward a deserted sports field.

Halting them close to where a vaulting horse stood, Wellstead walked over to lovingly pat the horse as if it was a living animal.

'You lot 'ave never seen lines of real fit soldiers clearing an 'orse, 'ave you?' Wellstead's eyes were as dreamy as a man thinking of his lover. 'It's a marvellous sight, that I can tell you. Before we leave 'ere today, you lot is going to be able to do it, I promise you. Rynedale, you show 'em 'ow to do it.'

When the sergeant tore the blanket off Rynedale, the naked soldier came close to collapse. In danger of dropping to his knees, but fearing a savage beating, he somehow found the resolve to remain standing.

'Start running from 'ere, laddie,' Wellstead told him, 'and you'll build up an 'ead of steam that'll lift you over the 'orse like a ruddy bird in flight. Now, *move!*'

Watching Rynedale ignore the order, Leon was torn between admiration for his stand and wanting the sick boy to comply to save himself from further punishment. But he realized that both of his thoughts were redundant. The vaulting horse was no more than coincidental. Rynedale and the rest of them were being tortured because they would not accept military service, and they would go on being tortured until they did, or until whatever the alternative was had happened.

Rynedale was sent off towards the vaulting horse in a staggering run. Six soldiers went with him, each punching him in turn. At the horse Rynedale stopped, defiance on his grey face as he refused to jump. At a barked command from Wellstead, the six soldiers picked him up and threw him over the horse. Landing heavily on the other side, a stunned Rynedale lay still.

'Liven 'im up, you men,' Wellstead shouted at the soldiers, who bent to pick Rynedale up and dash with him to where a full stream ran along the side of the field.

There was a splash as Rynedale was tossed into the water. Dragged out again by the soldiers, he was forced to run with them back towards the horse, his head flopping loosely, eyes rolling to the extent that Leon could see only the whites most of the time. At the horse, barely able to stand up, Rynedale again bravely refused to obey the order to jump.

On Wellstead's instructions, the six soldiers picked Rynedale up and ran a few yards back from the horse. Then they charged at it as if Rynedale was a battering ram. At a shouted command from Wellstead, they released Rynedale, who went high over the vaulting horse, head first.

Hearing the awesome crack of a bone as Rynedale hit the ground, Leon broke ranks to run across to him, with Wellstead yelling at him to come back. Leon was bending over Rynedale when Wellstead came striding up. 'Get away from him, Marriott,' the sergeant commanded and, when Leon made no move to obey, kicked him in the head, knocking him on to his back.

As Leon came up onto his knees, a bloody three-cornered flap from his scalp hanging over his forehead, Wellstead was yelling at Rynedale.

'On your feet. Show that you're a man. *Get up*!'

Still on his knees, Leon shouted at the sergeant, using a swear word for the first time in his life. 'He can't get up. He's dead. you bloody fool!'

Mouth drooping open, Wellstead turned his head to Leon, who watched the shock on the sergeant's face change to abject fear. The soldiers who had so eagerly picked up Rynedale to throw him, now moved back from the skeletal body as if afraid it would contaminate them in some way.

The letter he had written for the dead man came into Leon's mind. Was it possible that Rynedale had seen a premonition of his death? A more likely explanation was that his poor physical condition had convinced the clerk that he could not for much longer survive the brutal treatment. What did it matter? The poor lad was dead.

Sergeant Wellstead had taken on the sagging, wrinkled look of a half-deflated balloon. All of his bombast had deserted him and he seemed unable to drag his eyes away from the corpse lying untidily in the grass.

They were so far from the camp that it was quiet, very quiet. The air was so resonant that the slightest movement produced a sound that resembled an electrical crackling. Keenly aware of this, Leon couldn't believe what he was hearing when one of the Socialist conscientious objectors began to sing. Dismayed by so sacrilegious behaviour beside a recently dead comrade, Leon then recognized the words:

> *Though cowards flinch and traitors fear*
> *We'll keep the Red Flag flying here. . . .*

One by one the voices of the other Socialists backed the solo singer. Realizing it was a requiem for Paul Rynedale, Leon joined in, and James Hann followed suit. Their combined voices swelled to ring out over the fields, trees and buildings, as Wellstead and the other soldiers stood motionless, afraid and bewildered.

When the last note of the Socialist anthem sounded echoing over the hills, Leon, who fully appreciated and supported what his fellow objectors had done, wanted to add something spiritual to the secular performance. Prepared to go it alone, he sang the opening of 'Simply Trusting', and was delighted to discover that the others, including James, knew the words. They all sang together:

> *Trusting Him while life shall last.*
> *Trusting Him till death is Past.*
> *Till within the jasper wall,*
> *Trusting Jesus, that is all.*

There were tears in all their eyes by the time the hymn had ended. But then their souls were uplifted as a half-demented Sergeant Wellstead cried out in torment, '*Shut up! Shut up!*'

Judith came running up the road to meet him in that half-crying, half-laughing state of women when a crisis has come and gone. What she had gone through was evident to Bruce. His wife would have spent more than twenty-four hours praying, hoping, and watching. Yesterday morning a police-inspector and two lower-rank officers had come to the school to arrest him. For the sake of his pupils, Bruce had pleaded to be allowed to finish the morning's school. But the senior policeman had been adamant; he had to leave with them there and then.

They had taken him away, upsetting his class so that all the girls were in tears, and a number of the boys were sobbing. He had not been permitted to go to the infants' section to tell Judith what was happening. One of the constables had done that for him, no doubt distressing his wife much more than hearing the bad news from him would have done.

Now she collided with him head-on, wrapping her arms round him, hugging him tightly. Tilting her head back to look up at him, she gasped, 'Bruce, thank God, they've let you go.'

'You can't hold a good man down,' he joked, slipping an arm around her as they headed for home.

'What happened?' she asked anxiously.

'I'm cleverer than they are,' he replied, not boasting, but to take what drama he could out of the affair. 'I beat them on a technicality.'

'Thank God,' she said again. 'So it's all over now?'

Bruce delayed an answer. He had won a victory of sorts. Possibly because of his schoolteacher status, he had been allowed to stay in an hotel overnight, instead of the usual cell accommodation. In court that morning, he had asked for the arresting police inspector to take the witness box and the oath. Then Bruce had read to the court a circular from the Home Office recommending that conscientious objectors be brought to court by way of a summons and not by summary arrest. That Bruce had been taken by summary arrest could not be questioned, and the inspector had to admit that he had been given the wrong instruction by the recruiting officer.

Alarmed that they might put a foot wrong, the magistrates. on the advice of their clerk, had remanded Bruce on his own recognisance of fifteen pounds. This obviously wouldn't be the end of it, but he shrank from worrying Judith with that.

'It is all over?' she enquired for the second time.

'I think so,' he replied guardedly.

Hugging him tighter as they went in through the playground gate, heading for their home, she said, 'Do you know what I'd like to do to take us out of ourselves, Bruce?'

'Tell me.'

'I'd like to go to stay with Esther for two or three days by the sea.'

Bruce had no objection. School was breaking-up for the holiday tomorrow, Bournemouth wasn't that far away, and he got on well with Judith's sister. Nothing was likely to happen, for better or for worse, when they were not here in Marshlee. If it did, then they could be blissfully ignorant of it while strolling by the sea-shore.

'It would do both of us good,' he agreed, as she unlocked the door and they went in.

Four

It was a tranquil Sunday afternoon. The folk of Marshlee had gathered in the market-place for a short service arranged by the Reverend Paulton Penny, in memory of Lord Kitchener. Anne-Marie was there, regarding it as her final duty before leaving the town that evening until at least the war was over. Her mother was home from hospital. Although she was still poorly, Anne-Marie had been assured by the doctors that the old lady was no longer in any danger. Though saddened by the intended departure of her only child, Anne-Marie's mother had raised no objection. The same couldn't be said for her father, who vehemently blamed Vera Scanlon for poisoning the mind of his daughter. Reverend Penny's contention was that socialism could not be separated from anarchy, and he stipulated that if Anne-Marie should league together with a Socialist, then she would cease to be his daughter and the vicarage at Marshlee would no longer be her home.

This had caused her mother to cry, making Anne-Marie angry while strengthening her determination. Vera Scanlon had developed and completed the lessons Anne-Marie had learned when listening to Leon, James Hann, and the Seldons. Having always hated violence, Anne-Marie readily accepted the concept of militarism as belonging to a past when kings and nobles ruled supreme over workers who were slaves without voice or choice.

'Capitalism falsely claims that there must be enmity and animosity between nations,' Vera had told her, 'and our boys are being forced to suffer and die in the trenches to support that fiction.'

Seeing this as an unarguable truth, Anne-Marie couldn't wait to help constructively the enlightened ones who worked hard in the face of government aggression and media ridicule.

Looking to where her father stood now in his robes, her emotions seemed to have been neutered. If she felt anything at all for him, then it was pity. That worried her, as she believed that a feeling of dislike would somehow be healthier.

Though nothing would now change her mind about going to London, she wished that Judith and Bruce hadn't gone away on holiday. Bruce would advise her on how to leave Marshlee without totally alienating her father. Without achieving that, her days ahead would be blighted by regret over the rift between them, and worry about her mother.

'My friends,' her father's voice rang out, loud and clear as a church bell. It rebounded off the surrounding buildings to give a dramatic shadow effect to his words as he prayed for the repose of the old soldier's soul.

At the vicar's side throughout, Brigadier Lytton read out a eulogy in which he managed to mention his own name more times than he did Kitchener's.

The Brigadier ended with, 'Lord Kitchener wanted every man trained to arms. We must endeavour to ensure that his wish is fully realized. He would have drilled every male in the country. By gad, it would surprise me if that fine soldier isn't already organizing military training in Heaven.'

'We thank you, Brigadier Lytton,' said Reverend Penny, his ecclesiastical sensitivity in no way offended by Lytton's preposterous hypothesis, before continuing, 'I have gathered you here today to pray for the safekeeping of our men serving, and the souls of our men who have already fallen.'

Anne-Marie saw that the old man with the accordion had come back to Marshlee; had returned to the scene of the crime, as it were. With his instrument strapped on ready to play. he was in the front row of the crowd. Anne-Marie saw her father beckon to him. With his dancing walk the accordionist went towards the clergyman. His entourage of injured, dishevelled soldiers followed haltingly behind him.

'But first,' the Reverend Penny shouted, 'we will all pray to God that through His grace we will be worthy servants of our king, and responsible, worthwhile subjects of the great British Empire. Then I will ask our musician brother to play so that we may sing a hymn together.'

Leading the outdoor congregation in prayer, the clergyman then signalled to the accordionist, whose long white hair fell about his face as he bent to the vertical keyboard. As the hymn-singing began, Anne-Marie spotted Elsie and Beth Marriott in the crowd. She made her way to them. Astounded by how ill and strained the ashen-faced Beth looked, it took Anne-Marie a moment or two to be able to speak.

'Have you heard anything of Leon, Elsie?' she managed to enquire.

'Not a word. I worry so much about him, Anne-Marie.'

'I'm sure he'll be fine. He and James will be together.'

'Do you think so?' Elsie Marriott asked, seeking assurance that Anne-Marie couldn't give. 'They have been close friends since they were little, Anne-Marie, and I'd be comforted to know that they have each other now.'

'I'm certain they are together. What I hear of it they take them all to the same place,' Anne-Marie said before looking anxiously at Beth, then leaning close to the mother so that the child couldn't hear what she was saying. 'Beth looks absolutely terrible, Elsie. Has she complained of being ill?'

'Not at all. But she has become more withdrawn than ever. I was hopeful that working for Mr and Mrs Hann would bring her out, but it seems to have done just the opposite.'

'Do you think they might be working her too hard?'

Elsie Marriott shook her head. 'Not according to her. She's become quite fond of Mrs Hann, who she says doesn't ask a lot of her.'

'It has to be something that . . .' Anne-Marie began, but was shushed at by people standing nearby.

The singing had come to an end. Standing beside her father,

Brigadier Lytton was reading out a list of Marshlee's dead in the war so far. There were sixteen, a long Roll of Honour for so small a town. Lytton reached the last two names:

'. . . William Burden, Ronald Fletcher.'

Anne-Marie reeled inwardly from shock. She hadn't known that the slow-witted but likeable boy and the reserved but always friendly former railway porter had been killed. Neither had Elsie Marriott been aware. Moved to tears at the deaths of two people she had known all their lives, the older woman reached with one hand to clutch and hold Anne-Marie's arm. The soldier with the disturbed mind shouted the drill command. 'Bayonet exercise in close order front and rear back to back!'

On this occasion he raised no laughter. The air remained sombre, the crowd subdued as the accordionist softly played 'Roses of Picardy'. The Reverend Penny knelt on the hard ground, hands clasped in prayer. He'd set an example that the people felt obliged to follow. In an uncoordinated movement they went down on their knees, the old, arthritically, the young, self-consciously.

'Lord we beseech thee,' Paulton Penny called to the heavens, 'take unto Yourself the souls of our dear departed brethren.'

Anne-Marie noticed how old and bent her father looked, and she was disturbed by the sudden discovery. It stirred in her feelings that she hadn't known existed. Had this emotive service changed him or her? Perhaps they both had undergone some kind of kindred conversion.

'Amen,' came discordantly from the people.

As the Marshlee folk got to their feet, dusting off their clothes, massaging pain from their knees, two women held the sobbing, wailing mother of Billy Burden between them. Close behind Anne-Marie, Constance Fletcher, the late Ronald's spinster sister and only kin, wept quietly, a handkerchief pressed to her face. It was contagious sadness, with families as yet untouched by war weeping beside the bereaved.

Moved by what was happening around her, Anne-Marie's resolve began to ebb, and she considered remaining in Marshlee to avoid the traumatic experience of saying goodbye to her parents that evening. She was rescued only by a mental image of the strong-faced Vera Scanlon scolding her, telling her to be brave.

'I'm leaving Marshlee tonight, Elsie.'

Anne-Marie made the difficult announcement bluntly, because there was no other way. Wincing as she saw the reaction on Elsie Marriott's face, she felt terrible about abandoning the woman at a time when she sorely needed comfort and support.

About to soften the blow by saying that she wasn't going for good, and would come home as often as possible, Anne-Marie was surprised to see that her friend had turned away from her. Then her heart skipped several beats as she realized why. Beth had heard what she had said. Now, in tears and trembling, the girl was clinging to her mother with both hands. When Anne-Marie reached out to put a hand on her shoulder, Beth jerked away, hiding her face in her mother's breast.

'She thinks the world of you,' Elsie Marriott said, battling her own threatening tears.

'And I of her,' Anne-Marie said. 'I wouldn't hurt her for the world. I'll walk home with you both and try to put things right.'

'No, thank you, Anne-Marie, but you have things to do,' Elsie protested.

'There's nothing that can't wait, Elsie. London can wait.'

'No, Anne-Marie,' Elsie Marriott said bravely. 'We both love Beth, Anne-Marie, but I will not allow you to live your life for her. You go as you plan, and when Beth feels better I will explain that you will be back.'

'Please tell her that. Tell her I love her, Elsie.'

With a nod to confirm that she would do this, Elsie Marriott hurried away with her daughter, the two of them walking oddly as they held on to each other. Watching them go, Anne-Marie realized how infectious the outbreak of crying was. Beth had caused her to weep, but the reasons for Anne-Marie's tears were manifold.

Standing, lost and desolate in a world blurred by her own tears, Anne-Marie felt an arm go round her. Blinking her eyes to

79

clear them, she saw that it was her father embracing her. Giving way to a deep sob she wrapped her arms around him.

Paul Rynedale had, posthumously, won them a victory. Due to the scandal of his death, Sergeant Wellstead was moved from the barracks. Corporal Smythe was temporarily put in charge of the conscientious objectors. Smythe, a taciturn Irishman, was a disciplinarian but had none of the sadism of his predecessor. All of them were certain that Smythe had reported Wellstead, but they would never really know. Leon and the others had been given food and had their civilian clothes returned to them. In his pseudo-acrimonious fashion, Smythe had explained that they would all be facing courts martial, and advised them to make it easy on themselves until that time came. The corporal warned them that they might well be sentenced to death, a possibility they all acknowledged in a philosophical manner.

They agreed it would be best to get along with Smythe as well as they could without compromising the stand they had taken from the start. None of them had signed any papers, each of them had continually refused all payment and would not don a military uniform.

Leon was concerned for James. Despite now being fed, his friend was weakening in other ways. He was more seriously affected than any of them by the hardship they were enduring, and was increasingly missing his home and his parents. Resigned to James eventually cracking under the strain, it perturbed Leon to ponder on what form this collapse might take. He prayed that he would be close by when it did happen.

On a morning that had begun with a violent thunderstorm, Smythe took them out on the deserted parade ground. A regiment had marched out that morning behind a fife and drum band. Hearing the military music while in his lonely cell, Leon had been lifted by this strangely seductive aspect of the militarism he detested. He had balanced out that rogue reaction by praying for the young men following the drum at dawn.

Taking them to the square was a pointless exercise. For the corporal it was just a matter of going through the motions. The six of them had ambled to the centre of the massive parade ground, and there they stood talking among themselves in a group. Smythe knew that it would be hopeless trying to drill them, so he just stood off to one side.

They idly watched a battalion of cyclists pass. There were hundreds of them and the low swishing of their machines took on a surrealism in the vacant barracks. A passing orderly stopped for a short conversation with Smythe. Leon heard talk that a troop of Lincolnshire Yeomanry would be arriving that afternoon, and a battalion of the Royal Sussex were due in the morning.

Before he left, the orderly produced a packet of cigarettes. He and Smythe lit up, and when the orderly walked away the corporal continued to smoke furtively.

'What on earth is going on here, Corporal?'

Leon heard the question asked in angry, cultured tones, and was aware of Smythe's boot slamming into the tarmac as he came to attention and saluted before shouting at them.

'This is a sir,' the corporal yelled, as if they should be impressed. 'Stand to attention.'

All six of them turned indolently, leaving their bodies slack and standing with feet astride. Not knowing what to expect, and far from caring, Leon couldn't believe his eyes. Facing him, a wicked grin on his face, was Hubert Lytton, now showing the rank of captain.

'Well, well, well.' Lytton waggled his handsome dark head in disbelief. 'God truly moves in mysterious ways, Marriott, and now I've arrived, His wonders to perform. You too, Hann; the pair of you delivered to me like a brace of pheasants sent from a bush by beaters. This is an utter shambles, Corporal, and I hold you responsible.'

'These men won't accept discipline, sir. They refuse to obey any orders.'

'Do they now,' Lytton mused, tapping his swagger cane against the leg of his right boot. 'What would happen, Corporal, if you gave one of them a Mills bomb and ordered him to throw it?'

81

'He would refuse the order, sir.'

'I wonder, Corporal, I wonder,' Captain Lytton said quietly and questioningly. 'Go to the barracks and fetch me a Mills bomb, Corporal. At the double, there's a good chap.'

Spending a moment watching Smythe double off the square, Lytton then spoke to Leon and the others. 'Pay attention, you men. I have been sent here to break this ludicrous protest of yours, and break it I will. My orders are to employ whatever force, whatever means, necessary. If you capitulate now you can enlist as soldiers with your bodies and your minds still intact; decide to continue this nonsense and you will still become soldiers, but I will have broken you in the process.

'I promise that great pressure will be brought to bear upon you. You think that you're making a courageous stand, but each one of you is nothing but a wiggling little slug that could be impaled on a toothpick. I cannot impress on you enough the absolute insignificance of one individual in a modern army. Is that fear I see in your eyes, Marriott?'

'No, it's disgust, Lytton. Fear is what you'd be shaking with if you didn't have the army at your back, and it was just you and me here facing each other,' was Leon's contemptuous answer.

Though his face flushed, Lytton came back sarcastically, 'I say, that was aggressive. Not very Quakerish, what?' He broke off as Smythe returned with a Mills bomb, taking it from the corporal before saying, 'What you have to understand about a company of cowards, Corporal, is that they draw strength from each other. They huddle together for comfort like rabbits in a burrow. Divide them and they become gibbering wrecks, I will demonstrate. March everyone but Marriott off the square. Leave him to me.'

The corporal ordered the others to leave, but they remained motionless, looking to Leon for guidance. When he gave a nod they reluctantly walked away.

Waiting until they stopped beside Smythe on the edge of the parade ground, Lytton shouted, 'Take them along there by the water-tower, Corporal. I want you all further away.'

Suspicious of Lytton's actions, Leon conditioned himself for a bad experience. So far he had learned that cruel non-commissioned officers such as Wellstead were a rarity. The real viciousness lay with the officers, many of them from families with blood too blue to be wholesome.

When satisfied with the position taken up by the corporal and the other conscientious objectors, Lytton removed the pin from Mills bomb and held it out to Marriott.

'Throw it!' the captain ordered.

Making no move to take the bomb, Marriott put his hands behind his back and stared at Lytton. Beads of sweat bubbled up on the captain's forehead. From the corner of his eyes, Leon saw that the tension had reached the men at the side of the square. Their bodies were stiff with apprehension. As more seconds passed, a twitch started up at the right corner of Lytton's mouth, twisting the black moustache so that it wiggled like a hairy caterpillar.

'Throw it!'

This time Lytton screamed the order; Marriott continued to stare, but didn't respond.

Nerve suddenly giving way, Lytton dropped the live Mills bomb on the ground and ran off. Outwardly calm, Marriott stood motionless with the bomb hissing between his feet, but every nerve in his body was jangling. His thoughts were of his mother and sister. How would they cope when they were told of his death? How would they manage without him in the years to come? Anne-Marie came into his mind. She was beautiful, intelligent and understanding, all a man could want in a woman. Then he forced her out of his head. Waiting for the explosion that would tear him apart, blow him to pieces, he concentrated on prayer.

Having reached the edge of the square, Lytton threw himself face down on the ground, as Smythe shouted '*Down!*' and he and the five conscientious objectors with him did the same.

Leon ceased his silent praying to listen more carefully. Yes, the hissing had stopped. The Mills bomb had been faulty. It lay on the ground before him, silent and impotent. Fervently thanking God for his deliverance, Leon was close to fainting.

The most terrifying experience of his life had passed, and he never wanted to face anything like it again. Sweat streamed down his back and ran down his legs as he breathed deeply and slowly recovered.

When he was back in the barracks he found Smythe was in awe of him.

'Let me shake you by the hand,' the corporal pleaded. 'I've been around, but never in all my born days have I seen guts like that.'

'I couldn't do anything about it,' Leon said, worried because Hubert Lytton had sent him and the others back with Smythe, but had separated James from them.

'You could have run,' Smythe pointed out.

'Forget about me, what do you think is happening to James Hann?'

'I don't know, but I'll find out,' Corporal Smythe promised, then added in a whisper after taking a cautious look around to check that he couldn't be overheard, 'And I'll make sure that captain doesn't get away with what he did to you. Say nothing, Marriott, just leave it to me.'

The next morning Smythe came back to him to report that Lytton had placed James in a specially dug hole in the ground. It was eight feet deep and so small in circumference that James had to be lowered into it by means of a rope tied round his waist. Once in the hole he was only able to stand up. It had rained overnight, and James was now knee deep in water.

'Captain Lytton has told him that you and the others have been sent to France, where you will be shot,' Smythe reported.

'Do you think he believes that?' Leon asked, fearful to contemplate the dire effect this bogus information would have on his friend.

'After an hour or so in that hole you'd believe anything,' Smythe assured Leon. 'I'll do what I can for him, but it won't amount to no more than sneaking him some food and water to keep him going.'

Aware of the chances Smythe would be taking, Leon welcomed having the soldier on his side. But he didn't see

Smythe again for three days. In the interim, his chief guard was an uncomfortable, ageing sergeant whose indifference to conscientious objectors was so profound that he didn't seem to notice that Leon and the others were there.

Those three days and nights dragged by agonizingly slowly for Leon. The worry turned his thoughts constantly towards his friend, and those thoughts soon sparked off Leon's imagination. Certain that James didn't have the reserves of strength to survive the kind of ordeal he was being subjected to, Leon had a recurring mental picture of him crumpled in the hole, dead.

On the afternoon of the third day, Corporal Smythe made a hurried and unauthorized visit to Leon, answering his urgent enquiry about James with, 'He's all right. They took him out of the hole yesterday.'

'Thank the Lord,' Leon said on a long, sighing breath, but he then noticed that Smythe was behaving uncomfortably. 'Is there something else, Smythe?'

'Yes,' Smythe nodded curtly, 'Hann gave me a message for you. He said to say that he was sorry, and that he hopes you will forgive him. He said that being in the hole had driven him half mad.'

'I don't understand,' Leon frowned. 'Why would James need to apologize to me?'

Walking to the door, his military bearing deserting him, Smythe turned to look at Leon with haunted eyes. 'Don't be hard on the boy, Marriott. He was in a bad way. I didn't join the army to be part of the brutality that's going on here.'

'James gave in, didn't he?' Leon said hollowly.

'Yes,' Smythe confirmed as he left.

Alone, and experiencing a depth of loneliness he had never before sunk to, Leon understood why James had given in. It hurt, but it didn't demoralize him. If Hubert Lytton tried the same tactics with him, then he would find some way of surviving without surrendering.

An hour later, when Lytton and four soldiers came for him, he was resigned to being put in the hole recently vacated by James. But Lytton had other plans for him. The soldiers carried a valise filled with stones, which Leon was made to carry as a pack as he was force-marched to the field where Paul Rynedale had died.

On reaching the destination, already half exhausted, Leon was relieved of the valise, and ordered by Lytton to salute him. Leon refused. Lytton repeated the order, and Leon again refused.

Seething with rage, Lytton told him, 'James Hann is a soldier now, Marriott. I told you that I'd break you all. It means doing it one at a time, but I'm a patient man. Before this afternoon has ended I'll have you begging me to allow you to pick up the flag and carry it into battle against the Hun.'

'One day, Lytton,' Leon spoke in even tones, 'you and your fellow persecuters will be dethroned and we who love peace will triumph.'

Gesturing for two soldiers to hold Leon firmly, Lytton stepped forward to put the point of his swagger cane under Leon's chin. Pushing upwards, the pressure bending Leon's neck back so that it felt it was about to break, Lytton spat out his words. 'You speak of dreams, little man, while face to face with reality. Before another thirty minutes have passed I will have you crawling at my feet. You are the ringleader, Marriott, and once I have toppled you the others will fall.'

Removing the swagger stick so that Leon's head was able to drop back painfully into its proper position, Lytton once more ordered him to salute. When Leon yet again refused, Lytton punched him twice in the face, hard. Leon's nose bled copiously and he could feel his left eye closing as it swelled from a blow.

On orders from Lytton, the four soldiers stripped Leon. He stood staring steadily at Lytton, past being embarrassed by his nakedness when his clothes had been pulled off him. He was manhandled then. The soldiers bent him over, lifting his right arm and left leg above his head and holding them there. With a delighted Lytton pacing beside him, thus Leon was frog-marched by being compelled to move along on his left arm and right leg.

All the punishment Leon had endured had long ago merged

into one long and horrible experience, but right then he deemed this cruel indignity to be the worst of all. All his strength, reserve and resolve appeared to have been used up, and he was in a bad way when a shout came from a little way off and the soldiers suddenly released him.

Sprawled awkwardly and painfully on the grass, Leon saw a colonel and a major approaching together at a fast pace. When they were just a couple of yards away, the major snapped an order at the soldiers, who were standing at attention.

'You men! Put the prisoner's clothes back on and return him to the detention room.'

Handling him roughly, causing excruciating pain in his recently twisted arms and legs, the soldiers dressed him as he heard the colonel say, 'Captain Lytton, you will come with me to HQ Company lines.'

Later, when Leon was sitting on the floor of his cell, back against the wall as he manipulated his limbs in a futile attempt to push the pain out of them, a furtive Smythe entered.

The corporal passed him a newspaper. Peering at it in the poor light, Leon saw it was the local *Gazette*. On an inside page was the story of James Hann's suffering in the hole, and his own close-to-death encounter with a Mills bomb. No names were included in the report, but Leon could now understand why the colonel and the major had come to the field for Hubert Lytton.

'I don't know how them newspaper people gets hold of these stories,' Smythe commented, tongue in cheek.

'What will happen to Captain Lytton, Smythe?'

'He'll be on his way to France, Marriott,' the corporal said, imitating, badly, the accent of an officer to add, 'Spot of leave first, of course. old chap.'

'I pity him,' Leon exclaimed, causing Smythe to look at him in amazement.

'You what? After what he did to you lot? You should be hoping he gets a Boche bullet up his pampered backside, Marriott. But if he don't, don't go worrying: he's hated that much that one of our boys will get him.'

The viciousness of it all shocked Leon. He owed Corporal

Smythe a lot, not only for himself but for James, yet what the soldier had just said was so grievous that Leon had a problem in feeling grateful to him.

Both Judith and Bruce Seldon had benefited from the short holiday. Staying with Judith's sister in Boscombe, they had enjoyed touring the quaint and varied shops there. Only the shortage of several items hinted of the war raging so short a distance across the English Channel. They made an excursion to Christchurch, where they had picnicked on the lush green banks of the beautiful River Avon. The place had been packed with relaxed, happy holidaymakers, Here it was possible to forget the war completely until twilight when some perfunctory lighting restriction was a reminder.

Though they had been careful not to broach the subject to each other, Bruce recognized that the very real threat of conscription was in the back of his wife's mind just as it was his. The prospect cast a pale shadow over all their activities, which had included sampling the sandy-shored delights of Bournemouth and connecting up with maritime history on the quay at Poole.

With the pair of them reluctant to return and face whatever, if anything, awaited them at Marshlee, the discipline needed to bring them back came from their being required to officiate at the school sports.

An early warning that something was wrong came when they met old Clement Quincey outside the Memorial Gardens.

'I thought you two was back already,' commented Quincey, who had been in the Crimea with the Scots Guards and was abusing what remained of his memory by trying to equate that old war with this new one.

'Why do you say that?' Bruce asked.

'There's a right posh landau outside your house,' the old soldier replied. 'Had me thinking you'd come into money.'

Alarmed by this, Judith and Bruce quickened their steps. Turning into School Road they saw the landau. For Bruce, the stationary vehicle took on the guise of something predatory waiting to pounce. As they neared, they could see two men in the landau. One of the men got out as they approached. It was the police inspector who had previously arrested Bruce. The man was smiling, proffering a hand as Bruce came up.

'We meet again, Mr Seldon. Inspector Byrne.'

Taking the hand and shaking it, filled with trepidation, Bruce asked, 'What can I do for you, Inspector?'

'I'm afraid we have some unfinished business, Mr Bruce.'

'Oh no, I thought it was all over.' Judith breathed the words softly.

'In what respect?' Bruce enquired, although he didn't doubt that the policeman's presence could only mean trouble for him.

'I'm afraid that they want you back in court,' Byrne replied, with what looked like an expression of genuine regret.

'We've just arrived home from a short holiday, as you can see,' Bruce said, indicating the suitcase he was carrying. 'Don't worry, Mr Byrne, I'll be there in the morning. What time has the hearing been set for?'

Clearing his throat, Byrne looked away from Bruce as he replied. 'I'm afraid it is more serious than that, Mr Seldon. You see, sir, my orders are to take you with me now.'

'You have a warrant for my arrest?'

'I regret that is the case,' Byrne said, pulling a paper from his pocket and holding it out for Bruce to see, 'and I'm obliged to caution you that anything you say now may be used in evidence against you.'

To her credit, Judith didn't cry, but she looked ill with worry as Bruce kissed her tenderly, squeezed her arm as if transferring strength from him to her, and said, 'Don't fret, Judith, I'll be back with you tomorrow.'

When they were in the landau, Bruce was unable to prevent a brief, snorting laugh.

'Something amusing you, sir?' a surprised Byrne turned his head to ask.

'I was thinking how ironic it is that Herbert Samuel, the Home Secretary, wrote before the war that conscription is both wicked and inane, and here you are, arresting me under the Military Service Act.'

'All politicians change their tune when they achieve positions of power, Mr Seldon,' Inspector Byrne observed.

'Doesn't it trouble your conscience to have a turncoat for a chief?' Bruce asked.

Shrugging his wide shoulders, Byrne answered, 'I asked that question of myself, Mr Seldon, and decided that what I am presently doing is preferable to the alternative.'

'Which would be?'

'A trench in the front line,' Byrne replied wryly; then enquired 'And what of you, Mr Seldon? Will the war prove your judgment to be mistaken?'

Giving the question some thought, Bruce came up with a philosophical answer. 'Who knows! Maybe in a dim corner of one of the dark, dank dungeons of the judiciary I will meet a man who knows why men behave as they do.'

With his regimental march played by the elderly musicians of the local brass band, James Hann marched through the town as soldierly as the other members of his battalion. The pavements were lined with waving women and children, and the transport coming along behind the infantrymen lent an appearance of great strength to the column as it made its way to the railway marshalling yard.

Still having problems with his legs from the time spent in the punishment hole, more homesick than ever, and still feeling bad about having let down Leon Marriott, James occupied his mind with thoughts of the journey ahead. Never having been far from Marshlee, he looked forward to a train journey during which he could see something of England and then the landscapes of a foreign country, France.

But he soon discovered that his comrades and he would have only limited views of the countryside through slits in the sides of the closed railway wagons in which they travelled. There was only one carriage in the train, and that was marked Officers Only.

The two-day journey was stiflingly hot and uncomfortable. A lesson the soldiers soon learned was that the army valued horses more than it did men. The men were fed and watered, but even in that respect the animals took priority over them.

'How is it that you were late joining the rest of us, Hann?' enquired a wiry Birmingham boy named Bell.

As he was jerked about by the lurching wagon as it click-clacked along the rails, James considered what answer to give. He knew that in his position neither Leon nor Bruce would hesitate to say that they were conscientious objectors. James wished that he had the courage of those two friends. Yet here, amid hundreds of men but still very much alone, he didn't want to risk ridicule or hatred from his fellow soldiers.

'I was sick for a while.'

'Oh,' said Bell. 'Did you do the full training course?'

'Yes.'

That was a lie as well. Leon would be far from proud of him right now. Yet that didn't worry James as much as his lack of training did. Once he had dropped his protest he had, ill and weak from the punishment he had endured, been rushed into the army. James had been placed with an intake that had already completed four weeks training. James's fear was that his lack of military knowledge would let him down in the field.

They were enthralled by the novelty of the French town where they were billeted in a factory that sagged from years of disuse. Despite the constant coming and going of British troops, the town kept its identity with its shops and cafés, some familiar, others exotically fascinating. The language was amusing at first, but became frustrating when an attempt was made to communicate. James's initial response to dogs pulling carts was one of horror, believing it to be cruel. But soon he realized that they enjoyed tugging the little carts over the cobblestones.

They remained in the town for two days while supplies were brought up. The nerves of the young soldiers, all trained but untried, were stretched taut by the distant explosion of shells and the chattering of machine-guns. Aware that they were not far from the firing line, James found relief in the anti-climax that came with the order to move out for the trenches.

A brilliant display of starlights and Very lights fired into the air to illuminate No Man's Land told them that they were close to their destination. With the line stretching for miles and miles to the left and right, they were marched on as a battalion in column of fours. Relaxing into the feeling of comradeship, the absence of rigid military discipline as they sang and smoked, James discovered that his concerns about his parents and his home were less intense on this side of the Channel.

Then they met the London soldiers who were to be their guides. The order came 'No smoking and no talking', and they moved on in single file. James was amazed that the euphoria persisted even when they took up their respective positions on the Neuve Chapelle front. There was a constant crackle of machine-gun and rifle fire. A hard-faced sergeant serving with the London men warned them that the continual buzzing above their heads came from German bullets flying by.

'Keep dahn or you'll get your bleedin' 'ead shot awf,' the sergeant instructed.

Having expected war to be worse than this, much worse, James felt the dread that had built in him over days drain away in minutes. An hour later, he realized that he had wandered into a fool's paradise. Ordered to join a fighting patrol formed to flush out German machine-gunners from a railway cutting, he was soon to learn what war was really like. In the beginning there was nothing to it. As James and the rest of the patrol moved up the hill the only Germans they met were eager to surrender.

They popped up out of the ground with their hands raised. Not really sure how he expected a German to look, James couldn't adjust to the fact that none he saw here would appear out of place walking the streets of Marshlee.

'Disarm them and send them to the rear,' the captain leading the patrol ordered.

In the cutting, the enemy machine-gunners were not so ready to give up. They kept up fire, but the British machine-gunners were starting to stream bullets into the cutting.

At a shout from the captain, the patrol rushed the cutting and the Germans fled. A frightened James swung his rifle round as he saw two Germans staring at him from a shell-hole. But they had the vacant eyes of the dead. He was looking at his first corpses, and finding it unpleasant. Feeling both queasy and stupid, he lowered his rifle.

A corporal wearing the ribbon of the Military Medal had witnessed James's startled response to the two dead Germans. Expecting to be laughed at, instead James received a friendly, sympathetic smile and a pat on the shoulder.

There was one live German left in the cutting. Half-concealed in a dug-out, he spoke rapidly in German when the patrol found him. The corporal and another soldier got him out, and an interested James walked over as the captain questioned the German. He was young, probably around James's age, dark, when James had expected every German to be fair, with a blue/black stubble of beard. There was considerable trouble caused by the language barrier, but the smiling German seemed to be doing his best to answer the queries put to him by the captain.

The British, however, had forgotten to search their prisoner. Producing a small revolver he'd concealed in his hand, quickly the German fired the weapon.

Something hit James hard in the shoulder, spinning him round, coming close to knocking him off his feet. Feeling no pain, he clapped his hand to the shoulder and felt sticky blood oozing out. He watched the corporal kick the tiny gun from the prisoner's hand. while an angry soldier thrust his bayonet into the German's throat so hard that it came bloodily out of the back of the prisoner's neck.

There was a burning pain in James's shoulder now. Coming over to him, the corporal with the Military Medal cut his uniform away with a knife. Taking a quick look at the wound he said, 'You'll live, matey. It went straight through.'

Unsure whether it was the loss of blood that flowed from the wound, or the sight of it that made him feel faint, James leaned his healthy shoulder against a side of the cutting.

'Brace yourself, matey,' the corporal advised, as he broke a phial of iodine over the wound.

Tearing open a field dressing, the corporal skilfully bandaged James's shoulder, predicting, 'You'll be saying goodbye to the front line with this, at least for some time. How long you been up here, matey?'

'About one and a half hours,' a shamefaced James confessed.

'You lucky sod,' the corporal chuckled.

Five

There were faces present that were unknown to Anne-Marie, and she thrilled as Vera Scanlon put famous names to them. She was seeing in the flesh prominent people she had previously only read and heard about, such as Clifford Allen, Chairman of the No-Conscription Fellowship, Herbert Morrison, union leader and circulation manager of the now defunct *Daily Citizen*, Philip Snowden, of the Independent Labour Party, and his wife, Ethel, organizer of the Women's Peace Crusade, Penner Brockway, the handsome young editor of the *Labour Leader*, his lovely wife, Lilla, and Bernard Boothroyd.

The size of the crowd astounded her. She estimated there must be over 2,000 people in the hall. The fact that it was mostly men created an atmosphere of masculine camaraderie that forced her out toward the fringe of things. Anne-Marie remained a part of the meeting only by virtue of her friend's powerful personality. It seemed that just about everybody not only knew Vera, but held her in high esteem, In this gathering of dissenters, Vera Scanlon was looked on as one of the most resourceful and fearless activists of all.

There had been demonstrations outside when Vera and Anne-Marie had arrived. A loud chorus of chanted abuse was confusing rather than deafening. Most of the menace came from a mixture of full-time soldiers and Territorials who milled around in the street, but men and women civilians shouted foul, sexually orientated epithets as they waved Union Flags and banners with wording that denounced cowards.

'I feel right in the heart of things now,' Anne-Marie told Vera, inspired by the emotive but deeply meaningful speeches in which the politicians of the day were described as the 'new aristocracy'.

Her two weeks in London, marred at the start by missing her parents and worry about Leon and his young sister, had become increasingly exciting. The room she was renting, barren as a desert when she had moved in, had taken on the air of a second home after her few belongings had been in place for a while. With the promise of a responsible job on *The Tribunal* holding good, her only contribution to the cause had so far been an account of her meeting with soldiers on the train in Marshlee. Encouraged by Vera to write the story, she later learned that it had been widely distributed. Although she had not seen her words in print, there was an exhilaration in knowing that they were being read. As a foretaste of what was to come with her journalistic work, Anne-Marie found it to be quite heady.

'Anne-Marie, let me introduce Mr Edward Grubb,' Vera Scanlon said, during a short interlude as there was a change of speakers on the platform. 'With Leon in mind I'm sure you'd like to meet a Quaker of long standing. Mr Grubb was also, as you probably know, organizing secretary of the Howard League for Penal Reform.'

Aged around sixty, the grey-haired Grubb had kindly blue eyes that twinkled from an innate sense of humour. 'Anne-Marie,' he said musingly, going inward to search his memory. 'Of course, you are the author of that excellent pamphlet about soldiers supporting our movement.'

'I didn't realize anyone knew who I was,' Anne-Marie replied, with a self-conscious smile.

She was puzzled because her name hadn't been included when the pamphlet had been printed, but also delighted that her work had been recognized. Edward Grubb wagged a finger at her in mock reproval.

'Naughty girl,' he smiled. 'You're not going to make any friends in high places by putting the morale of the army into question. You have placed yourself in the ranks of those looked upon as enemies of the nation.'

'That won't worry me. I trust that the end will justify the means,' Anne-Marie said.

'The words of a strong spirit,' Grubb praised her. 'Let a veteran campaigner give you a small piece of advice, Anne-Marie. Noreen and those two men knew the risks, so you mustn't feel responsible in any way.'

Ignorant as to what he was inferring, Anne-Marie was sick with apprehension. Something bad must have happened that involved her, directly rather than indirectly from the way Grubb had spoken. She was about to question him when she heard raised voices by the door of the hall.

A group of soldiers were arguing loudly with stewards who were trying to prevent them entering. The current speaker, whom Anne-Marie felt sure was Ramsay MacDonald, pointed at the rabble-rousers.

'This is a private meeting,' the speaker stressed, 'please leave quietly or we will have no alternative but to call the police.'

This announcement was met with raucous laughter from the gatecrashers. The resistance put up by the stewards was over-whelmed by sheer weight of numbers, and then people, uniformed and in civilian dress, were rushing forwards in a stam-pede that scattered those who were sitting or standing nearby. The No-Conscription Fellowship platform party was ejected, and a smartly dressed man addressed the assembly at the top of his voice. He managed two or three indecipherable words, but then decided to wait until he could be heard when the disruption had settled down.

'That's the editor of the *Daily Express*,' Vera informed Anne-Marie in a hushed voice.

They had moved to the rear of the hall, standing not far from the exit. A distinguished looking man of average height, whom Anne-Marie had noticed on the platform waiting to speak, was also separating himself from the violence that was taking place.

'This is bad, this is bad,' the man said gravely, although the upturned ends of his heavy black moustache gave an impression of permanent amusement. 'Let me get you two ladies safely out of here.'

'In a little while, Will, I want to hear what he has to say,' Vera said, rising on tiptoe to look towards the platform.

'If you read the *Daily Express* you can guess,' the man with the black moustache muttered unhappily. He spoke to Anne-Marie. 'They refer to us as "pasty-faces" in that paper.'

'And what do you call them?' Vera asked cheekily.

'Nothing that I could say in front of two young ladies.'

A fight was going on close to them. Ignoring it, Vera leaned toward Anne-Marie. 'I'm choosing a poor time to make introductions, Anne-Marie, but this man will be your boss. He's Will Chamberlain, editor of *The Tribunal*.'

'Anne-Marie,' he repeated her name after overhearing it, 'I'll consider myself a lucky man if you write for me the sort of story you put on that pamphlet.'

Though nervous at what was going on around her, Anne-Marie enjoyed the compliment. 'I never realized that I had become so famous.'

'Our kind don't get famous, we get hated,' Chamberlain told her, his lips uniting with his black moustache in a smile.

'Shush,' Vera hissed urgently but politely. 'Your rival editor's about to start speaking.'

'Ladies, and gentlemen,' the interloper shouted over the tumult. 'Permit me to introduce Captain Wyndham, who is a recruiting officer.'

The uniformed captain took centre stage, but the backs of the whole assembly were to him as the No-Conscription Fellowship members made for the door. They found their way blocked by soldiers and Territorials, but they joined together to push past without offering violence.

'It's time to go, Anne-Marie,' Vera said, as disorder degenerated into violent chaos.

With Vera holding one of her arms and Will Chamberlain the other, both of them obviously no strangers to disrupted meetings, Anne-Marie allowed herself to be guided through the crowd. Heavy boots and shoes trampled her feet, and at times she was so crushed between a mass of bodies that it was difficult to breathe. They were close to the door when two grinning, taunting Territorials obstructed them.

Anne-Marie gave an involuntary, short scream as on her left two soldiers knocked a young civilian down and kicked him hard in the back. He was twisting on the floor, groaning in agony as they yelled at him that he was a 'cowardly, conchie bastard'. Not knowing what she could do, Anne-Marie wanted to help the man as he received another kick, but Vera pulled her to the left.

Believing that they were being side-stepped, the two Territorials facing them fell for Vera's ruse and moved quickly to their right. Quick as a flash, Vera and Chamberlain went to the right, dragging Anne-Marie with them. They were almost at the door when the fist of one of the Territorials skimmed across Anne-Marie's cheek, causing her pain before it connected with Vera's face.

Faltering for a moment, Vera, supported now by Chamberlain, recovered sufficiently for the three of them to escape through the doorway. They stood with their backs against the wall, taking in deep breaths of the cool, refreshing night air. A few people were loitering harmlessly out here, as the troublemakers were now all inside the hall.

'You're bleeding, Vera,' Anne-Marie gasped.

'All part and parcel of our work,' Vera smiled wryly as she dabbed with a handkerchief at her split, bloody top lip. 'Let's get away from here, shall we?'

A bus slowly trundled up, the woman driver looking out of place behind the big steering wheel. The conductor was also a woman, something that Anne-Marie hadn't yet managed to get used to. Chamberlain ushered them aboard and paid the fares.

'A cup of tea will perk us up,' he remarked pleasantly, as they took their seats. 'These interruptions of our meetings are increasingly well organized and are becoming more frequent.'

'What we'll have to do is publicise them by word of mouth,' Vera suggested.

Chamberlain pursed his lips dubiously. 'It will still be difficult, Vera. It was the *Daily Express* that made sure everyone knew about tonight's meeting.'

'And the *Daily Express* that broke it up,' Vera commented bitterly.

99

As a newcomer, a novice, Anne-Marie had nothing to offer. The City was still a novelty to her, and she felt childish looking avidly out of the window of the bus while sitting among Londoners who displayed total indifference to their surroundings. Despite the late hour, some provision shops were open, with long queues outside, evidence of how food shortages were now a part of life. Though dimmed by lighting restrictions, Oxford Street had a noticeable verve as the bus jolted along it.

When they alighted at Marble Arch, revellers with linked arms laughed and sang as they passed by. They weaved in and out of serious-faced men in uniforms and wearing strange helmets, ready to go into action should London be attacked from the air. Anne-Marie looked around at hoardings shared between hedonistic advertising and government exhortations and appeals to patriotism. She was unsettled, unnerved by this peculiar never-never land.

In a Corner House they drank tea which gave Vera pain from her cut lips. Much of the talk around them was of the war. A drunk with the appearance of a tramp stood swaying in a corner as he played a violin remarkably well. Both staff and customers were revolted by his looks but enchanted by his music. With the skill of a top-class virtuoso he played 'Roses of Picardy' so sweetly that the crowded café fell silent.

The tune returned a sad Anne-Marie to the day she had left home. She hadn't received the blessing of her father, but that afternoon had mellowed him so that a tacit truce had been agreed between them. Whether his new, softer mood had endured Anne-Marie didn't know. There had been no clue in the one letter she had received from her mother.

As the bewitching melody continued to be coaxed from the violin, her thoughts went to Leon, her parents, Beth, James, Judith, Bruce, and times that were gone, never to come again.

'A penny for them, Anne-Marie.' William Chamberlain masked his curiosity with a smile.

Anne-Marie hesitated. Unable to share personal thoughts that were causing her sorrow, she asked a question that had been nagging at her most of the evening.

'I was wondering what Edward Grubb meant when he was talking to Vera and I,' she fibbed.

'In what respect?' Vera answered. 'Whatever Edward says is worth listening to.'

'He's an interesting man,' Chamberlain agreed.

'That goes without saying,' Anne-Marie concurred, 'but I meant in particular. He mentioned something to do with the pamphlets.'

'Nothing that need worry you, Anne-Marie.'

'To be honest, Vera, I'm very worried,' Anne-Marie admitted. 'I really want to know.'

'Vera is too good a friend to tell you,' Will Chamberlain said, 'but now you are with us we must be open with you. Noreen Wellman, Jack Heastor and Denis Knight – an excellent trio in what might euphemistically be referred to as our front line – have been arrested and charged with distributing the pamphlets. You're safe. They wouldn't even think of involving you.'

'It isn't myself I'm thinking of, but them,' Anne-Marie said unhappily.

'As I said about my smack in the mouth, it's all part of the game, and that's how Noreen and the others see it,' Vera smiled at her. 'Now, the next tram going your way is just about due. Tomorrow is another day. Get a good night's sleep and I'll meet you in the morning. Put those pamphlets right out of your mind.'

'And I will be in touch soon to discuss you joining *The Tribunal.* It's been a real pleasure to meet you, even under the circumstances that prevailed.' Chamberlain held her hand as she took her leave of them.

He was a charming, erudite gentleman to whom Anne-Marie had taken an instant and real liking. Both he and Vera, most probably the closest friend she'd ever had, meant well when telling her to forget the people arrested. But Anne-Marie found it impossible to do so. Though she didn't know them, the three people filled her mind as she let herself in the front door of her new home.

Mrs Ralph, the landlady, wrapped in volumes of clothes that reeked of camphor. was in her usual position in the hall. The old lady's two cats continuously and mindlessly circled her feet, round and round. Sighing at the sight of her, Anne-Marie prepared herself to be delayed for at least half an hour. A natural gossip, Mrs Ralph used her tenants to relieve her loneliness.

Anne-Marie was dismayed when the landlady exchanged no more than a couple of pleasantries before hurrying away to her quarters. There was an uncharacteristic slyness to Mrs Ralph that Anne-Marie, too late, realized should have been a warning to her. But at the time she wasn't aware of anything to fear, and started up the stairs.

On the first landing, she saw Benny Crewe in his habitual grey with dirt singlet. A simple-minded, jobless creature was waving arms as thin as pipe cleaners in wild gestures. He was saying something, too; his jaw moving snaggy brown teeth from side to side.

Unable to hear his words, Anne-Marie asked, 'What?'

Not answering, Benny, suddenly looking very afraid, backed into his room swiftly and closed the door. Pausing for a moment, Anne-Marie gave a shrug and carried on her way. Who could tell what was going on in a mind such as Benny's? More to the point, it didn't really matter.

Reaching the door of her room on the second floor, Anne-Marie admonished herself when finding it unlocked. She had brought little of value with her to London, but it didn't pay to be careless. Going in, she froze with fear as a big man stood up from the room's one armchair. Anne-Marie, holding the door open, was ready to flee, but a second man, who stood propped by a shoulder against the wall, stopped her by speaking in calming low tones.

'Please, don't be alarmed.'

Glancing quickly around, Anne-Marie saw that though it would be an exaggeration to say that the room had been ransacked, her personal belongings had been disturbed and not replaced correctly. She looked at the. man who had spoken. He didn't in any way resemble the stereotype of a burglar. He was smartly dressed, had an athletic build, and was handsome in a rugged sort of way.

'Miss Penny?' he asked. 'Miss Anne-Marie Penny?'

Anne-Marie thought she was speaking up clearly, but her one-word answer was hoarsely whispered. 'Yes.'

Accepting this with a nod, he took a pocket book from his jacket. Opening it he showed her a card, speaking the words as she read them. 'Police Sergeant Williams of "G" Division.' Gesturing with his head towards the other man, he said, 'Police Constable Male.'

Male walked slowly round her to shut the door. Though in civilian clothes he had the look of a village bobby. Anne-Marie wanted to be angry with the pair of them. She wanted to protest, to complain, to be angry with them for entering her room without permission. But she was cowed by their presence. Maybe there was something of the violence in the hall remaining to frighten her so.

Taking something from his pocket, Williams held it out for Anne-Marie to see. Instantly and fearfully, she identified her wording on a pamphlet.

'What can you tell us about this leaflet, Miss Penny?' the sergeant asked.

'Nothing,' Anne-Marie answered, too quickly to sound convincing. Her mouth was dry and her legs shaking.

'I'm afraid that I can't accept that answer, Miss Penny,' the sergeant said, taking a second paper from the other officer and showing it to Anne-Marie, who felt she was about to faint. 'You see, we found this among your belongings. It is the original. We've checked; it is written in your handwriting.'

It would have been foolish to deny it. What Williams held was what Anne-Marie had written, and which Vera had returned to her when the printer had finished with it.

'What do you want me to do?' she asked despairingly.

'That is up to you, Miss Penny,' Williams's tones rang with officialdom. 'You can come with me down to the station voluntarily, or I can leave here now and return with a warrant issued for your arrest.'

The three months' convalescence planned for James Hann at Lord Clinton's estate near Torquay in Devon, was reduced to five weeks. His shoulder wound had healed rapidly. On a Friday morning, after a week carrying out hospital chores as one of the 'walking wounded', he was informed by the battleaxe of a matron that he had been granted three days' leave. On return to the hospital he would be sent back to France.

Allowed to wear civilian clothes for the visit home, James found they helped him adjust. Marshlee seemed smaller and distorted, the way familiar places are in dreams. Walking down the road the accordionist had used to lead the menfolk of the town away, the memory of that split him in two. The boy who had been labouring in the bakehouse with his father that day, was not the same man who had been bombarded by German artillery and machine-gun fire. James's difficulty came in trying to discover which of the two he now was. Unable to find the answer, his self remained divided.

Turning his head as he heard giggling behind him, to saw the three girls who had given white feathers to his friends and himself. They were holding another now, ready to pass it to him. Something in the look he gave them must have got a message through. The girls stopped giggling and hurried away.

Going into the house, breathing in the smell of the bakery, hearing the once so familiar rattling of tins, was almost too much for him. He needed to bite his bottom lip to hold it steady. Overjoyed at the sight of him, his father hugged him the way he had when James was a child. Yet there was something lacking for James in the warm welcome. He and this man had once spent most of the hours of each day together; now they were set apart by the fact that his father hadn't shared his army experiences with him.

These uninvited revelations came to James thick and fast, depressing him as he went up the stairs and into his mother's room.

Anticipating further discrepancies between the remembered and the real, James was relieved to discover the exact opposite. Perhaps because of the profoundly special love that had always existed between them, his invalid mother was exactly the same as when he had left her. Startled, she dropped the book she was reading and he ran to the bed to embrace her. The crippled woman was quietly crying when he released her.

'Oh, my dear James. You're home. Is it for good?'

'No, Mummy.' He shook his head sadly. 'I'm going back to France first thing Monday morning.'

'Oh, I don't want to lose you again, James. I just can't abide it here in my bed without you coming to see me each day.'

She was crying again, and he took her hand and sat on the edge of the bed. 'It won't be for much longer, Mum. The war will soon be over now, and the next time I come home it will be to stay.'

'I won't be happy until that day, James,' she told him before asking, 'What of Leon? Did he come home with you?'

Not wanting to discuss this subject, he replied, 'No, Mummy. We got separated soon after we left Marshlee. I haven't seen Leon since.'

'What a shame. It doesn't seem right that the two of you, always such great pals, aren't together,' she said. 'I hope Leon manages to get home for a while. How often do you they give you boys leave, James?'

They didn't, unless you got hit by shot or shrapnel, but James couldn't tell his mother that; it wouldn't be fair on a sick woman, so he wouldn't mention it to his father either, in case he let it slip.

Passing her question off was easy, because she wanted to talk of Beth. 'Oh, that girl's such a treasure to me, son. There's much more to her than folk would ever imagine. Mind you, we've been feeding her too well. She's filled out wonderfully since she's been with us.'

'Beth is a good girl,' he agreed.

'A perfect little angel, James,' his mother enthused. 'You go and find her, James, say hello before she's busy getting my tea.'

He found Beth at work in the scullery. Standing at the sink with her back to him, she was half again as broad across the beam as he remembered. Hearing him, her eyes lit up when she turned.

'Hello, Beth,' he said, smiling.

As he had many times before, he wished that he had a sister like her. Though most people mocked her, he found that being near to Beth soothed him. It was possible that his mother was right and she truly was an angel. In her open way she showed how pleased she was to see him. Her always round face looked to be swollen, but her sweetness, more potent than ever, was still there.

'Master James,' she gulped.

'There's no need for the master,' he chided her. 'I'm the same James you used to beat at every game we played when I came to your house.'

Beth giggled as silently and fondly she recalled those times. Looking at her, James was hit as hard by realization as he had been by the German bullet in France. The girl wasn't fat, she was pregnant! The limited possibilities as to who was responsible, and the likely dire implications of the whole sorry mess, moved him to despair. What would it eventually mean to not only Beth, but his bed-ridden mother, Beth's mother, Leon, and the family business?

James couldn't believe that his father was capable of something so despicable. Walter Hann hadn't had it easy over the years, coping with a business and a sick wife, but that didn't excuse his taking advantage of a slow-witted young girl. Filled with what was, or would shortly turn into, hatred, James was careful to avoid his father between speaking to Beth and bedtime.

Through that sleepless night and the following day, James sought a solution to a problem that he knew had no answer. Perhaps it would be easier if he was at home. He could not take care of things, control matters, from the battlefield. Meeting his father about the place was unavoidable. It strained James to the limit to act as if nothing was wrong.

Spending Saturday morning with his mother, he found it incredible that she hadn't noticed Beth's condition. It occurred to him that she might know, but had suppressed it in her mind because it was too terrible to contemplate.

In the afternoon, he called on Elsie Marriott. Ostensibly enquiring about Leon, the major reason for his visit was to find out how Beth's mother was handling the tragedy that had befallen the girl.

The news of Leon was – the last time his mother had heard from him – that he had been court-martialled and sentenced, subject to confirmation, to two years' hard labour.

'It must be hard on Leon, James. I've wished all along that he would relent and go into the army. He's so strong-minded.'

'He's safer where he is,' James remarked, and she looked at him sharply.

'Is it that bad, James? You are in danger over there, aren't you?'

'It's not as bad as you hear.' James tried to understate battle conditions. Feeling that he had failed, he changed the subject. 'I've had a chat with Beth.'

He had broached the subject lightly to sound out the mother. Welcoming her negative response, he was aware of his cowardice, as the terrible problem would have to be faced at some time. It would be better to deal with it now so that when he was back in France speculation wouldn't develop into frantic worry.

'Oh, good, she often speaks of you,' Elsie Marriott said, revealing that she didn't have an inkling about her daughter's pregnancy by adding, 'She's doing fine. Beth says your mother jokes that they are going to have to cut her wages down because of what she eats. But she looks well on it. It's only puppy fat that will disappear when she's a bit older.'

Beth's extra weight was going to dramatically disappear before that. James allowed his thinking to slip into cynicism in the hope that it would relieve his torment over Beth. It didn't.

'You're quite happy with her then?' He did a double-check.

'More than happy; Beth was lucky to have your father take her on.'

With that misplaced happiness ringing in his ears, James left after asking Elsie to remember him to Leon the next time that she wrote.

'Be sure to tell him that I am sorry, Mrs Marriott, and that I will explain everything to him the next time that we meet.'

'Why would you ever need to apologize or explain anything to my Leon?' Elsie Marriott scoffed at the very idea. 'Now you go along, and look after yourself, mind. I worry just as much about you as I do my Leon. Don't you forget that.'

Impulsively giving his friend's mother a kiss on the cheek, James walked off down to the schoolhouse. He found Judith Seldon as prettily charming as ever, but they were close enough for him to detect an underlying wretchedness in her.

'It's lovely to see you again, James,' she said, blinking tears away as she hugged him. 'I feared that you'd never come back home.'

'You heard that I was in the army?'

'Yes, Bruce found out before they took him away.'

'Where is he, Judith?'

'He's been court-martialled twice, and now he's in the Wandsworth Military Detention Centre,' she replied.

Flinching inwardly, James made sure that he didn't betray his misgivings to her. The inhumane way Lt Col Reginald Brooke, the commandant at Wandsworth, treated his prisoners was spoken of in hushed tones throughout the army, in France as well as in England.

James composed himself before asking the next question, terrified of the answer he might receive. 'What did he think of me letting all of you down?'

'Don't be silly.' She looked shocked. 'Bruce would never think of you like that. We heard about the awful things they did to you, James. You must have suffered terribly.'

'No different to what Leon and Bruce are going through,' he said miserably.

'You can't say that, neither can I, because we don't know. What I do know, James, is that you are beyond reproach. We could never have been so close all those years if we weren't the same.'

'Thank you, Judith,' he said, really moved by what she had said. 'It is really nice of you to say that.'

'It's easy to tell the truth, James.' She gave him the brightest smile she had managed so far. 'Now tell me how they came to let you home. I never expected to see either you or Leon until the war was over.'

Explaining that he had been wounded, though not seriously, James asked Judith to keep it to herself so as not to distress his mother.

'And you have to go back on Monday, James?'

'Yes.'

'To France?'

When he gave a nod she held his right hand in both of hers.

'May God keep you safe, my dear friend. I shall pray for you night and morning.'

'I take comfort in that,' he told her, thoughtful for a moment. Needing advice, guidance, help, he said questioningly, 'Judith. . . ?'

'Yes?'

Here was the opportunity to unburden himself, to deplete his troubles and his worries by sharing them. But he couldn't bring himself to do it. A fear of being disloyal to Beth, and a burning shame over his father, prevented him from going on. Backing away from the most pressing issue, he took a different line.

'I do hope that everything goes well for Bruce.'

Having spent seven days in hospital, Bruce was back in his cell. In so much pain because the strait-jacket they had put him into was too small, and from the beatings from which he was still spitting and passing blood, he paced the tiny room throughout the night. His attempt to pass the time by thinking of his wife failed miserably. It worried him that he was not able conjure up Judith's face in his mind. He had completely forgotten what she looked like. Attempting to remember his wedding day was a mistake that took Judith and his past life completely out of his head as a build-up of pain plunged him into unconsciousness.

When he came round, his memory had recovered, at least in relation to recent events. The previous evening the commandant had paid his usual visit. Lent courage by Bruce being incapacitated by the strait-jacket, Lt Col Brooke had been his usual abusive and insulting self. To people like Brooke, Bruce was an intellectual pretender with aspirations to join the upper classes. For a reason that eluded him, because of it Bruce was hated with an intensity that was absent where other prisoners were concerned.

Bruce had tried a hunger strike for forty-eight hours, which had proved to be debilitating and ineffectual. After this he had agreed to take food in the normal way, but they had unnecessarily forcibly fed him. It had been done as a punishment, and it had been a torture Bruce would not like to experience again. The acute soreness brought on by a too-large tube still affected his throat.

Each time he had been taken out on parade, he had been subjected to kicks and punches to force him to go through the motions when he refused to obey orders. When dragged before the medical officer to be vaccinated, four soldiers had held him down when Bruce had refused the treatment. The doctor had tried, but failed due to Bruce's struggling. The needle had snapped off, most of it remaining in his arm: it was still there.

Every time he was returned to his cell he had been put into the strait-jacket. Close to losing his self-respect because of this treatment, he had asked a sergeant why he, and none of the other prisoners, was in a strait-jacket.

The sergeant hadn't replied, but Lt Col Brooke had overheard while approaching the cell, and he had explained. 'Because you are a cowardly swine who has threatened to commit suicide, Seldon, Therefore I have a duty to ensure that you cannot harm yourself.'

Bruce understood what was happening. He hadn't threatened to commit suicide, but Brooke was trying to push him into doing so. He knew that he had to be strong, but was concerned that his reserves of strength were running low. It was easy to see why James Hann had broken, and Bruce wondered if Leon was holding out. Could it be that all three of them would be defeated? The army certainly seemed to have the upper hand.

Minutes later he hazily recalled thinking about James and Leon, but now he couldn't remember what his thoughts had been. Next, to his horror, he wasn't able to put faces to either James or Leon. Seconds later, he had no recollection of ever knowing men with those names.

In the morning, his head had cleared after a series of short, restless periods of sleep. As he watching an expanding dawn through a high, barred window, Bruce feared that he wouldn't be able to survive another harrowing day. Minutes later, six military policemen came into the cell and removed the strait-jacket. When the circulation of blood recommenced in his arms and shoulders, Bruce, who considered himself to have been in pain all night, could have screamed from the fresh agony he was suffering.

The military policemen, in fine spirits and no doubt having breakfasted well, were sorting his equipment prior to putting it on him. To take his mind from his pain, Bruce compared his own distressed condition and their rude health, and remarked, 'I'm beginning to think that Heraclitus was right.'

'Wot you on about?' a military policeman asked.

'He's a bleedin' schoolteacher,' another advised, as he wrapped webbing round Bruce's body and started to strap on his equipment.

'He's a raving lunatic,' the first military policeman gave his opinion.

Propped up partly by the man buckling his equipment, and also by the wall of the cell, Bruce closed his eyes and heard his seemingly disembodied voice quoting loudly, 'War is both father and king of all. It should be understood that war is the common condition, that strife is justice and that all things come to pass through the compulsion of strife. Homer was wrong in saying "Would that strife might perish from among gods and men", for if that were to occur, then all things would cease to exist.'

Tightening Bruce's straps cruelly, a military policeman said, 'By the time we've finished with you you'll be quoting King's Regulations, not bleedin' Plato.'

'Heraclitus,' Bruce corrected the soldier, and was hit across the head with a stick for his effrontery.

They took him to a small quarry nearby with the intention of putting him to work. When he refused, they tied a pick and shovel around his neck and tried to get him to run carrying the weight of the tools and his equipment. When Bruce exasperated them by not moving, they handcuffed him and tied his feet together. They brought a rope up from his ankles and threaded it through the handcuffs. Pulling the rope tight to double him up, they used their boots to knock him over sideways.

Bruce lay helplessly on the stony ground in this position under a searingly hot sun for three hours. He sweated, was so parched that his tongue swelled to twice its size, threatening to choke him. His already damaged body ached intolerably. At one time he panicked and tried to get away when he saw three Vikings in horned helmets advancing on him. Bruce could hear them conversing in a foreign tongue, and was aware of the clashing of their swords against shields as they walked. Then they became a tableau and he knew they were depicted in a history book at school. A split second later he had no idea what a school was.

When the same six military policemen came and took the ropes and handcuffs from him, he steeled himself for yet another beating. But they took him back to his cell, put him in the strait-jacket again, left him bread and water that he couldn't get to because he couldn't move his arms, and slammed the cell door shut behind him.

Next morning, the same soldiers came back for him. Taken out of the strait-jacket and down to the quarry, he was ordered to work. Bruce refused and was knocked to the ground. A military policeman first stood on his chest, then sat on it to hold Bruce down while the other military policemen beat him with sticks.

Battered and bruised, he was dragged to a wooden crane and ordered to turn the handle of the windlass to pull up a stone on a steel hawser. When he wouldn't do this, Bruce's hands were tied to the handle. which was then turned by one soldier while another rapped Bruce's knuckles hard with a stick at every rotation. With his blackened hands swelling to pressure the tight ropes so that they cut into his hands, Bruce fainted.

Embarrassed to the extent that he had stuttered and stammered throughout, James had explained the facts of life and her condition to Beth. They were at the riverside on the tranquil kind of summer Sunday afternoon made for boating and picnics. Sitting cross-legged, concentrating on arranging a posy of buttercups and cowslips she had picked for his mother, Beth showed no reaction. It had fallen far short of an informative medical lecture, but James was confident that he had strung together enough words in order to have even Beth grasp the gist of it.

'Do you understand what I've told you, Beth?' he enquired, daunted by the thought of needing to talk more sex with such a young innocent. It wasn't a subject in which he was either confident or knowledgeable.

A skylark did a vertical take-off from its nest in the ground behind her. Tilting her head back, exposing her thick, country-girl neck, Beth watched the bird rise into the air.

'Did you understand?' James repeated the question.

Plucking a teat-like petal from a cowslip she sucked on it, savouring the taste of pollen. She still hadn't answered and, as she threw away the damaged flower and reached to pick one to replace it, James was wondering what to do next. But Beth spoke then.

'That I have a little baby in my tummy?' she asked, placing a palm flat on her bulging midriff. 'Yes.'

At least she had learned something from him, but James concluded that she was taking it so dully, so calmly, that he still had a long way to go to convince her of the seriousness of the situation.

But she turned to look at him with the expression of an injured animal on her face. Seeing a tear building up in each of her eyes, ready to spill over, James hated himself for having come close to losing patience. The poor child had been crying on the inside all along.

'Why, Beth?' he asked, before deciding it was a pointless question. Poor Beth wouldn't know why, where or how.

But she proved him wrong. 'I didn't want to, but Mrs Hann said I must do everything that Mr Hann asked.'

Closing his eyes to shut out a horrible world, James was sickened by the way loyalty and a desire to do good so easily turned vulnerable people like Beth into victims.

'When will the baby come, James?' she asked in a shaky voice.

'Soon, Beth, very soon.' He took her hand to offer what small comfort he could.

'You will be here, James, won't you?'

Shaking his head, he said quietly, 'No, Beth. I'm so sorry, but I have to go away again in the morning.'

The terror this brought to her eyes made it clear how much she relied upon him. She had no-one else. For him to go to her mother and explain the situation would do no good. Elsie Marriott would collapse on learning the truth.

Holding his hand to her face, a sobbing Beth wet it with tears. 'What can I do? What can I do?'

Standing, James pulled her gently to her feet. Holding her in his arms he whispered reassurance in her ear. 'I'll take you home and then I'll go to speak to Anne-Marie Penny. She will take good care of you, Beth.'

'She won't,' Beth said miserably through her tears. 'Anne-Marie hasn't been to see me for ages.'

'She's probably been very busy,' he said, taking out a handkerchief to wipe the tears from her face.

'But you think that Anne-Marie will take care of me while you're away?' she asked doubtfully.

'I'm sure that she will,' James replied. 'Come on, Beth, I'll take you home and then go to speak to her.'

Nodding, Beth lingered for a while, looking around at the variety of flowers, the trees that were heavy with dark-green leaves, and the river that flowed so slowly that the glass-like service was only occasionally disturbed by a ripple. She seemed reluctant to leave.

'What's the matter, Beth?' he enquired, a little impatiently despite his good intentions.

'I just want to stay here for a while,' she said. Then she brought him close to tears by going on, 'I love it here. This has been the best day of my life, James.'

Those words of Beth's went through his mind, over and over again, as he walked to the vicarage that evening. They summed up the destitution of Beth's short life. Heavily pregnant through no fault of her own, with a bleak future – if she was to be allowed a future – she'd had her best day ever because someone had taken notice of her. Before leaving Beth at her home, he had promised to call later to say that he had seen Anne-Marie.

Knocking on the vicarage door, he explained his reason for being there to Mrs Penny.

'I'm sorry, James,' she said, 'but Anne-Marie has been in London some time now. If you are going there I can give you an address where you can find her.'

'No. Thank you, but I won't be going to London, Mrs Penny.'

With a heavy heart, James walked back into the centre of Marshlee. Pondering on what to say, starkly aware that there was no merciful way to tell the unfortunate girl that she was on her own, there was no one to help her.

He stood outside his home for a long time, not wanting to stay there in a thickening dusk, not wanting to go inside. Creeping soundlessly past the door to Beth's little room, knowing that opting out was no answer either for Beth or himself, he just couldn't face the girl only to destroy her.

Going up the stairs, he said a long goodbye to his weeping mother, then went to his own room to spend another sleepless night. When he arose early the next morning, Walter Hann, probably the only other person out of bed in the town, was at work in the bakehouse.

At the break of day, unable to bring himself to speak to his father, James Hann walked off slowly through the deserted streets of Marshlee.

Six

'If it pleases Your Worships, I am Jacob Gosling and I represent Miss Anne-Marie Penny in this matter.'

The solicitor making this statement to magistrates at Bow Street court was eccentrically anachronistic. His velveteen jacket and leggings were dated by about a century, and the style of his bush of hair was that favoured by the Victorian poets. He turned to crack his long-chinned face into something like a smile for Anne-Marie.

Standing in the dock, Anne-Marie couldn't understand how a solicitor came to be acting for her, but she was immensely relieved. Bewildered since having been arrested, she'd had no idea what to say in court, when to say it, or to whom. It was as unreal as a stage show, with her as a principal character instead of a member of the audience.

Both Vera and Will Chamberlain were in the public gallery. Bertrand Russell was with them, his sensitive face alert as he studied the participants preparing for the courtroom fray. Anne-Marie's first thought was that Vera and Will, possibly on the advice of Russell, had instructed Gosling on her behalf, but when she glanced at them they appeared to be as puzzled as she was. Both of them had warned her in the cells, where she had been guarded by the first policewoman she had ever seen, that she was on a very serious charge.

'The government's primary fear is of a revolution,' Chamberlain had explained to her, 'and your story of a meeting with soldiers disenchanted by the war could spread dissension throughout the army.'

'So I am likely to be dealt with severely?' Anne-Marie had asked, finding it difficult to be brave in the circumstances.

'If you are fined, it will be paid for you, Anne-Marie,' Vera had promised.

Anne-Marie was pleased to hear this. She had brought money with her to London, but it wouldn't stretch to meet a substantial fine. Her father wouldn't let her down in any emergency, but he wouldn't meekly pay to keep her from prison for an offence contrary to the Defence of the Realm Act. That brought a dire thought into Anne-Marie's mind: what if the court gave her no alternative but to go to prison?

'If I am sent to prison, would it be for long?' she had enquired, trying to keep panic from her voice.

'Probably six months' gad in the "first division",' the ever frank Vera had informed her.

About to enquire, Anne-Marie decided she would probably be happier if she didn't know what first division meant.

The trial had begun with exchanges back and forth that might well have been in Greek for all the understanding Anne-Marie had of it. But she became even more acutely aware of her situation when the magistrate, a jowled, middle-aged man who reminded her of Robert Kerr, Marshlee's bank manager, fixed her with a steely stare when the clerk of the court asked if her plea was guilty or not guilty.

Chamberlain had advised her that the court would expect her to plead guilty. This guaranteed them the least possible unwelcome publicity, and in return they would be lenient with her. 'Give them a fight, Anne-Marie,' he had cautioned, 'and they'll make you pay dearly for the bad Press the government will get.' Remembering this, she was about to plead guilty when Jacob Gosling spoke for her.

'My client pleads not guilty, Your Worships.'

Despite the position she was in, Anne-Marie got real pleasure from the chairman of the magistrates' reaction. His round cheeks lost their apple-red hue, and his public-image confidence deserted him. Consulting with the two male colleagues flanking him, he had somewhat recovered when he addressed Anne-Marie's solicitor.

'Mr Gosling, if your intention is to turn this hearing into a publicity stunt for the organization to which the accused belongs, and like-minded affiliated associations. then you will cause great harm to your client. Any defence entered into court must be firmly based. I will grant you time to consult with your client, who may well wish to change her plea.'

Affording Anne-Marie nothing more than another attempt at a smile, Jacob Gosling spoke confidently to the magistrate. 'Miss Penny and I have no need of consultation, Your Worships. Our defence will be that there is no case to answer. Telling the truth has yet to become a criminal offence, although doubtless it shortly will. My client, loosely speaking, is charged with sedition in that she falsely claimed to have spoken with soldiers who fully support the anti-war movement in this country. I have been successful in tracing eight of those soldiers, Your Worships.' The solicitor laid a significant hand on a bulging folder on the table. 'I, therefore, Your Worships, request an adjournment to allow time for these eight soldiers to be brought to court and sworn in as witnesses.'

Everything happened at a confusing speed then. After a quick exchange between them the three magistrates ordered 'Case dismissed', and uproar broke out in the court. There was cheering and applause from the many supporters of the cause. Vera and Will Chamberlain half lifted Anne-Marie from the dock, slapping her on the back in congratulations. They wanted to escort her out of the now chaotic court, but Anne-Marie insisted on speaking to Jacob Gosling.

'I can't thank you enough,' Anne-Marie told him. Up close he reminded her of Mr Punch from the puppet show.

'My pleasure.' He made a little bow.

Indicating the file he was picking up from a table, she enquired, 'How in the world did you find those soldiers I had been speaking to?'

'Soldiers?' he queried, mystification on his oddly-shaped face. 'I saw some troops marching through Long Acre on my way here. I don't imagine it is those soldiers you are referring to, Miss Penny.'

'The soldiers I was speaking to on the train,' Anne-Marie protested, feeling foolish although she had no reason to. 'The men you told the magistrates you had traced.'

'That was sheer bluff on my part.' He gave her a covert wink. 'I took it for granted you would prefer to remain as Anne-Marie Penny and not become a Joan of Arc. Parliament is ready to burn dissenters like yourself at the stake.'

'But . . .' Anne-Marie pointed at the bulging file.

'In here,' he leaned close to tell her quietly, 'are the papers relating to the case of a farmer who accidentally shot his labourer in the private parts with an humane killer.'

'But . . .' she gasped, 'what if the case had gone on?'

'It would have become very confused,' Gosling chuckled.

Anne-Marie found it easy to laugh with him, but difficult to stop her laughter from becoming hysterical. It was evidence of how much strain she had been under.

'If you will kindly let me have your address,' she told the solicitor, 'I will arrange for you to be paid.'

'No need, miss, no need.' Gosling wagged his head as if Anne-Marie was playing Judy to his Punch. 'My fee was paid in advance.'

'By whom?' Anne-Marie queried, wondering why Vera and Will Chamberlain had allowed her to become fraught with worry when they had already arranged for a defence.

Nodding at someone who had come up behind her, Gosling said, 'Captain Lytton instructed me and settled my account, miss.'

Unwilling to believe what was happening, Anne-Marie turned quickly to discover Hubert Lytton standing there. Resplendent in his uniform, his face was paler than she remembered, contrasting drastically with the neatly trimmed moustache.

'You are a difficult person to find, Anne-Marie,' Hubert said, 'but thank heaven I located you in time to save you from prison.'

'Hubert.' Anne-Marie's voice let her down squeakingly. 'It was you who paid for a solicitor.'

'Under the old pals' act.' He gave what he'd done a desultory dismissal.

This was ludicrous. A serving officer with a predominantly military ancestry had engaged a solicitor to defend an anti-war campaigner. Anne-Marie concluded that Hubert had acted without checking on the circumstances.

'Did you know what the charge against me was, Hubert?' she asked.

'Of course,' he replied. 'I wasn't assisting someone alleged to have sinned against the defence of the realm, but helping Anne-Marie, the love of my life.'

Hoping that his final five words had been said light-heartedly, but fearing that this wasn't the case, Anne-Marie enquired, 'What are you doing in London, Hubert?'

'Looking for you, actually. You see, Anne-Marie, I'm on a spot of leave before going to France.'

Anne-Marie felt a chill begin somewhere at her centre to spread throughout her body. It was now common knowledge that the battlefields of Europe offered the ordinary soldier only a modest chance of survival, but meant certain death for officers. The prospect of the handsome and charming Hubert Lytton being torn bloodily apart by bullets or a shell, appalled her. 'But shouldn't you be with your parents at this time?' she queried, knowing that the deep love the brigadier and Claudia had for their son would ensure they would want to share every one of what could be Hubert's last minutes with them.

'I've had a few days at Farley Grange,' Hubert replied. 'The brigadier and Mother actually urged me to come to London and look for you. They know how I feel about you. Now I've found you, Anne-Marie, and we have two days. I'm going to take you to all the places we enjoyed together that wonderful August.'

Two eventful years had passed since then. In addition to the international upheaval, Anne-Marie had met and grown close to Leon. It was always folly to go back, to try to relive magic moments that belonged to the past. Convinced beyond any shadow of doubt that both Hubert and she were facing a major disappointment, she lacked the courage to trample on his high hopes.

Meekly, Anne-Marie permitted the uniformed captain to take her arm and guide her out of the court.

Leon regarded the heard-but-not-seen arrival of an army lorry as portentous. It was a warm morning when Dartmoor was at its best. Absent so far that day was the infamous moor mist that could drop as quickly as a theatre curtain, and rise in the same swift manner. Welcomed by prison escapees of old, the sudden fog blotted out the landscape to intensify the isolation that was a harrowing part of being a conscientious objector.

He and his comrades enjoyed the illusion of freedom that came from working on the new road at Two Bridges. They worked neither hard nor diligently. The government's ideal of settlements in which men who refused military service were to be usefully employed for the good of the country, had wilted. It required the co-operation of the conscientious objectors, which hadn't been forthcoming. At most times now disobedience was passive, becoming confrontational only when a particular occasion demanded. The locals, more of them friendly than hostile these days, had already labelled this cutting of a highway as 'Conchies Road'.

When they'd arrived at lonely Princetown the empty prison had been totally disorganized. They had moved in with the resentful ghosts of the 1,500 French and American prisoners of war who had suffered and died in that huge sepulchre. Initially there had been weeks of enforced idleness. During this period the militant Socialists had formed a Men's Committee that they dominated. The sole purpose of the committee was the wrecking of the government scheme. With no interest in politics, Leon avoided any active role by placing himself firmly in the large group of religious prisoners.

Princetown was to be the largest of the Home Office settlements, and close to 1,000 conscientious objectors were moved in. Order was gradually introduced, and life became tolerable. Leon and the others worked in the workshops, the farm, and on outside projects like the road, ten hours per day for five days a week, and six and a half hours on Saturday. Unlike convicted criminals, the conscientious objectors were at liberty after finishing work each evening. They could go out, but in the beginning it had been risky to do so, as 'conchy bashing' had become the favourite local sport. The prison rules required them to be in their cells, or 'quarters' as the Home Office preferred to call them, by 9.30.

After the torments endured in army barracks following his arrest, Leon appreciated the leniency at Princetown. Life wasn't good, but it was bearable. Of late, however, there had been talk of a revision of regulations at the prison. The national newspapers had publicizd complaints from various quarters that the men held at Dartmoor were being 'coddled' and 'pampered'. A warning that harsh changes were afoot came when two retired army officers were sent by the government to inspect the place and advise on bringing it in line with army standards. Since that visit there had been an atmosphere of impending doom at the prison.

That morning as Leon swung a pick-axe and heard the strained whine of the approaching lorry's gearbox and the groaning of its springs, he had more than a suspicion that the good times were just about to end.

'Don't look up, Leon,' Johnny Cave, a Seventh-Day Adventist, said from out of the corner of his mouth as he shovelled beside Leon, 'but a lieutenant has got out of the lorry and is heading this way.'

'I don't like it, Johnny,' he whispered his fears, able only to see the prematurely balding top of his comrade's head, with the jagged white scar running diagonally from above the right eye to behind the left ear.

In need of spiritual contact of some kind, Cave had joined a party of Anglican conscientious objectors who had attended a Sunday service one evening at Walkhampton. The small group from the prison had been set upon by the congregation, and Cave's head had been laid open by a scythe. The obvious question asked at the time was 'Couldn't the vicar have stopped it?' Cave had been the one to give the truthful but incredible answer. 'It was the vicar who incited them to attack us.' The churchgoers had not been hurt so badly as their friends who had been assaulted and hospitalized by marines in Tavistock, but they probably suffered more because there was a certain ignominy to being beaten up in a church.

With a sergeant at his side, the lieutenant came to a halt beside where Leon and Cave were bent at their work. The officer was too young for the straggling growth of fair hair on his upper lip to attain moustache status. When he ordered them to stop working there was a choir-boy's squeal to his voice.

'Pay attention. Listen for your name, and if it is called fall out and line up behind the sergeant. Go ahead, Sergeant.'

The sergeant read out six names. Leon knew all of them, and silently wished them well wherever they were bound. The seventh name read out was that of Cave. and Leon reached out to touch him on the shoulder as he went over to join the short but growing line. It was the only form of farewell that could be risked in front of the guards.

The lorry, carrying some ten soldiers, all armed with rifles, was turning in readiness for driving back in the direction of the prison. With the manoeuvre completed, the driver stopped the truck and waited.

'Leon Marriott.'

'Marriott?' the lieutenant shouted, because Leon, stunned at hearing his own name, hadn't moved.

With no other choice. he walked over to put himself on the end of the line. When the named men numbered fifteen, the soldiers were ordered down from the lorry to march them under armed escort down to the wide, dusty main road of Princetown. There they were halted and left formed up as a major stepped from a motor car and walked across to return the boyish lieutenant's salute before taking over from him.

'You fifteen men are your own worst enemies,' the major began. He had the brittle eyes of someone who has seen too many men killed to have any human feelings left. 'You are the hard core, the ringleaders here at Princetown who are responsible for bringing hardship down on your fellow prisoners. It is due to your anarchistic activities that discipline will be tightened here. Rations are to be cut, the allocation of books greatly reduced, and the prisoners made to sleep at ground level at the mercy of rats, mice, and insects.'

Aware that none of the fourteen men he was with, nor himself, had incited, led, or even taken part in any organized disobedience, Leon accepted that he and the others were scapegoats. They had been selected to be made examples to deter, frighten, and control the 16,000 men who were refusing to fight for Britain. Pondering on what way they were to be used caused Leon to shudder. His worst fears were confirmed when the major continued.

'Your days of disobedience have ended. Tomorrow you will leave here for France. Once you are across the Channel you will find things very different. Over there the cowards who run your various associations and your pals in Parliament won't be able to do anything for you. In France, even a hint of disobedience on your part will result in the death sentence.

'Yet, and I personally deplore this, Parliament in its wisdom has decided to give you a chance that none of you deserve. You can be saved from what is certain death by giving an immediate undertaking that you will obey orders, take the king's shilling, and serve your country like real men. Now, on my command, all those wishing to avail themselves of this undeserved mercy – one step forward, march!'

Not one of the fifteen men moved.

'Very well,' the major said. 'Take over, Lieutenant.'

They were escorted to the ancient and notorious dungeon at Lydford Castle, where they were to be held overnight. Confined in irons they were kept in darkness and fed nothing other than bread and water. Completely deprived of sight affected Leon's mind in a way that frightened him. Shut off by the blackness, his mind rejected rational thought. At first it spun alarmingly, thoughts passing through at such a speed that they were impossible to identify. Then it was as if his mind had crept off to hide in a corner of his head. The result was that he felt very small, perhaps no more than a baby. For the first time ever in his life, Leon discovered what it was like to be afraid.

There were eerie sounds in the night that were unaccountable and unidentifiable, and his fellow-prisoners whispered in a terror made worse by the total blackness. He, never given to imagination, several times felt his scalp and the hair on the back of his neck prickling icily as he felt a menacing presence close to him.

It was an immense relief when they were taken outside in the early hours of the morning while it was still dark. A noisy colony of jackdaws filled the air with their harsh cawing and throat-rattling. Leon heard an awed Johnny Cave repeat a superstition often spoken of in the prison.

'They say that the souls of dead convicts have passed into them jackdaws so that they can return to the prison.' Cave's voice had a tremor as he shivered from the early morning cold.

'As a religious man you shouldn't be talking such nonsense, Cave,' a prisoner scolded.

'Anyway,' another commented acidly, 'even a bloody ghost wouldn't be daft enough to want to come back here.'

'Stop talking, you men,' the lieutenant came up to shout at them before giving his soldiers orders.

Leon and his comrades were handcuffed and packed into a train for Southampton with several hundred men of the 7th Royal Fusiliers. A few of the soldiers were scornful of the conscientious objectors, but most of them were friendly. As well as offering cigarettes to the handcuffed prisoners, they held them to their mouths. They shared their hard tack, too, and Leon thanked a diminutive soldier who had a single stripe on his arm and spoke with a close to incomprehensible Scottish accent.

'No need ta' thank us, mac,' the soldier said. 'After all, this is a one-way trip.'

Leon tried to console his new comrade. 'Not necessarily, my friend. Many of you will survive, and I will pray that you will be among them.'

'You got hold of the wrong end o' the stick, mac,' the Scotsman said with a laugh that mingled harshness and sadness. 'It's you fellals who's going one way. Have you not seen the papers? No, of course, you wouldna have. You lot are being taken across to the other side to be shot. There's been questions asked in the House, as they say, but no answers given. There's them that's protesting on your behalf. but it looks pretty sure that you've had it. Sorry, fellas.'

This information depressed the conscientious objectors. Most of them remained silent, staring out at landscapes they passed without seeing. They tried to come to terms with their own thoughts and worries brought on by what the fusilier had said.

On arrival at Southampton in the afternoon, they stood on a quay, under armed escort, while a military band that had just played the 7th Royal Fusiliers aboard a troopship, stayed standing, holding their instruments in a way that said they would soon recommence playing.

'I'd say they're waiting to play another regiment on board,' Johnny Cave said, 'which means we'll be lined up here for quite a while yet.'

A tall Yorkshireman who was a Quaker, made a fervent confession. 'I could kneel and kiss the ground of the country I was born unto and love so.'

'The country that's going to have you shot,' Johnny Cave reminded him. 'I'd say spare your kisses.'

'I'd sooner kiss my missus,' a stocky, flame-haired Cockney Socialist raunchily declared.

'That's something you'll never do again, but don't worry, somebody will be doing it for you soon enough,' a wild man by the name of Mullaly – who insisted that he was Welsh despite his Irish brogue – callously informed the redheaded Londoner.

Listening to this banter, Leon's curiosity as to why the band had stayed behind was satisfied when he and the others were ordered to board the troopship. As they made their way up the gangplank the band played the 'Dead March', while bystanders jeered. There was a shout followed by a concerted movement in the crowd. The conscientious objectors were pelted with rotten eggs and over-ripe tomatoes.

An egg smashed against Leon's neck. He felt its contents running stickily down his chest. The stench was nauseous. A tomato squashed as it hit his face. the juice squirting into his eyes so that he had to blink rapidly to clear his vision. The others suffered just as badly, some of them even worse. Johnny Cave looked to be in danger of vomiting from the smell of two eggs that had smashed messily against his chest. It would have been a humiliating experienced if Leon and the other conscientious objectors hadn't by then become inured.

They cleaned themselves up as much as circumstances would permit, and were resigned to their fate on landing in France. Lined up on a quay, breathing in the aroma of the sea, they were largely ignored by everyone except for their armed guards. Some women wearing aprons gutted fish not far from them, and male workers who were probably dockers were engaged in an argument that involved much arm waving. They were standing outside a factory that, to their consternation, had the Union Flag flying from its highest point. Mike Dornley, a man who had caused the authorities considerable consternation by ceasing to be a soldier to become a conscientious objector while previously in France, was able to explain.

'That place was taken over by the army as a field punishment barracks,' he informed them.

That was depressing news, and they were eyeing the iron gates morosely when, to their relief, they were marched away and taken to a huge camp. Standing in line outside the guardroom, they were told by a sergeant that the officer commanding was coming to have a word with them.

When the colonel arrived, a small, round, fussy little man who spoke so fast it was difficult to catch all his words, they were surprised when he addressed them in conversational rather than military tones.

'You men didn't realize it at the time, but crossing the Channel was a momentous point in your lives. Each and every one of you comes to me with a clean sheet. Your past disobediences mean nothing here – they are forgotten. You will be taken from here to your billets. Within the hour you will be on parade with the British Expeditionary Forces, as a part of the British Expeditionary Forces, as soldiers of the king.'

When they were in a barrack-room, they looked to Leon as their leader and asked what they should do. Dornley stated rather than asked, 'We don't go on parade, do we, Marriott?'

Leon shocked Dornley and the others by replying, 'Yes, we go out on the parade ground,' he repeated the officer commanding's words, 'with the British Expeditionary Forces, as a part of the British Expeditionary Forces, as soldiers of the king.'

Dismayed by Leon's attitude, the disgruntled conscientious objectors were ready to rebel. Johnny Cave, a long-term friend of Leon's, challenged him almost aggressively. 'Are you saying that we give up the fight now, that we start taking orders, is that what you are saying?'

Leon just looked at his friend without saying a word. They wanted instant answers, while he needed time to think. This was possibly the most crucial time of the war for them. Whatever Leon decided now would determine the degree of suffering they would have to withstand in the near future. He had learned a lot in England, but had to accept that little or none of it would apply here. His ignorance in a foreign country was threatening to undermine his self-confidence. Still undecided, he answered Cave delayingly.

'I'm not saying that,' Leon shook his head. 'All I am saying is that we join the parade. Once we're out there on the square just do as I do.'

When they reached the gigantic parade ground they had a clear view of the white cliffs of Dover. It was a sight that distressingly emphasized their exile. They stayed together when falling in beside smart, well-drilled soldiers. Leon fought not to fall under the influence of the collective dread of common soldiers, men who were the victims in a disciplined force, as tension built up while waiting for the parade to start. They were no longer individuals, but had been crushed by the military system into an unthinking mass. To remain separate would require a super alertness, but Leon intended to succeed.

The parade was taken by a regimental sergeant-major who, by design or chance, was the image of the late Lord Kitchener.

'A–tten–shun!'

At the yelled order, the parade snapped to attention, the slamming of boots onto tarmac as loud as a shot fired from a cannon. Only fifteen men, Leon Marriot's cohort, remained at ease. Aware of this, the sergeant-major decided to ignore it for the time being. He gave them the opportunity to change their minds by standing the parade at ease and bringing it to attention twice in quick succession. When Leon and his men didn't respond, the sergeant-major stayed calm and chose a different tactic.

He ordered: 'Right turn! Quick march!'

The soldiers of the British Expeditionary Forces marched smartly away. Left standing together in an irregular line, a red rag to the bull of militarism, were the fifteen conscientious objectors.

The regimental sergeant-major came striding over to them on legs stiffened by rage. 'Your country needs you,' Johnny Cave said under his breath, for the likeness to Kitchener was even more remarkable close-up.

'We don't need him,' Mike Dornley muttered.

There was no further levity as the RSM descended angrily upon them. As he ranted and raved, other NCOs came up to join him in his verbal abuse of Leon and his fellows.

'You spineless apologies for men aren't aware that you are now in a war zone,' the sergeant-major, red in the face, yelled at them. 'Here the military authorities have absolute power. You are also ignorant of the fact that in a war zone the penalties for disobedience are severe. I will personally see to it that every man-jack of you is executed for the blatant disobedience you have shown here today. Take them down to the field punishment barracks, sergeant, and clap them in irons.'

Late evening had mellowed the French town, but the sounds of not-too-distant gunfire, and a constant stream of distressed civilian refugees, precluded even a deceptive sense of peace. In the cobblestoned main street, two military policemen paced up and down beside the long queue of soldiers. Their presence was unnecessary as there was no disorder. The troops were patient and well behaved as they moved slowly toward the open door of the big house. Close to the front end of the line now, James Hann was having timorous second thoughts. He was doing a quarter turn with the intention of walking away when the man behind him put a restraining hand on his arm. James turned his head to find himself looking into the harsh, chiselled lines of a dark face that was elderly by army standards.

'What's up, son, getting cold feet?'

James replied with a nodding and shaking of his head that was as confusing for him as it was for the veteran who had spoken. But James didn't want to appear gauche, so he denied the suggestion.

'No.'

'Good thing, son, good thing,' the veteran said. 'These places are for married men like me, who's missing it, and sproggs like you who ain't never had it. Your first time, son?'

James gave a clearly confirming nod this time.

The veteran looked as sympathetic as his hard face would permit. 'No need to worry your head about it, son. A bit of grumble and grunt ain't nothing like as frightening as a salvo of Jack Johnsons, old Jerry's heaviest shells, coming your way.

'Any road up, son, do you hear those guns firing off there in the east? You'll be going over the top again in the morning. You don't want to get killed without ever finding out what it's like, do you?'

Those last words were in line with James's own thinking, and he moved back into the queue, getting a congratulatory slap on the back from the veteran as he did so.

He was wondering if, like most things he had experienced in life, the anticipation would prove better than the realization in this venture. Finding Beth coming into his mind yet again, he tried unsuccessfully to push her out. The sweet, young, inadequate girl he had been forced to abandon weighed heavily on his conscience at all times. In some ludicrous way, what he was about to do now struck him as a betrayal of her. Remembering Beth made him feel ashamed. Yet he owed her no more than protection and care, certainly not his life.

James's thoughts were becoming fixated on Marshlee. The surrounding countryside here, rolling chalk downland, wooded valleys and scattered villages, was reminiscent of home. What would Leon think of him right now? James tried to excuse himself by reasoning that Leon wasn't in the front line. But that didn't work, because Leon was fighting his own stressful war in another way.

'Go on in, son, or these rampant bastards behind me will trample us both into the ground.'

Until the veteran had spoken, James had been so engrossed in his thoughts that he hadn't realized he was at the door. Summoning his nerve as he had the first time he'd clutched his muddy rifle to slip and scramble up out of the trench towards the German lines, he stepped inside.

He was in a long room that was crowded with soldiers. A long bar stretching down one side of the room was heavily patronized. On the flight of stairs opposite, girls in flowing dressing-gowns stood in an uphill line looking down boredly at the troops by the bar, many of whom were the worse for drink. There were girls of all sizes and complexions, the common denominator being their youth. A few of the more enterprising ones had pushed a bare leg through the rails, and others, leaning on the bannisters, had pulled their gowns down to reveal the smooth skin of their shoulders and give a shadowy hint of breasts. They held no eroticism for James; the sight of them left him completely unstirred.

'Two francs, love.'

A woman who looked eighty but was probably aged about forty, held out her hand beside James. He paid her and she made a half gesture towards the girls on the stairs. James interpreted this as a signal for him to take his pick.

Walking slowly across the room to the stairs, James looked up into a row of faces. All the girls were attempting to appear welcoming, but none of them could hide an underlying hostility and contempt. As he looked, their faces blurred for him so that he could not distinguish one from the other.

Then one girl came sharply into focus. A veneer of tiredness couldn't disguise the loveliness of her face. Her jet-black hair was bobbed. Her looks and stance reminded James of a girl he must once have known but had long forgotten. His memory refused to help him, but the conviction was so strong that he wondered if he had met the girl, or someone very like her in a dream.

Pulled by what seemed to be a type of magnetism, he moved towards her. Then Beth, plain by comparison and with none of the mystique and allure of this French girl, invaded his mind. He saw a vision of Beth's swollen body, her flat-footed walk of pregnancy, the anguish on her childishly bewildered face. Hatred for

131

his father welled up in him, jolting him into the realization that, though in different circumstances, he was about to use this girl the way Walter Hann had used Beth.

It hurt him to read in her brown eyes that he was just another lustful male to her. He would have liked to explain to her that he was different, have her see him in a different light. But that was ridiculous, for what value was there in one girl's opinion of him? James couldn't answer the question, for at that moment how she saw him was of the utmost importance.

Forcing himself to break off eye contact with the girl, it disappointed James to discover they had exchanged nothing, except perhaps his guilt and her dislike. Wondering if he would regret it during the days ahead, throughout the long years to come, James walked away.

The guffaws and catcalls that followed him out the door had the men in the queue cheer his failure loudly. Uncaring, beyond reaction to criticism, James headed off to where his unit was under canvas. He felt strangely light-headed. It was a dizzy feeling of triumph at having overcome, albeit with little difficulty, his carnal urges.

James had reached the guns of an artillery battery, and the slit trenches dug for taking shelter should the retaliatory fire become heavy. Not far away he could see by starlight the silhouettes of gunners stacking shells. He stepped off the track to permit the passing of an old Frenchman pushing a wobbly-wheeled cart, with his aged wife half-lying on it, surrounded by bundles of their personal belongings. Though they passed within inches of James, their staring eyes didn't see him. War had destroyed their home and their lives.

A little further on, James's giddiness increased, disturbing his stomach. Hearing the whistle of an incoming shell, his reflexes were too slow for any reaction. There was a crump in the middle distance, and he heard the easily identified sound of stones and soil falling back to earth in the wake of the explosion.

'Everyone under cover!' came the cry, and he saw the gunners tumbling into their trenches as the booming whistle of another shell rose to an ear-shattering pitch.

This time the danger was so threatening that James dived for whatever protection a wide-boled tree could give him. The shell exploded in an eruption of earth away from the trenches, somewhere back along the track he had just passed along. As always, the noise was louder than a soldier remembered from before, or had prepared himself for since. There was the smell of scorching and the agriculture odour of freshly churned earth.

Peering back through the night, James could see no sign of the aged couple with the cart. But there was a yawning black hole where they would have been, should have been. Two wispy spirals of smoke rose from the hole.

Feeling ill, James clung to the trunk and was violently sick. It left him so weak that a blackness filled his head. He became aware of two figures approaching. They were Germans, white teeth gleaming in their dirt-streaked faces, rifles held ready to lunge at him, close enough to gut him with bayonets rather than fire their Mausers.

Trying to push himself away from the trunk of the tree, a terrified James found that he was paralysed. He tried to shout, but could make no sound. One German was staying back to permit his comrade to have the first thrust. As the Hun bayonet came at him so did James regain the use of his vocal cords. He released a piercing scream.

Then two pairs of hands were each holding one of his shoulders, shaking him. Opening his eyes, wondering why his captors had decided not to bayonet him, James saw the men shaking him were two British gunners.

'Reckon as 'ow you had a bit of a skinful in town, pal,' one of them grinned. 'I reckon's you deserve it. You're with the infantry up there under canvas, ain't you? Poor blighters.'

'I'm not drunk,' James defended himself indignantly.

'We'll believe yuh, thousands wouldn't,' the other gunner chuckled.

'Hill Seventy is our objective in the morning,' James said, to prove he was clear-headed.

'Rather you lot than me,' one of the artillery men sighed fervently. 'Like I said, poor blighters!'

133

A sudden recall struck James and he glanced around. He asked, 'Where are the Germans?'

'And you reckon as 'ow you ain't pissed?' a gunner chuckled. 'The Hun is only near enough to hurl them bleedin' Jack Johnsons at us.'

That was no doubt true, but James had seen those two Germans as clearly as these two Britishers, even if it was only in his mind. His whole body suddenly went cold. His weird experience had to be a bad omen. He should have heeded the old soldier in the queue at the brothel. James had a premonition that he would die on the morn without having discovered what it was like.

In one of his lucid times, which were becoming less frequent and of shorter duration, Bruce had listened to the other conscientious objectors smashing prison furniture as he lay in his damp and filthy cell. They were on hunger strike in rebellion against the system, and he was too weak to join. Now they were coming back in rowdily from an exercise period. Having sung 'The Red Flag' at the top of their voices on the way out, they were belting out another revolutionary song, 'The Internationale', as they were brought back in.

As the raised voices and pounding of feet on the landing outside caused him to shake, Bruce began to escape by shutting out the world. He was passing through the hazy, nonsensical phase between waking and sleeping, when he was jerked back into panicky alertness by the glass in the spy hole of his cell door being shattered.

Drawing up his knees, wrapping a blanket tightly around himself, Bruce surveyed the slivers of glass on the floor like a child tearfully looking at a broken toy.

Then his cell door was slammed open and two angry warders leapt in. One pointed to the smashed spy hole, shouting angrily at Bruce, 'You see the damage you've done. Couldn't resist joining the rebellion, eh?'

Given no chance to protest his innocence, Bruce was pushed outside. Hitting the landing railings hard, he was grabbed by four other warders. One wrapped an arm round his neck, pulling it tight, choking him, to drag him along the landing. Another was punching him, a third kneeing him in the back, while the fourth hurried on to wait at the top of a flight of steps going down to the next landing.

When they reached there, the waiting warder seized him and braced himself to throw Bruce down the stairs. As he felt himself about to hurl through the air, an instinct of preservation had Bruce grab a rail with both hands. This checked him so suddenly that the warder who had been in the act of throwing him, went hurtling down the steps himself.

Bruce and the other guards stood shocked into immobility, looking down on the warder lying prone below. Slowly, the warder jacked himself up on to his hands and knees. When he turned his head to look up, his jaw was crookedly out of line and dark red blood was pouring from his mouth. Every bit as slowly as he had carried out the first movement, he got himself to his feet. Standing for a moment, swinging his bloodied head from side to side like a wounded bear, he suddenly burst into life and came rushing up the stairs.

The other warders pinioned Bruce by the arms as their enraged colleague, snuffling and snorting on his own blood, grotesquely disfigured by the dislocated jaw, laid into him with fists and boots.

Aware of his nose giving way crunchily under one blow, and agony knifing through him as a knee was driven into his crotch, Bruce knew no more until he came round in a punishment cell. His face felt sore and swollen, and his head ached abominably. There was no way of telling how damaged he was in the body as he was in a strait-jacket that had been strapped so tightly that his shoulders were cramped and breathing was painfully difficult. There were two warders in the cell with him, and he weakly made a request.

'Could you slacken the straps a bit?'

'It's not up to us,' one warder replied. 'Ask the doctor when he comes. He'll be here in a short while.'

When the doctor arrived, his hurried manner showed that he wanted to be somewhere else at that time, and visiting Bruce was an annoyance. He was a tall man whose chin was pulled in like he was permanently belching. There was a reek of whiskey on his breath and an irritated frown on his face as Bruce complained.

'This jacket is too tight. Will you take it off me?'

'Most definitely not,' the doctor answered hotly.

'This is an injustice, Doctor,' Bruce complained. 'There is no reason for me to be strapped in a strait-jacket.'

'That may be your opinion, but you have to be restrained. You went berserk and did considerable damage to prison property before violently attacking a prison officer. Plainly you are not responsible for your actions, being a lunatic.'

'I didn't break that glass. Somebody passing my cell did it,' Bruce protested.

'This entire prison is filled with men who are innocent of everything,' the doctor said sarcastically.

'I am not a lunatic,' Bruce objected.

'If you act like one you must expect to be treated like one,' the doctor told him coldly, before getting ready to leave and telling the warders, 'If he wants to make water, then release one of his arms, but strap it tightly again afterwards.'

Jumping to his feet as the doctor reached the cell door, Bruce tried to shout further protests at him. But a retching began deep down. Bent double he retched hollowly, the effort knotting his stomach in agony. There was no vomit, just an exhausting series of spasms.

Turning, Bruce tumbled head first onto the dirty mattress that had been placed in a corner. He felt a minute or two of relief, but then he had to stand in an attempt at easing new pain. In this way he was up and down all through the long night. He would fall onto the mattress, feel his agony abate, then get up to walk the cell as it returned with renewed viciousness.

His pleas to use the WC were ignored, and wetting himself added to his distress. This disgusted the warders in the morning when they freed him from the strait-jacket. He was taken out into the yard, where one guard turned a hose on him while two others scrubbed him down with a stiff yard brush. When this ordeal was over, his flesh red raw in places, Bruce was told to wash his clothes.

Having done this he draped them over a rail for whatever drying was available while he went to the WC. When he returned, his clothes, even his socks, had been stolen.

Breakfast was brought for him, but he was unable to eat it. For this involuntary offence, and for losing his clothes, a naked Bruce was lashed back into the strait-jacket, even more tightly and painfully than before.

'Behave yourself and we'll take that off you at breakfast tomorrow, giving you another chance,' a warder told him.

On his knees, Bruce dug his head into the mattress, finding that this position temporarily eased his physical distress. He knew that he couldn't face a full day followed by an endless night. Unable to flee, he could only retreat inside himself, but that was also a daunting prospect because he had experienced terrifying visions in that state.

Conversely, as he struggled to banish rational thought, his mind suddenly became clearer than it had been for some time. Bruce had a distinct memory of sitting in the schoolhouse at breakfast with Judith. They were discussing the work ahead of them that day. It all seemed very alive, as if he was living it right then. The only problem, a mind-shattering one, was that the Bruce Seldon sitting eating toast and chatting with his wife, was an entirely different person than the Bruce Seldon, whose nose had started to bleed copiously for some reason, here in a prison cell.

When the doctor came into the cell, Bruce was curled in the foetal position, tears pouring from his eyes to dilute the blood flowing from his nose. His tightly restricted body was jerked by convulsive sobs.

Looking down on him contemptuously, the doctor said, 'I told you that you are a bloody lunatic.'

When the doctor left the cell, Bruce began to scream loudly, over and over again. Even the hardened warders couldn't stand the sound, and one went running off to fetch the doctor back.

Seven

As she knelt blacking the massive grate in the Hanns' front room, Beth Marriott was happy in the knowledge that this was going to be a good day. She didn't feel well, and was finding it difficult to move her heavy body around. She had no problem in kneeling, but it was causing her more and more strain and effort to get down and then back up. Though she hadn't told her mother or anyone else, she had been sick a lot. It was possible that Mrs Hann had heard her vomiting in the outside toilet, for the crippled woman had taken to studying her intently of late. Beth wondered if Mrs Hann had noticed what James had explained to her. Though she had forgotten much of what James had said was happening to her, Beth felt sure that it was nothing to do with what was worrying his mother.

But none of this mattered to Beth right then. She had been terribly disappointed when James had left and Anne-Marie hadn't come to see her as he had promised. Beth had been left feeling so lonely that she had cried herself to sleep every night for weeks. But she could forget those times of misery now, for she knew that something wonderful was about to happen.

Since early morning, the talk in the Hann house had been of James. Beth had heard it once removed, as it were, hearing James's name without understanding what was being said. Walter Hann had been in and out of the bakehouse countless times. On each occasion he had gone up the stairs two at a time, although he always came down slowly. When Beth had his wife's breakfast ready, he had taken it up to her, saying that Mrs Hann had to be left alone for a few hours.

Beth had guessed what it was all about: James was coming home again. That was what was making Walter Hann restless, while Mrs Hann wanted to be alone to prepare a welcome for her son.

With the invalid woman off her schedule, Beth had time on her hands. So she made some treacle tarts the way her mother had shown her. When they were cooked she put them on one of the fancy plates that normally stood upright on display along the top shelf of a dresser. She hoped that James would arrive home while the tarts were still fresh and warm.

The grate finished, she reached to a chair with both hands and pulled herself to her feet. Her ankles were badly swollen and stiff to move. Beth looked up from examining them, and gave a little start. Her mother and Walter Hann were standing together in the doorway, looking at her. This was the first time since Beth had been working for the Hanns that her mother had visited the house.

Beth was pleased. Thinking that her mother must have come to see how she was getting on, she wanted to show the work that she did, and hoped Mr Hann would leave.

'Come along, Beth,' her mother said, stepping into the room. 'You can come home for the rest of the day.'

'But it's not Sunday,' Beth objected, jerking back from her mother's reach, frightened that she was going to cost her her job.

'It's all right, Beth, go with your mother,' Walter Hann said gruffly.

Permission given this easily surprised Beth. It would be nice to be at home and spend time with Kipsy. Even so, she wished she knew how to object. She wanted to be here when James got home. She couldn't give that reason, of course. Then there were the tarts. Beth looked at them, a mouth-watering golden brown. They wouldn't be so nice tomorrow, but she found consolation in a plan to make some more in the morning.

Stepping close, her mother wiped some blacking from Beth's face. It was an automatic movement. Her mother's eyes were blank, but the hair-sprouting mole on her top lip held a familiarity for Beth that made her feel secure.

'Come along, Beth. Mr Hann has things to do.'

What was so special about that? Walter Hann had lots of things to do all day, every day. Having Beth around had never impeded him before. There was nothing different now, but Beth allowed herself to be led out of the house by her mother.

When they were inside their own door, Beth's mother turned her sideways and stepped back to look at her. Feeling foolish, Beth started to move, but her mother spoke sharply to stop her.

'Stand still, Beth.' The older woman kept staring at her daughter as she walked round to the other side of her, frowning as she stopped to view her from another angle. She sighed, 'Oh, good Lord, what they've been saying is true!'

'Why do you keep looking at me?' Beth was nonplussed.

'Oh, Beth, what have you been up to?' her mother wailed. 'Did you walk out with James when he was home on leave?'

'Yes,' Beth replied enthusiastically. 'It was nice. We went down by the river. I picked flowers for Mrs Hann.'

Eyes brimming with tears, Elsie Marriott took her simple daughter in her arms, saying, 'Oh how I wish Leon was here to help me. You poor child, you don't know what's happening to you.'

'I do, Mam, don't cry,' Beth returned her hug. 'James told me lots of things. He promised to help me, Mam. It will be all right, you'll see. James is coming home again today.'

Letting out a mournful cry that made her daughter jump with fright, the mother cried, 'Oh, Beth, what will we do! James isn't coming home today, dear child. He won't be coming home ever again. James has been killed in France, Beth.'

They had visited all the places that they'd so enjoyed during their London holiday of just before the war. As dashing as ever, an officer and a gentleman throughout, Hubert was excellent company. Absorbed by recent history and a mine of interesting information, he tutored Anne-Marie on a London that had slipped away, a London she had never known. Explaining the recent American phase, he showed her the London Opera House that Hammerstein had built in Kingsway. Hubert had seen the City's first full American revue there in 1909. It had been called *Come Over Here*, and his description was so colourful that Anne-Marie lived the memory with him.

Hubert knew his London, and she had listened avidly. Anne-Marie learned that when Clare Market, Holywell Street, Wych Street and Newcastle Street had been demolished and the new crescent and highway cut through to Holborn, the crescent, given the Saxon name of Aldwych, was designed to link with the past, while the highway had been futuristic with huge white buildings in the American style.

They covered the route from Hampstead to Euston Road that had been travelled by London's last horse-tram right up to 1913. Then they had taken the halfpenny ride on the only surviving horse-bus from Somerset House, across Waterloo Bridge, to Waterloo Station.

Afterwards they had walked to stand on the south side of Westminster Bridge, where Hubert recalled what had been a great day in his childhood and the highlight of his parents' lives. On special invitation they had ridden on the capital's first electric tram. Highly decorated, it had run from where they were now standing to Clapham Common with King George V and Queen Mary, then the Prince and Princess of Wales, as passengers.

'I was old enough to enjoy myself but too young to appreciate what an historic occasion it was,' Hubert said ruefully. 'The brigadier and my mother felt greatly privileged, of course, to be a part of high society. To the best of my memory I was most fascinated by the fully equipped fire-engine that accompanied us on the journey.'

He had brought his story alive, too, and a fascinated Anne-Marie asked, 'Why was the fire-engine needed?'

'It wasn't, thank goodness,' Hubert replied with a laugh that brought the boyishness she liked to his handsome face. 'The brigadier explained to me when I was much older that the engineers weren't confident of the monster they had created, and had feared it would catch fire.'

Anne-Marie laughed with him, welcoming the chance to be lost for a while, however brief, in merriment. Her time with Hubert had been dimmed by a letter she'd had from Judith. It reported that Bruce was ill in a military hospital, but Judith could learn nothing of substance from the army. 'This may surprise you, Anne-Marie,' Judith had written, 'but the Reverend Penny has offered to find out what he can for me. Your father has changed quite a lot in recent times.'

That had to be an understatement, Anne-Marie had thought on reading her friend's letter. For her father to help a conscientious objector and his wife was a miracle that Leon would find difficult to believe. It was news of Leon in Judith's letter that had depressed Anne-Marie. He had been sent to France, and Anne-Marie, in close contact with Vera and the others, understood fully what that meant.

Anne-Marie was aware of Sir George Cave, the Solicitor General, having made the chilling statement that conscientious objectors were not subject to the death penalty, but men conscripted into the army were.

Now, as she sat in a Leicester Square basement café with Hubert on the eve of his departure for France, she was gloomy with worry over both him and Leon. Will Chamberlain had reluctantly told her that Harold Tennant, the Under-Secretary of State for War, had admitted to the House of Commons that the death sentence had been pronounced on thirty-four conscientious objectors in France. It was Chamberlain's belief, and many agreed with him, that the British Government had lost control of the British Army.

An unusually subdued Hubert was studying her across the table. Feeling guilty because these were their last hours together before he embarked for France, Anne-Marie made an effort to lift her mood.

'I feel a little out of place here,' she remarked, with an apologetic little laugh.

Looking around him at women wearing provocative clothing and with heavily painted faces, Hubert managed a smile. 'We certainly don't seem to fit in, Anne-Marie.'

'Thank goodness,' she breathed her words out gratefully as a group of homosexuals minced past their table. 'Are they born that way, Hubert?'

'A good question. Legatees of Oscar Wilde, the brigadier calls them.' Hubert smiled fondly as he referred to his father. 'He says the world would be a better place if they were taken outside and sh—'

The way he broke off when realizing what he was about to say told Anne-Marie that Hubert was aware of the situation Leon was in. Had he been waiting for her to introduce it into their conversation? His normally pale face had reddened now. Feeling sorry for him, and forgiving because he was culpable only of a near slip of the tongue, Anne-Marie wanted to say something reassuring if not cheering. He was as down as she was this evening.

Hubert had staked all his hopes on this time together in London rekindling what had been between them two years ago. Anne-Marie had known from the start it was a failed exercise. She had tried unsuccessfully to convey this to him all along. It had taken him until that evening to recognize the truth.

It came as a shock for Anne-Marie to discover she could no longer picture him in anything other than an officer's tunic and Sam Browne, his legs encased in puttees. How had he once looked in a sporting blazer and flannels? She felt that if she was able to remember him in more relaxed clothing she would cope better with this new Hubert Lytton.

'I was worried that you would want nothing more to do with me when I joined those who opposed the war,' she commented.

'That would have upset you, Anne-Marie?' he asked, the expectant way in which he awaited an answer making her uneasy.

'Naturally. Good friends are rare, Hubert, and I wouldn't want to lose you.'

'Most people are losing someone each day, every day,' he said abstractly.

Though reluctant to broach the subject of France, Anne-Marie wanted him to tell her truthfully how he felt about going to war. His martial family upbringing and military training had provided him with a mask of duty that he wore most of the time.

Anne-Marie needed a glimpse behind that protective disguise so as to know how to think about him when he had gone. Even though she didn't love him, they were close enough for Anne-Marie to want to discover his inner feelings.

'You are quiet,' she said blandly, though hoping to draw him out.

'Doing some deep thinking. I'm a fraud, Anne-Marie. I've been a fraud all along, and still am right up to this very minute,' he told her self-critically.

'How can you possibly say such a thing, Hubert?'

'It comes easily because it's the truth,' he answered. 'I've strutted around in a uniform, playing the big I am, trying to impress all and sundry. My arrogance on the night of the Christmas ball cost me your love and respect.'

'That isn't true, Hubert.'

'I think that you'll find it is, Anne-Marie. I've never behaved other than as a spoilt brat,' he said. 'I was the fine army officer, son of a brigadier, but I am afraid now the time has come to face the Hun.'

'Apprehensive, which is perfectly natural,' Anne-Marie corrected him. 'You could never convince me that you are a coward.'

Reaching across the table, he put a hand over the back of one of hers and gave it a gentle squeeze. 'You are a true friend, Anne-Marie. I am not afraid of the Germans. The fact that I'll be joining old Plummy, Alex Plummer, who has already seen action, puts me at a disadvantage. What frightens me is that, despite all my military preparation, I don't know how I will react under fire. The brigadier tells me that one forgets oneself completely when battle commences. But the brigadier is more of a man than I'll ever be.'

'I won't have that, either,' she protested. 'You are a chip off the old block, as they say.'

'I'd like to be able to believe that.'

'There's no reason why you shouldn't,' Anne-Marie told him, disturbed as the café's Hungarian band deepened their despondency by striking up the mournful tune 'Destiny'. 'Would you like to dance, Hubert?'

'Perhaps later, Anne-Marie. There are two things that I'd like to ask you. Do you mind?'

'Not at all,' she replied, fibbing a little because she knew that he would ask about their relationship, and she feared hurting him.

'Actually, it's one question and one request,' he said, pausing before tentatively asking, 'The question is about us. Do I stand no chance with you?'

'You'll always have a special place in my heart, Hubert.'

'But. . . .' He filled in for her with a sad smile.

'But,' she agreed with a nod, moving away from the subject by asking. 'And the request?'

'I won't be seeing the old folk at Marshlee, as I'm sailing for Le Havre first thing tomorrow,' Hubert said. 'I wondered if you had any plans for a visit home, Anne-Marie?'

'I was hoping to do so this weekend, Hubert. I'm still a trifle worried about my mother.'

'I see.' His thoughtful face showed signs of encouragement. 'I wonder if you would be kind enough to take something back to Farley Grange for me?'

'I'd be happy to, what is it?' Anne-Marie enquired.

From a tunic pocket he took a small Bible and placed it on the table. It was aged, the cover was creased and worn. Hubert lifted the cover. Glimpsing an amount of handwriting in ink on the fly-leaf, Anne-Marie attempted to read it but he had closed the Bible again.

'This has been in the family for years,' he said. 'I wouldn't have brought it with me had Mother not insisted.'

'You want me to take it back?'

'If you would, Anne-Marie.'

'Your mother won't be very pleased,' she pointed out. 'Are you afraid that you'll misplace it, Hubert?'

'Something like that. It's a kind of talisman that my ancestors always took with them into battle. I suppose there was a Lytton with it in the pocket of his bright-red tunic at Bunker Hill, maybe even Waterloo.'

'A good luck charm!' Until then Anne-Marie had suspected

that the Bible was a ruse to return her to the Lytton family fold, but now she realized that it went much deeper than that. 'Obviously it kept all the earlier Lyttons safe, Hubert, so you should carry it with you.'

He gave a doleful shake of his head. 'This is a messy war, Anne-Marie, and I can't take responsibility for so important a family heirloom.'

Anne-Marie understood. Hubert feared that he would be blown to pieces in France, depriving the family not only of a son but a vital part of their heritage.

'I'll return it to your parents for you,' she consented, reaching for the Bible.

'Thank you,' he said gratefully.

They both knew that the time had come to go, for them to part. The evening had sped past. They sat quietly for a while, each storing memories of the past few days to carry with them.

'I don't know if I can stand a goodbye at the station,' she told him truthfully.

'I can make it easy on you, Anne-Marie,' he offered with a kindly smile. I'll walk away now as if I was simply going out to buy us a bottle of wine; I'll arrange a taxi-cab to wait outside for you.'

'No,' Anne-Marie was adamant. 'That would be letting both you and myself down. I'll come with you.'

'It might prove easier on your conscience,' he agreed, failing to inject the intended levity into his remark.

Chased by six sergeants armed with sticks and revolvers, Leon and the others were rushed to the field punishment barracks. The sticks were used freely along the way, cracking against heads, arms, backs and legs. The sergeants got fun from putting the sticks between the legs of the running men to trip them. Once a prisoner was on the ground they laid into him with sticks as well as brutally kicking him.

When they were inside of the improvised prison, a quarter-master-sergeant strode up. As lean and curved-backed as a whippet, he bellowed an order as he came, his voice booming out to bounce off the walls and high ceiling of the former factory as an echo.

'Put them in "figures of eight"!'

He was referring to irons of various sizes made to grip the wrists one above the other behind the prisoners' backs. A sergeant approached Leon, ready to secure him, but the quartermaster-sergeant stopped him with a shout. 'Not that man. Not the ringleader.'

Held by two sergeants, one of whom whispered gleefully in his ear, 'This ain't your lucky day, curly, that's Quartermaster Wilson.' The inference was that Wilson's cruelty was too well known to require an introduction.

Leon watched his comrades' excruciating pain as the irons were screwed up. Every time one of them jerked from pain or struggled, they were punched severely about the face and body. Johnny Cave lay on the floor, his old head injury re-opened and leaking blood. His eyes were glazed as he was pulled to his feet. A sergeant pushed the end of his stick cruelly along the track of Cave's gaping wound, expecting a cry or a plea for mercy, but the Seventh-Day Adventist denied him the satisfaction.

'May God forgive you,' Cave said breathlessly, before a blow to the mouth prevented him from saying anything else.

One by one, the manacled men were dragged away and tossed into tiny cells that had concrete floors and iron walls.

When he was the only conscientious objector left, two sergeants held Leon's arms while the quartermaster-sergeant came up to give a display of exaggerated surprise as he looked Leon over.

'Well, well, a conchy with muscles. Is there some fight in you, son, or are you the same as the others, prepared to have your arse kicked from here to breakfast time while you wait for the meek to do their inheriting?'

An anger flared in Leon as he found himself no longer able to turn the other cheek. Though he and the others had long ago learned that passive resistance was the wisest choice, it was eroding his self-respect. When this was over, if it ever was over, he was going to ask Anne-Marie to be his wife. Though she now shared his pacifism, he would be unable to look her in the eye if he wandered across the line from peacemaking into cowardice. He stared directly into the fox-like narrow face of Wilson.

'That you have knowledge of the Bible gives me hope,' he replied, asking as if moved by mild curiosity. 'Who read it to you?'

Seeing Wilson's bunched fist coming at him, he made no move to evade it or retaliate. The hard knuckles caught his right eye with a force that knocked him off his feet. Back hitting the iron wall, he slid to the ground but came quickly back up on his feet.

'Ah, so you do want to try your luck.' Wilson gave a crooked-toothed smile as he squared up to Leon with the stiff-backed stance of a bare-knuckle fighter of old.

Leon was ashamed of himself for being sorely tempted. He knew that even after the hardships he'd endured he had sufficient strength remaining to crush Wilson like an insect. But so unintelligent an action would solve nothing. Even contemplating fighting was lowering himself toward Wilson's thuggish level.

Even so, noticing the flash of fear that his hesitation brought into the eyes of the quartermaster-sergeant, Leon wanted to strike back hard, to take revenge for all the insults and physical abuse he and his friends had suffered. But to do so would be to betray the code by which he had lived all his life. Relaxing the muscles he had bunched in readiness, he turned away.

'I thought as much,' Wilson said tauntingly, though his relief was evident.

Waiting until the sergeants had screwed a very small pair of figure of eights on to Leon's wrists, cutting and ripping the flesh, all but stopping the circulation, Wilson used his hands and one knee to send Leon flying.

Hitting the iron wall dug the manacles harder into his flesh sending acute pain coursing through his body. Determined not to go down. Leon leaned his back against the wall for support. That was a mistake, for Wilson and the others leapt on him, not letting up until they had battered him to the ground. Even then they kicked him in the back several times.

Leon lay where he had fallen all night, his arms and hands numb. He slept intermittently, each period of sleep ending with distressing dreams of him being back in Marshlee but invisible, his loved ones totally ignoring his approaches. Frustration at not being able to communicate with his mother, Beth, and Anne-Marie woke him each time. Then, when his mind was still slightly out of focus, fear set in. Leon was certain that he had died and he was visiting his home town as a phantom.

Shortly afterwards, the cold and the pain of his battered, manacled body told him that he was still alive. His swollen face hurt, but the effect of the steel biting into his wrists was nullified by numbness.

This numbness seemed to him to be as bad as the pain, but he readjusted his thoughts in the morning when Wilson returned to his cell with a staff-sergeant and a sergeant. They took the figure of eights off him and he twisted his body this way and that in failed attempts at escaping the agony of returning circulation.

'A new day,' Wilson announced, 'and a new regime. Out on the square right now, Marriott, and then we'll have you off to work.'

'No,' Leon objected. His agony had abated, but his wrists still hurt, his lips were so swollen that he could barely part them, and his right eye was closed from a punch from Wilson the previous evening. 'I refuse to obey any orders, or do any work.'

A hard blow to his stomach from the staff-sergeant winded Leon. He dropped to his knees. Wilson, his eyes burning with a brightness Leon didn't doubt was fuelled by insanity, drew a revolver and placed the barrel against Leon's forehead. Leon heard the hammer click back.

'Right, curly,' Wilson hissed, frothing at the mouth, 'this is self-defence.'

Wilson pulled the trigger; Leon's ears rang from the report the gun made, but he felt nothing. Then it was apparent that Wilson was in an even greater rage then before. But this time his anger was directed at the staff-sergeant, who had knocked Wilson's arm to one side as he had fired the gun. The bullet had brushed past Leon's knee, hit the floor and then ricocheted to flatten itself against an iron wall.

'What did you do that for?' Wilson complained. 'We was safe enough. Dead men don't tell tales.'

'He wouldn't be able to, but the others can hear what's going on,' the staff-sergeant said, then added logically, 'You can't kill 'em all.'

'More's the bloody pity,' Wilson mumbled. 'Come on, you two, help me get this yellow-gutted bastard outside.'

They pulled Leon out of his cell to where the other abused and dejected conscientious objectors were assembled. They were a ragged bunch, all wearing the cut and bruised badges of having been beaten, but in better shape than he was. Exhausted from prolonged pain, Leon fell to his knees as he was led along. Mullaly, the Welsh/Irishman, helped him to his feet, whispering information into Leon's ear as he did so. 'Johnny Cave died in the night.'

Leon, having considered himself at an all-time low, felt his spirits plummet to even greater depths at this news. During their incarceration, he and the dour but unselfish Johnny Cave had become close friends. It was probable that all of them would soon be dead, but that thought couldn't salve Leon's immediate, harrowing grief.

He was kept apart from his comrades, held by the staff-sergeant and sergeant while Wilson addressed the other conscientious objectors. 'Take a look at your leader!' He waved a hand to indicate Leon. 'Do you still want to follow a wreck of a man like him? I give each and every one of you fair warning. Do as you're told from this minute on, otherwise you'll suffer as Marriott is about to. Our military superiors have, in their wisdom, prescribed Field Punishment No.1 for him. If any of you don't know what that means, I'll be happy to describe it.'

It meant, Leon was well aware, that he was to suffer what soldiers referred to in awed tones as 'crucifixion'. He saw how anxious his fellow prisoners were. But their sympathy couldn't help him. Leon was on his own, facing what was sure to be the worst ordeal of his life.

My dear Judith
Just a few hurried lines to let you know what I have learned through our intelligence system here. What I have to say is not meant to add to your worries, and I pray that it will give you hope. Sad to say,

some thirty COs have been sent to lunatic asylums. Some have been driven mad by the treatment they have received, but a high number have not been certified as insane. Bruce is among the latter. He is confined in the Epsom Asylum.

You must go there, Judith. I can't get away to go with you, but you have to remonstrate, insist on Bruce being released from that place. If he is sent back to prison, then that is better than where he is now. Let me know what happens. I will do all I can at this end.

I am working for The Tribunal *with Mr Bernard Boothroyd now that Mr Will Chamberlain has been sent to prison. The hours are long, but I enjoy the work. I was coming home last week, but we were too busy. I hope to make it down on Friday and will see you then.*

As ever, Anne-Marie.

Watching the Reverend Paulton Penny reading the letter written by his daughter, Judith Seldon wondered why she had ever feared or disliked the elderly clergyman. There was a childishness to the way he was sitting in the armchair. the thin knees of his long legs raised high. She had heard folk of late expressing concern over his health. The fire and brimstone sermons were no more; the man was not what he once was.

He passed the letter back to Judith, clearing his throat nervously. Both of them were awkward in each other's company. Maybe the yawning chasm between their beliefs had been closed or bridged, but the memory of yesterday's animosity lingered on to make their attempted conversations stiff-lipped and stilted.

'I would like to go with you to Epsom, Mrs Seldon,' the old preacher said, his eyes fixed on the distempered wall just above her head.

'Why?' Judith asked. It sounded rude, she was conscious of that, but it was difficult not to be suspicious of a man who had long been the implacable enemy of Bruce, Leon, and the tragic James.

Misunderstanding her, he replied, 'I feel that a man will have more chance at Epsom. These days those with authority bestowed upon them by wartime emergency measures can be quite unhelpful to women.'

'My meaning, Reverend Penny,' Judith forced herself to make a point, 'was why would you want to help either my husband or myself?'

He stood without answering. Tall and gaunt, a little stooped these days, he walked to the window to stand looking out on a dark-orange sunset, hands behind his back. Some minutes passed before he spoke without turning to her. The powerful voice he once had was now muted and sounded strained.

'I have come to view a number of things differently, Mrs Seldon. It was a gradual process, no blinding lights along the road to Damascus for me, I'm afraid,' he said in a way that suggested to Judith he was having a problem keeping his emotions in check. 'This war has become a veritable nightmare. Robson Jewell, the vicar over at Bremminwell, has lost four of his five sons. Fine lads they were – Bartholemew, Richard, Norris, and Roland. I baptized all of them, and they grew up as young gentlemen, each with so much promise, so much to offer the world, and now they have gone. I've known Robson for years, we were at Oxford together. This has broken him, Mrs Seldon, he will never recover. Robson Jewell will die a broken man.'

'When will it end?' Judith sighed.

'When did it begin?' the clergyman sorrowfully turned her question. 'It all started long before the fourth of August, Mrs Seldon, but we who profess to know the ways of man were too arrogant to see the signs. Even now we are no wiser. Vanity of vanities. A man loses four sons and we can do nothing but cry with him.'

'So many people have suffered loss,' Judith bleakly sympathized.

If Bruce were here now he would reduce the sorrow philosophically by questioning if dying was really what everyone believed it to be. Judith could actually hear him quoting Euripides: 'Who knows if life is not death, and death life?'

Reverend Penny amazed her then by saying, 'Quite so, but this town can't afford to lose your husband, Mrs Seldon. He is a gifted teacher, and after this war is over the young people will need him to shape them for a new future, to fit them for a new world.'

'I never thought the day would come when you would praise Bruce, Reverend Penny.'

'I admit that I couldn't condone the attitude that he and others took to this war,' he said, 'and I would be dishonest to say that my feelings have completely changed, but I am beginning to see the other man's point of view.'

'That was something Bruce Seldon was always capable of,' she said in praise of her absent husband.

'I accept that, and I am humbled by it, Mrs Seldon. That is why I want to help. We must do everything we can to preserve the brilliant mind your husband possesses. We have to get him out of that asylum as quickly as possible. It is inconceivable that Bruce Seldon is mentally afflicted, but being in such a piace could have a dire effect on him.'

Judith had been thinking the same thing, and she had been dreading going to Epsom alone. She said, 'I will gratefully accept your kind offer to go with me to see Bruce, Reverend Penny.'

When he turned to face her, Judith was moved when noticing that the old clergyman must have wept a little during their conversation. He reached out a bony-fingered hand to place it gently on her shoulder. 'It is me that must be grateful to you, Mrs Seldon, for raising an old man out of his uselessness. The distress this war has caused me has in a sense been secondhand. With no sons to worry over, I am made to feel guilty by the sacrifices of other fathers. I thank the good Lord that I have just a daughter.'

Pouring from the pot of tea she had made when the vicar had arrived. Judith passed him a cup, asking, 'Sugar?'

'Please.'

Taking two spoonfuls, the clergyman stirred his tea far more vigorously and for much longer than was necessary.

'Are you still against the work that Anne-Marie has chosen to do?' Judith enquired.

Continuing his aggravated stirring, keeping his head down in a way that suggested to Judith that he didn't want to discuss a family situation with her, Penny remained silent. Then he removed the spoon from the cup, tapped it lightly on the saucer, and laid it down. Looking up at Judith, an uncertainty on his grey, lined face, a luminous honesty lighting his pale-green eyes, he answered her question.

'When I consider the work, many reservations abide, but where my daughter is concerned I am proud that she has the resolve to follow her conscience.'

'She followed her conscience with Leon Marriott, too, Reverend Penny,' Judith said, aware that she was treading on dangerous ground. 'I ask this not out of idle curiosity, but because I love Anne-Marie as a sister. Will you continue to oppose that relationship in the future?'

Concentrating on this question seemed to age him yet another ten years, a fact that made Judith regret asking it. Embarrassed, she apologized.

'I'm sorry. I shouldn't pry.'

'Not at all. You asked with the best of motives, but I confess to not having a ready answer,' he said, a wry little smile twitching at his thin lips. 'It would be necessary to know the outcome of the war to consider the possible combined futures of Anne-Marie and young Leon. Making predictions is the prerogative of the warlock not the clergyman, so I am at this time unable to give you any kind of an answer, Mrs Seldon. Perhaps this is something we could discuss on our journey to Epsom.'

'When will we be going, Reverend Penny?' Judith asked eagerly, wanting to be with her husband, to rescue him, as soon as possible.

'First thing in the morning, Mrs Seldon, if that is agreeable to you?'

'Most agreeable,' a delighted Judith assured him.

Leon knew that the way his powerful physique had enabled him to make a swift recovery had enraged Quartermaster-Sergeant Wilson. On a blisteringly hot afternoon he had been strapped to the wheel of a gun carriage. His legs were spread out and fastened by the ankles to the spokes of the wheel, and the same was done to his wrists: the military's infamous crucifixion. Not being able to move as much as an inch was a torture exacerbated by the blazing sun.

Four passing soldiers risked punishment themselves by tying the corners of some old blankets to the carriage to erect a crude sunshade for him. Still able to speak at that time, Leon thanked them before they left, feeling that it was only fair to tell them that he was a conscientious objector.

'Makes no difference to us,' one of the soldiers said with a friendly grin. 'We'd do the same if you were a bloody Jerry, mate. It's you being crucified today, tomorrow it could be any one or all of us.'

Being shielded from the sun brought him relief, but only for a matter of minutes. A major spotted the construction from a distance. By moving his eyes to the right, Leon saw the officer pause, heard him bellowing for Wilson.

Then Wilson, body shaking in one of his frequent fits of rage, came running up to rip the blankets down and aim kicks at the defenceless Leon. He was left alone then, totally ignored as his body reacted agonizingly to being strapped tightly. Drained by the sun, only semi-conscious, he was vaguely aware of two of the soldiers who had helped him earlier, creeping back. Keeping themselves concealed from view as much as possible, they loosened his straps a little.

Either due to having witnessed this, or some super-sadistic instinct, Wilson came charging up within minutes to retighten the straps.

An hour later, when Leon was no longer interested in living, and the military authorities had apparently lost interest in him, the four soldiers returned and cut him loose. Carrying Leon down to the rear of the cookhouse, they laid him on a table and brought him round by bathing his body with cold water. Rationing him severely for his own good, they gave him sips of water that eventually revived him fully.

Soon afterwards, Wilson caught up with him and Leon was put back into his original cell. In the afternoon of the following day, Leon and the other conscientious objectors were marched up a hill from the top of which they could see the sun-sequined blue water of the English Channel. This sight increased the sense of separation from his homeland in Leon, and he assumed it had the same effect on his friends. All of them were subdued as they were doubled down the grassy slope of the far side of the hill.

Up ahead of them was a sprawling military camp. They were marched towards and into the camp, all of them puzzled. Why had they been brought here? They could not be kept so secure here as they had been in the field punishment barracks.

There was not a cloud in the bright blue sky as they were lined up on one side of a large open, flat space that, despite a rough surface, was obviously used as an improvised parade ground. Though they stood alone, they were aware of activity in other parts of the camp. After an hour standing in the broiling sun, they were joined by soldiers who were marched up to stand along the other three sides of the parade ground. This went on until there were thousands of men present, apparently there as spectators.

Aware that the other prisoners and himself were being gazed at curiously by countless pairs of eyes, Leon anticipated that something big was about to happen. Whatever it was, it would be bad for the conscientious objectors.

It dawned on him at the same time as he heard Mullaly mutter his assessment of the situation to the others. 'We're about to be sentenced, lads. It'll be the firing squad for us in the morning.'

A captain, the camp's adjutant, walked to the centre of the square, as Wilson collected a stack of papers from a soldier before marching over smartly to salute and then stand beside the adjutant.

By chance it was Mullaly who was first taken to the centre of the square, where he was stood in front of the officer and Wilson. The adjutant read out Mullaly's rank, army number, and the unit he had been forced to join.

The adjutant continued reading and Leon went cold, despite the heat, when he heard Mullaly's sentence: '. . . tried by field court martial for disobedience whilst undergoing field punishment. Sentenced to death by being shot.'

A white-faced Mullaly turned his head to look back at them, until Wilson screamed at him, 'Face the front, Soldier!'

'Confirmed by General Sir Douglas Haig,' the adjutant said finally, 'and commuted to ten years' penal servitude.'

Leon couldn't be sure whether the mass sigh of relief was silent or not. One thing he was certain of was that it came from the soldiers at the side of the square as well as the conscientious objectors waiting to be sentenced.

Three more men were taken forward, then it was Leon's turn. As he reached his position, he saw the papers of the previous man passed back by the adjutant to Wilson. The word *Death* caught his eye because it was in slightly larger letters than the rest of the text. Watching Wilson pass his paper to the adjutant, Leon's heart seemed to stop beating as he again saw the word *Death*. This time it was in huge letters that were penned in brilliant red and thickly underlined.

Once more he had been singled out to be made an example of. The only consolation, which was no consolation at all, was that this would be the last time. He wilted inside as he thought of how his execution would affect his mother. How would she and Beth get along without him? It would have been easy to weep for his mother and young sister there and then, but he was determined not to betray the slightest weakness. Anne-Marie came into his mind. As much as he loved her and longed to be with her, he didn't want his death to cause her a lifetime of unhappiness. If Hubert Lytton was the antidote to a life of misery for her, then Leon prayed that the captain would be spared in the war.

He heard the crisp, upper-class tones of the adjutant reaching the end of his sentence. '. . . sentenced to death by being shot.'

A great hush had fallen on the assembly. Leon waited, hoping that the adjutant had only paused for effect as before. He expected the commutation of his sentence would follow.

But too much time was passing and there was still silence. From the corner of his eye he saw the adjutant exchange a glance with Wilson. The latter then roared out a command. 'About turn!'

Defiant to the last, though he felt really sick deep inside, Leon turned casually on his heel, and when Wilson ordered, 'Quick march', he ambled back towards his friends.

The hush had, if anything, deepened, and horror was registered on the faces of the other conscientious objectors as he approached them.

'Halt.'

At this order from Wilson, Leon took a few more steps before halting. He turned as casually as before when Wilson issued the about turn command.

Raising his voice to cover the distance that was now between Leon and himself, the adjutant held up Leon's paper to read,'Confirmed by General Sir Douglas Haig, and commuted to ten years' penal servitude.'

An immense relief robbed Leon's legs of their strength. His knees sagged but he didn't go down. They had played a cruel game with him, and he heard his fellow prisoners shouting angry protests. There was a muttering that was growing in volume from the thousands of watching soldiers, too.

Close to panic, Wilson was issuing orders fast to NCOs. There came the sound of rifle bolts being worked as a number of sergeants and corporals surrounded the incensed conscientious objectors. At the sides of the square, fear of mutiny had officers and NCOs bringing various groups of soldiers to attention and marching them off.

Within minutes, the square was almost deserted and Leon stood alone. In the distance, turning to look back at him as they went, his friends were being marched back up the hill to return to the field punishment barracks from whence they had come. The fact that he remained behind told him that once more he had been singled out for special treatment. He waited without anxiety to face whatever was in store for him. After what had seemed a very real sentence of death, nothing seemed to matter very much.

A small petrol-driven truck came lurching up to the side of the parade ground. The private soldier behind the wheel was so bereft of driving skills that he had difficulty in stopping the lorry for Wilson and his staff-sergeant to alight. They strode over together to manacle Leon and put him on board the truck.

They journeyed for miles. Leon took an interest in a mining village of brick terraced houses. Water pumps stood at intervals along the deserted street of the evacuated village. The gardens of the houses had been well tended. Wilson ordered the driver to stop the lorry. Getting out, leaving the staff-sergeant to guard Leon, he jumped into several gardens to collect fresh vegetables and fruit.

Back in the lorry, Wilson shared the vegetables with the staff-sergeant and the driver. They had a feast, with ripe cherries as a dessert. Leon was not offered even one cherry.

On the move again, they kept going until late afternoon when they passed through hills that were yellow with dandelions and buttercups. Here the lorry halted and Leon was taken to a barbed-wire fence that crossed the terrain. Wilson and the staff-sergeant placed him face against the fence. They tied his wrists to the actual wire instead of the thick wooden posts it was strung between. This allowed them to lash him so tightly that the side of his face was pressed hard against the wire. To turn his head without ripping open his face on the barbs was impossible.

Satisfied that Leon was secure, Wilson told him, 'Try not to worry. We'll be back in the morning. You'll find the fresh air will do you the world of good.'

For a short time the lorry refused to start up again. The cursing driver swung the starting handle, yelling abuse at the vehicle when the engine kicked back and the handle was sent spinning out of his hands. Finally the engine fired, the three soldiers climbed into the truck and it drove away. Leon listened to the sound of the engine fading. Then there was nothing but the special quiet of the wilderness.

Left all alone as dusk began to settle around him, Leon tried to relieve his tortured body by rising on tiptoe, but he had been tied too tightly to succeed. He had no idea where he was, and conjecture as to why Wilson had brought him here failed to produce an answer. Darkness fell to add to his loneliness. Leon's sole company were unseen creatures of the night whose cries were incessant and varied, but mostly mournful.

Rain heralded a summer storm. Great splashing drops hit his face, soaking his clothing in a matter of seconds. A blinding flash of lightning lit the terrain for a split second. A crash of thunder followed and Leon gave an involuntary jerk that sent a sharp barb of wire into his cheek. The birds and animals had ceased their calls, but as the storm ended as swiftly and unexpectedly as it had begun, he discovered that it had worked some magic on the air to make it super-conductive to sound.

At first he believed that he was hallucinating. But then he was certain he could hear men's voices coming from not too far away. Someone started to sing 'There's a long, long trail a-winding, into the land of my dreams . . .' but was quickly hushed by a harsh voice that declared the singer was a 'bloody idiot'.

What he was hearing could mean only one thing: Wilson had deliberately left him helpless just behind the front line. A terrific clap of thunder startled him. But a minute later, as an explosion occurred to his right, he knew he had been mistaken. This wasn't a return of the earlier thunder, but the opening of a German artillery barrage.

Soon the earth was shaking. There were brilliant orange flashes all about him as shells exploded. From where the sound of singing had come to him, there now came the blood-curdling screams of wounded and dying soldiers as the British Expeditionary Force was blasted by German shells.

After a futile struggle with his bonds, Leon resigned himself to certain death as the shelling went on. One shell exploded so close that his face was peppered with earth and small stones. All he could do to protect himself was to close his eyes.

The night had become one great rushing, roaring noise. In the flashes from the exploding shells, he saw the silhouettes of soldiers scrambling up out of the trenches to run staggeringly in retreat. They were heading his way. The war that it had cost Leon so much to avoid, was coming to find him.

Eight

'Are you the father of a patient?'

The Royal Army Medical Corps sergeant asked Reverend Penny this when the old man protested at having been kept waiting. He and Judith Seldon had been at the mental hospital more than an hour without finding anyone prepared to deal with their request to see Bruce. Though desperate to be with her husband, Judith was now regretting having come to Epsom. She was still upset from having looked out of a window on arrival. Out in the grounds three men in the bright blue uniforms of army hospital patients had been giggling like children as they chased each other round in circles. Now she could still hear their inane laughter, and because the horrible has a compelling attraction all its own, she couldn't resist taking an occasional peep out. Each time she did, the three men were still completing the same circle at the same speed. Though satisfied that Bruce would have complete control of his mental faculties, she hated the thought of him having to mix with men like the three out in the garden.

'No, I am not the father of anyone here,' Penny was replying to the sergeant. 'I am the Reverend Paulton Penny, Vicar of Marshlee.'

'That don't cut no ice in this place, mister.' The sergeant, a tubby little man whose round face was made to be pleasant but wasn't, made a show of tapping his shoulder with one hand. 'It's pips and crowns on here that counts, not' – he pointed to his head – 'haloes up here.'

'I am not asking for special favours, but I surely qualify for at least a modicum of respect from you, Sergeant,' Reverend Penny said with enough of his old fire to make the sergeant wilt.

'Can I be of any help, sir?' A captain who had been passing by changed direction and came to Penny with an offer of assistance.

Judith stood and walked to the clergyman's side. There was something kind about the captain's face. It had a pinkish complexion suggesting the hair under his cap would be ginger. She felt that they were about to get somewhere at last. The officer gave her an unofficial salute that she took as the equivalent of a gentleman's raising of his hat.

'We have come a long way to see a patient here, Captain,' Penny explained. 'A Mr Bruce Seldon.'

Putting his hand to his chin, the captain did some thinking. Things clicked together in his mind and he said, 'Of course. We don't have titles like mister here, it's all ranks you see, sir. But Seldon is a patient of mine.' He looked quizzically at Judith. 'And you are Mrs Seldon, madam?'

'Yes,' Judith answered.

'Ah,' the captain nodded, losing much of his positive, military manner. 'I'm afraid that I have an emergency to attend to. I will see you in my office in, what shall we say . . . ten minutes? Perhaps you would care to wait here.'

'Mrs Seldon has been kept waiting long enough, Captain,' an emphatic Reverend Penny responded. 'If you would kindly have someone show her the way, I would like her to see her husband right away.'

'I would prefer you to wait, Mrs Seldon. I do like to have a word with relatives before they go on our wards.'

'Nevertheless . . .' Penny said, in a way that made it plain he would brook no argument.

'Very well,' the captain said with a sigh, calling to the sergeant Penny had been speaking to earlier. 'Sergeant Pierce. Take Mrs Seldon and this gentleman to Private Seldon in Mafeking ward.'

'Just Mrs Seldon. I am content to wait here,' Reverend Penny told the sergeant.

'I'd like you to go along with her, sir,' the captain said so pleadingly that he gave Judith her first intimation that all was not well.

But that was silly thinking. Bruce was as strong in the mind as the powerfully built Leon was in the body. Bruce could cope under any circumstances. She could recall Bruce explaining to her a survival technique when under intolerable pressure: 'The soul is no larger than a single dot made by a pencil on paper, Judith. When under great stress, mentally contract to a dot and no one can get at you. To effect complete escape, move to the far side of that dot and you will be back where you were before birth.'

Though the last method had sounded frighteningly irreversible to Judith at the time, Bruce's knowledge and understanding of such matters gave her confidence now.

With Reverend Penny at her side she followed the sergeant down a long corridor that reeked of cheap disinfectant. The RAMC man wore soft-soled shoes, but the ringing footfalls of the clergyman and herself on the stone floor of this weird place were somehow as offensive as a shouted oath in church. Judith's heart skipped a beat as they turned into a crowded ward. She averted her head as a vacuously grinning patient stood in front of her and dropped the trousers of his pyjamas. A stern-faced nurse pulled him out off Judith's way, but he was hobbled by his own trousers and fell heavily to the floor. Reverend Penny held her arm to assist her in stepping over the patient, who was being scolded by the nurse because he was urinating all over the floor.

They passed a bed on which a patient sat, appearing to be concentrating hard on writing a letter. But each time he wrote one word he tore the paper from the pad, screwed it up and threw it on the floor before beginning the whole pointless process again.

Relying on the clergyman's hand to guide her, Judith closed her eyes briefly to offer up a prayer for Bruce who had to endure these deranged people around him.

The sergeant stopped by an armchair in which an ageing man was slumped, his head hanging lifelessly to one side. Impatient, Judith wanted to move on, to find Bruce. In her distress she was about to berate the sergeant when she heard Reverend Penny speak beside her.

'Oh, Judith!' the elderly clergyman moaned emotionally, using her Christian name for the first time.

The sadness in Penny's voice made her take a second look at the man in the chair. As thin as a starving man, he was made to look old by the ravages of illness. A mighty tremor shook her. With difficulty, Judith identified this human wreck as her husband.

'Oh, Bruce,' she cried, dropping to her knees and grasping one of his skeletal hands in both of hers.

His eyes were open but unseeing. 'It's me, Bruce; Judith,' she implored. He didn't move. His only response was to dribble copiously out of the side of his mouth.

Stunned, dry-eyed, she permitted Reverend Penny to gently bring her up on her feet. Speaking very calmly, she said, 'Bruce has moved to the far side of the dot, Reverend Penny.'

'I'm afraid that I don't understand, child,' the vicar said apologetically. 'Come. He doesn't know you, and it will only serve to increase your distress to remain here.'

Judith made no protest as her companion hurried her away, taking her out of the ward. They had to walk round an orderly who was mopping the urine-stained floor. A screwed-up piece of writing paper thrown by the man on the bed landed in the bucket, and the other patient was advancing on Judith again, loosening his trousers. The nurse from earlier dragged him away as they hurried out of the ward.

In the corridor, the captain, his face anguished, was hurrying toward them. Trying to study Judith without staring rudely, he seemed to find her composure incredible.

'I'm so sorry,' he told Judith. 'I wanted to prepare you.'

'I don't think there is any way you could have prepared her for that, Captain,' Reverend Penny said in a kindly way. 'How long has he been that way?'

'He has deteriorated a lot in recent weeks.'

'Did he leave anything for me, a letter perhaps?' Judith heard herself enquiring, amazed by her own self-control.

'I'm afraid that he was too ill to put pen to paper when he was admitted, Mrs Seldon, but' – the captain reached into his pocket to take out a scrap of paper – 'he insisted on giving me this, which I assumed he wished me to pass to you.'

Hand shaking, Judith took the paper and read the two lines on it that was written in a spidery hand barely recognizable as that of Bruce:

What weight of ancient wisdom can prevail
When private judgement holds the public scale?

'Dryden, I believe?' the captain said softly.

'It's Dryden. Bruce was a great one for quotations,' Judith said just prior to hearing an unearthly howl filling the corridor.

She wasn't aware until she felt Paulton Penny's arms supporting her, that it was she who had howled. Clinging to the clergyman, deep sobs racking her body, she let him and the solicitous captain lead her, feet dragging, into an ante-room.

Hanging on the wire like a bird trapped by its wings, Leon prayed to God over and over again as German shells continued to explode all around. His prayers were answered, for he remained unscathed as shrapnel flew through the air past him, sometimes so close that he could feel heat from the shell fragments. The barrage had become an absolute roar, while separate from it came a new sound, the rattle of machine-gun fire. A rocket went shooting up into the night sky, bursting as brightly as a carnival spectacular. Bruce guessed it was a British Army SOS fired by the soldiers he had earlier heard talking and singing.

There was an almighty explosion nearby, the blast from which flung him around so that the barbed wire jabbed viciously into his wrists. Leon felt this pain, then knew no more until he opened his eyes to find himself lying at the bottom of a shell hole. His nose and ears were bleeding, which told Leon he was concussed, and his face felt strange because it was peppered with powder dust driven into the skin by the explosion. Sitting up, he discovered that the explosion had freed him. The blast that had knocked him out had torn down the barbed-wire fence. The wire he was fastened to was now loose, and he could bring his hands together to untie the ropes.

Taking a little time out to get his shattered senses together, Leon then clambered up out of the hole. As he saw soldiers running towards him, he was about to drop back into the hole and hide when he saw that they were British. Eyes as wild as those of stampeding cattle, they came on in droves, parting to go round him then closing up together again.

They kept on coming, running as fast as they could, most of them without rifles or equipment. The German artillery still came whistling over, taking its toll on the fleeing men. Horrified, Leon watched pieces of men, limbs, torsos, heads, all tossed high into the air by exploding shells. He saw a sergeant, standing bemused just a yard or two from him. The shelling had ceased suddenly and now only the pounding of running feet could be heard.

A young lieutenant stood a little way off, talking loudly to himself.

'The Hun counter-attacked. A complete breakthrough, a rout, damn it,' Leon heard the officer say as he tilted his head back to look up into the sky. 'The Boche is barraging with 5.9s.'

'5.9s, sir,' the sergeant agreed in dull tones.

Brandishing a revolver, the lieutenant pointed at the fleeing men and cried out in disgust, 'Look at them, Sergeant. Soldiers! They're not soldiers! Damned if I can believe that British soldiers are behaving like this. I want the name of every man, Sergeant. Every damned one of them will face a court martial.'

When the sergeant remained standing as still as a statue, making no response to the officer's ludicrous order, the lieutenant yelled at the running soldiers, 'Get back to your guns, you men, or I'll put a bullet in every one of you.'

Not a single man paused in his headlong flight. The sergeant still stood undecided for a moment longer, then jogged off with the last of the soldiers. Seeing this, the lieutenant said, 'Damn, damn, damn,' and joined his men in their flight.

Now knowing in which direction safety lay, Leon was ready to move off when a lone soldier approached him in a shambling run, pleading in a weak voice, 'Stop it bleeding. Please help me.'

A single shell, as if fired by afterthought, came whistling over. Dropping to the ground until he heard it explode some way off,

Leon came up again to see that the soldier remained standing.

'I'm wounded,' he declared superfluously, when Leon went to him.

'I have no bandages,' Leon spread both hands in a gesture of helplessness.

'There's a field dressing packet in my pack,' the soldier told him urgently. He was young, possibly not yet eighteen. 'I've got to go back. There's a patrol out there cut off by Jerry. They won't know that the line has moved. We have to guide them back to here. Will you help me?'

Saying nothing, Leon was in a quandary. The boy was mistaken. There was no field dressing packet and no pack. He took a closer look to see that the soldier's right arm had been all but torn from the shoulder. The muscles had been severely lacerated, a large amount of flesh was hanging loose, and blood was flowing fast. Unless the flow was staunched the boy would bleed to death.

The soldier made it plain that he knew this by making a confession to Leon in a shaky voice. 'I'm frightened.'

No sooner had he said this, than the boy pitched to the ground on his face. Bending with the intention of helping the soldier to his feet, Leon peered curiously through the darkness at a stain that covered the back of the fallen man's tunic. Reaching out to touch the boy's back lightly with his fingertips, Leon recoiled. His fingers had sunk into a soft morass of blood and mangled flesh. There was a huge hole where the soldier's back should have been. Some after-death reflex must have got the soldier this far. Now he was dead.

Standing up straight, Leon looked to where the last of the running soldiers were disappearing over a hill. He started after them at a steady lope that he knew he could keep at for hours. As he went, he thought of the stranded patrol that the boy had spoken of. They didn't have a hope of surviving if somebody didn't go to their rescue. But there was no one to go except him, and he had neither military training nor experience. He would not be saving their lives but throwing away his own.

Leon had not covered one hundred yards when his conscience halted him in his tracks. Turning, he ran in the opposite direction, with no plan in mind but aware that he had to do something to help the men lost behind enemy lines.

They had tea on the lawn at Farley Grange that warm late-summer Saturday afternoon. Sitting between the brigadier and Claudia Lytton, Anne-Marie was now convinced that Hubert had an ulterior motive when he had asked her to return the Bible. Arriving here had been like walking into a trap that the Lyttons quickly sprung. Ever since, even now when Gladys Plummer had joined them, the old couple were employing nuance and innuendo in an attempt to influence her where their son was concerned. She knew that the couple must thoroughly disapprove of the work she was doing, but were prepared to overlook it in their quest for a daughter-in-law. But Anne-Marie could detect an underlying tension. The brigadier and Claudia were suffering like all parents with sons in the front line. They lived under a constant dark cloud of fear that bad news might arrive at any moment.

Gladys Plummer, too, was on edge. Accepting that the woman profoundly loved her absent husband, Anne-Marie could understand the nightmare Gladys was living through. This understanding permitted her to forgive the woman her behaviour at the troop train, and to strike an uneasy truce with her.

Taking a gold sovereign and half-sovereign from his pocket, the brigadier had a small, sad smile on his face as he pointed to the coins and asked Anne-Marie, 'What do they mean to you, Anne-Marie?'

With a shrug, aware that it wasn't what he wanted to hear, Anne-Marie gave the only reply she could think of. 'Money. Just money.'

'No, no, much more than that.' He shook his round head of sparse grey hair. 'Those coins represent quality, my dear. They have been taken out of circulation and a vital part of our way of life will go with them. Quantity not quality is all that counts these days. What sort of person do we expect the next generation to produce? By gad! Anne-Marie, they will be people who have never heard that magic sound, that resonant ring, of a sovereign on a shop-counter.'

This seemed a trivial complaint in comparison to all the horrors going on in the world, but Anne-Marie had long placed the brigadier as one of those people who make use of small talk to keep black thoughts at bay. The brigadier's wife mildly rebuked him.

'It always puzzles me why you waste your intelligence on things so unimportant, Cecil.'

'Unimportant!' the old man snorted. 'I'm talking of a transition, my dear, the exchange of the finer things of life in return for expediency, the fast, trashy, American way of life. You remember better times, don't you, Evans?'

This question was directed at the Lyttons' aged butler, who had shuffled up to put a replacement pot of tea on the table. Anne-Marie watched the loose jowls swing and the drooping bags under barely visible eyes quiver as the old servant shook his head.

'I'm afraid that I remember very little these days, Brigadier,' Evans replied.

'Of course you remember, dammit, Evans,' the brigadier protested. 'You remember when men looked proper in silk toppers. Then there were the taximen in their brilliant blue coats with silver buttons, their shining peaked caps and yellow chamois gloves. Standards have already slipped, and I shudder to think what life will be like when this war is over.'

Holding her saucer high, Claudia delicately sipped tea before saying, 'We'll put up with anything to have the war over and our boys back home. Do you hear from dear Alexander fairly regularly, Gladys?'

'Very often,' Gladys Plummer answered with a pleased smile. 'I imagine it's the same with Hubert?'

'Oh yes,' Claudia agreed, then turned a knowing smile on Anne-Marie. 'But we don't hear much news from him. All he writes about is what a wonderful time he spent with Anne-Marie in London.'

'That's something we'll always be grateful to you for, Anne-Marie. You made our son so very happy before he went off to war,' the brigadier said.

'It was just . . .' Anne-Marie began, biting her tongue before she could reveal that she had in a way repaid Hubert for saving her from prison. If she told the Lyttons this, and detailed the anti-establishment charge she had been on, they'd probably both have a heart attack there and then.

'We were so pleased for you both when we heard about it, my dear,' Claudia simpered. 'You'll be spending the evening with us I trust, Anne-Marie?'

Reluctant to refuse her old friends, Anne-Marie knew that she must. On arriving home her mother relayed a message that Elsie Marriott urgently wanted to see her. Thinking that there could be news of Leon, Anne-Marie was ready to go at once, but her mother explained that it was something to do with Beth. Anne-Marie paid a boy to take a message to the Marriott home saying that she would call that evening.

'I'm sorry, but I promised to help a friend this evening.'

'What a pity. We wanted to hear all about what you and Hubert did in London. Never mind, it won't be long before the two of you are together again.' The brigadier took a lot for granted in his prediction. 'By all accounts our boys are giving the Germans what for right now.'

'That's what I've been hearing,' a pleased Gladys put in.

'And you heard right, Gladys. No country can withstand the losses old Jerry is having inflicted on him now.'

The idiots, Anne-Marie moaned inwardly, although she pitied them. They were living in a fools' paradise created by casualty figures doctored by the government. From her work in London she knew that the people were being fed propaganda in what they took to be news bulletins.

'He can't say, of course,' Gladys said, 'but reading between the lines I think Alex is where the Germans are falling back fast. That pleases me, for I know that means he is so much safer.'

With an animated nod of agreement, the brigadier said, 'Of course he'll be safe, Gladys, just as Hubert will be. They are from fine English stock, my dear, far superior to the Hun they are facing.'

'I haven't heard a word from Leon since he was sent to France,' Anne-Marie said, upset because they hadn't enquired after him.

'That's different,' the brigadier commented a little angrily. 'That young man may have been forced into the army, but he'll never be able to call himself a soldier.'

Annoyed by what was intended to be criticism, Anne-Marie put the matter in perspective by saying, 'Leon has never wanted to call himself a soldier.'

'Never mind, Anne-Marie, they say it takes all sorts to make a world.' Claudia Lytton offered unwelcome sympathy in a way that insulted Leon and all he stood for.

'You have no . . .' Anne-Marie began, angrier than she would like to have been, but a cry of delight from the brigadier made her break off.

'Here comes the Reverend Penny,' the brigadier said with a laugh, as he watched his old friend come across the lawn to where they sat. 'Do you know, I'm sure Paulton can smell a fresh pot of tea from a range of five miles.'

Having noticed the unhappy expression on her father's face, Anne-Marie ignored the brigadier's banter. Something was wrong, badly wrong.

Reaching the seated group, her father exchanged the briefest of greetings with the others, then turned a sorrowful face to her. 'I've just returned from Epsom with Judith Seldon, Anne-Marie. I have taken her home, but she is in a really bad way.'

'Whatever has happened, Father?'

'It's her husband. His mind has gone.'

'Gone?' Anne-Marie gasped, finding it impossible to envisage the erudite Bruce Seldon without his razor-sharp mental faculties.

'Completely gone, Anne-Marie. He didn't recognize us. In fact, he is barely in the land of the living at all. There is no hope for him I'm afraid.'

Anne-Marie stood. 'I should go to her.'

'I think you should,' her father concurred. 'To be truthful, I was uneasy about leaving her alone to come here.'

Alarmed, Anne-Marie started to make her hurried excuses. Elsie Marriott and her daughter came into her mind, but she accepted that she had to get her priorities in order. Judith's need was the greatest, and Anne-Marie would postpone her visit to the Marriott home until tomorrow evening.

As night gave way to day, a blanket of thick mist meant that Leon could not see further than a few yards ahead. There was not a breath of wind to dispel it. As he made his difficult way over ground pitted and churned up by the German bombardment, he found that visibility improved as he moved away from the river that was on his right. Moving on, he found himself passing arms and equipment strewn about, abandoned by the troops in their headlong flight. Leon came upon death at its most grotesque. The awful stench of it was in the air, and he had to step carefully over bodies that had inflated like balloons, bulging so much they had split their uniforms. He was aware that the British retreat before an enemy advance must mean that the Germans were just up ahead. He was in No Man's Land, and to go on would mean blundering straight into the German lines.

Leon was trying to think of a plan of action when the guns started firing again. But there was a difference, for the guns were firing from behind him, and the shells were exploding up ahead. The British had begun a bombardment and would soon launch a counter-attack. But that would come too late to help the patrol the dying soldier had told him about.

Thinking that at least the barrage would force the Germans to keep their heads down, Leon moved on. The artillery fire was increasing, and the mist thinning. As he got closer to where the shells were exploding up ahead, a brilliant sun came out and the last remnants of mist conceded defeat and cleared away.

About a mile ahead and to his left, he could see a couple of German gun teams and limbers on a hill. This was a sign that the British bombardment was driving them back. Leon prayed that he would find the patrol in hiding and intact.

He was crossing ground now that was littered with bodies. Leon was walking through the land of British dead. They were lying with heads away from the enemy, most of them face down. It was hard to accept there could be so many dead. Leon found himself thinking sadly of the homes to which these men would never

172

return. Hesitating, with the shells still whistling and roaring overhead, he wondered if there was any point in him going on. From a logical viewpoint when standing among all these corpses, the few men of the patrol became unimportant. But he knew better than that. Every human life was of the utmost importance. Leon moved forward again.

Glancing to his left, he saw the two German teams had made slow progress with the limbers. As he watched, they received a direct hit from the British artillery. The top of the hill was capped by swirling smoke. When it cleared away there was nothing there. Men and horses had died violently, silently and remotely. Perhaps because he had witnessed them, those distant deaths affected him more profoundly than the bodies he was stepping over.

Coming up on the trenches vacated by the British soldiers, Leon at first thought he had found one member of the patrol. But it was a guardsman lying on his back in part of a trench half blown in. Chest soaked in blood and with his head hanging loosely, the guardsman was dead. The only way across was for Leon to use the chest of the corpse as a stepping stone.

Hating himself but having to move on, Leon closed his eyes and took a step. As he trod on the chest his weight compressed the lungs of the corpse and the dead guardsman let out what started as a groan and seemed to become a cackling laugh.

Landing on the far side of the trench, Leon, terrified for the first time in his life, ran. Shells landing closer to him now, but unnoticed, the dead man's laughter bouncing about inside his head, he went crashing through undergrowth into a wood. He kept running, puffing and panting, weaving in and out of the trees, until he had no breath left and had distanced himself from the guardsman so that the laughter had ceased to reverberate and was just a harrowing memory. Then he stopped, supporting himself with one hand against the trunk of a tree as he bent forward, dragging in air to ease his lungs and steady his pounding heart.

Not far away in the wood an exploding shell shattered trees. When the ear-splitting roar of the detonation died away, Leon, now almost fully recovered. could hear damaged trees creaking and splitting as they fell.

Then he heard a different sound nearby. Close to inaudible, it was no more than the crushing of a dried leaf under a foot. But it became a loud crackling in Leon's head. Turning to where the noise had come from, his whole body went rigid.

Standing there, a Mauser rifle held at the hip and aimed at Leon's chest, was a German soldier. The face under the spiked helmet was young, and the German looked as apprehensive as Leon felt. He looked to be a nice kid whose company, with the borders of nations removed, Leon would have welcomed at some social or sporting event.

The two of them stood looking at each other. They were silent because there was nothing to say, and neither would be able to understand the other anyway. Slowly Leon began to raise his hands, prepared to surrender if that was what the situation called for. But an instinctive or intuitive impulse came to him, and instead of lifting his hands he spread them wide to show that he was unarmed.

For a moment the young German appeared puzzled. But then he smiled a really friendly smile. Leon smiled back. Lowering the rifle, the German waved his hand like a schoolboy bidding his mother goodbye. When Leon waved back, the German turned and walked off into the trees. Before the wood hid him from Leon, he turned and they again exchanged waves.

A little shaken by the odd encounter, Leon realized he had just seen the words of Bruce Seldon proved true. 'The workers of the world have no reason to fight each other. German Socialists are our loyal friends and we should greet them across the roar of guns.'

Coming cautiously out of the wood, Leon reached a canal. With no forward observers, the co-ordinates of the British artillery had probably been changed by educated guesswork, the shells dropping much further ahead so that they were no longer a danger to him. There was no sign of any Germans. Leon reasoned that they had been driven back by the bombardment. The boy with the Mauser in the woods must have been a straggler left behind.

Although with scant understanding of warfare, Leon recognized that he had been granted only a brief respite. When the British guns stopped firing for the infantry to counter-attack, the Germans would speedily return to take up defensive positions.

If it was possible to find the lost patrol, then he must do so quickly. Moving along a hedge that had great chunks bitten out of it by shells, he came across a fresh body. It was that of a British lieutenant, and Leon turned it over. The left side of the face of the corpse had been blown in, and lacerations to the neck had torn the jugular vein apart. Yet enough of the facial features remained for an astonished Leon to be able to recognize Alex Plummer.

'It's a small world, Plummer,' he heard himself say to a man beyond conversation.

He walked a little way off. Standing, looking at the tops of the trees in the wood he had just left, Leon pictured Plummer the last time he had seen him. It was a Christmas that seemed more than a century ago now. Plummer had been a boy then, excited over a new car bought for him by his father. Despite never having liked him, Leon found it an unbearably sad experience to link that half-drunken, fun-seeking young man with the shattered, bloody body in the grass behind him. He thought of Gladys. If he never got back, and it seemed more and more likely that he wouldn't make it, she would probably never know what happened to the man she loved. This deceptively peaceful stretch of land beside the canal would shortly return to being a battlegound. When the guns stopped firing, the smoke had cleared, and the dead had done their dying, it was unlikely that anything of Lt Alexander Plummer would remain.

A low but dreadful groan snapped Leon back into alertness. Estimating that it was most likely a German who had made the noise, Leon wondered what the chances were of a second one being as friendly as the first. The odds wouldn't seem to be in his favour.

Going on a slow, careful search, Leon heard a second groan coming from an area of long grass. Walking over, his movements mechanical rather than thought-controlled, he wondered if meeting the young German and finding the body of Plummer had been part of a dream that now had him looking down on a wounded Captain Hubert Lytton.

Not far from Lytton, in the blood-soaked grass, was a torso with nothing but a head left attached to it. Recognizable on an empty, ripped and bloody sleeve were the two stripes of a corporal. Lytton, who was conscious, had the flap of his holster open and his revolver in his hand. He lowered the gun as, eyes wide at the shock of seeing Leon, he tried to say something. The words came out as a groan.

Kneeling beside the captain, Leon saw a fragment of shrapnel was embedded in his cheek. A thin, straggling line of blood ran from it. But Lytton's major injury was a shattered right leg. When he saw Leon looking at the leg, Lytton was able to gasp out a few words. 'Caught in machine-gun fire.'

Combat and injury had changed Hubert Lytton. Gone was the arrogance and the bombast. In great pain, he was plainly as spell-bound as Leon was at the two of them meeting here. It was too much for coincidence, but beyond the understanding of men like Lytton and himself. Bruce Seldon would be the man to offer a clue, probably provide an explanation, but Bruce wasn't here.

Gently, not wanting to cause him more pain, but having to do so, Leon grasped the captain's shoulders and raised him to a sitting position, back resting against a boulder. The wounded man was strong enough to keep a grip of his revolver.

Finding no field dressing pack on Lytton, Leon scrambled to where the torso and head lay. Avoiding looking at the face that had been burnt black, with teeth showing bright white in a grimace that was set for eternity, Leon went through the corporal's kit until he found the pack he needed.

Back beside the wounded captain he ripped open the field dressing. Tending to Lytton's face first, he put a thumb each side of the shrapnel and applied pressure as if squeezing a boil. The additional agony this caused Lytton was registered in his eyes. Then the jagged-edged fragment of shrapnel popped out like a pea from a pod. Breaking a phial of iodine over the now bleeding wound, Leon placed a pad of lint on Lytton's cheek and held it there until slowly congealing blood acted as an adhesive.

Moving a little, Leon ripped open the blood-soaked trouser leg. He could see that the leg was badly injured, but as a layman could not judge just how badly. It looked as if bullets had ripped away flesh and parts of the bones from the thigh down to the ankle. Reaching for the dressing, he paused as Lytton asked him a question. The captain's voice was so weak that he asked three times before Leon heard.

'Plummy?'

'Dead.'

'I thought as much,' Lytton said, somehow regaining strength. 'We were the only two left. The rest of the patrol was wiped out in Crapouillots Wood when we got caught in a crossfire. The machine-gun has a hellish sound.'

Hubert Lytton appeared to have lost all of his earlier enthusiasm for this war. The wood he had mentioned must be where he had met the German, Leon thought, as he worked on the leg. Cleaning the torn flesh as best he could, he tenderly, but most probably pointlessly, fingered splinters of bone back into what he considered might be their place. Then he bandaged from the ankle upwards, using up all of the available dressing before sitting back on his heels to take a break while viewing his handiwork.

'Thank you, I feel less pain now,' Lytton said. 'But it won't help much. If I had to gamble who'll get here first, our boys or the Hun, my money would have to be on the Hun.'

'That makes no difference, for we won't be here,' a confident Leon told him.

'You can get away,' Lytton agreed, then pointed at his injured leg, 'but how could I go anywhere on that?'

'You won't need to use your leg, I'll carry you.'

Having said that, Leon told himself that he should be enjoying having the upper hand. Out here, the family status and wealth that had put Hubert Lytton much more than a cut above the working man back home, had been superseded by Leon's physical prowess. It was something Leon would be justified in gloating over. Yet he felt no sense of triumph, just an urge to get the wounded Lytton out of here.

As he was rising to his feet it was a change in Lytton's facial expression that warned him. Aware of Lytton raising his revolver to point it at something behind him, Leon turned and for the second time that day saw a German with a levelled Mauser rifle.

This man was very different to the boy in the wood. Wearing no helmet, he had short blond hair above a tough face marked by fists as well as hard experiences in life. Aware that this soldier wouldn't be content with an exchange of smiles and a wave of the hand, Leon, positioned between the German and Lytton, dreaded the violence that was certain to happen. His own life depended on Lytton firing the first fatal shot, but he hated the thought of the German, a living, breathing creature, dying in front of him.

Waiting for the inevitable sound of a shot, Leon instead heard Lytton's whispered, 'I can't do it.'

Turning his head, he saw the hand in which the captain held the revolver dropping slowly. Understanding came to Leon in a split second. All soldiers could fire from cover at shadows and silhouettes that seemed to have no connection with human beings. That was impersonal, and something that officers like Lytton shone at. But, face to face with one of the enemy, looking into his eyes, glimpsing his soul, Hubert Lytton, who came from a long line of military men stretching back to the gallant William the Conqueror, could not kill him.

Seeing a smile crack apart the hard face of the German, Leon recognized that he was savouring the moment in the knowledge that he was just about to kill both the Englishmen in front of him.

It was a Sunday afternoon, but so very different to Beth from the one she had spent here at the river with James. With Kipsy in her arms she had at first wept quietly as she told the doll of her hopes and wishes. Beth wanted James to come home. She had heard women talking, saying that the word 'missing' didn't necessarily mean that the soldier concerned had been killed. Mrs Crandal, who knew so much about the war because her husband, Clarence, was an important man, had said to Beth's mother, 'You'll see, Mrs Marriott, mark my words. When this war's over they'll find thousands of our poor lads wandering around, lost in a foreign country. They'll bring them home then. All them lads ain't dead, Mrs Marriott. Oh no, all them ain't dead.'

Did that mean that Leon would be coming home, too? That was another of Beth's wishes. When it all happened, James and Leon coming home, she wanted to feel well again just like she used to.

Pain, sudden and overwhelming in its severity struck her, shooting her legs out straight, knocking Kipsy off what lap Beth's swollen stomach had let her keep. This was something new, and it frightened Beth, but then it was gone and she leaned sideways to pick up Kipsy and cuddle her.

With only the soft rippling of the flowing river to listen to, Beth heard a new sound. Initially unable to identify it, she then recognized accordion music. Beth desperately hoped it was the funny man who had come to town with some soldiers a long time ago. It had been fun listening to the music and watching the soldiers fall over.

Struggling to her feet, she climbed to the top of a little hillock. From here she could see further. There was a little procession heading her way. It had to be them, Beth was excitedly thinking, when the terrible pain came again. So bad was it this time that her legs gave way and she fell to the ground. Lying there, Beth screamed out as she seemed to be splitting apart in the middle. The bottom half of her body, from the waist down, was being pulled by something she couldn't see, and agony was knifing through her.

Then the pain left her as quickly as it had arrived. Though feeling sick she was able to stand up. Something warm and sticky was running down the inside of her thighs. Badly frightened, Beth saw that it was blood. Pulling a broad dock leaf from its stalk, she wiped her legs with it. The sound of singing took her mind off the bleeding.

The white-haired man, swaying as he walked and played the accordion, was coming along the riverside path. Behind him were the same soldiers, the one-legged man, the one with the bandaged head, and the daft one who had kept shouting before. They were singing a lively hymn:

Shall we gather by the river, the beautiful,
beautiful river . . .

As they went by her, Beth fell in behind the last soldier. Swinging Kipsy from side to side, she marched along behind them. She giggled as she thought of how amused James and Leon would be if they saw her now. Anne-Marie would laugh her lovely laugh if she were here.

Thinking of Anne-Marie took all the fun out of Beth. She started to cry again. Her friend had promised to come to see her last night. Beth and her mother had waited up late, but Anne-Marie hadn't arrived. Remembering how disappointed she had been, Beth was shaken by a mighty sob that brought on another bout of intense pain.

Unable to continue with the marching men, Beth dropped to her knees. They carried on, still singing the hymn as an even greater pain gripped her and blood gushed out from under her skirt.

The crazy soldier on the end of the line turned his head and saw her. He shouted, 'Keep on shooting until you have no more ammo left. Get them before they can get you.'

They carried on, still singing, going away from Beth unaware that she had joined them, ignorant of that fact that she had fallen by the wayside.

She waited for the agony to leave her. It took longer this time. Up on her feet, her legs, shoes and the grass around her covered in thick blood, Beth looked around her. Expecting to see Leon, James, or Anne-Marie there, she cried out in despair when finding herself alone.

Waddling awkwardly because something had gone really wrong with her body, Beth headed towards the water. Turning, she was about to go back to retrieve her doll from where she had dropped it on the ground, but she felt too terribly ill to go back.

Staggering to the edge of the bank, Beth half jumped, half fell into the water. She made a splash, but the farcical procession had gone too far away, and the music was too loud, for the men to hear.

Looking from Hubert Lytton, who had completely given up and was prepared to die, to the German soldier with the lust to kill on his face, Leon felt a strange sensation burst like a fiery balloon inside of himself. Years of being brutalized while turning the other cheek generated a churning anger that built to a white heat of rage. This was something he had never known, and it had taken him over completely. He wasn't prepared to allow the protracted ordeal he had gone through as a conscientious objector, and his efforts to rescue the patrol, come to naught. A German bullet wasn't going to end everything for Leon.

With an angry roar he leapt at the German, taking him by surprise. Snatching the rifle from the soldier's grasp, Leon held it by the barrel to swing it like a sledgehammer and shatter the weapon against a rock.

Swiftly recovering, the German, a big fellow, confidently struck a fighting pose to deal with Leon. But he had no chance. Never before having either the occasion or the drive to fully employ his considerable strength, Leon did so now. As the long-established dams of frustration gave way, he reached to grasp one thigh of the German's trousers with his right hand, and the soldier's tunic at the chest with his left. Bellowing like an enraged bull, Leon lifted the German over his head, his arms straight. Then he threw him.

Shouting as he went through the air, the German landed face up on a cluster of jagged boulders. To the horror of a now calmer and regretful Leon, a pointed rock thrust upwards through the German. Hands flailing wildly, trying hopelessly to push his innards back into the space now filled by the rock, the soldier began to scream.

Terrible in volume and intensity, the man's screaming went on and on. His rage having subsided, Leon desperately wanted to help the German, but there was nothing he could do. The sound of the soldier's suffering was too much for anyone to bear, and Leon saw Hubert Lytton holding his revolver in both hands, aiming it at the German.

Leon was so tense that the sound of the shot startled him. He noticed the recoil of the gun drive the weakened Lytton back against the boulder that supported him in an upright position. The right side of the German's skull imploded bloodily. He seemed to suck his last scream back in so that it became a rattle in his throat. His body convulsed twice, then he was still and silent.

Mortified by his act of violence, Leon told Lytton in a half whisper, 'You've killed him.'

'No, I merely stopped him making that damned-awful noise,' Lytton, now much like he had been in the old days, corrected Leon. 'Make no mistake about it, my Christian friend: *you* killed him.'

Nine

A suspected tragedy in Marshlee left Anne-Marie with no alternative but to delay her return to London. Beth Marriott had been missing since leaving her house to go for a walk alone after Sunday lunch. The local police had searched through the night without success. At daybreak, they had begun acting on reports from people who claimed they had seen the girl on Sunday afternoon. The shell-shocked soldier who had been with the accordionist, insisted he had seen Beth throw herself into the river. He had Police Sergeant Haines convinced until he had broken off his testimony to cry out, 'First objective taken with very few losses.'

Yet the man had been rational when referring to the girl jumping into the water, and Haines could not ignore what he said.

On a Monday morning that carried the first chill of autumn, Anne-Marie stood beside the river with her arms tight around a sobbing Elsie Marriott. She turned the distraught mother away from where three men standing knee-deep in water lifted what had the appearance of a bundle of sodden rags up onto the bank. It was the body of Beth Marriott, and Anne-Marie had to fight not to avert her eyes as she saw a dead baby floating on the surface of the water. It wasn't until one of the men had reverently placed the tiny little corpse on the grass that Anne-Marie was traumatized by the realization that it was still attached to Beth by the umbilical cord. United in death she thought hollowly – one who had never been born, the other who should never have been born.

'Is it my girl?' Elsie asked in a strangled voice.

'Yes, it is Beth,' Anne-Marie confirmed miserably.

A respectful, small, silent group of townsfolk had gathered beside the water. They were the kind of sensitive people who are drawn to a crisis but are at a loss to know what to do when they are there. Anne-Marie saw Walter Hann detach himself from the others to waddle over to her and Elsie, his prominent belly swinging from side to side as he walked.

'You have my sincere condolences, Mrs Marriott,' the baker said. 'Beth was a lovely child, and all of us, Mrs Hann especially, unite with you in your sad loss. I hope that it will be some consolation for you to know that I have arranged with the Reverend Penny for a service to be held for Beth this evening.'

'That is most kind and thoughtful of you,' Anne-Marie said, a little surprised because she had never imagined Hann to be a man of fine feelings.

'Yes, thank you, Mr Hann,' Elsie mumbled, her face half smothered against Anne-Marie's breast.

'This isn't the time to talk of such things,' Walter Hann was continuing, 'but this war has hurt us all. Though Mrs Hann and me still grieve deeply over our beloved son being taken from us, I want you to know that will not cause me to shirk my responsibilities. I will take care of you financially, Mrs Marriott. You will want for nothing. I see it as my duty after the way James behaved toward your little girl.'

Head spinning as she heard this, Anne-Marie had to cling to Elsie Marriott for support. Until that moment she had not given a thought as to who might be responsible for Beth's condition. Had she done so, then her suspects would include the tramps, many of them obviously disturbed men, who often passed through Marshlee. Or the itinerant knife grinder who had badly frightened little Joanie Brown. Anne-Marie just could not credit that it was a boy who had been one of her closest friends. Never would she have believed that the gentle, caring, altruistic James Hann could do such a thing. Yet she had just heard a father condemn his recently dead son. That had to mean something.

What she had learned about James perplexed Anne-Marie for

the remainder of the day. Her father arranged for carpenter-cum-funeral director Will Stumont to take Beth and the baby to his premises. Elsie wanted to comply with tradition by having her daughter taken home to lie at rest in the parlour. The Reverend Penny thought this would be too much for the bereaved woman, and Dr Collette agreed with him.

It was left to Anne-Marie to explain this to the weeping Elsie, and take her home. This proved to be a crushing experience. Entering the Marriott house was like returning from a funeral, only worse. Its emptiness suggested a contradictory haunting by absent rather than present spirits.

Able to remember seeing Beth's legs when she sat in her favourite place on the landing, Anne-Marie, normally sensible and well balanced, had to force through a paralysing fear to go up the stairs. But she was able to conquer this icy-cold feeling and put the grieving mother to bed.

Anne-Marie knew that in these circumstances it would be callous to enquire about James, but had difficulty battling with the urge to do so.

Even more pressing was her need to get back to London. She had risen to a high position on *The Tribunal*, and the controversial newspaper had been more and more subjected to sinister inter-ference from both government and the police. After a police raid in which every copy of the paper had been confiscated and the printing press dismantled, they had moved to shared premises south of the Thames.

In recent weeks, at first believing that her imagination was playing tricks, she had finally accepted that she was being constantly followed by two men. Believing them to be detectives, she mentioned it to Vera Scanlon. Expecting friendly ridicule from her phlegmatic friend, Anne-Marie was surprised when Vera accepted what she said with a nod, and said that she was also being followed by two plain-clothes policemen.

'I thought that I was becoming paranoid,' a relieved Anne-Marie had said.

'It's the British powers-that-be who are paranoiac because of what is happening in Russia,' Vera explained.

They had tested their theory by spending alternate nights at each other's lodgings. It had amused, but unnerved, them to discover that they were followed home by four detectives each evening when leaving the printing works at Streatham.

This pressure from the Home Office made it essential for her to return to *The Tribunal* without delay. As she had to take responsibility for much of the editorial, Anne-Marie didn't want her subordinates to undergo harassment that was meant for her.

Nothing seemed to have gone right on her weekend visit home. Brigadier and Claudia Lytton's unabashed promoting of their son as a husband for her had been so obvious it had been off-putting. Having spent all Saturday evening attempting to comfort the stricken Judith Seldon, she was filled with remorse because Beth had needed her and she had let the child down. Though she had been in terrible trouble, Beth might well still be alive if Anne-Marie had gone to see her as promised.

Music, soft and slow enough to be a dirge, filtered into the bedroom. Going to the window to look down, Anne-Marie saw the three crippled soldiers across the street. They were sitting on the doorsteps of houses, holding their heads in their hands. The accordionist was standing, his back propped against a corner of the baker's shop, his head bowed over the instrument as he played. Anne-Marie caught the melancholy tune of the hymn 'Abide With Me'.

Moved to tears by the lament, she hurried down the stairs to busy herself in the scullery. Making tea and finding a few home-made cakes, Anne-Marie took them up to the bedroom on a rusty tray. Elsie Marriott had ceased to cry, but only because she had slipped into what was or resembled a coma. She lay like one of the living dead. Assuming that this was the way in which the mother was escaping from the death of her young daughter, Anne-Marie left her.

A knock on the door brought her relief in two ways. First, being all alone in this house of death was depressing. Secondly, and selfishly Anne-Marie had to admit, it could well be Mrs Crandal, Elsie's friend, which would mean that she could go home and prepare to return to London.

She opened the door to find Gladys Plummer standing there, asking sheepishly, 'May I come in?'

Puzzled, Anne-Marie stood back and gestured the other woman into the cramped front room. Gladys looked around, shocked to see for the first time the conditions in which the other half lived, but her face showed neither distaste nor criticism.

'You've heard about what's happened to little Beth?' Anne-Marie asked to break the uncomfortable silence between them.

Nodding and ill at ease, Gladys replied, 'Yes, I've come to see if I can help in any way.'

'I don't understand,' Anne-Marie said truthfully. Normally Gladys Plummer would avoid this part of town.

'Perhaps I should begin by trying to make my peace with you, Anne-Marie,' Gladys said hesitantly. 'I'm ashamed at the way I behaved at the railway station that time. It's a poor excuse, I recognize that, but I was upset and angry because the war had taken Alexander from me.'

'I can appreciate that, Gladys. I know how much you and Alex mean to each other.'

'It's sweet of you to say that,' Gladys said, pleased. 'I want to apologize for the way I treated you, but I will understand if you reject me, Anne-Marie.'

'Of course I accept your apology. I'd like us to be friends once more, Gladys,' Anne-Marie said, welcoming a spontaneous embrace from the anxious girl.

When they parted, standing at arms' length but both of them still wanting to hold hands, Gladys asked, 'Might I enquire about Leon?'

'I haven't heard anything of him for quite some time.'

'Oh dear, that must be worrying for you, Anne-Marie,' Gladys said sympathetically. 'It would help his mother so much if he was home at this time. I expect that she's very upset?'

'Terribly so.'

'That's why I came. I was talking to your father this morning, Anne-Marie, and he tells me that you should have gone back to London last night. Well, I'll stay with Mrs Marriott, and you can be on your way now.'

187

'I'd like to do that, but . . .' Anne-Marie started, but couldn't finish. Previously Gladys Plummer had never given the slightest indication that she would be an ideal recruit for the Salvation Army.

'But you're wondering why a selfish little bitch like me would want to help in this way?' Gladys said with a sad, wry little smile.

'I wouldn't use those words,' Anne-Marie replied, adding, 'What I wonder is whether you understand just what kind of work I'm doing in London?'

'I think I do, and it doesn't worry me. So many of us had the wrong idea about this war at the beginning, but we have become wiser. Perhaps my honest reason for coming here is that. . . .' Gladys stopped talking while delving into her handbag and pulling out an envelope to show Anne-Marie. 'I had this letter from Alexander this morning. He writes that he was spending his last hours in the front line. His unit is being pulled out, and he estimates that he'll be back home within a month.'

'That's wonderful news.' Anne-Marie was delighted for her regained friend.

'When so many people are suffering so much, I can't believe that I am so lucky,' Gladys said self-deprecatingly. 'I am so happy that Alexander is safe that I feel I should help someone who is less fortunate. I would really like to comfort Mrs Marriott, Anne-Marie.'

Nothing was all bad, not even war, Anne-Marie thought. It had helped Gladys find her true self. Nevertheless, Anne-Marie had found it difficult to leave Elsie Marriott, and she felt that she was abandoning the woman now as she headed for the railway station and the 6.30 p.m. train. It had amazed her how quickly people can adapt to changing circumstances. The first time she had left home it had been an emotional wrench for her parents and herself. This evening all three of them hardly noticed the parting.

Before leaving, she asked her father to let her know the date and time of Beth's funeral so that she could come back home to attend. In turn, he had promised to visit the bereaved mother often.

James Hann was much in her thoughts, too. It hurt her badly

to think that the memory of the brave, upstanding James would be blackened when Marshlee remembered her war dead. She had been tempted to ask her father how the rumour about Beth and James had come about, but discussing things sexual was among the many taboos that formed at least a half-barrier between the occupants of the vicarage.

'Is that you, Miss Penny?'

About to turn in the station gateway, Anne-Marie stopped as she heard her name called. Raymond Plummer, grey-haired and distinguished-looking even without his mayoral chain, came hurrying toward her from a side road.

'Mr Plummer,' she greeted him respectfully.

'Do you know where I might find Gladys? Earlier today she said she was to see you, Miss Penny.'

'Yes,' Anne-Marie nodded. 'You'll find her comforting Mrs Marriott in her loss, Mr Plummer.'

'Thank you. What a shocking business that is,' a plainly distressed Plummer said.

Moving off, fearing she would miss her train, something about Raymond Plummer made Anne-Marie pause. He was a kind man, but not the type to be so positively grief-stricken over the death of Beth Marriott.

Maybe that wasn't the reason at all. With the sound of a railway engine snorting steam increasing her sense of urgency, and dreading hearing a porter's whistle, Anne-Marie frowned as she enquired, 'Is something wrong, Mr Plummer?'

'We've had some terrible news, Miss Penny,' he answered, his voice breaking as he went on, 'Young Alexander has been killed. I dread having to tell Gladys.'

It was dusk and the sound of approaching horses carried clearly on the thin air. Although having spent four nights and three days making his way back to the British lines carrying Hubert Lytton across his shoulders, Leon was still a battleground novice. Taking no chances, he eased himself down into a ditch running beside the road, and laid the unconscious Lytton beside him. Being relieved of the captain's weight momentarily made Leon feel so light that he could float upwards.

Yet the wounded man was nothing like the burden to Leon that his conscience had become. Telling himself that it was a case of kill or be killed did nothing to ease his shame and regret over slaying the German. It would never do so, for Leon was keenly aware that he could have taken the Mauser rifle and temporarily disabled the soldier. The fact that he had killed the German in a fit of uncontrollable rage was unforgivable. Worse still was that he wouldn't have dreamt himself capable of such a violent act.

All of this was made worse by his immense weariness. He had taken only brief half-naps in which he had stayed alert throughout, and had eaten nothing but wild berries and a few vegetables pulled from abandoned gardens.

Head low, he peered through a ridge of roadside grass. Passing along the road before him, mounted on small, lightly built horses, were wild-looking men with dark, foreign complexions. They wore flowing crimson cloaks over khaki trousers. It was the oddest sight Leon had ever seen, and he was completely mystified until Lytton, in one of his conscious periods, eased himself up weakly beside him to take a look.

'A brigade of Algerian calvary,' Lytton identified the horsemen in a low whisper.

Not sure whether the foreign horsemen were on the side of the British or the Germans, Leon didn't want to betray his ignorance by asking. Anyway, the effort of propping himself up to take a look had taxed Lytton's strength. He had slipped into unconsciousness again.

With no more bandages available, Leon had not touched the dressing on the captain's leg. It had become blood encrusted and had patches of yellow pus. Fearing that the leg was rotting, Leon could do nothing other than push on to where Lytton could have medical attention.

Assuming that the Algerians were allies, discretion nevertheless made Leon stay hidden.

When the horsemen had gone by, Leon reached to pick up Lytton. He was eager to move on, to keep going through the night in the hope of reaching the pulled-back British lines before dawn. But more horses were approaching and he had to leave the captain where he was and drop down to conceal himself yet again.

There were more of these horsemen, two brigades guessed Leon, who was learning fast. This time he didn't require Lytton's military knowledge. From pictures he had seen, somewhere and at some time, he knew that these mounted men were French Chasseurs. Despite being a man who despised all things military, Leon had to admit to himself that they were a splendid sight. A parting in the clouds added drama and the moon gleamed briefly on their lances. They were definitely on the side of the British, but it was possible that if they saw him they would shoot or use a sword on him first, and find out his nationality later.

A panicking hare ran swiftly past Leon to cross the road, causing horses to rear and whinny, while the soldiers cursed in French and then laughed as they regained control of their mounts. It was the sound of camaraderie among men, but Leon was on the periphery, isolated. Always self-sufficient, he suddenly felt very alone and vulnerable.

Then they were gone. Leon, feeling better after the short rest, stood Lytton up and ducked in front of him to get the captain lying across his shoulders once more. Starting off, he kept to the road for a couple of miles on the assumption that it must be safe otherwise the two lots of cavalry wouldn't have passed through without trouble.

Later, when an overcast sky thinned to permit a new moon to shine brightly, Leon left the road because he could be seen easily. Squeezing through a hedge, he started to climb a hill, bending low and using the shadows cast by bramble bushes as he went. A barbed-wire barrier that had been broken by a wire-cutting shell warned him that he was nearing some kind of fortification. He didn't doubt that it was British. Though he may know who they were, they didn't know him, and he was likely to be cut down by 'friendly' machine-gun fire before the soldiers ahead discovered that he wasn't a German.

As he climbed higher he noticed a parapet above him. Realizing it was likely to be a gun emplacement, Leon shifted

Lytton into a more comfortable position on his shoulders, and started on a diversion that would take him round the side of the parapet.

He had only taken a few paces when there was the crack of a rifle, a dart of red/yellow flame up on the parapet, and a bullet screeched by close to Leon's head. Dropping to his knees he rolled Lytton off his shoulders on to the ground and shouted, 'Hold your fire. I'm English.'

Everything remained quiet for a while, then came an Australian-accented yell of annoyance. 'Hogan's ghost, digger! I near shot your bleedin' arse off! What you doing out there?'

'I'm bringing a wounded officer back.'

'What's he want to do something like that for?' another Australian voice complained.

The first soldier called to Leon, 'Take no notice of him, matey. Come on up.'

When Leon reached the top, willing hands came out to lift Lytton off him. Then they were pulling him in over the parapet, shaking him by the hand, slapping him on the back. They looked not only to be the roughest of rough men, but they were all half-drunk.

'What you gonna have, digger?' one of them asked, sweeping a hand along a row of bottles as if Leon was paying a social visit to his house. 'We've got just about everything, including champagne.'

'Don't be afraid to drink up; it didn't cost us nothing. Been helping ourselves from abandoned farms and houses,' another informed him.

Feeling his exhaustion more than ever now that he had stopped moving, Leon wanted only to be on his way. He said, 'Thanks, but I don't drink.'

'Now's the time to start, matey,' a tall, thin Australian with a pointy face advised as he looked down at the unconscious Lytton. 'You need something in your guts. If you don't get him to a sick bay soon you'll be carrying a corpse on your back. That sore leg of his stinks like a Brisbane brothel.'

'I must get going,' Leon said. Though he had suspected for

some time that Lytton's leg was gangrenous, the reminder depressed him.

He was glad that they had stopped trying to force alcohol on him. If he had to protest that it was against his religion, these ruffians, who appeared to him to be mad, would laugh at him. One of them, a squint-eyed man, was running his eyes admiringly over Leon's physique.

Reaching out a hand to squeeze Leon's bulging deltoid and bicep admiringly, the Australian asked, 'Were you with a circus before the war?'

'Not before the war,' Leon replied with meaningful emphasis, causing a roar of laughter.

'Go that way,' an Australian pointed west. 'You'll come to a village. On the far side of that is the 22nd Casualty Clearing Station. We pushed the Hun out of the village early on today.'

A squat Australian with his head tilted back to drink, lowered the bottle to issue a warning. 'You take care passing through that village, digger. The Germans often leave machine-guns and gunners in the cellars so they can come out and attack us from the rear.'

'Thanks,' Leon acknowledged the advice as two of them lifted a semi-conscious, groaning Hubert Lytton up onto his shoulders.

'Cheerio,' they were saying drunkenly as an officer came striding up.

'What's going on here? You lot appear to me to be drunk,' the officer said angrily.

Not wanting to get involved in any disciplinary action that would hold him back, Leon moved away.

'Would you like a drop, sir?' a soldier enquired.

'If you've some to spare,' the officer replied, to Leon's surprise.

'More than enough, sir, more than enough.'

'What's that galah up to?' the officer pointed at Leon, and when the soldiers told him he walked over to Leon.

'Do you know tonight's password, Soldier?'

He was a lieutenant, every bit as rough-looking as the soldiers. Only the single pip on each epaulette distinguished him from the others. One of his eyes was so bloodshot that Leon doubted he could see with it. While Leon was replying that he didn't know the password, a soldier came up to hand the officer a bottle.

Pulling the cork, the lieutenant lifted the bottle to his mouth to drink long and deep. Smacking his lips, the Australian wiped them with the back of his hand, saying, 'You could do with a shot of this.'

'I don't drink,' Leon explained, regretting being delayed while he had the weight of Lytton on his back. 'I want to keep a clear head.'

'You'll have a clear head all right, when a Hun bullet ploughs through it to knock your brains out,' the officer said cynically. 'Now, you'll need to know the password or you'll never get through to the casualty station. It's "thistle", remember that.'

'I'll remember,' Leon assured the lieutenant.

'Don't you ever say sir or salute?' the officer asked, as Leon started to walk off.

'No,' Leon told him flatly.

'Good on you,' the Australian lieutenant called after him, chuckling.

Leon had reason to be grateful to that officer after passing through the deserted village safely. The sun was edging above the horizon when Leon topped a rise and saw what he took to be the field hospital about a quarter of a mile away. It had been set up in a shell-shattered factory, the grounds of which was crowded with huts, marquees and tents.

Being able to see his destination re-energized Leon and he was making good progress until he reached a ridge from behind which a voice barked harshly, 'Halt, who goes there?'

'Thistle,' Leon replied.

'Advance and be recognized,' the unseen sentry commanded.

When Leon went forward, using the last of his strength, a group of soldiers hurried up to take Lytton from his back.

'Stone the bloody crows, mate,' an undersized Londoner exclaimed. 'How far have you come?'

'Too far,' Leon answered wearily as, practically asleep, he allowed them to take him to the casualty clearing station.

The place was such a shock to Leon that he became immediately wide awake. There were wards, huts and tents all with rows and rows of stretchers. In the corner of one tent he could see human legs and arms stacked high the way a farmer stores logs for the winter. He stood bemused, his nostrils filled with the blood-reeking stench of the place, his ears ringing with the cries of agony.

A hatless captain who had seen Leon arrive with Lytton, came up in his shirtsleeves holding out a blanket to him. He was a middle-aged man with kind eyes. Leon immediately put the officer down for the surgeon, for though he had washed his hands the upper parts of his bare forearms were stained the rusty colour of dried blood.

'You've had a tough time, Soldier. You did well bringing that wounded officer in,' the captain said. 'Find somewhere quiet to curl up in this blanket. You're safe here and could do with a good sleep.'

Taking the blanket, Leon said, 'Thank you, sir.'

'Don't bother with the sir, my friend,' the surgeon said with a hard smile. 'All men become equal in the extremity of suffering. I'm Kenneth Robbins. How far have you come. . . ?'

'Leon,' Leon answered the unspoken query about his name, warmed by the friendly approach. 'I found Captain Lytton near Crapouillots Wood.'

'My word, and you carried him all that distance. I'll see that you get a medal for this, Leon.'

'I'd rather you didn't,' Leon said, watching Robbins frown and shrug. 'Will the captain be all right?'

'I was about to say that the kindest thing we can do for him is amputate the leg,' the surgeon said, 'but what's kind about cutting off someone's leg?'

'If you don't?'

'Unless the leg is removed he'll die,' Robbins replied. 'Maybe that's what he would choose to do, but we don't ask them, Leon. The wounded soldier has no more rights than the dead soldier. Take no notice of me son! Being out here has made me a cynic. Go and get your head down.'

Finding a lonely corner, Leon was amazed that sleep threatened to overtake him even as he lay down. When he awoke it was twilight and nightingales were singing in some nearby woods. The charming sound was completely out of context with the grim surroundings, and Leon had to shake himself to be sure that he was awake.

Standing, mind refreshed but finding his joints and muscles stiff, he strolled back through the tents and huts to the centre of the ground. The same horrible smell of septic limbs and torn-open abdomens was on the air. but Leon found it less nauseating now. Coming to two large tents that had been laced together to make one huge one, curiosity made him reach with the intention of lifting the flap. But, breathing in the pleasant smell of tobacco, Leon was stayed by a hand resting lightly on his arm.

'Best not go in there, son.'

It was a chaplain, pipe clenched between his teeth, who had spoken. An elderly man, too old to be here in the front line, he had the round, chubby, reliable look of a country parson.

'That's the moribund ward.' The chaplain took the pipe from his mouth to explain.

'I don't understand, sir.'

'It's for officers and men who are dying, son. The surgeons have given them up as hopeless, but they don't know that, of course.' The chaplain extended his right hand. 'I'm the Reverend Michael Millhope.'

'Leon Marriott,' Leon shook the proffered hand.

'Ah,' a smiling Millhope pointed the stem of his pipe at him. 'You're the young fellow who carried that captain in. You're already spoken of as a hero around here, Leon. The 22nd Casualty Clearing Station's most outstanding soldier.'

'I'm not a soldier,' Leon said quietly. 'You're not going to like this, Reverend Millhope, but I'm a Quaker, a conscientious objector.'

'On the contrary,' the chaplain gave a closed-toothed smile around his pipe, 'I'm absolutely delighted to meet you. I long for the day when the men of all nations refuse to serve as soldiers, my son. That will leave the pot-bellied politicians to scratch each other's eyes out.'

196

This made Leon smile. He had taken an instant liking to the man. The flap of the tent opened and a tired-faced nursing sister came out. Taking a covert look inside the tent, Leon saw a madman who was swearing and kicking, fighting the blanket that was wrapped around him.

The nurse was the first female Leon had seen in a long while, but, though she plainly was a woman, he couldn't see her as one. He put that down to her unusual, nun-like uniform.

'Time for me to go in, I'm afraid,' Millhope said, taking the tent flap from the sister's hand before she let it fall back. 'I'll squat or kneel beside stretchers, saying a few words, offering prayers, administrating Holy Communion, absolutions, blessings.'

Moved by what he heard, Leon felt an overwhelming need to help men who had been blown almost to pieces. 'I'd like to go in with you, Reverend Millhope.'

'No, son,' the elderly clergyman shook his head. 'You have been through enough. This is something that I wouldn't wish on anyone. Just inside is a man who has no face left from the nose down, while another has had the back of his head blown off. No, Leon, Ken Robbins gave me a message. He wants you to go to the mess tent where there's a meal waiting for you. I daresay some time has passed since you had a substantial amount of food in you. Off you go now.'

Leaving the chaplain, Leon felt humbled. Always having considered himself to be a good Christian, compared to Millhope he had done no work for the Lord. He was undergoing a change of mind, or possibly of heart. Once his anti-war protest as a conscientious objector had been enough, but it was a negative campaign and his nature demanded something positive.

Leon felt that he needed a purpose in life. Previously having refused to join a non-combatant corps, he was now ready to do so if he could work in this hospital as an aide to the chaplain. Never anything but self-aware, he realized that this was probably a reaction to killing the German, a need to make atonement. He wondered if it would help him if he shared his trauma over breaking the Sixth Commandment, but decided that it would be selfish to do so.

He turned the idea of working here at the hospital over in his mind as he ate a meal in the mess tent. Sitting just inside, under a swinging oil lamp that attracted flying moths, singeing the unwary among them, he had cleaned his plate. Satisfying his hunger for the first time in ages had a relaxing effect. Leon was feeling pretty good when Captain Robbins came up to him. With the surgeon was a young Grenadier captain, with a row of medal ribbons on his breast and a detached manner that Leon found unsettling as he stood up from the table.

'I've heard about your exploits,' the Grenadier captain said to him. 'It was an action above and beyond the call of duty, and I will see to it that your valour is suitably recognized. In the meantime, you'd make me a proud man if you would permit me to shake you by the hand.'

Bewildered by the unexpected status he had achieved, Leon shook the hand of the Grenadier officer, who gave him a wan smile before walking off while saying to the surgeon, 'I'll see you in the mess shortly, Captain Robbins.'

As soon as they were alone, Leon was keen to follow up on his recently conceived plan. He said to Robbins, 'There's something I'd like to speak to you about, sir.'

'By all means, but I'm afraid it will have to wait until morning.' Robbins patted him on the shoulder. He started to walk off in the wake of the Grenadier captain, but paused to grin at Leon and say, 'Now you have something to tell your grandchildren, Leon.'

'What's that, sir?' Leon was more bemused than puzzled.

'You don't know? Leon, my friend, you have just shaken the hand of the Prince of Wales.'

A dumbfounded Leon slumped back into his seat as Robbins left him. The son of the king had shaken his hand, the hand of a man judicially branded a criminal. The surgeon seemed too genuine a man to be taking a rise out of him, but he still couldn't believe it was true until the Reverend Millhope confirmed it when he came to join him.

'Recognition in wartime is as fleeting as fame in times of peace, Leon.' The chaplain looked intently at him. 'I would make you no promise, of course, but this might well be a time when you could have all your previous civil and military convictions waived, and be returned to civilian life without a blemish on your character.'

It was both possible and tempting, but Leon had reservations. To pursue the matter would be to gain from having saved Hubert Lytton. Leon did not want to profit from what had been, and must remain, an unselfish act.

He and Millhope strolled together through the grounds. There were many walking wounded about, a number of them limping badly. The chaplain indicated the latter. 'Some of them have compound fractures of the femur, Leon, but they hobble around in agony rather than lie still like those waiting to die. They find it easy to believe that death is contagious in a place such as this'

'I'd like to volunteer to assist you here, Chaplain.' Leon seized the opportunity to broach the subject.

'You value me too highly.' Millhope shook his head sadly. 'There is not much that makes for Christian living among men out here. Aside from a fear of death, these soldiers do not want religion, and who can blame them? There are hundreds of men here who could attend my services, but I usually take matins and evensong alone.'

Disappointed, Leon was thinking of something to say when an artillery barrage started. The heavens and earth were rolling up in the night, the ground shaking and the roar deafening until pained ears managed to adjust to it a little.

'The crazy hour has begun,' Millhope informed Leon, his face even more sorrowful. He was out of place here. The chaplain was better suited to the scented garden of a rural vicarage in England. 'When the guns stop you will hear the cavalry and infantry passing on yet another push. Then the casualties will begin to come in.'

'How many?'

The chaplain's reply crumpled Leon's spirit. 'It varies little each night – one hundred officers, ten times as many men.'

They paused beside some flower-beds that to Leon's mind were less suited to this place than the caring, gentle padre at his side. Millhope explained. 'I help the nurses plant and tend this little garden. This is a tiny corner of sanity in what is a gigantic madhouse, Leon. War paints vicious contrasts, with these flowers representing the beauty of nature, while just a yard or two from them are those two tents filled with officers and men who have contracted venereal disease.'

Able to understand the distress being hospital chaplain caused Millhope, Leon was searching for something to say when a voice behind him rose above the sound of guns: 'Well, well, well, if it isn't Marriott.'

'My, your fame is spreading,' the chaplain commented between puffs as he lit his pipe.

Leon was unable to answer. He was in a state of shock where everything around him, including the clamour of the artillery, alternately faded from him and returned. With the blood pounding inside his head louder than the guns on the outside, Leon recognized the man who had spoken. It was Quartermaster-Sergeant Wilson.

'Come, I will let you into a little secret, confess a sin to you,' Millhope said, taking Leon's arm to move him along.

Hesitating, expecting the worst to happen, Leon breathed a mighty sigh of relief when he saw Wilson was walking away from them. Unsure as to what this meant, he let the chaplain take him to a small shed that was heavily padlocked.

'This is where the drugs are housed, Leon. I have keys, and in the night I creep down here to steal morphia which I use on the dying in the moribund tent, or the wounded German prisoners who lie neglected in that tent over there. I just cannot bear seeing those boys suff—'

The chaplain stopped speaking as Wilson returned, marching up in the company of two military policemen. As he felt his arms pinioned from behind, Leon saw the look of surprised indignation on Millhope's face.

With his wrists tortured by figure of eights yet again, and with Wilson standing close, leering into his face, Leon knew that his brief period of freedom was at an end.

'As wise men we must follow the bright star of hope now visible in the sky over Europe. The Tsar has been forced to abdicate, the Russian autocracy has been overthrown, and I say to you that

Labour must not delay in dispatching messages of congratulation and solidarity to the Petrograd Soviet.'

As the orator paused, seeking approval for his proposition, he was not disappointed. A mighty roar from thousands of throats rose up to the high ceiling of the Albert Hall. A need to conform that she could never defeat impelled Anne-Marie to raise her hand to join more than ten thousand others. Although an ardent supporter of the cause to which Vera Scanlon had recruited her, she didn't understand politics well enough to be certain of what Russia's March revolution meant now and for the future.

She had read the newspapers. The banners round the hall reminded those present that George Lansbury's *Herald* was sponsoring this enthusiastic rally, and her friends and colleagues had welcomed success of the revolution. Lansbury had met her as she had come into the hall, showing her to a seat he had reserved for her, apparently regarding her as an important guest at this momentous rally.

But Anne-Marie had reserved all personal comment until she had a better understanding of the situation. She was adept at handling the narrower issues publicized in *The Tribunal*, but was at all time conscious of her political limitations.

Having done her share in preparing *The Tribunal* for press, she had left the others at work to come alone to the Albert Hall that evening. Her main purpose in being there was to further the fast-growing petition demanding an end to the persecution of conscientious objectors. Though she had received no word of Leon since he had been taken to France, she felt sure that he was still alive. That being so, she was determined to do everything possible to prevent him and others like him from continued suffering.

Another of her worries was Hubert. Claudia had written to say that she and the brigadier hadn't heard from their son for a long time, and the War Office was unable to offer any explanation. Worse still, although one personal tragedy is no different to another, it had come close to destroying Anne-Marie when a letter from her mother reported the death of Bruce Seldon, who had cut his own throat in the lunatic asylum at Epsom.

The letter had gone on to say that Judith Seldon was not only drinking heavily, but had been seen wantonly consorting with soldiers passing through the area.

Lowering her right arm as the others did when the proposal had been endorsed, Anne-Marie was for some reason fascinated by the fact that the young man sitting at her side had raised his left arm. Forgetting herself, she stared at him.

Noticing this, the man brought his right shoulder forward so that she could see the sleeve of the jacket dangling emptily. Handsome, though very pale and ill-looking, he gave her a rueful smile. 'I have to be the odd man out here. I'd have raised my right arm had it still been there.'

'I do beg your pardon,' a blushing Anne-Marie stammered. 'It was rude of me to stare. I didn't mean to give offence.'

'None taken,' he assured her, his smile broadening. 'What effect do you think this Russian thing will have on the war?'

'You'll regard me as terribly stupid, but I haven't come close to grasping the situation yet,' Anne-Marie confessed, still blushing.

'Neither have I, and I suspect that those who say they do know what's going on are no more informed than you and me. On a personal note, whatever happens I won't get my arm back.'

'I feel that I should apologize to you again.'

'There was no need to the first time,' he assured her. 'I'm Richard Bell, by the way, formerly Lieutenant Richard Bell.'

'How do you do. I'm Anne-Marie Penny,' Anne-Marie replied, before cringing with embarrassment as she proffered her right hand toward where his was missing. 'Oh, my God, I'm so sorry.'

Taking her hand in his left one, he laughed gently at her. 'Don't be embarrassed, please. I'm not touchy. On the bus coming here some young fellows were calling me "Lefty".'

'That's really cruel,' Anne-Marie commiserated.

'It's a cruel world, but let's not talk about me. You're a much more interesting person. That accent of yours isn't London, is it?'

'No, I come from a small town that you'll never have heard of, called Marshlee.'

'I've never been there, but I've certainly heard of it,' Richard Bell frowned. 'I met a captain over in France, he was in the twenty-second Casualty Clearing Station with me. Lytton, Hubert Lytton.'

'Good heavens!' a completely dismayed Anne-Marie gasped.

'It seems that you know him?'

'Yes, I do. Did he: Is he...?' Frightened of the answer she might get, Anne-Marie left her questions unformed for her new companion to take up.

'It's all right, Anne-Marie. He didn't die.'

'Thank the Lord,' she sighed out her words. 'Was he badly hurt?'

Studying her carefully, he replied with a string of questions of his own. 'What is the captain to you, brother, cousin, uncle, sweetheart perhaps?'

'None of those things.' Anne-Marie gave a shake of her head. 'Hubert is just a friend since childhood.'

'In that case I can tell you, but I'm sorry to have to do so: he lost a leg, Anne-Marie.'

'Poor Hubert,' she whispered. 'Is he still in France?'

'No, the last I heard he was in a hospital at a place called Sherborne, in Dorset.'

'That's not far from my home town,' Anne-Marie said.

'Look, you will probably resent me being so forward,' Bell said, studying her anxiously, 'but when this rally is over perhaps we could go for a cup of coffee and I could tell you all I know about Captain Lytton.'

'I'd like that,' Anne-Marie smiled at him. 'Not just to hear about Hubert. I would really like to be with you. Oh dear, I'm blushing again.'

'At least it's for a better reason this time,' he chided her with one of his soft laughs.

Anne-Marie felt apprehensive as she saw George Lansbury making his way through the seats in her direction. From the look on his face she knew he carried bad news. But it couldn't be from home for nobody there could know that she was at the Albert Hall.

Coming along the row behind her, Lansbury bent over to speak quietly in her ear. 'You had better get over to Streatham, Anne-

Marie. The print shop has been raided and the police are using sledgehammers to smash the press to pieces.'

Alarmed by the news, afraid that Vera or some of the others might be arrested at best, injured at worst, Anne-Marie stood. Reaching out to catch hold of Richard Bell's remaining hand, she said, 'I'm sorry, we won't be able to have that coffee together.'

'Some other time,' he suggested brightly, though his acute disappointment was plain to see.

'Some other time,' Anne-Marie agreed before hurrying away.

Both charming Richard Bell and she knew well that that 'other time' would never come.

Ten

Someone was coming up the path toward the schoolhouse. Clinging to the inside frame of the window for support, Judith Seldon blinked her bleary eyes several times before recognizing the Reverend Paulton Penny. That's right, he had promised to come to see her today. Or was it yesterday? She couldn't be sure. Maybe it was tomorrow, but what difference did it make? Every day was just a blur to her now, merging with other days to become a confusing kaleidoscope of dull colours that had no readable pattern. He was at the door now. The clergyman wouldn't knock in the knowledge that she was unlikely to come to the door. Anyway, the door was unlocked. It was always unlocked now. Every Tom, Dick, and Harry in a khaki uniform felt free to wander in at any time. The trio of names amused Judith. She began to laugh, too loudly and too wildly, and by the time the tall figure of the vicar entered the room, her laughter had turned to tears.

Holding her by the shoulders, he looked intently at her. There was no condemnation, no anger, no pity in the clergyman's eyes. Yet she saw something there that was more disturbing than any of those three things. It was probably the drink, Judith told herself fuzzily, but she was sure that she saw her own suffering reflected in the depth of the Reverend Paulton Penny's eyes.

Easing her down into an armchair, he sat himself sideways at the desk where Bruce used to sit writing. It would have upset, most probably angered, Judith had anyone else taken such a liberty. But the vicar merited that special seat. Maybe it was a God-given right, for in some mystical way it seemed that the dead Bruce had bestowed it upon the vicar.

'Are you able to fully comprehend what I say, Mrs Seldon?' the clergyman asked, and Judith, looking at him owlishly, wondered if it was her alcohol-distorted vision that was fooling her, or had Paulton Penny aged ten years since he had visited her a day or two ago?

'My head is fairly clear, Reverend Penny,' she assured him with what was probably slightly more than a half fib.

'Good, good. Then you will recall that I visited the Epsom Asylum where I questioned the staff and drew the conclusion that there was something suspicious about your husband's death.'

'I do remember that, yes, of course.'

'Well, I wrote to the authorities requesting particulars of Bruce Seldon's death,' the vicar said, taking a letter from his pocket, holding it out to her, then, apparently regarding doing so to be a pointless exercise, replacing it in his pocket. 'Today I received a reply curtly informing me that military hospitals are under no obligation to provide relatives or other enquirers with particulars of the cause of death of any patient.'

'That sounds typical of officialdom,' Judith commented.

'It doesn't satisfy me, and I would be willing to take the matter further, Mrs Seldon,' the clergyman told her. 'But, first things first. It is generally agreed that the present all-out military offensive will bring a swift end to four years of bloody warfare, and it is you and your future that concerns me.'

'I have no future,' Judith murmured, her eyes going longingly to a half-empty bottle of alcohol standing on the sideboard.

Neither did she have a present. There was no grave in the local churchyard for her to kneel beside or place flowers on. They had buried Bruce in an impersonal, distant military cemetery. Maybe Judith would pay a visit one day, but she knew her husband would abhor his army resting place. Judith doubted that he would want her to go there.

'That isn't so. Harsh though the old adage that tells us we can't live with the dead may be, it is very true.'

'I can't live without the dead, Reverend Penny.' Judith had a little choke in her voice. 'My life is completely empty without Bruce, and I see nothing but a vast emptiness stretching ahead of me.'

'I appreciate that and you have my sympathy, Mrs Seldon.' Penny reached out a bony hand to cover the hand Judith had resting on her knee. 'It would be silly of me to promise that you will get over it entirely, but it would help you here, and ensure that Bruce can rest there, if you pick up the pieces of your life and put them together.'

'You have an advantage that eludes me, Reverend Penny. I know the *here* only too well. but I'm afraid I don't believe in the *there.*'

'I can help you find faith, Mrs Seldon. I'm available to you at any time you wish, either at the church or the vicarage.'

'You have been very good to me, and I shall be forever grateful,' Judith said, tears stinging her eyes.

Looking imploringly at her, the vicar said, 'I want to do more. The school committee meets next Tuesday, when a decision has to be made as to whether Miss Lyons, who has temporarily taken your husband's position is to become head teacher permanently. I am of the opinion that you are the person most suited to that position. It will help you, Mrs Seldon, for without work, without a purpose to keep it occupied, the mind rapidly deteriorates. Gladys Plummer has found faith, and she finds caring for Mrs Marriott and the invalided Mrs Hann fulfils her. I am convinced that you can manage our school better than anyone else.'

'Take a look at me, Reverend Penny,' Judith cried, 'and you'll see an immoral drunkard.'

'No. I see a widow demented by grief. But I knew and respected the Judith Seldon of old, and I want you to become her again. Anne-Marie is back from London, Mrs Seldon. She is staying at Farley Grange at the moment, but I understand that she will be coming home in a few days' time. She can give you a lot of support.'

'I can't let Anne-Marie see me like this,' Judith protested.

'All she'll see is a dear friend understandably in need of help, Mrs Seldon,' Paulton Penny said as he stood up from his chair.

'You have a few days before Anne-Marie will be along to see you. I know that it is easy for me to say but hard for you to do, but please, make an effort. Anne-Marie will soon coax you back to normal, I'm sure of that. Will you try for me?'

'I'll certainly try. Reverend Penny.'

'You promise?'

'I promise.'

When the vicar left, Judith watched him go. There were two soldiers loitering in the lane that ran alongside the school playground. Taking the bottle from the sideboard, she watched Penny stop beside them to speak sternly. The soldiers walked off. Replacing the bottle without removing the cork, Judith tentatively congratulated herself on a minor victory in her battle for recovery.

For the first time in ages she tidied and dusted the sitting-room, lovingly putting Bruce's chair back into position beside the desk. Life could never be the same without her husband, but now that the Reverend Penny had expressed his confidence in her, she felt that she owed it to Bruce to retrieve the best of herself and make the most of the future.

Fetching long-neglected school books from a cupboard, she sat down with them at the table. Judith was aware that she would not attain the position of head teacher automatically. She could rely upon the Reverend Penny and Anne-Marie, who was also on the school committee, to explain and excuse her gross behaviour since the death of her husband. Nevertheless, the committee would want to interview her before reaching a decision, and she intended to make sure that she impressed them.

Ten minutes and two cups of tea later, unable to remember the last time she had drunk anything other than alcohol, she was making good progress when she heard the latch on the garden gate click. Getting up and going to the window, Judith saw the two soldiers coming up the path. They had avoided the vicar by circling the school and coming back.

Stepping away from the window, Judith hurried past the books that were open on the table and went to the sideboard. Holding the bottle by the neck she took the cork out. As she drank straight from the bottle she heard the front door open and close. Then there was the sound of boots crossing the linoleum in the hall.

With plenty of spare time for contemplation, the imprisoned Leon had reached an agreement with himself. Thinking didn't come easy to him these days, and because odd ideas entered his mind from time to time he vetted every thought carefully before accepting it.

But he knew that this assessment of his incarceration could be depended upon. It wouldn't be accurate to say that eighteen months in prison had changed him. It had been a convoluted process. He had been brought to the Maidstone gaol as his old self. The hard labour part of his sentence, that had worn weaker men down by degrees until they had become gibbering idiots, had weakened only his passivism. But now he had returned to being the same Leon Marriott who had made an enforced departure from Marshlee.

What had made prison and its barbaric regulations tolerable in the beginning had been his certainty that Captain Hubert Lytton would intercede to have him released. With that in mind he had obeyed most of the rules. Being reunited with old friends with whom he had originally been imprisoned, including Mullaly who was now a very sick man, had been a pleasure diminished by the prison's 'no speaking' rule.

Hoping for an occupation of mailbag sewing or mat-making, Leon's powerful physique had him immediately assigned to stone-breaking. There had been a feeling of security in those early days, being one of 200 conscientious objectors walking in file round the exercise yard. Since then death, illness and mental break-down had drastically reduced that number.

When dragging weeks had drifted into endless months and it became obvious that he'd been abandoned by Lytton, a frustrated Leon had led a rebellion. There had been hunger strikes, refusing to come back in after exercise period, the smashing of prison furniture, and noisy protest achieved by rattling tin mugs against bars and the slamming of doors.

Beaten senseless many times by prison officers wielding

batons, Leon was eventually put into solitary confinement for eight months, and spent three months on bread and water. In his long and enforced loneliness he resigned himself to having lost the sustaining Quaker faith the day he had killed the German soldier.

On coming out of solitary he learned that Mullaly, who despite being a chronic consumptive, had been fearlessly at his side throughout the prison rebellion, had died. Two more conscientious objectors had also succumbed to tuberculosis, five to influenza, while one had gruesomely committed suicide. With the other prisoners so weak from ill-treatment and starvation that they barely had the strength to shuffle round the exercise yard, Leon had called a halt to the protests.

After the first two months in prison he had been allowed to write one letter a month and receive one personal visit. Leon had written to his mother for three consecutive months, but she had not answered his letters. Though tempted to write to Anne-Marie, he had resisted because her goodness would have made her respond and she didn't deserve to be involved with a convict.

It occurred to him that his mother could be dead. Initially that possibility, and worrying over what might have happened to Beth, made him fraught with anxiety. But his thoughts began to wander as prison starved his brain of activity so that it had become partially inoperative. Now he was unable to conjure up a clear mental image of his mother, his sister, or even Anne-Marie.

Yet in one of his more lucid moments he had conceived an idea that would bring about his freedom. Leon remembered Michael Millhope, the chaplain at the 22nd Casualty Clearing Station in France. With the Reverend Millhope's age in mind, Leon had assumed that the clergyman would now be back in England. He had asked the prison chaplain to obtain Millhope's address for him.

Three weeks later, Leon had the address of a parish close to Exeter, and wrote off at once to tell Michael Millhope of his plight, and asking him to intervene on his behalf. Leon regarded freedom from prison as the first step. After that he had to face the fact that he had killed a man. Though he felt in his heart that there was a way to absolution, he accepted that Millhope wouldn't have the answer.

Leon didn't know who could help him. It was all a matter of faith, and he found that gradually returning to him. He wondered if Hubert Lytton had died while his leg was being amputated. If not, why hadn't he helped the man who had saved his life? Should Lytton have lived, would he have reported the death of Alexander Plummer? It could be that Gladys was still hoping, praying that her husband would be found alive and well.

Prison has few bright times, but this particular morning was the most exciting Leon had known in a year and a half. He had received his first letter since being imprisoned. It bore an Exeter postmark, and he sat on his hard bed studying the envelope, teasing himself, building up to the moment when he would open it.

'Normally hearsay and gossip wouldn't be entertained here,' Claudia Lytton said, indignation triggering the habit of pulling in her chin close to her chest, 'but from what is being said around the town, and I say this with the utmost respect for you, Reverend Penny, more than verbal assurance is required before we can as much as consider re-employing Mrs Seldon, let alone promote her to head teacher.'

Putting friendship to one side, Anne-Marie had to agree in her mind with what the brigadier's wife had put into words. Arriving home that afternoon she had paid an immediate visit to the schoolhouse, where she had found her friend in a drunken stupor. Yet she hadn't given up on her. Anne-Marie was convinced that Judith Seldon was fundamentally too sound to be regarded as a lost cause. Once she'd had a chance to talk with her in depth, Anne-Marie was satisfied that she could coax Judith back from the wayward path.

'With the years of service Mrs Seldon has given this town,' Anne-Marie said, 'I feel that we owe her another chance.'

'So may that be, Miss Penny,' Walter Hann dissented, 'but I have heard people comment that soldiers hang around the schoolhouse like, begging your pardon and that of Mrs Lytton, dogs around a bitch on heat.'

'I'm sure it will be best if we dispense with such crudities, Mr Hann,' the Reverend Penny objected with a touch of anger in his voice.

'I regret any offence I may have caused the ladies, but I felt justified in using whatever is necessary to get a valid point across,' Hann said. 'We must give Mrs Seldon fair consideration while remaining conversant with the fact that we have a greater duty to the children of Marshlee.'

'That cannot be argued against, but we have to bear in mind what this young war widow has been through,' the Reverend Penny pleaded.

'I am not without sympathy, that goes without saying, but another member of this committee' – Walter Hann used a sideways wag of his head to indicate Raymond Plummer – 'has a daughter-in-law who is also widowed. That woman, as I above all people have reason to be grateful, has since been a tireless worker for the less fortunate in our community. She has been a constant, comforting companion to poor Mrs Marriott, and I don't know how my wife and myself would have managed without her valuable help.'

'I don't think that this committee should debate on a personal level,' Raymond Plummer objected.

Listening to the cross-exchanges, Anne-Marie couldn't instantly come up with a suggestion that would help her friend. Everything had moved too fast of late. After fleeing London for her own safety when the police had wrecked the printing press, she had lain low for a while. First staying at Farley Grange while visiting Hubert in hospital, she had returned to London to find that the war was plainly coming to an end. At the time a number of schisms and divisions began to show in the pacifist organization she had worked with and for. The No-Conscription Fellowship had been weakened by so many of its members having been sent to prison. In addition, the circulation of *The Tribunal* had undergone a dramatic drop even before the police had smashed the machinery at Streatham.

Most worrying of all for Anne-Marie was the fact that some of her former colleagues had been inspired by the new Soviet

Union. They anticipated that revolution would follow war. That kind of reasoning was too extreme for her.

The ailing movement no longer had a star to follow. Vera and she both accepting that it was a hopeless situation, had agreed to go their separate ways. Vera had dedicated herself to suffrage, while Anne-Marie had returned to Farley Grange and Hubert, who was now the local hero.

Their relationship was still one of friendship, though Hubert, in his rare lighter periods. still wanted it to be more. His parents, together with many others, seemed to regard Hubert and Anne-Marie as already betrothed.

Claudia regularly said things like 'Hubert needs a good wife more than ever now'. Though never actually stating who she believed that wife to be, Claudia tacitly left Anne-Marie in no doubt about who she had in mind.

It was taking some time for Anne-Marie to adjust to the Hubert who had come back from France. As was to be expected in a young, formerly super-fit man, he often went into deep depression over the loss of his leg. There was something else, too, an inner torment that Anne-Marie attributed to the horrors undergone and witnessed by Hubert in the action during which he had been wounded. So far he hadn't said a word about his part in the war. She had discussed the situation with her father, who agreed with her that it would be therapeutic for Hubert to talk about his experiences. But the brigadier was adamant that his son should be left to choose when he was ready to talk.

'I agree with Mr Plummer,' Anne-Marie heard her father say. He had really changed and now there was a hitherto absent warmth between them. 'Not only shouldn't we talk of people who are neither here nor in any way connected with the matter under discussion, but the effect of grief is not something that can be compared between individuals.'

Aware of the assistance her father had given to Bruce and Judith, Anne-Marie judged that he must have relented toward conscientious objectors. But he carefully avoided all mention of Leon, and when Anne-Marie surreptitiously slipped the name into a conversation the Reverend Penny turned a deaf ear.

Walter Hann gave a snort of annoyance. 'Then what are you saying, Paulton, that we just blindly appoint this woman as head teacher?'

'Of course not. We are here to discuss objectively and reach a decision democratically,' the Reverend Penny replied haughtily.

'With the emphasis on democracy,' Claudia stressed. 'As the brigadier is unable to be with us this evening, and in the light of his very strong views on lewd behaviour and drunkenness, I will strongly object to any attempt to put this matter to the vote at this meeting.'

'Yes, it should be put before the full committee,' Raymond Plummer concurred.

'Well let us at least try to construct a basis for resolving the issue,' the Reverend Penny urged. 'Have we any proposals?'

Anne-Marie had a scheme, but it was as yet half-formed because her thoughts kept straying. When the No-Conscription Fellowship had been at its operational zenith its intelligence system had been second to none. In the offices close to Fleet Street the important movements of every conscientious objector had been written down. Though Anne-Marie was puzzled how she had come by it, Vera had sent Anne-Marie the record card of Leon Marriott. It had arrived in the post that evening just before Anne-Marie had left home. After years of wondering and worrying, she now knew that Leon was in Maidstone Prison.

Though welcome, this news put her whole life asunder. Unsure yet as to how she would act on it, Anne-Marie helped the committee meeting along with a proposal. 'I visited Mrs Seldon before I came here this evening, and that visit encourages me to suggest a way of handling this. I move that we ask Mrs Seldon to attend to be interviewed by the committee at a meeting convened in the next week or so.'

'I second that,' Raymond Plummer said.

'I will concur providing no more than a week passes,' Claudia made the proviso. 'To prolong the issue further would be unfair to Miss Lyons, who has much to lose or gain, depending on the decision we reach.'

'That is a good point. So shall we agree to return here, say, next

Wednesday evening?' the Reverend Penny studied each of them in turn.

There was no dissension, and Anne-Marie's motion was carried. Yet she was already having misgivings. Considering the state in which she had found Judith, her suggestion had been unwise. Though her powers of persuasion were good, and Judith respected her, Anne-Marie knew that it would be a close to impossible task to present a sober, coherent and cognizant Judith Seldon to the school committee in just seven days.

A loud noise brought Judith Seldon instantly awake. As always on waking she reached out a hand to Bruce. As always in the past year or so, her husband's side of the bed was cold and empty. As always this reminder of her loss brought a numbing spell of grief.

The noise happened again. Mentally pushing through a haze of alcohol fumes, Judith struggled to identify the sound. It was gunfire. Tumbling out of bed in a panic, she staggered out onto the landing to unwittingly increase the aching of her head by squinting at the grandmother clock. It was half past eleven in the morning. Judith had slept late again.

As she washed and dressed, the ringing of bells and blowing of trumpets had joined the roar of guns. From her window she saw children bouncing around excitedly in the school playground. In the street beyond, people were waving flags and cheering. An open car went slowly by with Raymond Plummer in it, standing beside the driver. Complete with the mayoral chain, Plummer, holding the top edge of the windscreen for support, was shouting at the top of his voice, 'The war is over!'

Though frail from her heavy drinking of the previous night, Judith wanted to be a part of it. Out amid the laughing, crying. cheering, ecstatic crowd, she was surprised when Gladys Plummer ran up to embrace her.

'It's ended, Judith. It's all over,' the previously aloof Gladys, her voice over-loud, announced. 'We're going to make this a day for Marshlee to remember, Come and help.'

Amazed by this show of friendliness, Judith allowed Gladys to link arms with her. United in recent widowhood, they went down to the centre of town together to join a throng of happy people. Seeing Anne-Marie standing with her parents, Judith gave a wave. Anne-Marie came running across the road to join her and Gladys.

'Isn't it wonderful?' a smiling Anne-Marie shouted over the tumult. 'They're putting trestles out on the green, and the trades people are going to give all the food they can spare.'

Then she stopped, embarrassed, and apologized. 'I'm sorry. There can't be anything wonderful about this for either you, Judith, or you, Gladys.'

'This is a landmark in history that Alexander and Bruce, in their different ways, had a part in the making of, Anne-Marie,' Gladys smiled while blinking away a few tears. 'I think Judith will agree that we can keep our private thoughts, no matter how sad, separate to join the celebrations.'

'That's the way I view it,' Judith agreed, pleased at being accepted as her former self. 'There's Leon, too, Anne-Marie, and, like me, I expect you have James on your mind.'

Anne-Marie nodded, and Judith could tell her friend was unable to trust herself to speak for a moment. Judith could understand why Anne-Marie was upset. In the tragedy of war, James was a calamitous figure. If his name appeared at all on the roll of honour there would be a black mark against it. The only way she could come close to accepting that James was responsible for Beth's pregnancy, was to blame the ordeal he suffered when first pressed into the army.

Raymond Plummer passed by, heading for the town hall, still shouting, hoarsely now, 'The war is over.'

Standing in the centre of the road, the white-haired accordionist was moving animatedly as he played a tune that no one could hear. The one-armed soldier was making a pretence of conducting the music with his remaining hand, while the one-legged soldier was being largely ignored as he held out a collecting box. With tears streaming down his face, the unbalanced soldier somehow managed to appear all alone despite standing in the thick of the crowd.

Then some people were shushing others, asking for quiet as

216

Raymond Plummer appeared on the balcony of the town hall, with the officious Clarence Crandal at his side. The pair were flanked by the Reverend Paulton and Mrs Rachel Penny on their left, and Brigadier and Claudia Lytton on their right.

Only a snatched word or two reached the noisy crowd as the mayor read the official telegram. Then Clarence Crandal had more success in getting through to the people by shouting.

Addressing a sea of waving flags, the clerk said, 'The welcome news has come upon us so quickly that nothing could be officially arranged for this day of days. However, the town council will not be expecting any of our men to work, and I imagine the same applies to all of Marshlee's employers.' A mighty cheer of approval went up, and Crandal had to raise both hands to appeal for silence. 'There will be festivities later, but in our desire to mark this occasion as a joyous one, we must not forget to give thanks to the Almighty for our deliverance. Accordingly, the Reverend Penny would like to say a few words.'

Judith was aware of Anne-Marie putting an arm around her waist, and the other around Gladys, and knew that her sweet friend was providing what comfort she could to two young war widows.

'I will not keep you away from your festivities for long,' the Marshlee vicar promised the crowd. 'I will be holding a short thanksgiving service and look forward to seeing you all in church.'

There was a diversion then as some soldiers came up to the town hall in a wagon. Amid laughter and wild cheering, the soldiers hoisted a life-sized effigy of the Kaiser. With one end of a rope tied round the neck of the dummy, the soldiers threw the other end up to the balcony. Deftly catching the rope, a smiling Clarence Crandal secured it to the balcony's balustrade.

They roared approval and shouted hysterically as the soldiers set the effigy alight. As the grotesque figure swung from side to side, blazing, Judith had to turn away. Anne-Marie and Gladys shared her distress. As the crowd yelled and jumped up and down, a number of people who were old enough to know better, began to throw stones and other missiles at the burning figure. It was some kind of collective madness as people gave way to the pent-up repressions of four dreadful years.

Frenzy made for bad aiming. A young boy fell to the ground, bleeding at the temple, injured by a thrown bottle, and a stone caught Brigadier Lytton's hand up on the balcony. Clarence Crandal's appeal for moderation went unheeded.

Judith heard a saddened Anne-Marie ask a question. 'What have we gained if they celebrate peace with violence?'

'Fools never learn,' Judith replied. With her head clearer than it had been for a long time, she felt that on this special day she owed it to Bruce to make a quotation. ' "All things tremble before danger, all fear death. When a man considers this, he does not kill or cause to kill".'

'The Buddha,' Anne-Marie identified the quote. 'It's nice to see you continuing the Bruce Seldon tradition, Judith.'

This pleased Judith. She aptly replied, ' "One repays a teacher badly if one remains only a pupil". That's Zarathustra.'

'Thanks, I wouldn't have known that one,' a laughing Anne-Marie pleased Judith by giving her a one-armed cuddle. 'You're doing fine, Judith.'

'I didn't know the Buddha one,' Gladys ruefully confessed, and all three of them were laughing together when Brigadier Lytton came up.

'Right, ladies. You are invited to the mayor's chamber, where we are about to crack a bottle of fizz,' the brigadier said. 'We shall drink to victory over the Hun, and toast absent friends.'

Misgivings quelled the fun of the day so far in Judith. It was now gone one o'clock and she hadn't had a drink. That was something of a record. But she realized that just one glass of champagne could mark the point of no return as far as she was concerned. Not for the first time, that day and in the past, she realized how priceless Anne-Marie was as a friend as she heard her saying, 'I'm sorry, Brigadier. We'd love to come, but we've promised to help with putting up the trestles and laying out the food.'

Waving a magnanimous hand, the brigadier replied, 'Feel free to do as you wish, Anne-Marie. I'll wager that whatever you are going to engage in will be more interesting than patronizing a bunch of old fogies like us.'

'Not at all, Brigadier. It's just a case of a prior engagement,' Anne-Marie diplomatically assured him. As an afterthought, she enquired, 'Has Hubert come into town with you?'

Worry crumpled the brigadier's round face. 'I'm afraid not. I don't know why, but he was in a difficult frame of mind before, and hearing that the Armistice has been signed seemed to darken his mood. Both his mother and I begged him to join the celebrations, but I'm afraid he remained adamant.'

It surprised Judith to hear Gladys say, 'I think I might be able to persuade him, Brigadier. He and Alexander were very close.'

'I'd really appreciate it if you tried, Gladys. You could be just the one to work the miracle.'

'If Anne-Marie has no objection,' Gladys said awkwardly, having overlooked the fact that Anne-Marie had been looking after Hubert at Farley Grange.

'Of course I don't mind,' Anne-Marie assured her friend.

Judith could sense that Anne-Marie was pleased that Gladys had volunteered. She suspected that Anne-Marie wouldn't feel right enjoying herself if he wasn't there.

'Most commendable, most commendable, Gladys,' the brigadier expressed his gratitude. 'Come with me to the town hall and I'll have Dobson drive you out to the Grange.'

Saying goodbye to Gladys, assuring her they would meet up with her again later in the day, Judith and Anne-Marie walked on to where trestles had been set up on the village green. There was an excited buzz of conversation from the women busily laying out food. They stopped to look at the centrepiece, which was a huge iced cake decorated with the lettering *Marshlee Rejoices. 11th November 1918.*

'Isn't that a marvellous cake?' Mrs Crandal came up behind them to say. 'As soon as dear Mr Hann heard the good news he set to and baked the cake in what must be a record time.'

'It's really very nice,' Judith agreed.

'Most kind of Mr Hann,' Anne-Marie said.

Mrs Crandal leaned her head between theirs to whisper confidentially, 'Us ladies from the church choir intend to repay him, at least in a small way. We are going to sing a selection of hymns under Lou Hann's bedroom window this evening.'

'That will be lovely for her,' Judith said absently, as a woman standing alone and a little apart from the others caught her eye.

Following the direction of Judith's gaze, Anne-Marie gave a little gasp of a sigh as she recognized the woman. 'Elsie Marriott. Whatever must be going through her mind right now. I must go to speak to her.'

When Anne-Marie walked off, Judith stayed put. She was fully aware of the fragility of her surprising recovery of that day. Small, thin and bent, old and lined before her time, Mrs Marriott was a pathetic figure. Judith saw her as the straw of misery that would break the back of her own emotions.

She walked slowly away from where Anne-Marie stood talking to the elderly woman.

Unable to hold out any longer, Leon used a thumb to slit the pale-blue envelope open. The little square of ruled paper inside was the same colour. His heart leapt as he unfolded it and read the address of the vicarage at the top right-hand corner. The letter was written in a well-formed hand, but the letters were small and in the dim light of his cell he had to screw up his eyes to read:

My dear Mr Marriott

I was pleased to receive your letter, and was most appreciative of the kind words you had for my husband.

Sad to say, the Reverend Michael Millhope passed away two months ago. He was invalided from France just three weeks before his death. Although I had him back for so short a time, I thank the Lord for the many years we shared together.

I was sorry to learn of your plight, and you will be in my prayers.

Yours in Jesus

Sybil Millhope

As a dispirited Leon slumped on his hard bed, the single sheet of blue paper slipping from his fingers to float to the floor, there was sudden uproar in the prison.

It sounded as if both prison officers and convicts were shouting at the tops of their voices. The thud of running footsteps on the landings rose to a crescendo. Someone was banging on his door. An eye came to the spyhole to peer in at him, and a voice, high-pitched with excitement shouted in at him.

'It's over, Marriott. They've signed the bloody Armistice.'

Uninterested, Marriott turned away from the door, facing a blank wall as the man by the door, officer or convict, Marriott didn't know and didn't care, yelled at him once more, 'Don't you understand? It's over!' When Marriott made no response, the man shouted, 'Bugger you, then, you miserable sod,' and went running off along the landing.

'No thank you,' Judith said as firmly as she could.

As if not hearing her, Walter Hann half-filled two tumblers with whiskey; one for her and one for him. They were alone in his bakehouse because Mrs Crandal had volunteered Judith to collect more rolls for the victory feast. It was dark now, and an occasional squib was being let off on the green, to accompanying 'Oohs' and 'Aahs' from the townsfolk. Judith could faintly hear the ladies from the choir singing outside the thick walls of the Hann house. It was a scratchy-voiced rendition of 'Hark the Herald Angels Sing'. The women had been arguing among themselves when Judith had come in, some claiming that it was too early for Christmas carols, while others protested that it was exactly what Mrs Hann would love to hear. Apparently the pro-early Yuletiders had won.

'Drink up. Not one of us will see the likes of this day again,' Walter Hann urged as he held the glass out to her.

The enticing, compelling aroma of the alcohol reached Judith. She wanted it, needed it, couldn't do without it. Today had been pleasant enough, but a terrible strain. She could have relaxed, enjoyed it much more with a drink or two inside her. That wasn't true. She was fooling herself. One or two drinks wouldn't have been enough. She would have been incapable within a short time, shaming herself instead of continuing to regain respect as she had been doing all day.

A dough-mixing machine was producing a hypnotically drumming aural background. Judith discovered she was tempted. No, it was more than that. Temptation gives you a choice, but with the scent of whiskey in her nostrils and the glass of drink just inches from her, Judith had no control over herself.

She was about to reach for the glass when Walter Hann made a misjudgement. Wrongly assessing her slight delay in acceptance as a budding refusal, he decided to force her to take the drink. Slipping one of his heavy arms behind Judith's neck, he pushed the glass towards her mouth. The rim of the tumbler clinked against her teeth, giving her slight pain that was nothing compared to having the obese baker so close.

The whiskey that ran into her mouth was as revolting to her as Hann was. Angrily knocking the glass away, out of his hand so that it smashed against the stone floor, she spat out the whiskey. Judith struggled but he held her tightly. His grossly fat, horribly wet lips were searching for her mouth, and with his spare hand he was frantically groping her body, pulling at her clothes.

He smelled. His smell filled her head and her stomach, sickening her. He stank of whiskey, yeast, and a combination of every foul stench it had ever been her misfortune to encounter. Reaching blindly behind her with one hand, she identified a pair of scales by feel. Her fingers curled round a heavy weight he used for weighing dough. Swinging the weight up, she slammed it hard against his forehead.

Involuntarily releasing her, Hann took a staggering half step backwards. His hand went to his forehead, but the blow hadn't broken the skin. His massive bulk was between her and the door. Judith couldn't believe that the frightening creature before her was Walter Hann, businessman and one of Marshlee's dignitaries. He was totally consumed by lust and rage.

'What's up,' he asked deridingly, 'you suddenly found yourself some morals? What's one more man to you?'

'Man?' she laughed, detecting more than a trace of hysteria in her voice, but not afraid of him any more. 'You're old, a fat monster, a load of sweaty blubber. No woman would let you near her.'

'Whore!' he yelled, beside himself with anger.

His eyes bulged out at her like a frog's, becoming increasingly bloodshot as she looked at them. From outside came the sung line 'Peace on earth and mercy mild'.

'No woman would look at me, is that right?' He kept his thick lips tight together as he spoke. Like all people who put themselves before the public, he couldn't handle being criticized. 'I suppose you think you're worth having. Well, I made a mistake and I've changed my mind. You can get out of here.'

A relieved Judith squeezed between him and a still warm oven. But his temper hadn't subsided. Hann jabbed a thick forefinger at her. 'I don't need worn-out whores like yourself. I can do better. Old, am I? Well, I could surprise you. Who'd you think Beth Marriott took into her bed? She was a young girl, and pretty, but she liked me.'

Faint at hearing this, Judith had to lean against a wooden dough trough for a moment. Looking at Hann, whose shoulders were drooping as the lust drained quickly from him, taking his psychotic rage with it, she got strength back into her shaking legs and made for the door.

'Mrs Seldon,' he called after her, his voice croaking. 'Please don't go. You don't understand. I'm a man broken by taking care of a sick wife for long years. I lost a dear son in the war. Come back, Mrs Seldon, please. What I said about that girl was nonsense. It was just the boast of a silly old man trying to impress you. I'm sorr—'

Judith heard no more as she dashed out, slamming the bakehouse door closed behind her. Outside she came face to face with Mrs Crandal and five other women. Smiling at her, wagging their heads from side to side like badly controlled string puppets, they sang. '. . . bring me my arrows of desire'.

Hurrying past them, Judith dashed up the road to where she knew she would find Anne-Marie.

Eleven

It wasn't until the train reached the outskirts of Marshlee that a sudden realization came to Anne-Marie. When she had mentioned Hubert Lytton to Leon, he knew that Hubert had lost a leg. How could he have known? Why hadn't she seen how impossible it was for Leon to have that knowledge, and asked him about it there and then? There might well be a simple explanation; perhaps as Leon had learned about Hubert's injury on the prison grapevine, but that was unlikely as conscientious objectors were uninterested in serving soldiers. Intuition warned Anne-Marie that the truth was far more sinister.

As the train pulled into the station she saw the car from Farley Grange parked under a gas lamp, waiting for her. She welcomed the prospect of time alone with the taciturn, doddery old Dobson driving slowly back to the estate. It would give her the opportunity to mull over this mystery. Also she needed to recover from her dismal visit to Maidstone Prison.

Late December was probably the worst time of year to go there. She had used everything black in her imagination to prepare herself, but the gaol was more forbidding than the worst imagery she had dredged up. The dark interior of the building had echoed hollowly. Every slight sound was magnified. Even a gentle clearing of the throat made a thunderous noise that bounced from wall to wall. At all times there had been a background of concerted noise with an aggressive tone.

A sympathetic prison officer had assured her while she was waiting that the prison was centrally heated, but she could detect not the slightest warmth. The tiled floor was like ice under her feet, striking uncomfortably through the soles of her shoes.

Though she had known that she must, she had dreaded seeing Leon. She was the bearer of bad tidings, both from their home town and in general. Lloyd George had made the abolition of conscription an election issue, reminding the people that he had led the nation to victory, and promising that conscription would end. The election had come and gone, and Lloyd George had reneged on his pledge. With men continuing to be called up and a new crop of conscientious objectors being sent to prison, it seemed that the wartime objectors such as Leon would never be released.

Worst of all was the death of the sister he loved so dearly, and the circumstances surrounding it. Anne-Marie was in a dilemma about how much of those circumstances to reveal. To be told that James had taken the blame for what had happened to Beth would distress Leon. Judith had related her shocking experience with Walter Hann, and had confided in Gladys and Anne-Marie what the baker had claimed regarding Beth's pregnancy. Yet all three of them had no idea how to use that information to restore James's good name without destroying his mother and the trust the people of Marshlee had in his father. This was certainly something that she couldn't tell Leon.

A happy side-effect of Judith's unpleasant encounter with Hann was that it had jolted her out of the semi-trance she had been in from the time Bruce had died. Not having touched a drop of alcohol since, and having no wish to, a brilliant Judith had faced the school committee – Walter Hann having sent an apology for his absence – to be unanimously appointed as head teacher.

When a warder brought him to face her through a small barred window, Leon blinked hard as he saw Anne-Marie. At first she had been worried that he wouldn't remember her, but she reasoned that after so long in prison he was experiencing problems separating daydreams from reality.

Just as her preconceived idea of the prison had been inadequate, so had she failed to ready herself for the inevitable change in Leon. It was evident how badly he was suffering from the cold. His face revealed the agonies he was enduring, and his hands were terrible to look at. They were disfigured by countless chilblains that had been painted with iodine.

Their first ten minutes together had been awkward and stilted. In a matter-of-fact way, totally devoid of self-pity, he had told her how bitterly cold it had been in the prison since the onset of winter. Leon said that he survived only by pacing his cell all day, and again at intervals during the night when the cold awoke him.

He looked leaner and older, but it was in his eyes that Anne-Marie could gauge how much he had changed. There was no depth to them. It was as if he had brought down a shutter to keep secret behind it all that he had endured. Displaying no interest In what had happened to her, or what had been going on at home, he made an obvious attempt to stop her from talking of such things by telling her of the prison routine.

'They wake us at half-past five in the morning, Anne-Marie,' he had told her leadenly. 'We are marched outside to the lavatories to wash ourselves. Then we have to scrub out our cells and what little furniture is in them, before polishing our cutlery and pails. The bedclothes have to be folded as per regulations. Then break-fast is at six o'clock.'

'What do you have?' she had asked.

'One pint of porridge without milk. After that there's three-quarters of an hour supervised exercise in the exercise yard, then off to work in the quarry. Lunch is at midday and is never much in quality or quantity. Then it's back to work until a quarter-past four. For supper there's a pint of porridge and half a pound of bread. Then we're locked up for the night and the routine goes on just the same the following day.'

Hearing this, Anne-Marie came close to tears when recalling Leon's well-organized, productive working day in his forge at Marshlee. She tried to think of something to say. Something of interest to them both so that it would create a diversion.

'Have you met a man named Will Chamberlain in here, Leon?' Anne-Marie asked. 'I worked for him on the production of *The Tribunal* in London before he was arrested.'

226

'I've never met Chamberlain, but I've heard of him. Bernard Boothroyd often mentioned him.'

'Bernard! He took over from Will until his own arrest. Is Bernard Boothroyd in here with you, Leon?' Anne-Marie was excited.

'He was, Anne-Marie,' Leon replied, 'but he was moved. I think he's in Pentonville now. I didn't know that you gave that kind of support to the movement.' He gave her a pensive smile. 'I just can't imagine Marshlee's Anne-Marie Penny working in London, opposing the Establishment, too.'

'I admit I had misgivings at the time, but it worked out fine,' she told him.

'I'm sure that it did,' he praised her. 'I've been wondering recently if my protest was worthwhile. I like to think, perhaps immodestly, that I made something of a stand for the brotherhood of man.'

'I am absolutely certain that you did, Leon,' she assured him.

'But I am being a coward now, Anne-Marie.'

'In what way?'

'By being aware that there are things about home that you have to tell me, and trying to put that moment off,' he replied unhappily. 'But time is short, so I'm ready. Is there any news of Bruce?'

At that moment Anne-Marie's courage threatened to desert her, but she steeled herself. He knew that James had been killed, but was worried over the fate of his comrade.

'I'm so sorry, Leon,' she replied tearfully, 'but Bruce is dead.'

Concealing his sorrow, Leon said tersely, 'Bruce wouldn't have given in and joined the army, so they must have executed him.'

'It wasn't like that, Leon. Bruce was tortured so badly that he lost his mind. He killed himself.'

'I can't believe it, not Bruce,' Leon, no longer able to hide his shocked grief, exclaimed in a rasping whisper. 'Judith?'

'She took it badly at first, but she's started to cope now,' Anne-Marie assured him.

It had been tough up to then, but it immediately became worse. Although she had unlimited sympathy for Leon, she hadn't shirked her responsibilities. Her hardest task was to tell him about Beth. Leon's face was without expression, but Anne-Marie suspected that he was crying on the inside.

That was when he had deliberately changed the subject and asked about Hubert. 'Is he managing to cope with just one leg, Anne-Marie?'

'It's a problem,' she replied, not finding anything unusual about his query at that time. Now she excused herself by blaming the fact that she was talking through iron bars to a man she had known in free and happy times.

'Can he get around, Anne-Marie?'

'He has an artificial leg now, but finds it difficult to get used to.'

With there being no point in lying to Leon, Anne-Marie had said that she was spending time at Farley Grange assisting with the rehabilitation of Hubert. But when leaving Leon, both of them needing to touch hands, which resulted in Leon being rebuked by a warder, Anne-Marie had made it clear.

This had saddened rather than reassured Leon. Looking at her glumly, he told Anne-Marie, 'I appreciate you coming all this way to see me, but I don't want you to make the journey again. Your life is at Farley Grange now, Anne-Marie.'

'No, Leon!' she had gasped, taken aback. 'Through these past years, with so many terrible things happening, I've got through it all by telling myself that one day, no matter when, you and me will be together. They can't keep you in prison much longer.'

'We will never be forgiven,' he said solemnly. 'In France, Anne-Marie, I saw some soldiers, little more than schoolboys, running from a German attack. I later learned that the British Army had shot to death dozens of those boys as deserters. Until that moment of panic, they had been willing soldiers who had fought well, yet they were executed. With that as an example, what chance have people like myself got? There are one and a half thousand of us still in prison.'

'You mustn't give up.' Anne-Marie had done her best to sound positive. 'A lot of influential people have signed a petition for an amnesty for conscientious objectors. It may take a little while, Leon, but I will wait for you.'

'I don't want you to wait for me, Anne-Marie. There is something else, something really bad that I can't tell you about. Believe me, it means we can never be together.'

'Nothing could keep us apart,' she had argued. 'This doesn't sound like you. You have your faith, Leon.'

'No,' he said flatly. 'I have forfeited the right to call myself a Quaker, and cannot lay claim to being a pacifist.'

Before she could ask Leon what he was talking about, a prison officer had led him away. It made no difference, as Anne-Marie could sense that Leon wasn't going to tell her. But there had been something final in their exchange of glances when they had taken him from her. It was plain that Leon didn't expect to see her ever again.

Finding this too much to bear, she had cried quietly several times on the journey back to Marshlee. Knowing Leon as she did cancelled out any possibility that he had done anything wrong, anything that he was so ashamed of that he couldn't be with her. She wondered if it was a case of illness, some terminal disease he had contracted when undergoing the vile punishment to which he had been subjected. Even as she was telling herself that speculation was pointless, another part of her was desperately seeking the answer to the conundrum.

Standing as the train slowed, she checked her looks in a mirror affixed between maps on the wall of the carriage. Alighting, she walked out of the station, her footsteps faltering as she neared the car to see that Claudia was sitting behind the wheel. Hubert sat in the back, looking less moody than he had for some time.

He had been improving fairly rapidly of late. As he more and more mastered his artificial leg, Hubert had eased himself back into community life. He had quickly, and most deservedly ln the opinion of all who knew him, including Anne-Marie, become Marshlee's war hero. Though remaining taciturn about his soldiering, he had developed a maturity that gave him an impressive military presence.

'Hello, my dear, hop in,' Claudia greeted her smilingly. 'We've had some great news. Arnold Goadsby, head of chambers at Harley, Goadsby & Fulton, Lincoln's Inn Fields and an old friend of the brigadier, has offered to take Hubert on as a junior.'

'I'm so pleased for you, Hubert,' Anne-Marie said, as she got into the car to sit beside him. 'We will all miss you, of course.'

'I trust that you won't be missing me,' Hubert said significantly, but Anne-Marie couldn't grasp his message.

It was Claudia who, after beckoning over a railway guard to turn the starting handle of the car, let Anne-Marie know what the Lyttons had planned for her.

'The thing is, my dear, that you have played an invaluable part in Hubert's recovery. Without you he wouldn't be ready to take advantage of this opportunity.'

'It is Hubert's own determination that's responsible,' Anne-Marie said humbly.

'You are too modest, Anne-Marie,' Claudia fondly chided her. 'In fact, I was going on to say that both the brigadier and myself fear that Hubert's remarkable progress may not continue without you. Which makes us ask if you would consider moving to London with Hubert as his companion?'

Reaching for her hand, Hubert clasped it briefly in support of his mother's suggestion. Maybe they would be content to have her as the companion of Captain Hubert Lytton today, but what had the brigadier and Claudia in mind for her tomorrow?

'It won't be for at least another six months yet, my dear,' Claudia said consolingly. 'That will give you plenty of time to settle your arrangements here before you leave.'

'I am thankful that Walter Hann isn't here with us this morning,' Clarence Crandal said fervently. 'A most unpleasant business this, most unpleasant.'

'To me it smacks of deceit and treachery, though I confess that I can think of no alternative,' the Reverend Paulton Penny complained, hands clasping his flowing clerical robes as a keen December wind plucked at them.

Amid the grey, leaning tombstones of Marshlee's dead of yesteryear, they were holding an impromptu council meeting outside the church. The service was over and the rest of the congregation had gone to the warmth of their homes and the comfort of their Sunday dinners.

Face purpling in the cold, the brigadier said tetchily, 'We've agreed the three basic essentials, that it will take the form of a cenotaph, be made out of Portland stone, and located on the green, so I see nothing to be gained by this *ad hoc*, as it were, discussion in Arctic weather.'

'It is probably the only opportunity we will have with Mr Hann not present, Brigadier,' Claudia reminded her husband.

'Yes, I feel we must come to a decision on the vexed question as to whether or not the name of James Hann is to be included on the memorial,' the Reverend Penny said, lips pursed dubiously.

'James Hann!' The brigadier spoke the name as a snort of disgust. 'That bounder would have been horse-whipped in my day. Were he here now we would make sure that the courts dealt with the fellow.'

'But he is not here, dear,' Claudia said reasonably. Her reasonableness gained her an angry glare from the brigadier.

'Why not do the whole thing in style?' he fumed. 'Carve the name of Leon Marriott at the top, and that other coward, the schoolteacher – what was that apology for a man's name?'

'Bruce Seldon, and I'd prefer that we didn't talk ill of the dead,' the vicar said quietly.

'We march to different tunes, sir,' the Brigadier informed Penny. 'In my book death doesn't forgive a man. If he was a coward when alive, then he's Just as much a coward dead.'

Inclining his head, the Reverend Penny said, 'I'm pleased to disagree with you on that. But let us consider the pros and cons of omitting young Hann's name from the planned memorial.'

The vicar waved a signal, hand clutching a prayer book, and the others turned their heads to see Rachel Penny closing the vicarage door.

'My little woman telling me that dinner is on the table,' the Reverend Penny said self-effacingly.

Taking a hunter watch from his pocket, Clarence Crandal used a thumb to flip open the cover, and pulled a face of consternation as he studied the dial. 'Oh dear, I must not keep Mrs Crandal waiting for much longer. Perhaps we should discuss this at another time.'

'I think that it can, and most definitely should, be settled right now.' Penny wasn't going to be put off either by his own wife or Crandal's.

'I agree. The way I see it, Walter Hann is a sensible fellow who is able to judge public opinion. He'll raise no objection.' The brigadier was confident.

'I have his wife in mind, the dead boy's mother,' Claudia said.

'She'll never see the memorial,' Clarence Crandal put in.

'That is hardly an admirable comment, Mr Crandal,' the Reverend Penny admonished the council's clerk.

'What I meant was. . . .' A red-faced Crandal was stuck for something to say.

'Your meaning was perfectly clear,' Penny said stiffly. 'Now, what do you all say?'

'James Hann's name must not be included on the Marshlee memorial,' the brigadier spoke up fiercely.

'Having regard to what happened, I have to go along with that,' Claudia agreed.

'The memory of poor little Beth Marriott convinces me that it would be wrong to include the name of the man who wronged her.' Clarence Crandal spoke in a more positive manner than was usual for him.

'And you, Reverend Penny?' Claudia enquired.

'As I am outvoted, I suppose it falls to me to inform Walter and Lou Hann of the decision,' the Reverend Penny replied resignedly.

'But what of Anne-Marie?' Claudia asked. 'James Hann was a close friend of hers.'

'My daughter is strong-willed, Mrs Lytton, and I have learned to respect her views. But this is a council matter, and Anne-Marie has no vote.'

'Nevertheless, I'm sure that she'll have something to say,' Claudia Lytton cautioned the clergyman.

Having served a full two-year sentence, Leon Marriott was among the first twenty-four conscientious objectors to be released from Maidstone Prison. Bowing to public pressure it had until then ignored, the government ordered the start of releases in batches that were to be staggered over several weeks. Taken by surprise, Leon found himself free and on the streets with little money and no time for psychological preparation.

Stepping back into a world that had been insane when he'd left, Leon was soon telling himself that it was even crazier now, albeit in a different way. Physically weakened, and accepting that it would take time for his thinking to straighten out, he realized that it would be a mistake to go home. Accepting that this decision was unfair on his mother, he needed to recuperate before he could face a Marshlee where there would be no Beth, and his best friends had gone forever.

Then there was Hubert Lytton, who had betrayed him by not making an official report of what had happened at Crapouillots Wood. Though Lytton's inaction had blighted Leon's life, he felt no animosity toward the captain, only a colossal pity.

Not least important in his reasons for not returning home was Leon's conviction that he needed to give Anne-Marie time and space to settle her life before he came back on the scene. That was only part of it, Leon had to admit to himself, because his feelings for Anne-Marie were sure to get the better of him. It would be easier for him to return after she had made her decisions, chosen the course she would follow for the remainder of her life. That would make it simpler for him to stay separate from her.

Making his way to London, Leon found the unbroken rows and rows of buildings to be claustrophobic. Without knowing where he was or where he was heading, he found himself at Crystal Palace. The spendidly Victorian railway station fascinated Leon. His blacksmith's heart was stirred by the ornamental ironwork, but when he walked away from the station to find himself in the strangest area of the strangeness of South London, he was hit by a homesickness such as he had not known for years.

He found himself a room in a tall house that stood beside the road that ran along the edge of the steep declivity just below the Crystal Palace. It was a dingy room, but a vast improvement on the prison cells he had known for so long. As a country boy he was pleased by the view from his window. Beyond the clutter of the imperial city he could see the pleasant green hills of Hampstead and Highgate. In the middle-distance there were numerous parks. Though all of modest size they were open spaces, and Leon appreciated that.

That evening after dark, he sat at the window and marvelled at the spectacular panorama that was the lights of London. It was a scene so alien that it brought back to him the oddly detached feeling he'd had during most of his time in prison. Though this was an eerily unsettling experience, he welcomed the fact that it dulled the edge of his thinking about home.

Early the following morning he went out job-seeking, but soon learned that finding work wouldn't be easy. Army demobilization had been going on for some time before the conscientious objectors had been freed. Consequently, the soldiers returning home had filled just about every vacancy.

'You can blame Winston Churchill for that,' the foreman at a forge in Battersea told him.

Not wanting to blame anyone, which would be a pointless exercise, Leon had walked away. Day after day he was turned away from business premises all over London. But on the afternoon of the fourth day his luck seemed to change when he went into a Wandsworth café for a much needed cup of tea.

'I can't say for sure that they're still taking men on, but they was certainly looking for more hands this morning,' a toothless man, bent like a question mark by a tubercular spine, told him about a brick-making company in Enfield. 'They turned me down, reckoned I weren't fit enough because it's right hard work. You shouldn't have no trouble. You look as strong as a bloody horse.'

Getting precise instructions, Leon set off for Enfield on foot. Energy boosted by the thought of obtaining work, he walked at a fast pace and arrived there before the brickworks closed for the day.

'I sure could have used you, yes by gosh, indeed, mister,' a man with east European features and a barely decipherable accent said, looking Leon over appreciatively. 'But this day I tek on two chaps, weedy chaps, to do job that fella like you do on own, easy. Sorry I am.'

He made his disappointed and weary way back to his room at Crystal Palace. There was a letter in an official envelope awaiting Leon. It was a curt note from the War Office advising him that he had been dishonourably discharged from the army. A warning was added, absolutely unnecessarily in Leon's case, that he would become liable to two years' hard labour if he ever tried to join the army in the future.

This letter confirmed what he had been told by many employers, and had heard disgruntled job applicants moan about on his long tramp in search of work. The twin infamy of a prison sentence and a dishonourable discharge from the army reduced the chance of employment to somewhere around nil.

At the end of his first week in London, late on Saturday afternoon, a dispirited Leon was walking past Olympia when he heard his name called. At first the well-dressed man hurrying toward him was unrecognizable; then something in Leon's head worked a transformation for him. He briefly saw the man approaching him dressed in prison garb, his appearance changed from poise to dejection. Then that peculiar sensation passed, and Leon knew that he was shaking hands with Bernard Boothroyd.

'What are you doing in these parts, Leon?' Boothroyd, overjoyed to see him, enquired.

'London?'

'No,' Boothroyd replied. 'London is the only place to find work. I meant here in Hammersmith. If I remember rightly you were a blacksmith. I thought south of the river would be a better hunting ground for you.'

'I've hunted everywhere, north and south of the river. I've just come from a motor-car works in Russell Gardens.'

'No luck?'

'The same as ever,' Leon said with a despairing shrug. 'If there was a job they didn't intend to give it to an ex-convict with a dishonourable discharge from the army. I'm coming to the end, Bernard.'

'*Nil desperandum*, Leon,' Boothroyd urged. 'It is a scandal that there are no pensions for CO ex-servicemen, and many of them, family men in particular, are literally destitute. The No-

Conscription Fellowship has been revamped, and a national committee will shortly be able to offer help to those who need it.'

'Let the married men with children be helped first. I'll still keep trying to find myself a job,' Leon said.

'That's commendable,' Boothroyd nodded, 'but treat yourself to a slap-up supper this evening, Leon. There's a big reunion of conscientious objectors at the Central Hall. I'm heading there now, so come along with me.'

Taking up the offer, Leon fell into step beside Boothroyd. He could use a proper meal, and looked forward with pleasure to meeting some of his old fellow protestors.

In the hall, filled with what Leon estimated to be close to 2,000 men, Boothroyd put him in the picture. Indicating the central table at which sat six Labour mayors of London boroughs, he said, 'There's the Attlee brothers. A bit of family difference there, but no trace of acrimony. Clement, the reserved-looking little man, was a major in the army, whereas Tom was one of us, a conscientious objector.'

Studying those seated at the main table, Leon couldn't believe his eyes when he saw what should have been a familiar figure but wasn't. It was an ashen-faced, frail, young/old man who looked terribly ill. There was something remaining of a prominent activist who had been a thorn in the side of the government both before and while he was imprisoned.

'Is that Clifford Allen?' he enquired of Boothroyd in an uncertain voice.

'It is,' Boothroyd confirmed. his face anxious. 'Prison treated him harshly, Leon. He lost more than two and a half stone in weight while inside, and is very sick. It is terrible to see so great a man suffer in the way Clifford Allen has. But he still has the fire, Leon. One good man like Clifford Allen is worth twenty irresponsible militants like Winston Churchill. Allen is a seeker after peace, whereas Churchill is a menace to the peace of the world.'

Leon was agreeing with Boothroyd when the latter was called away. Sitting down between strangers to enjoy an excellent meal, Leon listened to the political speeches afterwards. There was a long and extremely moving address by Clifford Allen, who, when referring to the suffering of conscientious objectors, made a point of placing that suffering a poor second in comparison with the men who had fought in the trenches. The fact that Allen was speaking to an assembly of conscientious objectors gained him Leon's admiration.

Though he agreed with most of what Clifford Allen and the other speakers said, Leon felt no spark of interest. Had Bruce Seldon been there he would have delivered an oration to inspire the listeners. It was Bruce who had battled in the political arena, and he would fight no more.

When the speeches were over and the socializing had begun, Leon searched in vain for a familiar face. Once he believed that he had spotted Johnny Cave, but it was an illusion. Beaten and broken by the army, Johnny Cave had breathed his last during a terrible night in France. The crowd was noisy with talk and laughter. It was split up into groups that were engaged in animated conversation. Having anticipated a fitting, sombre requiem, Leon was disappointed by a hedonistic festival.

A voice at his side observed, 'A collection of footprints, young sir.'

Turning to the speaker, a bespectacled, elderly man of distinguished appearance, Leon said, 'I'm afraid that I don't understand.'

'Michelangelo compared himself to God's footsteps in the mud,' the elderly man said. 'From the way you were surveying our friends, I wondered if that is how you see them.'

'I want to believe that man holds more potential than that,' Leon protested.

'I share your hope, my friend,' the man smiled, light reflecting from his spectacles to deny Leon a glimpse at what his eyes were saying. 'Which has me puzzled by your consternation.'

'I was wondering how many here are remembering the dead.'

'Ah, the dead.' The man wagged a finger like a schoolmaster praising a pupil for having raised a moot point. 'I once met a man who was of the opinion that we are the dead. He saw the living as the ghosts of those who had died at conception, and believed that we will be conceived into life at our deaths. I suppose there is considerable comfort in such a view, young sir.'

'But no evidence to support it,' Leon commented.

Laughing quietly, the elderly man put a hand on Leon's shoulder. 'Young sir, if evidence was a requirement there would be neither theology nor religion.'

'I had a friend with whom you could have debated for hours,' Leon smiled, liking his uninvited companion.

'*Had?*' the man asked sympathetically, and when Leon used a nod to confirm his use of the past tense, went on, 'Might I enquire if he was with the Society of Friends?'

'No, he was a Socialist.'

'And you, young sir, am I correct in judging you to be a Quaker?'

'Not any more,' Leon replied, harshly enough to deter the elderly man from continuing on the same theme.

'I see.' The man gave a little nod of his grey head. 'Whatever, you are the dynamic type needed in the vanguard of the movement if we are to rebuild society, a just and a fair society.'

'Not me,' Leon announced emphatically. 'All I want to do now is find work and lead a quiet life.'

'One man's revelation is another's anathema. We must follow our inner light, my friend, with that I agree. From your fine physique I take it that you once followed an occupation that demands prodigious strength?'

'I was a blacksmith. But I can find no work.'

'Would you consider any other kind of employment on a temporary basis?' the elderly man asked. 'Gruelling work in an iron foundry, perhaps?'

'Anything at all.'

Taking a notebook and pencil from his pocket, the grey-haired man wrote on the top page, tore it out of the book and held it out to Leon. 'There is the address of a foundry in Nine Elms Lane. If you care to present yourself there on Monday morning, I can guarantee that you will be taken on.'

'I thank you most kindly, sir,' a delighted Leon took the scrap of paper. 'Should we not meet again, may the Christ within be with you always and forever.'

Clasping Leon's hand, the elderly man said, 'We both have the word of God written on our souls, young sir, and I feel sure that we will meet again.'

Before Judith and she started up the dark, narrow stairs of the Hann house that evening, this had seemed like a good idea to Anne-Marie. Now that the time had come she wasn't so sure. Gladys had picked a time to arrange a visit when Walter Hann was out of town on business. With an urge to back out now, to abandon the mission at the eleventh hour, and certain that Judith felt the same way, Anne-Marie pushed on. Time was pressing. In a little over a month, at Eastertide, the town of Marshlee would officially celebrate the end of the war. On that day the war memorial would be unveiled on the green. Anne-Marie and Judith were calling on Lou Hann with the intention of having James Hann's name carved on the local cenotaph. How this was to be achieved they did not yet know.

Having neither seen nor met Mrs Hann, Anne-Marie and Judith didn't know what to expect. Different people had given descriptions of the baker's wife that covered a scale that had a sweetly benign, crippled woman at the bottom, and a foul-smelling, wicked witch at the top. Tapping lightly on the bedroom door, Anne-Marie took a deep breath as the moment of truth arrived.

Propped up, the invalid woman's body spread across the bed like a gigantic jelly wrapped in a human skin. Her layered chins drooped on her chest, her lips flopped loosely over toothless gums as she talked, while her eyes were little black beads glistening out of slits in the fat on each side of a surprisingly tiny nose.

Glancing around the room, Anne-Marie imagined Beth Marriott working in this room, caring for the sweating, gross woman in the bed. It was inappropriate employment for a young girl, to say the least. Could she have prevented the tragedy? Or would any intervention on her part have been looked upon as interference in family business? Unable to answer either of these

239

questions, Anne-Marie felt a shudder of guilt run through her, nonetheless.

'It's not often I get visitors,' Lou Hann said wheezingly.

The woman seemed so pleased at having them there that Anne-Marie felt terrible about the purpose of their visit. A sideways glance at Judith evinced that she was equally as discomfited.

'You are the vicar's daughter, aren't you?' the woman pointed the chubby finger of a trembling hand at Anne-Marie.

'Yes. I'm Anne-Marie Penny.'

'I thought as much. I've seen you pass by, when I used to be able to get to the window. But I don't know you.'

'I'm Judith Seldon,' Judith introduced herself. 'I'm head teacher here at Marshlee. My late husband used to hold that position: Bruce Seldon.'

'Oh yes, I've heard of him,' Lou Hann said in a way that suggested she had formed a definite opinion of Bruce, but wasn't prepared to state it.

'I don't want to upset you, Mrs Hann,' Judith began, 'but we have come to talk about James. He was a very good friend of ours.'

'He was my son,' Lou Hann said so pointedly that it dismissed their friendship with James as irrelevant.

Anne-Marie's unease at being there was churning inside of her to become a panic. If Lou Hann asked after Leon, Anne-Marie felt sure she would flee the room. Leon had been released from prison several months ago, but he hadn't been in touch. Not even his mother had heard from him. Remembering how disturbed he had been by something when she had visited him in prison, Anne-Marie had accepted that Leon would never return to Marshlee. She cited phantoms of the past as partially to blame for this, but the main reason had to be whatever was plaguing Leon. It was a cross he was finding too heavy to carry, yet he had refused to talk about it to her. Womanly intuition made her suspect that Hubert could answer some of the questions that had been nagging at her since going to Maidstone Prison. But you didn't speak the name of Leon Marriott at Farley Grange.

It was all academic now, for circumstances had forced her to get her life into perspective. Under pressure from her own parents, as well as the brigadier and Claudia, she had agreed that her engagement to Hubert be made public on 6 June, exactly four weeks before they left for London.

'Do you know what they are saying about your son, Mrs Hann?'

Hearing Judith put this question to the bedridden woman, Anne-Marie braced herself for an explosive response. A clock downstairs boomingly marked the hour. As if waiting for the reverberations to die away, Lou Hann delayed her answer. She was emitting a smell, an unidentifiable sweet odour that tempted Anne-Marie to breathe it in, and sickened her when she did.

'What are they saying about my James?' she asked. 'Surely no one in Marshlee would have a bad word to say about a boy who gave his life for his country?'

Having assumed that Walter Hann had reported the rumours about James to his wife, such a move being useful to cover his own involvement and guilt, Anne-Marie was at a loss when she discovered this wasn't the case. But Judith was determined to achieve what they had come here for. Anne-Marie winced as she heard her friend press on regardless.

'They are saying, Mrs Hann, that it was James's baby that Beth was carrying. As friends of James we know that isn't true, just as you, his mother, must know that it was a lie.'

Eyes closed, tears squeezing out between the swollen lids, Lou Hann started to cry. She made not a sound, but the great mounds of flesh quivered and occasionally jerked. Moved by a combination of pity and revulsion, Anne-Marie turned away. It took a callousness that she lacked to distress a woman so ill that she had been confined to her bed for years. Though keenly aware that it would be a betrayal of the memory of James, she was anxious to leave this room, to flee this dark and forbidding house. But Judith would not be detracted. She sat by the bed, outwardly unmoved.

'Not James, not my James, no, no, no . . .' Lou Hann began to moan, rocking her massive bulk from side to side in the bed.

Anne-Marie's heart skipped a beat as she listened to Judith apply pressure on the invalid. 'No, it wasn't James. We know who interfered with poor little Beth, and I think you also know, Mrs Hann.'

Muttering a few unintelligible words, Lou Hann then set up a long, wailing cry. It became a howl, the agonized cry of a wild animal caught in a trap. Shivering, Anne-Marie made to stand up, ready to run, but Judith put a firm hand on her shoulder to press her back down in her chair.

'Because of what folk believe about James, Mrs Hann,' Judith said, 'his name will be left off the Marshlee War Memorial. That isn't fair on your son, is it?'

There was more noisy crying from the invalid, but then she spluttered words wetly. 'I don't know what to do.'

'You know who it was,' Anne-Marie gasped in surprise. 'You know that your husband was responsible, Mrs Hann.'

A sudden terror gripped Lou Hann, instantly switching off her crying. Eyes pushing through rolls of pudgy fat to bulge out at them, she said, 'I can't live without him. Please, don't tell anyone. Walter is all I have left. If they take him away I'm finished.'

In complete sympathy with the frightened old woman, Anne-Marie turned an imploring look on her friend. 'We can't do this, Judith. What would this poor creature do without her husband to take care of her?'

'We have to consider James,' Judith reminded her.

'I know what Walter did was terribly wrong,' Lou Hann admitted, 'and he deserves to be taken to account. But I have done nothing. Do you think James would wish you to punish me?'

'That's true, Judith,' Anne-Marie made the superfluous statement, for both her friend and she knew beyond all doubt what James's answer would be if asked to choose between his name on the cenotaph and his mother.

'But we can't just ignore this,' Judith objected.

'I am not asking you to overlook it forever. All I want is that you leave things as they are until I'm dead and gone. What you decide to do after that is no concern of mine,' the fat woman said, the effort in making so long a speech exhausting her.

'That's a reasonable compromise, Judith,' Anne-Marie said persuasively. 'We can always have James's name included at a later date.'

'I suppose it's the only way,' Judith conceded with a shrug.

'We will bow to your wishes, Mrs Hann. No mention of this will be made while you are alive,' Anne-Marie told the bedridden woman.

'Do I have your promise?'

'You have our promise,' Anne-Marie assured her.

'Both of you?'

Anne-Marie and Lou Hann both looked to Judith for her answer. Giving the matter some thought, Judith said, 'You have my promise.'

Standing more than six and a half feet in height and built like a latter-day Samson, the mulatto took on an aggressive stance in front of him. It was one of those inconsequential disputes; that men who toil together use petty dislikes and jealousies to blow up out of proportion. Leon was aware that if he permitted the argument to continue the original cause would be forgotten before the fighting started.

Months of hard work in the foundry had restored his strength and put the bulk and elasticity back into his muscles. The heat from the fires had trimmed every ounce of fat from him so that his physique was a superb example of manhood. His mind, fractured by the army and prison, had healed, too. Originally having felt anger towards this belligerent half-caste, he was now perfectly calm.

'If you'll just step aside,' he suggested, reaching for his jacket, the altercation with the dark giant having caused him to reach a long-overdue decision.

Unmoving, his heavily muscled arms folded across his chest, the mulatto taunted him, 'What if I was to call you a coward, matey?'

'You certainly wouldn't be the first to do so,' Leon replied laconically.

In anticipation of a fight, the other men in the foundry stopped work. They stood around, watching and waiting. The mulatto was a trouble-maker, and they believed that the more agile, and most probably just as strong, Leon, could take the bully.

This was an opinion that Leon shared, but had no interest in putting to the test. Turning, he walked away in the direction of the rear door, a massive sense of relief putting a spring into his step. Although still haunted by the knowledge that he had killed a man, he had now extinguished the fire of violence that ill treatment as a conscientious objector had ignited in him.

Leaving a shocked, disappointed silence behind him, Leon went out of the foundry. Crossing the yard he entered the office. Tod Geddes, the owner of the foundry, looked up from where he sat at his desk. Ash from a cigarette in his mouth spilled down his waistcoat like dirty dandruff. A gruff, insular man, Geddes had taken Leon on without hesitation and had treated him fairly since.

'What you doing here, Marriott?' the owner asked.

'I've come for my time. I'm calling it a day, Mr Geddes.'

Frowning, Geddes rubbed the knuckles of his right hand across the dark stubble on his chin. The rasping noise was surprisingly loud. 'What's wrong? If you're having trouble with that mulatto, then I can fix it.'

'It's nothing to do with him,' Leon answered. 'It's just time I moved on. That man who sent me here, is he a Quaker?'

'Edward Grubb. Yes, he's with the Society of Friends, as I am,' Geddes replied. 'Why do you ask?'

'I want to speak to him.'

Writing with a fountain pen, Geddes then passed the paper to Leon. 'You'll find Edward there.'

'Thank you, Mr Geddes,' Leon said, pleased to have the address.

Opening a drawer, Geddes took out a battered black metal cash box that had gold lines painted on it, and placed it on the desk. He began to count money, taking it from the tin with one hand to place it in his other hand.

'I don't want to lose a good worker like you, Marriott. Are you sure about this? Seems to me there's less work here in London now than there was when I gave you a start.'

'I'm not staying in London,' Leon said. 'I'm going home.'

'Well, here's what I owe you.' Geddes passed over the money he had counted out. 'I hope you know what you're doing.'

'So do I,' Leon said, meaning it with all his heart.

Twelve

They rode slowly through Marshlee on an evening in the first spring of peace. They passed little cottages, clothed in Virginia creeper, the windows glowing redly in the rays of a lowering sun. Along the banks of the swelling and darkened river, where the townsfolk strolled on Sunday afternoons and Beth Marriott had died, the horse-chestnut trees were proudly regaining their leaves. In the air was a happy restlessness stirred up gently by the promise of summer. Anne-Marie saw it as an evening to be stored in the mind, treasured as a golden memory. But she knew that, like yesterday's newspaper headlines, it would soon perish under a welter of new sensations.

As a precaution, pre-planned between Gladys and herself, they rode with Hubert between them, keeping their horses in tight to his. An artificial leg made being on horseback precarious. Anne-Marie was sure that he had noticed their strategy, but he made no comment. Hubert had every reason to be proud of his achievement in getting back into the saddle. From a window at Farley Grange, Anne-Marie had seen him try and try again over long hours. His biggest challenge had been to master mounting on the 'wrong' side due to his disability. Often Hubert had fallen, so heavily that he must have hurt himself. But every time he got up, frustrated but undaunted, to try again.

Hubert had also struggled back into public life. At first, acutely conscious of his peculiarly shoulder-swaying, leg-dragging gait, he came to accept it once those around him had become accustomed to seeing him walk. Occasionally he would revert to being embarrassed when there were strangers around, but otherwise he was coping excellently. The whole of Marshlee regarded Hubert as the ideal choice to unveil the war memorial on the day victory was to be celebrated. The only other name put before that council had been that of Clarence Crandal. With the brigadier abstaining, the council had voted unanimously for Hubert to perform the task.

The self-important Crandal had afterwards declared that he was pleased to have lost out to the heroic Captain Lytton. He hadn't convinced anyone, least of all himself.

In addition to having ridden horses all his life, Hubert, Anne-Marie had recognized, was determined to get back into the saddle because his false leg was unnoticeable when he was on horseback. He often said, 'Up on a horse I am once again the equal of all other men.'

'Give it a season or two, Son, and you'll rejoin the Hunt,' the brigadier had predicted.

Hubert, Anne-Marie, and most probably the brigadier, were starkly aware that Hubert would never again have that kind of mobility. Yet, as much as she would have liked Hubert to be whole again, this was something that gladdened Anne-Marie's heart. She had always detested hunting, and would have hesitated to marry a man prepared to join in what she saw as a barbaric practice. The wise Judith had pointed out, in no way maliciously, that the fact Hubert *couldn't* ride with the hounds was very different to Hubert deciding that he *wouldn't* go hunting.

Anne-Marie hadn't needed her friend to raise this distinction. She was already aware of it – and other things that the Lyttons accepted as the norm but to which she had an aversion. The anomalies were due in some part to her having been raised as the daughter of a clergyman, but largely came from a personal philosophy that she had begun to shape at puberty. As a result she had found it easy to embrace the pacifist views of Leon, James Hann, and the Seldons when the war had begun.

With minor incidents, a snatch of conversation, or a barbed jibe at Farley Grange temporarily alienating her from Hubert and his parents, she had reasoned that in marriage, just as in life, a certain amount of adaptation was necessary. These, at most times insignificant differences, were far outweighed by Anne-Marie's admiration for Hubert. 'An indomitable spirit bred down through generations of fighting men', was the brigadier's proud boast about his son, and there was no one in Marshlee who had cause to disagree with him.

'The pair of you will be sacrificing so much in moving to London,' Gladys observed, as they moved away from a river that was reflecting the image of dark pines and bright yellow birches.

As they headed towards the church steeple beyond which lay the grounds of Farley Grange, Anne-Marie felt sorry for Gladys Plummer. Widowed, alone and very lonely in young years designed for happiness, Gladys dreaded the time of more loss when Anne-Marie and Hubert left her. In the beginning, official notice that Alexander was 'missing' made her live in hope.

'I have this feeling – no, it is more than that,' she used to tell Anne-Marie and Judith, 'that Alex has been held prisoner by the Germans, and he'll be home one day soon.'

Hubert, aware of how traumatic Gladys's ultimate disappointment would be, had not been prepared to allow her sanguine belief to continue. In the only reference Anne-Marie had heard him make to his time in France, he had tenderly told Gladys that he had not been present when Alexander had died, but he had it on good authority that he had been killed outright.

'We'll come home regularly, you can be sure of that,' Hubert assured Gladys now. Anne-Marie had noticed how considerate he was to Gladys, and how the widow had come to depend on Hubert. In a kindly, diffident way he was doing his best to be something of a substitute for Alexander. 'I'm never likely to get used to London. Anne-Marie has more experience of it than I.'

'To be honest, we were so busy that I didn't really notice where I was most of the time,' Anne-Marie said. She was about to add that she'd had a purpose in life then, which would have amounted to a confession that this was no longer the case.

With a shock she realized that it wasn't just a matter of not wanting to worry Hubert. To hear herself admit it aloud would depress her. For months she had been achingly aware that something was missing in her life. Initially attributing it to an anti-climax after four years of war, she had recently accepted that wasn't the cause. Had it been, then passing time would have brought about a remission of her distress, not an exacerbation.

'Have you decided what you will do, Gladys?' Hubert enquired, referring to plans the widow might be making for the future. Gladys, who was rich enough not to have to earn money, was still doing charitable work in Marshlee. One of her most successful acts of mercy had been to gradually, very gradually, coax Elsie Marriott back into something approaching a normal life. Gladys also spent hours making life more tolerable for Lou Hann, whose health was failing fast.

'I just can't make up my mind,' Gladys answered. 'Everyone tells me that I should be thinking constructively, and I suppose I agree with them. The trouble is that nothing really interests me.'

'All in good time,' Anne-Marie said, some crocuses growing abundantly round the bole of a tree catching her eye. She would pick some to take to Elsie Marriott later that evening. She reined in, saying, 'You two carry on. I'll catch up with you. Please ride carefully, Hubert.'

Dismounting, Anne-Marie dropped to one knee to pluck the colourful little flowers. Elsie Marriott, who would never fully recover from the death of her daughter and the uncertainty of what had happened to her son, always welcomed a visit from Anne-Marie, and the flowers would bring at least a little bright-ness into her life. They would talk of Leon and Beth as if they were both still there, and the trauma of the past few years was a myth. Having to revert to facing the truth was upsetting for them both.

In the tree above her, a bird chirruped a song in praise of the beautiful evening. A squirrel heading for home scurried past her to climb the tree with admirable agility. Kneeling, Anne-Marie was glad she had stopped to gather flowers. She was in a timeless zone, away from the pressures and the decision-making that demanded a certain urgency. She was able to view her life with a startling clarity. She scolded herself that by harbouring doubts she was being both ungrateful and ungracious. The Lytton family couldn't have been kinder to her, and service in the war had smoothed Hubert's arrogant edges. Now he was as considerate as his father, but untainted by the war-mongering belligerence that bubbled just below the surface in the brigadier.

Amid the after-war emotional debris, with relationships ended forever and grief the order of the day, Anne-Marie was among the fortunate minority. It would be a woeful mistake for her to lose Hubert Lytton by seeking the indefinable something that she believed was absent from and vital to their relationship.

Stretching an arm to pluck a flower, she let out an involuntary, muffled gasp of fear as two booted feet stepped close to her hands. They were brown, dust-covered boots. Anne-Marie's mind raced. It could be a harmless traveller, lost and weary, needing to ask directions. Or it might be far more dangerous, perhaps an untamed half-bred gypsy intent on rape. She took heart in the knowledge that Hubert and Gladys could not have gone far. A scream from her and they would come galloping back. Knowing that she was in danger, Hubert wouldn't give a thought to his own safety, to the very real possibility of him being unseated.

Fearfully raising her head to take in worn, faded trousers up as far as the man's knees, she determinedly tilted her head back further. With a start she recognized who was standing there. A name burst from her in a strangled cry.

'Leon!'

Trying to still her mind, Judith walked between the desks to set writing for the children to continue with while she spoke with the Reverend Penny. He had arrived with the astonishing news that Leon was back in Marshlee. According to the clergyman, the young blacksmith had walked all the way from London. What would his return mean to the town? Doubtless most people would respond badly and in ignorance, subjecting Leon to virulent abuse. How would Leon's return affect the marriage plans of Anne-Marie and Hubert Lytton? Head spinning with possibilities and probabilities, Judith returned to her desk and Paulton Penny.

He was sitting on a child-size chair she had given him because she had no other seat to offer. It was the chair she kept beside her desk for when a pupil required individual tuition. When the lanky clergyman had first sat he'd made such a long-legged comical figure that the children had laughed. Already filled with respect for the Reverend Penny, Judith had admired him even more when he had laughed at himself with the children.

'Does Anne-Marie know that he is back?'

'Yes,' the clergyman answered. 'She was the first to inform me.'

'I've no wish to pry into your family business, Reverend Penny, but as Anne-Marie's closest friend, I wonder what this will do to her plans to marry Hubert Lytton?'

'What can it do, Mrs Seldon?' Penny replied with a question of his own. 'Let us look at the situation. Captain Lytton is a war hero, a member of a prominent and influential family. Anne-Marie will be marrying into her own class, so to speak. That may sound ludicrously snobbish to you.'

'It certainly does,' Judith gave an honest answer. 'You would neither expect nor want me to be other than straight with you, Reverend Penny.'

'Indeed not. I find straight talking to be one of your many admirable traits, Mrs Seldon.'

'If I didn't know you better I would suspect that you have an ulterior motive in flattering a widow,' she told him, fun twinkling in her eyes.

'You overlook the disadvantages of my being fifty years too late and wearing the wrong sort of collar,' he said parrying her joke with one of his own.

As he did so, the stern set of his face was dissolved by a smile. Not for the first time she saw a side of the local vicar that probably none of his parishioners had ever been privileged to witness. Judith thought it unfortunate that through the years his public image had concealed the private person, who was truly a man of God. With a need for revenge strong in her, Judith had wanted to take up his offer to find out how Bruce had died. But in his quiet way he had explained that revenge was self-destroying, and that it was enough to know that the army had killed Bruce, without knowing exactly how.

'My duty as a father requires me to consider this matter logically, Mrs Seldon,' Penny said, becoming his old rigid self again. 'The very fact that Marriott walked the one hundred and forty miles or so from London says that he is penniless or next to penniless. Added to that, is that he has served a lengthy term in prison, and has been dishonourably discharged from the army.'

Judith felt pain but not bitterness at hearing this uninspiring assessment of the staunch friend of her late husband and herself. If it wasn't for the injustice of the stigma attached to James Hann, it was easy for her to consider right then that Bruce and James were better off dead than they would be here facing what the brave Leon Marriott had come back to Marshlee to deal with.

'But Leon is a strong, determined fellow, Reverend Penny,' she argued. 'Are you really saying that he has no future?'

'I don't see any possible way in which he can re-enter our community, Mrs Seldon. Perhaps he would be wise to go back to London and seek a career in politics. But he would be of the exiled left-wing. The Independent Labour Party is already extinct, and it won't be long before the Labour Party wanders into the wilderness, too. They will remain there a good deal longer than forty days and forty nights. Revolution will never happen in this country.'

'Poor Leon,' Judith sighed, before saying musingly, 'Forgive me for straying into your terminology, Reverend Penny, but I wonder who will cast the first stone?'

'I'm afraid that it's already been cast, quite literally.' The vicar's face showed sadness. 'Young Marriott stayed with his mother last night, and I regret to say that every single window in the house was smashed.'

'Oh, no,' Judith cried.

'As if that poor woman hasn't suffered enough.'

'If Leon remains in Marshlee, Reverend Penny, he is going to get hurt, or worse. When school is over for the day, I will try to find him and suggest he lies low before leaving town.'

'You'll be too late, Mrs Seldon.' The clergyman shook his head wonderingly from side to side. 'I have to give that boy credit for a specific kind of courage, no matter how misguided. He reopened his forge first thing this morning.'

Coming home had been tough. Meeting Anne-Marie in the woods had eased things in one way, but added to his woes in another. The barrier he had put between them on her prison visit was still there, though no longer necessary. They had conversed in the over-polite manner of strangers. When Anne-Marie had swung up into the saddle to ride after her friends, Leon was sure that she was as relieved to go as he was to have her leave.

Their disturbing meeting was still troubling him when he had walked into town. While still obsessed by guilt over killing the German soldier, his intention had been to briefly visit his mother. But his second meeting with Edward Grubb had altered that.

'I said when we talked at Central Hall that I felt certain we would meet again,' Grubb said welcoming Leon into his home.

'I'm glad that you've been proved right,' Leon had replied, 'as I need your advice, perhaps help would be a better word.'

'As a good Quaker should, I try to emulate Christ, but I must warn that I am a complete failure in the miracle department,' the Quaker said, half in truth, half in joke.

'I don't think I need anything so extreme as a miracle,' Leon explained, though uncertain.

Leon, who appreciated the clever mind and altruistic outlook of the Quaker, had been surprised to learn he had known Anne-Marie in the war years. Knowing this made it easier for Leon to be taught by Grubb how to come to terms with the killing of the German trooper. Grubb had assured him that, though it may take a little while for his mind to adjust, his faith would return when it did. Sceptical at the time, Leon had since been delighted to discover that both of the predictions made by Grubb had proved to be true. Now his plan was to remain in Marshlee and reopen his business.

He had stood at the start of the main street for a long time. Having expected his homecoming would be an overwhelmingly emotional experience, Leon couldn't understand why he was completely unmoved. There was an emptiness, as if he was about

253

to enter death. Marshlee was everything and nothing both at the same time. The town was a black hole – zero.

His feelings had coldly mocked him, eluded him, leaving him devoid of motivation. Then, in the manner in which a forgotten name pops unbidden into the mind, so had his emotions returned.

Moved close to tears, Leon had striven to imagine his friends hurrying to meet him. He struggled to see James Hann's slow smile, to hear Bruce Seldon quote the great thinkers, to have Beth waiting for him at home, making sure that Kipsy was included in the cuddle he gave her. He remembered the impromptu recruiting campaign when they had stood together and defiant on this road. Maybe they hadn't been innocent on that day, but they had been naïve, which had to be the second cousin of innocence.

The loved faces didn't appear by magic. Walking to his mother's cottage on dragging feet, he passed people without seeing them. But some of them noticed him. When he was in the house with the painfully thin, haggard, white-haired woman who had once been his mother in his arms, the first rock had shattered a window.

It had become worse. Eventually every window in the house was smashed. Though he had dashed out into the street, the culprits ran off into the darkness. Passing a sleepless night, he had risen early to make breakfast for his mother. There was an eerie, vacant feeling to the house. Several times he thought he'd heard Beth, and had a joke ready for her when she would appear.

But his sister now existed only inside of his head. Beth had gone forever. With his mother still in bed, Leon sat at the kitchen table, head in hands, and cried for the first time since he could remember. He wept not only for Beth, for Bruce, and for James, but for what once was but could never be again.

When it was over, he felt more at peace with himself than he had for years. Glad to leave the house of sad memories, he walked through the deserted streets of Marshlee to his forge.

The day started better than Leon had dared hope. There had only been time to gaze at and fondle the trappings of the forge that he had missed so much, when Ronald Starza, a smallholder, brought in a plough to be repaired. Starza had greeted Leon as if he had never been away.

Next to arrive was Les Sanders, the boy who worked for quarry owner Tom Macby, trundling a wheelbarrow filled with pickaxes and other tools for sharpening.

With irons heating in the fire and sweat on his brow, Leon was back in business. Feeling a kind of spiritual and physical renaissance, he heard the roaring of a motor-car engine and an anguished squeal of brakes. Edward Lee, passing in his hire car, had noticed that the door of the forge was open. He came running in to embrace Leon.

No sooner had his old friend gone, the hire car groaning in protest as an elated Edward Lee drove it away too fast, than Owen Newgate did his usual slow walk to enter the forge.

'I've three horses needs to be shod, young Leon,' said Newgate, who had a haulage contract with the Plummer flour mill. 'Can you fix me up tomorrow morning?'

'How would first thing suit you, Mr Newgate?'

'That's fine,' Newgate said, turning to add as he was leaving, 'It's real good to have you back, young Leon.'

'Thank you,' Leon said.

Never having anticipated such a reception, to have so much work come his way right from the start, Leon was pleased. It was a great feeling that lasted only until he looked out of the door to see Brigadier Lytton and Mayor Raymond Plummer, both of them stern of face, striding resolutely towards the forge.

'Lou Hann breathed her last this afternoon.'

Gladys blushed with shame at her own lack of respect after coming into the schoolhouse to excitedly make this announcement. An eager Anne-Marie exchanged glances with Judith. This was what they had been waiting for, but to start any action too quickly would be like coffin-jumping. The knowledge they held would shake the town to its roots. Contrite now, Gladys apologized to Lou Hann rather than them.

'I didn't mean it to sound like that,' she stammered.

'We know that, Gladys.' Judith stood to put an arm round her, 'I have a shrewd suspicion Mrs Hann would be pleased we are free to clear the name of her son.'

They both turned expectantly to Anne-Marie. Now that they were able to ensure that James's name was included on the Marshlee cenotaph, the enormity of what they had to do to make that happen made Anne-Marie shudder.

'What are we going to do, and when?' Anne-Marie asked quickly, wanting it to be a joint decision.

Judith paced about the room, hugging herself with folded arms as she said, 'When something like this comes up I try to think on it the way Bruce would have. If we release the story of Walter Hann in a small way, then as it spreads it will be regarded as pure gossip and wither away. I'm all for it being announced during the celebrations.'

'Do you think your father will do it, Anne-Marie?' Gladys enquired.

Holding up her hands to prevent any further talk, Anne-Marie replied, 'If I as much as mention this to my father there would be no celebration. He would deal with it in his own way, ensuring that the town suffered as little as possible.'

'With the consequence of Walter Hann getting away almost scot free,' Judith commented bitterly.

'Exactly,' Anne-Marie nodded. 'not because Dad would support Hann, but he would have the benefit of everyone else in mind.'

'Which isn't what we want. There is no taste in nothing,' Judith declared. 'I feel strongly enough to stand up and denounce Walter Hann myself.'

'And lose your job in the process,' Anne-Marie warned of the likely outcome of such a move.

'It would almost be worth it.'

'It wouldn't,' Anne-Marie said firmly. 'We have to do this right, without any repercussions.'

'That's agreed, but it should happen at the victory celebration, Anne-Marie,' Judith insisted.

'It would have the most impact then, but how to do it is the question,' Anne-Marie concurred.

'Hubert!'

An idea came suddenly to Gladys, who shouted the name.

'You're not suggesting that we ask Captain Lytton to help us?' Judith gawped at Gladys in utter disbelief. 'James started out as a conscientious objector, Gladys. The poor lad was ever a reluctant soldier.'

Gladys gave an emphatic shake of her head to invalidate Judith's argument. 'You haven't been in Hubert's company since he came back from the war, Judith. He's a changed man, honestly. I do believe that you could persuade him to speak up for James, Anne-Marie, don't you?'

'I'm not sure,' a dubious Anne-Marie said, horrified at the very thought of putting such a proposition to Hubert.

'I'm surprised you came alone, Reverend Penny,' Leon remarked cuttingly, leaning against a bench because he had no work to do. 'The brigadier and the mayor have already been here to do most of the dirty work.'

'I find your implication that I would put my hand to anything underhand as offensive, my son,' the clergyman objected without malice.

'Whatever,' Leon shrugged. 'They'd only just left when Starza sheepishly arrived to take back his work, and Maeby called in to pick up his tools and say I could not expect any more business with him. I had Owen Newgate bringing horses in for shoeing tomorrow, but I don't suppose that will happen now.'

'And you think Brigadier Lytton and Raymond Plummer had something to do with that?'

With a short laugh of disgust, Leon answered, 'I know that they did. From what I remember of you, you always sided the brigadier.'

'People change, my son, even clerics,' the clergyman said with humility. 'I bear you no ill will, and I am not a party to whatever others have subjected you to.'

'They told me to leave Marshlee, Reverend Penny. It was plain that I will be tarred and feathered, although they didn't put it into so many words, if I don't get out quickly.'

'I regret that you were subjected to that, but I feared it would happen. In fact I have come here in peace to suggest, with the kindest of intentions, that you would be wise to reconsider your position.'

Looking past the clergyman, out into the street where Marshlee life was going on almost as he remembered it. Leon said quietly, 'There were many times during the war that I wondered if I was doing the right thing, Reverend Penny, and on more than one occasion I came close to capitulation. But I didn't then, and I won't now. I still stand by my principles. Should another war begin tomorrow, then I will do exactly the same as before.'

'I wasn't referring to your pacifism,' the clergyman put in quickly, going on to astound Leon. 'In fact, I'm prepared to admit that I was wrong. You, Bruce Seldon and the others had grasped reality, and we reacted badly because you represented a threat to our illusions. I have not spoken of this to anyone before, my son, but it shames me to contemplate the time it took me to recognize the bane of patriotism and that no man, a man of the cloth in particular, should follow a flag.'

'It takes a big man to admit something like that,' an impressed Leon said.

Shaking a sad head, Penny disagreed. 'That's not true, my son. There is no achievement in a man learning that he has done a foolish thing. The true victory comes to a man when he learns that he is nothing but a fool.'

'That's a harsh bit of self-judgement, Reverend Penny.'

'But of vital importance,' the clergyman emphasized. 'Now, I came to suggest that the best thing you can do for everyone concerned—'

'Your daughter especially,' Leon put in mildly.

'Yes, I confess that Anne-Marie is uppermost in my mind. You won't be given a chance should you stay in Marshlee. Bigots have long memories and vicious tendencies. There are men here who will hound you, deprive you of a living, rob you of all happiness. Go somewhere and make a fresh start. Anne-Marie and myself will take care of your mother.'

'There are certain other considerations involved,' Leon said.

'I am not unmindful of that, which is why I would like to invite you to dinner at the vicarage, perhaps tomorrow evening? Anne-Marie will be there. I feel that we will all gain from a constructive discussion.'

Staggered by the invitation, Leon took a while to answer. Then he said, 'I'd like that. Thank you.'

'Very good. I shall look forward to it, my son.'

The clergyman was at the door, ready to leave, when Leon made an observation that made Penny pause.

'I have to say, with the greatest respect,' Leon began hesitantly, 'that you are not what I expected the Reverend Paulton Penny to be.'

Locking glances with Leon, the Reverend Penny's severe expression did not change for a long time. Then the old, lined face did a gradual softening before it shaped itself into a genuinely pleased smile.

'And I must return the compliment by saying that you are not what I expected Leon Marriott to be.'

Stepping back into the forge, the Reverend Penny shook Leon warmly by the hand.

They moved away from the graveside making small talk the way mourners, frightened by the dead, remind themselves that they are alive. The sky had quickly greyed and now a light drizzle fell as a gloomy mist. Why did the sun never seem to shine on a burial, even an interment of the righteous?

Judith linked arms with Gladys, pleased that she had paid her last respects to a woman she had met only once. She had really been there for James. Looking over to where a sagging Walter Hann was being comforted by a number of Marshlee's business-folk, she felt hypocritical.

'Did you notice, Judith,' Gladys asked, 'that the vicar made not one reference to James? That was terrible, not including her son.'

'Anne-Marie told me about that. Her father fought to acknow-ledge James in the service, but Walter Hann forbad it.'

'What sort of a father can he be?' Gladys queried. 'I suppose that he also insisted that the eulogy contained no mention of James?'

'With Brigadier Lytton reading it, Walter Hann wouldn't need to,' Judith said cynically.

That was true. Despite the eulogy at the graveside being a moving tribute to a woman who had spent so many years of her life housebound, the absence of any word about Lou Hann's dead son spoilt it for Judith. She didn't doubt but that the brigadier had delighted in making sure that a one-time conscientious objector be excluded from the funeral.

As they mingled with the other mourners making their straggling way to the parish hall, Judith pondered on why Hubert Lytton hadn't attended. His father had been pushing him before the public, and this had been a missed opportunity. She knew that Anne-Marie would be with Elsie Marriott on an occasion that held many reminders for Beth and Leon's mother. Leon had, of course, stayed away. She had hoped to bump into him, keen to have a chat as Judith had not seen Leon since his return to Marshlee.

Inside the hall, Judith and Gladys each took a daintily cut sandwich from a tray being passed round. The mourners had split up into groups. The tradespeople talking business, the less wealthy enjoying gossip. Fittingly grave of face, Walter Hann stood nodding his head repeatedly as a woman dressed all in black stood close to impart what was probably advice on how to cope with being a widower.

Raymond Plummer, holding a plate high against his chest and bending his head forward vulture-like to bite at a sandwich, was looking in the direction of his daughter-in-law. Of late, by what appeared to be a natural process rather than a planned move, Gladys had been drifting away from Plummer and closer to Judith and Anne-Marie.

Judith fretted Gladys. They were both young widows, but she had her work at the school, something that encapsulated enough of Bruce to sustain her, while Gladys had nothing to cling on to.

'Not long to go to the big day,' Judith heard Clarence Crandal exclaim pompously.

'We have to attain the ultimate,' Raymond Plummer was saying, 'the perfect blending of joy and solemnity. We have to jolly our people into forgetting the horrors of war, while at the same time remembering our illustrious dead.'

Covertly watching the two men as she stood with Gladys, Judith saw Crandal take a furtive look around before bending his head closer to Plummer. The council clerk lowered his voice, but Judith could still catch his words, and was upset by them.

'More than a few folk have approached me, Mr Mayor. They fear that our thanksgiving will be marred, even ruined, by the return of this Marriott fellow.'

'Then you can put their minds at ease, Mr Crandal,' Raymond Plummer said in the confident voice he used for speeches. 'The name of my son is on the war memorial that Captain Lytton, disabled in war, is to unveil. It would be a gross insult to have an outright coward present.'

'I agree most heartily, Mr Mayor, but how can we be sure that it won't happen?'

Gladys started to speak to Judith, who put her hand on her arm to stop her. Keeping her breathing shallow so as not to miss a word, Judith waited for Plummer's reply. When it came she shivered.

'Don't lose a minute's sleep over it, Mr Crandal,' a grinning Plummer advised. 'There's nothing here in Marshlee for Leon Marriott, the brigadier and myself have seen to that. He'll be gone from here before the victory celebrations, and gone for good. I promise you.'

'Thank you.' Anne-Marie gave a little sigh as she expressed her gratitude, turning her head to peer at Leon in the scant moonlight that filtered through the trees. 'You are not angry?'

'No, not angry,' he replied reflectively. 'Perhaps confused – uncertain.'

'Disappointed?'

'Of course.'

'So am I,' Anne-Marie agreed, 'but it would only have made matters so much worse, complicated everything so terribly.'

As if they weren't already too complicated for her to get to grips with. The evening at the vicarage had been a pleasant one. There had been a convivial ambience at the dinner-table that had both pleased and astonished her. The Reverend Paulton Penny, throughout her life a clergyman first and a father second, had been wonderful. At first, the talk had been general, and then it had narrowed to Leon's position in Marshlee. Though she was aware that it was breaking his heart, Leon had accepted that old hatreds may have at one time died, but had now undergone a terrible resurrection: he could not stay in the town.

Though it hurt her as much as Leon, she knew he'd had no argument against her father's well-meant point that he had nothing to offer Anne-Marie. It had seemed cold and business-like, similar to the making of an arranged marriage. Yet it wasn't anything of the sort. Anne-Marie had genuine feelings for Hubert, and only the return of Leon had caused her to reconsider her wedding plans.

The discussion and the decision made at the vicarage had been easy without any of the stiffness she and Leon had experienced when meeting in the woods the night he had come home. In contrast, something warm and really special had flowed between them. This last walk together, the chance to say goodbye, had received her father's blessing.

Everything had taken a bewildering turn when they had reached the wood and went down a small, twisting path. With the moonlight cut off, Anne-Marie had caught her foot against a molehill and stumbled into a tree.

Shaken out of proportion to the trivial incident, she had cried out, 'Leon!'

'Take my hand, Anne-Marie.'

She felt his firm grip, pulling her towards him. Then the mix-up in Anne-Marie's head brought on by her half-fall, turned everything into a blur. She was lying beside him on the ground and they were kissing passionately. Underneath she felt the cool grass, her elbows pressed against knobbly roots, and in her back the sharp pressure of a stone. It was the intense hurt caused by that stone which had saved them from making a terrible mistake.

The pain between her shoulder blades made her push Leon away. The movement brought them to their senses. Standing, Leon had helped her to her feet. He was contrite, as embarrassed as a man who has made an unwelcome pass after reading the signs wrong. This wasn't so. Anne-Marie was aware that all her signals had been inviting. When he had tried to apologize she had insisted that she was just as much to blame as he for what had happened, or had almost happened.

Coming out of the wood they stopped by the stile which she would climb to enter the Farley Grange estate. She hadn't hidden from Leon that she was going to see Hubert when they parted.

In the brightness of the moon she pulled the bottom of her dress round, making a face as she looked down to examine it. 'Grass stains.'

'What will you do?' Leon was concerned for her.

'I think they'll wash out of this material all right.'

'That wasn't my meaning,' Leon said. 'I meant how will you explain the stains when you get to the Lyttons' place?'

'I don't have to explain myself to them,' she assured Leon, at the same time proving that she was still very much her own woman. Then she asked, 'Can you tell me now what you couldn't tell me at Maidstone?'

'It's no longer important, Anne-Marie.'

'When will you leave?' she enquired sadly.

'Tomorrow night.' She saw his hand reaching for hers, and she drew back a little. 'Can I kiss you goodbye?'

Her body quivered with desire for him, but she managed a firm reply. 'I think that would be dangerous.'

'Then can I see you again before I go?'

This was becoming more difficult for Anne-Marie. Everything had seemed simple, clear-cut, when they had talked with her parents at the vicarage. Their emotions had been on the periphery then, now they were churning at the centre of their highly charged relationship. She knew that she had to end this quickly or they would both become lost.

'That would be even more perilous,' she told him, turning away and climbing over the stile.

Anne-Marie hurried away without saying goodbye or looking back. She could sense that Leon was standing there in the night, waiting for her to turn. To give way would be to let both of them down. Steeling herself, she kept staring rigidly ahead as she quickened her pace.

'It's out of the question,' Hubert Lytton said with annoyance, if not anger, in his tone. 'I am shocked that Anne-Marie asked me. It's probably no more than malicious gossip.'

'What if it's not, Hubert?' Gladys asked, unafraid.

'If it isn't, then I am not prepared to ruin the day, not just for Walter Hann, but for every man, woman and child in Marshlee by making so horrible an announcement, Gladys.'

With Anne-Marie in town engaged in some preparations with her father for tomorrow's celebrations, Gladys had accompanied Hubert on one of the long walks designed to strengthen his remaining leg. Now they sat in the drawing-room at Farley Grange, drinking homemade lemonade. Having seized the opportunity to broach the subject of denouncing Walter Hann, Gladys hadn't known that Anne-Marie had already spoken to Hubert about it.

'We will find another way,' Gladys told him, not as a threat but in the hope of swaying him.

Hubert stood to make his awkward way across to the window. Looking out, he shrugged and said, 'You must do as you think fit, Gladys. Even if I did subscribe to this ridiculous character blacking, which I most certainly don't, it would still be a case of horses for courses. Unveiling the cenotaph deserves a great solemnity, Gladys. When doing the honours tomorrow, I would not consider even for one moment announcing the betrothal of Anne-Marie and myself; so I wouldn't besmear the proceedings with this ridiculous conjecture about a respected businessman.'

'I agree that it is a solemn occasion, which is all the more reason for James Hann to be included.' Gladys refused to be put off.

'I've accepted that it will take me some time to wean Anne-Marie from the doctrine of those she had the misfortune to mix with in the past, but you disappoint me, Gladys,' Hubert said wearily. 'I wouldn't expect you, the widow of an officer and a gentleman, to be waving a banner for one of that wishy-washy crowd.'

Leon made a diversion on leaving town. Very conscious that he was tempting fate, he passed through the grounds of Farley Grange in the hope of meeting Anne-Marie going to or from the house. After a harrowing, tear-filled farewell with his mother, he suspecting that he would never see her again, she convinced that this was so, he had left home at ten o'clock on what was a dark night. Leaden clouds were packed tight in the sky, and the air was uncomfortably humid. Distraught at having to leave, Leon's short-term plan was to go back to London.

As he went behind an avenue of trees flanking the drive leading to the house, Leon's pulse quickened when he heard approaching hoofbeats. It could well be Anne-Marie, who was an ardent equestrian. Standing behind a tree. it was so dark that Leon knew he could only hope to identify her from a silhouette as the horse went by.

The pounding hoofs came closer, and the head of the horse was level to where he stood when a mighty flash of lightning turned the darkness as bright as day. Close behind it came a deafening clap of thunder.

Screeching in terror, the horse reared up high on its back legs. Instinctively, Leon leapt out from behind the tree to grab the animal's head and swing with his full weight to bring it back down. Quick though he was, he wasn't in time to save the rider, who slid off the back of the horse to land with a thud on the drive.

Battered by rain as the heavens suddenly opened, Leon, fearing that it was Anne-Marie and that she was badly hurt, hurried over to peer down at the prone figure.

Another flash of lightning illuminated the night and he saw Hubert Lytton lying on his back. The captain was unable to move. His artificial leg was twisted at a grotesque angle from his body. Kneeling, the rain pelting against his back, Leon straightened out the leg. It was practically unhinged, with possibly only Lytton's trousers keeping it attached to the stump.

Fully conscious, Hubert pushed himself up to a sitting position to pull up the trouser leg. With the rain soaking them both, and the time between lightning flashes shortening, Leon turned his back so as not to embarrass the crippled man as he securely strapped his dummy leg.

When Leon bent over to offer his hand, Lytton looked almost deranged as he tried to say something. But the words were garbled and the noise the storm made prohibited Leon from catching what the captain said. Though Lytton gripped Leon's hand, he lacked the strength, and was handicapped by the artificial leg, to assist Leon In pulling him to his feet.

Stronger than he'd ever been through working in the forge, Leon ducked lower. Getting Lytton across his shoulders, he straightened up and walked with him to where the horse was standing nearby, its eyes still rolling in fear of the storm.

Hair plastered by the wet, rain running down his face, Leon manhandled Lytton up onto the back of the horse. Then he helped the disabled rider to scramble into the saddle. When Leon handed up the reins, Lytton took them in one hand while pointing a finger at Leon and saying: 'You. . . .'

Lightning showed up Lytton's white face, giving it a ghostly translucence. But it was the man's eyes that worried Leon. They had a brightness that Leon had never before seen in anyone. They shone like beacons of hatred, or perhaps fear, Leon couldn't decide. Maybe it was lunacy that made Lytton's eyes glow in this strange way. Whatever it was, it disturbed Leon greatly.

Holding his horse steady, reins in both hands now, Lytton's lips moved as he looked down at Leon. If he had said something, then a crash of thunder snatched the words away.

Pulling the horse's head round hard, Hubert Lytton rode off fast into the stormy night.

After what the old-timers agreed was the worst spring night in living memory, Marshlee's big day dawned bright and sunny. A light tarpaulin still covered the new memorial, and a farm wagon had been parked close to it. A bunch of eager women had decorated the cart, the finishing touch being a gigantic Union Jack draped across the front. George Holland, the undertaker, had manufactured a set of wooden steps for the dignitaries to use getting up onto the wagon, while Raymond Plummer's foreman had rigged up a system of ropes so that Hubert Lytton could perform the unveiling from where he would stand on the wagon.

With everyone in Marshlee assembled by early afternoon, the band of the Devonshire Regiment, specially engaged for the event, played stirring martial music as the prominent men of the town climbed up the steps to the wagon.

It was a men-only occasion, and Anne-Marie watched together with Judith, Gladys, and, to her surprise, Claudia Lytton. The people cheered as Clarence Crandal, as officious as ever, stood alone on the makeshift stage and beckoned for the brigadier to join him. Then Anne-Marie's father drew a reasonable amount of applause as he climbed the steps, as did Walter Hann and Raymond Plummer.

A surge of pride electrified Anne-Marie as Hubert, fighting to disguise his undisguisable limp, mounted the rostrum to rapturous applause. He, the Reverend Penny, Brigadier Lytton, Walter Hann, and Raymond Plummer, stood in line behind Clarence Crandal, who addressed the crowd with a shout that made his voice thin and tinny. His words did a delayed action echoing from the surrounding buildings.

'On this very special day,' Crandal began, 'which during those four wearying years of war, most of us thought would never come, it is my more than pleasant duty to first introduce the men who have made this event possible – our Victory Mayor, Councillor Raymond Plummer, the Vicar of Marshlee, the Reverend Penny, Mr Walter Hann, who, despite his recent sad bereavement, has worked tirelessly and has so generously donated most of the food that you will be enjoying later today. . . .'

A mighty cheer for Hann went up, and Judith leaned close to Anne-Marie to say, 'We have to show that man up for what he is, Anne-Marie. How are we going to do it?'

'I don't know,' Anne-Marie confessed despairingly. Her mind was in turmoil. Wanting to support Hubert on this auspicious occasion, her thoughts kept straying to Leon. His mother had said that he had walked away from Marshlee just prior to the beginning of the storm.

'I'm angry enough to go up on that platform and let everyone know,' Gladys said.

'No, we agreed that no one of us will take the blame,' Judith reminded Gladys. 'Let's try to think of a way we could do it together. Like they say, there's safety in numbers.'

'What are you three talking about?' Claudia Lytton enquired.

'We were just saying how kind Mr Hann is,' Anne-Marie lied.

'Last, but by no means least,' Crandal restarted his oration when the applause for Walter Hann had died down, 'I give you Marshlee's senior and, until his son challenged him for the title, most venerated soldier.'

The cheering for the brigadier didn't amount to much, but the crowd went wild with enthusiasm when Crandal introduced Captain Hubert Lytton as 'Marshlee's own courageous war hero'.

'Do you think there's a chance Hubert might have changed his mind, Anne-Marie?' Judith asked.

'Definitely not,' was Anne-Marie's emphatic reply.

'Not a hope,' Gladys supported her. 'He was adamant as well as angry when I put it to him.'

'It will be too late once the memorial is unveiled,' Judith said unhappily. 'I want it to stay covered until James's name is included.'

'That's what we all want, but there's no way to do it.' Anne-Marie looked helplessly at her two friends.

'There is,' Judith argued. 'I'm prepared to run forward and shout the truth the moment Hubert takes hold of the cord, but before he can do the unveiling. Will you join me? If not I'll do it on my own.'

Gladys laid a hand on Judith's shoulder. 'I'm with you, Judith, but we can't ask Anne-Marie to embarrass Hubert like that.'

'I'll join you,' Anne-Marie answered. Though horrified at what the outcome of such an act was likely to be, James Hann was all that counted right then.

Hubert Lytton, a novice at public speaking, began falteringly, but swiftly gained confidence. 'No individual, no one soldier, can really lay claim to heroism in war. Every man or woman, whether they were in the trenches, driving ambulances, nursing, or carrying out some vital task on the Home Front can rightly be called a hero.'

Captain Lytton waited for the applause to die down, then he began again. 'Although I am most honoured to unveil Marshlee's cenotaph today, and as much as I appreciate the work of Mayor Plummer and the others, I have to say to them that the list of names carved on that stone with pride, is not complet. . . .'

A concerted gasp of awed surprise came from the crowd, and Anne-Marie, Judith and Gladys looked at each other, eyes widened by shock. Anne-Marie went to say something but her voice wouldn't work. She saw the perplexed expressions on the faces the other dignitaries turned to Hubert. She could sense they were preparing themselves to face the unexpected. An unholy glee bubbled inside of her at the thought they would not be expecting the bombshell Hubert seemed about to drop.

'There are, in fact, two names that must be added before this ceremony can be justified. The first is not that of a soldier doing his duty, or a sailor battling the Hun on the high seas, but it is the name of a little girl.'

The crowd waited in silent expectancy. To the consternation of Claudia Lytton, Anne-Marie, Judith, and Gladys, laughingly embraced each other. People close by hissed at them to be quiet as Hubert Lytton went on.

'Beth Marriott took no part in the war, yet she was every bit as much a victim, perhaps more so, than those who died on the battlefield. The man most of you hold responsible for that child's death, did die in action. His name must be included on this cenotaph because he fell not only to the German guns, but also to the cruel gossip in this town. There is no guilt that can be attached to James Hann. That guilt belongs to a man who has put himself before you this day as an upright citizen.'

There was uproar as Hubert pointed an accusing finger at Walter Hann. Amid booing and cries of 'Shame!' that mingled with shouts of disbelief and support for the baker, Hann hurried down the steps. The men he left behind him on the makeshift rostrum looked totally bewildered.

'Leave the man be,' the Reverend Penny shouted commandingly, as an angry mob surged towards Hann when he reached the ground.

The people fell back for him, leaving a wide space as if he were a leper. Hann walked off towards his premises, head held down.

With the noisy assembly now totally disorganized, Clarence Crandal yelled at the top of his voice for calm. It took him some time to get the people under control. His nose was bleeding from the effort he had put into shouting, and his voice hoarse as he said, 'Captain Lytton has more to say.'

'Thank you, Mr Crandal,' an amazingly calm Hubert said. 'I am sure that the gentlemen here with me, including the Brigadier, my father, will agree that this ceremony must be postponed. Not only for the reasons I have already stated, but for another very personal, and long overdue, purpose to be served.

'Last night, at the height of the storm, I was thrown from my horse—'

He was interrupted by the crowd's calls of sympathy for a one-legged man in such a situation.

'I would have lain there all night, and no doubt perished,' Hubert said, 'if a Good Samaritan had not happened along. That man picked me up bodily and carried me to my horse. He saved me, ladies and gentlemen, but as God is my witness, I didn't deserve to be rescued.'

Anne-Marie and her two friends were as puzzled as everyone else now. The pleasure at hearing Walter Hann denounced and the good name of James restored was overshadowed by the mystery announcement Hubert was making.

'For that was not the first time that same Good Samaritan saved my life. In France I lay injured, the only living man among more dead than I care to think about. It was just a matter of hours until I, too, would die from my wounds. But, just as he did last night, this man came along and picked me up onto his back. He carried me that time, too, but not a few yards to a horse: my Good Samaritan carried me untiringly for many days and nights until he reached a casualty clearing station.'

Caught up in the compelling atmosphere, the people of Marshlee began applauding without knowing who they were praising and why. Captain Lytton raised his hands and made a gesture for them to be silent.

'I would be a fraud were I to pull this cord. That honour must be given, some time in the near future, to that brave man who rescued me. You all know him, ladies and gentlemen. That man is Leon Marriott.'

Pandemonium broke loose. People were milling around and yelling. Claudia ran to the platform, going up the steps two at a time to where the brigadier was slumped holding his head in his hands. Raymond Plummer said something to Clarence Crandal, who jumped down off the cart to run to the bandleader.

Anne-Marie saw her father clamber down and hurry away. She guessed that he was going in search of the stricken Walter Hann. The military band struck up with 'John Brown's Body', a totally inappropriate tune. Horrified, she saw Hubert keel over sideways on the platform. With Gladys running at her side, Anne-Marie made her way to the wagon, where Hubert's parents and Raymond Plummer were helping him to his feet.

Hubert's pale face was ashen, and his dark eyes hollow as he watched Anne-Marie and Gladys come up the steps side by side. Behind Anne-Marie, there was the roar of a motor, and above it was her father's voice calling her name.

'Anne-Marie!'

Halfway up the steps, Anne-Marie turned her head to see Edward Lee driving his car recklessly through the crowd. As it stopped close to the foot of the steps, her father jumped out. Holding open the passenger door, he used a swinging arm to urge her to get in the vehicle. When Anne-Marie still hesitated, he said, 'Come on, Anne-Marie. Go after that young man and bring him back to Marshlee.'

Still uncertain what to do, Anne-Marie looked up to the platform, where Gladys was now holding Hubert in her arms, supporting him. Jerking back into life, Anne-Marie ran to hug and kiss her father before she clambered into the car and closed the door.

As Edward Lee drove away at speed, a huge cheer rose up from the people. Clinging on as the car swung round a corner, Anne-Marie saw a weeping Elsie Marriott waving to her. A happy smile broke through the old woman's tears as Anne-Marie waved back.